About the author

Grigory Kanovich is one of the most prominent Lithuanian writers and winner of the Lithuanian National Prize for Culture and Arts for 2014. Kanovich was born into a traditional Jewish family in the Lithuanian town of Jonava in 1929. Since 1993 the writer has lived in Israel. He is a member of the PEN club in both Israel and Russia. He is also a renowned playwright.

'Shtetl Love Song' won the Liudas Dovydenas Prize, awarded by the Lithuanian Writers' Union.

About the translator

Yisrael Elliot Cohen, B.A. Harvard College, Ph.D. Yale University, taught Russian literature and humanities at the University of Illinois. He settled in Israel in 1979, working as a professional translator from Russian into English and as an English-language editor. At Hebrew University he was co-editor of 'Jews in Russia and Eastern Europe' and worked on a bibliography project for the Centre for the Study of Anti-Semitism. Currently at Yad Vashem, he is working on 'The Untold Stories: Holocaust Murder Sites in the Soviet Union'. Dr. Cohen has translated several books. His non-academic interests are his grandchildren and attempting to apply the teachings of the Biblical prophets to the contemporary social and political situation.

Grigory Kanovich

Shtetl Love Song

Translated from Russian
by Yisrael Elliot Cohen

Noir

First published in Russian as Местечковый романс

Text copyright ©Grigory Kanovich
English translation copyright © Yisrael Elliot Cohen
The moral rights of the author and translator have been asserted.

Published by Noir Press Ltd
www.noirpress.co.uk
noirpress@hotmail.com
Company number 10622391

Cover design by Le Dinh Han
Editorial work by Marija Marcinkute, Joy Collishaw and Susan Last
Typeset by Hewer Text UK Ltd, Edinburgh

978-0-9955600-2-4

Today, Kanovich is the only writer in the entire world capable of depicting the life of the pre-war Jewish shtetl with the documentary precision of an immediate witness and the deep emotional passion of a lover mourning his loss. He survived the Holocaust almost by a miracle, and made it his mission to serve, against all odds, as a custodian of the collective memory of generations of Litvaks, Lithuanian Jews. Set in the rural Lithuanian landscape on the eve of World War II, Shtetl Love Song is full of tender affection, soft irony, and sharp observations. Guided by the memory of his beloved mother, the masterful narrator takes us into the very midst of his enchanted family world, recreating the past that is irrevocably destroyed and yet fully alive in his memory.

Mikhail Krutikov, Professor of Slavic and Judaic Studies, University of Michigan, Ann Arbor

BOOK ONE

"My Yiddish mama! You overcame so many troubles!
My Yiddish mama! There's no better in the world."

From a Yiddish folk song

1

For a long time I have been intending to write about my mother with that joyous enthusiasm and the kind of abundant detail with which it is fitting to recall one's parents, the people closest and dearest to you. But to my great shame, for one reason or another, I have kept putting it off and putting it off. Or, if I have started, then I have written nothing more than casual scraps, limiting myself to separate episodes that dealt with my relatives and the other people from my hometown. Wanting to somehow soften my feeling of guilt, I began to recall things, conjuring up memories even when I was sleeping. However, the following morning I would mercilessly erase the words that had seemed so appropriate the night before.

So now, in my declining years, I have finally decided that I have no right to put it off any longer. Rather than sitting gnashing my teeth, I had better get moving, to at least partially atone for my guilt before Mama. Otherwise, God forbid, I might not be spared long enough to do so.

However, even when I had begun to start collecting together, in my failing memory, everything I knew about Mama up until the time of her premature death, I must admit I did not have a good idea where to begin the story.

Before getting down to work, I decided that it would be neither chronological nor complete, since the path of her life was neither straight nor smooth.

Perhaps, I thought, it would be best to begin in that far-off time before I appeared in the world, with that riddle that still puzzles me of how Mama succeeded in becoming the daughter-in-law of my imperious and pernickety grandmother Rokhel Kanovich, née Mines, to whom even the men in our shtetl gave way. It was not without good reason that, following the example of our local doctor Isaac Blumenfeld, the villagers referred to her by the strange and awe-inspiring nickname of Rokha the Samurai.

Grandma Rokha considered her eldest son Shleimele – Solomon – the most eligible bachelor in the tiny shtetl of Jonava. He was as precious to her as a lost ring in the immensity of the universe and she carefully guarded him from making any fateful mistakes. She was convinced that there was no one as handsome as he – not only in Jonava, but in all of Lithuania, from its border with Latvia all the way to its border with Poland. From the latter country, freedom-loving Hasidim in long dark coats occasionally arrived, uninvited, in law-abiding Jonava. They sang prayers in a far from harmonious chorus and, with legs that seemed flexible as rubber, stomped wondrous, hieroglyphic dances on the cobblestone pavements, in praise of God who had commanded the whole tribe of Israel to always and everywhere be fruitful and multiply.

The ragged, twisted shape of my narrative grew from the stories and the late-in-life admissions of Mama, who now and then liked to return to her distant youth: she never missed an opportunity to disappear into the past, like a squirrel with its provisions into a favourite hole. The point of departure was often the strained relationship between the undesirable daughter-in-law, Hennie Dudak, and my grandmother Rokha and the circumstances connected with my mother's marriage and my appearance in the world. So, I figured, this was as good a place to start as any.

Unable to hide her worry, Grandma Rokha asked her husband who, gloomy as a late Lithuanian autumn, was bending over his shoe tree, "Dovid, do you perhaps know where our dear son Shleimele spends his evenings?"

Dovid stroked his thin reddish beard, thinking it over, and then, indifferently, as if there was nobody else in the room besides himself, continued to punch the heel of a customer's worn out shoe with his awl.

As was his habit, he preferred not to reply to questions that had no direct connection with his trade, or, if he deigned to do so, then it was only with a glance of his tearful, sad eyes or by nodding his head.

"Why don't you say something? Isn't Shleimele your son too?"

The autumnal sorrow in my grandpa's eyes did not diminish, but behind the lenses of his eyeglasses in their faded horn-rimmed frame there dimly glimmered the wisp of a smile.

Dovid did not waste his words. He used to say that while it was a sin to keep the money he earned with his awl and hammer from his wife – as a matter of fact, he would give her everything, down to his last *litas* – words were another matter altogether! Who needed words? They produced only misunderstanding and unpleasantness. If you tell someone close to you what you believe is the truth, he not only won't thank you but, pay attention to this, he will get angry and might well give you a resounding slap. And if you say something untrue, it's as if you are spitting into your own soul with your nonsense. It was simply best not to say anything. Not for nothing does the Lord in heaven remain silent. He also commands us sinners to keep our tongues locked behind our teeth – in any case there are never enough words. If you are going to follow someone's example, then follow Him, not Taibe, next door, who didn't close her mouth the whole day long.

"Rokha, use your brain. What would it be like if the One above replied every day to everyone who asks Him something? Our Taibe alone would drive him out of His mind."

"You're mad, you old fool!" Grandma Rokha raged at her husband. "What has God to do with any of this? He's in heaven and I'm well aware of the fact that he's no chatterbox without your wise observation. God sits in His house, on a golden throne, surrounded by angels and cherubs, who have blessed conversations with Him while He, out of the corner of His eye, still manages to keep watch over all of His sinners, to see whether we're ruining His creation. The Heavenly Father doesn't go strolling around the shtetl at night with young women or smooch with them in the dark on the banks of the Vilija.

"Leave God in peace! He's no less tired than a cobbler. You'd better answer my question, where is our beloved son Shleimele hanging around?"

Mama would always recall her mother-in-law's arguments with her father-in-law with heat and passion. Those endless arguments and sharp exchanges, peppered with witty details, protected her from the terrible memories of the war years. She seemed to grow younger before our eyes, transported from shattered Vilnius to her warm Jonava, to the banks of the wide Vilija which sang, with its quiet, blessed gurgling, wedding songs to more than one loving couple.

"So tell me, oh wise one, didn't the idea ever enter your head that one fine day your dear son might bring home some blonde *shiksa* wearing a cross on her breast? That he might show up with his wench, push her toward you with his elbow and say, 'Papa, meet Morta or Antanina . . .' and ask for your blessing! What will we do then? Give them our blessing? Chase them away? Or set out for the church, to your old customer, Vaitkus, the priest, with his brothers Motl and Isaac and his sisters Leah and Hava? He'll marry them and sprinkle the newlyweds with holy water, while we can ask them and all those churchgoers forgiveness for the way, long ago, we dirty Jews crucified their good, divine Jesus with iron nails, which, by the way, were neither for sale nor in use back then?"

Dovid reacted to his loyal partner's threats with a calm that was both steadfast and offensive. For quite some time he himself had had no interest in women, either goyish or Jewish. For entire days his elongated head, with its shining bald oval, like a pond on top and the rust-coloured growth along its sides, was filled with other thoughts, like heels, soles and wax ends, the price of leather and the damned cough he was suffering from. Hoping to mollify his all-too-ready-to-explode wife, Grandpa reluctantly scrambled out of his safe corner of silence and, taking courage, said, "It's natural, Rokha, that every man of his age has to find a woman to settle down with. Otherwise, how could we be fruitful and multiply? Sometimes the search for a partner takes time and sometimes she is found right away."

Satisfied by his wife's surprised silence, he slowly wiped his sharp awl with his patched apron and added, "I found you right away, without having to look high and low, even though all kinds of women were dancing around me! He's been looking around. Our son will find his Rachel. You don't need a watchman with a club to encourage young men in this matter."

"In what matter?"

"In this matter . . . the one that involves kissing and . . ." he mumbled.

In contrast to his irritable and temperamental wife, from whose mouth vulgar expressions and curses emerged like a swarm of wasps, the vocabulary of Grandpa Dovid was as pure and unblemished as a yarmulke used only once a year, on Passover. He never used unseemly expressions because, as he tried to convince his foul-mouthed customers, the soul of a person becomes overgrown with brambles.

"Don't you remember," he continued, "how you and I . . . until dawn on the grassy springtime bed under the bridge over the Vilija . . . It was the kind of pleasure you don't easily forget! The long and short of it is, you must remember how the two of us snuggled . . ."

"You should be ashamed of yourself!" Grandma muttered, embarrassed. "Snuggled? Ugh!"

"It's no shame to speak the truth," Grandpa said, shrugging his shoulders. "Your mother-in-law, my late mother, didn't want you as a daughter-in-law either. Really didn't want you. She thought you were as mean as a witch and quite small and that your breasts were small and not fit for nursing babies. As she put it, your face had a wart like a raspberry and your rear-end stuck out like a chair."

He sighed after such an effusion of words and grew silent. But no matter how much you twisted your tongue you couldn't convince Rokha. Grandpa's wife dreamt not of a cobbler's daughter for her son, but of a princess, a niece of Rothschild or, in the worst case, Zlata, the heiress of the miller of Jonava, Mendel Vasserman. Or Hannah, the stepdaughter of the pharmacist Nota Levita, so that her father would give Rokha, who suffered from a dozen different ailments, a discount on the medicines she needed.

Translucent clouds hung over our communal apartment on Generalissimo Stalin Boulevard. Our three destitute families had been settled together in one apartment by the Vilnius city executive committee, having returned from a gloomy exile. Every day they shared their funny, painful memories about times gone by. In the evenings the refugees reminisced about their prewar lives with pleasure. They resurrected memories to drive from their heads the woes they had suffered and the worries that piled up with each new day. There descended into their communal apartment from the bare, recently repainted walls, on which there were neither pictures nor mirrors, a crowd of their fellow townspeople and their neighbours with whom they had lost contact during the war.

From the corners, piled with unpacked bags and containers, from a miraculously preserved photo album and from yellowed photographs, in groups or individually, their murdered fathers and mothers, brothers and sisters appeared, as if they had risen from their shallow graves in ditches and ravines. The deceased rushed forwards to greet their living relatives, who had miraculously survived and returned to their homeland. Their different fates became wondrously intertwined. Ineradicable grief and unfulfilled hopes. The past merged with a present that promised new, unforeseen experiences and terrifying, unpredictable dangers.

Still, the beautiful past, which has always served as a consolation and inspiration for Jewish souls in distress, was much better than a future that was so unclear. Eagerly, happily, the inhabitants of our apartment immersed them-selves in the past, as if they were bathing in the peacefully flowing Vilija River, warmed by the rays of the summer sun. Memories of suffering washed over them too, and they were tortured by terrible losses, which beckoned them back to Vilija's banks, which were overgrown with thick shrubbery – the banks of their first trysts and first love.

In the evenings on Generalissimo Stalin Boulevard both of my grandmothers and grandfathers, resurrected in this memoir, sat at the table, brought to life by my aunts and uncles, along with their neighbours and fellow shtetl-dwell-ers who had disappeared into oblivion. They recalled their voices and their manner of speech, which my mother, that eternal entertainer and the life of all the get-togethers, took pleasure in imitating. Those voices could be heard like a distant echo and didn't grow quiet until dawn.

Time after time Mama would wind time backwards, as if it were a clock, to find herself far away in the frozen *auls*, the native Kazakh villages, scattered across the endless steppe, which echoed with the calls of hungry jackals and were blanketed with the poisonous coal dust of the Trans-Urals, far from the strange, silent Vilnius.

"A person is alive as long as he remembers that which he should in no circumstances forget," my mother loved to say.

"You're getting yourself upset for no reason. Your favourite will choose his better half for himself."

Great amateur actress that my mother was, it was as if I could hear the hoarse baritone of Grandpa Dovid from a distance, along with the high, fervent alto of Grandma Rokha, who exhausted him constantly with her fears and whom he spoiled their whole life together.

"Shleimele? That dumbbell! Any girl could easily wrap him around her little finger. It would be good if he met a nice young woman from a decent family and not some whore who would present us with a bastard!"

Exhausted by her uncertainty, Grandmother decided to set up a round-the-clock surveillance of Shleimele. She encouraged her youngest son, Motl, and her oldest, Itzik, not to let her 'King Solomon' out of their sight and, if they caught sight of him with some profligate local wench, then they were instructed to report it immediately so that their mother would know with whom their brother was going around. Although the brothers had to agree (if they had tried to refuse, their mother would have kicked up a storm) they were hardly going to gossip about or report on their brother.

In order to discover her son's sweetheart, the determined Rokha resorted to all kinds of sleuthing devices. On the Sabbath she made every effort to dig out information from her elderly peers, who didn't mind gossiping. Casting a keen eye at the men and women worshippers, Grandma considered who had an eligible daughter and to which of the latter her handsome son might be directing his attention. There was no shortage of potential brides in Jonava; poor ones whose parents could not afford a dowry, complete fools with decent dowries and young ladies with stupid, painted faces. Not one of them, according to the picky and demanding Rokha's judgment, was a suitable match for her son. There was Zlata, the daughter of the miller, Vasserman, but she was studying to be a dentist in either Germany or France and visited the shtetl only during the summer vacation, when she would have nothing to do with the local yokels.

You can imagine Rokha's disappointment when she finally found out from the *balagula*, the wagon driver Peisakh Shvartsman, who was well acquainted with everybody in Jonava, the identity of the fortunate young woman with whom her favourite son was visiting the banks of love.

It was Hennie, the daughter of the cobbler Shimon Dudak! She was the object on whom her Shleimele, her 'King Solomon', was casting his eyes.

"So, Shleimele, I heard that you've found your life-partner. Is that true?" his mother asked accusingly. Rokha the Samurai was transformed suddenly from clever detective into a scrupulous and relentless prosecutor.

In neither his features nor his behaviour did my father, Solomon, called either Shleimele or Shleimke, differ from his father. Instead of responding clearly and without evasion to his mother's questions, he only bit his lip, inhaling the smell of shoe-polish and borscht. However, in contrast to the mournful, funeral silence of Grandpa, his offspring, it should be said, adorned his silences with either a life-affirming or a condescending smile.

But, what can you do? Secrets don't stay secrets long among Jews! However hard you try, some *balagula*, or the grocer, Chaim Lutsky, will smell it out and tell absolutely everyone. Jews are Jews and they learn about everything before anyone else in the world. Or at least they try to. Otherwise, God forbid, a pogrom could take place and how would they then save themselves from the cutthroats?

"So, can we make arrangements with the Rabbi? Should we get ready to put the *chuppah* up? Invite guests?" Rokha asked ironically, bombarding her handsome son with questions and cutting off any honourable way for him to retreat.

"What are you talking about, Mama?" was all he said by way of reply.

"What? Does the sun shine in a special way on that hefty Hennie Dudak? Maybe all the men in the shtetl are lining up for her and you're afraid you'll be last?"

"Hmm . . ."

"Don't 'hmm' me! I'm speaking to you seriously and you can only say 'hmm' and 'hmm'? Is your tongue caught in your behind?"

"I guess it is," Shleimele replied cheekily and then left to go to see his employer, the well-known tailor Abram Kisin, to ask for his salary.

For a long time Rokha couldn't recover from the extraordinary audacity and willfulness of her son. She couldn't get that sparrow, that short-legged, tail-wagging Hennie Dudak out of her head. Where were his eyes? she wondered. "Of all the daughters of Shimon Dudak, second cobbler in the shtetl, eternal rival of Dovid Kanovich, he chose that one? He could have waited a year or two while her sister, the beauty Feiga, grew up." At 16, Feiga already had what matchmakers called a 'come here, big boy' look. "But Hennie? When you go to market, do you buy something from the first wagon you see? Smart people look over all the wagons first, examine the merchandise, feel it, evaluate it, and only then, after scratching the back of their heads for a while, reach into their pocket for their wallet."

"Don't be sad, Rokha! Life has a way of putting things into place without our interference. What is fated to be cannot be avoided," Dovid murmured imperturbably, as always. "After all, Rokha, did our parents act any differently?"

"Well, if you are so clever, maybe you can tell me how our newlyweds will live?" Rokha asked, as if playing a trump card. "We're seven in two rooms. Dudak has six children: four potential brides and two potential grooms – Shmuel and Motl. Let's say Shleimke and Hennie do get married, Dovid, where can we put them? In the attic? In the cellar with the mice? Or maybe we'll give them our bed and we'll spend the night walking around and hugging under the stars?"

"It's not a problem. If they really love each other, they can live separately for a while, he with us on Rybatskaya Street and she with her father, Shimon, on Kaunas Street. Shleimke will leave his employer, Abram Kisin, and set up for himself, then they will rent a room . . ."

Grandma Rokha didn't let her husband finish his sentence.

"Separately? Maybe, Dovid, it's time to have your brain seen to. I'd like to know how, if they live separately, they will fulfill God's commandment to be fruitful and multiply?"

"Don't worry!" Dovid interjected. "They will, they will."

Grandma Rokha still hoped Shleimele would change his mind; that after courting and kissing, he would get rid of her. But he didn't change his mind.

When for the first time my father decided to bring my terrified mother to Rybatskaya Street to meet her future father and mother-in-law, Grandma Rokha looked her over from head to foot as if examining a calf for sale in the shtetl or brought to the district town from a distant farm.

"Child, you look better than I thought," she muttered gloomily. "You're no beauty, but you're not a beast either."

Hennie blushed and lowered her head.

"I understand that you two have already decided everything," said the future mother-in-law with a barely concealed threat rather than a friendly reproach. "You've already decided that you'll live together without any need for a parental blessing, like honourable people would ask for. You've wished yourselves *Mazal tov!* exchanged rings, poured some wine out and shouted, *l'chaim*! and jumped into bed!"

Dovid stood silently to the side holding his awl, from which he was inseparable, as if he was considering using it at any moment to stab his partner of many years.

"Yes," the groom said firmly. "The time has long passed when parents had the last word in such matters, when they, so to speak, took their children by the horns like animals and mated them."

"Those were good times," Grandmother Rokha pronounced. "Isn't that so, Dovid?"

"As well as I can remember, Rokha, there were never any good times," her cautious husband responded, avoiding a direct answer. He scratched his unshaven cheek with his awl. "But during all those bad times, you could still find some good people."

"Hennie is a good person," said our Jonava King Solomon, who had not been known for his boldness, expanding on his father's comment. "She *is* good," he repeated. "You can be sure of that."

Her son's praise didn't convince my stubborn grand-mother, however.

"A rooster is a rooster," she said, "because he breaks into song before the foolish hens in the yard." She required more than a simple statement from her offspring as proof. "Meanwhile, my girl," she continued her interrogation, "what else can you do, other than win the hearts of young men?" She paid no attention to Dovid's strange winking and awkward grimaces, which were intended to say, 'Enough, Rokha, of tormenting a person.' Grandpa was tempted to remind her that before she stood under the marriage *chuppah* all she knew how to do was to boil potatoes in their jackets and to pray.

"I know how to love," my mother replied, dumbfounding not only the incorrigible Rokha, but also her husband. "When you love, you can learn anything."

"You know how to love, but do you know how to cook? To wash clothes? To iron? Or how to clean the floor and tidy up?" Grandma Rokha grew weary, choking over the lengthy list of things that had to be done. She had suddenly become hoarse.

"Everything I do, I do with love," Hennie said with simple-hearted dignity. She focused her gaze on the old people who stood like statues, motionless. "I will also love you both," she added with enthusiasm.

Dovid seemed to melt and almost stuck his awl into his sunken cheek, while Grandma began to sniff noisily, wiping her eyes for some reason, not her nose.

"We'll live and see," she mumbled. "If we live."

2

Rokha tried to convince her son to put the wedding off. After all, they didn't have a single bit of free space in the house for the newlyweds. All the beds were taken. From outside the termite-eaten walls you could hear not only the whistle of the locomotive and the rumbling of the carriages of the trains passing through Jonava, but also every fart and snore. How could he, Shleimele, fulfill his conjugal obligations in such a crowded house? Grandmother suggested that he wait a bit, get started in his profession, find a number of customers and begin to earn enough to rent an inexpensive corner in a house, perhaps from that turkey-cock, the landlord, Ephraim Kapler, for whom Dovid, may God grant him many years, had mended shoes and boots his whole life. Or perhaps from Kleiman, that other rich man, the one who owned horses and rented out apartments. Meanwhile, she concluded, he and Hennie would have to live separately.

"Separately?" the bridegroom exclaimed, wide-eyed.

"If Hennie really loves you, and I see she does from the look in her eyes, I don't believe she will object. Your delicious little pastry won't go anywhere. Nothing will happen to her. Girls don't throw away lads like you, or exchange them for someone else," Rokha remarked, trying to butter her son up.

"Anyway, so far no one has thought about setting up the *chuppah* or contacting Rabbi Eliezer. We're getting married as soon as I return from my national service."

"What? Don't the Lithuanians take married men into the army? Or do they leave them so that their wives, full of yearning, don't go running elsewhere to fling themselves into forbidden embraces?"

"They do take married men."

"And what do they need tailor-soldiers for, and Jewish ones at that? You don't repair a pair of trousers with a bayonet."

Shleimele laughed.

The stubborn Rokha was prepared to grit her teeth and give her blessing to the couple, since Hennie was wild and capable of anything – even running away from Jonava and eloping or getting pregnant before the wedding. In order to keep Shleimele, Rokha was ready to make concessions; she might have agreed to have the house even more crowded. With the help of Motl and Isaac it would have been possible to drag the sunken double bed, almost as old as Moses, into the entrance hall. The bed, if it was good for anything, was only good for the chickens to nest in. On the other hand, perhaps there was no rush and she could wait; maybe the army would part Shleimele and Hennie. Maybe that nanny goat wouldn't wait for his return and would go and turn someone else's head.

But the ancient double bed remained where it had been. Shleimke was called up into the army and set off for the district centre, Alytus, on the Neman River, not far from Jonava. To the amazement of all the Jews in the shtetl, he was assigned to a cavalry regiment, either to the *Uhlans* or the dragoons, despite the fact that he wasn't tall and had never ridden a horse in his life.

"The commanders know best who should serve where," her eldest son, Isaac, the family's advisor and comforter, consoled his mother. "There's nothing wrong if my brother Shleimke, in addition to knowing how to sew, learns how to ride a horse as well."

"But why?" Battling her fear, Grandma Rokha importuned not Isaac, but God Himself. "Why does a Jew need to gallop around on a horse? Where did you, Isaac, ever see a Jew on a horse? I've known the *balagula*, the wagon driver Peisakh Shvartsman, for a million years already and not a single time have I seen him on horseback, even though he has three healthy dray horses in his stable. He always holds their reins and leads them down to the Vilija River. Any normal Jew will pay for his horses to take them somewhere, but not to ride on horseback around Lithuania like wild men. *Vei iz mir, vei iz mir*. He'll fall right off and break his head open and become an invalid!"

Grandma Rokha had nightmares. She jumped up screaming and then wandered around the house, whispering prayers. It was neither her sons nor her husband that calmed her in the end, but the swift local postman, Kazimiras, who, one month after Shleimke had been called up, brought Grandma a letter from Alytus. The grey envelope contained a small photograph, carefully wrapped in paper, of her handsome son in military uniform and army cap, riding on a horse.

"A real general!" Rokha the Samurai uttered, kissing the photo three times and bursting into tears.

It was highly likely that Shleimke had sent the same photograph to Hennie. How could he not have done so? As a matter of fact, he must have sent it to her first. So why didn't she come then to visit them on Rybatskaya Street, to boast and share her happiness, saying, "Look, Rokha, how handsome Shleimke looks! A real lancer!" Evidently, the poor thing was not that clever. Joy should be shared with everyone; not only does this not diminish the joy, it increases it!

But Hennie did not appear on Rybatskaya Street, even though she had assured them that she would love them.

Rokha watched out for her, kept an eye out, but she had disappeared like the wind. When she inquired about Hennie from her friends, neighbours, fellow worshippers and shop-keepers, they just shrugged their shoulders. No one knew anything about Shimon Dudak's eldest daughter. Then, tormented by curiosity, Grandma Rokha decided to abandon her roundabout methods and float, like a duck, right up to Shimon Dudak himself in the synagogue yard with an attractive proposal for Hennie. Her old acquaintance Reb Yeshua Kemnitzer, the owner of a haberdashery store, was, people said, looking for a good Jewish girl to take care of his grandson Raphael. Perhaps the unemployed Hennie would be interested in this job? After all, an extra penny for a hungry family of eight would never do any harm.

"But Hennie isn't here," replied Shimon simply.

Shimon Dudak was known in the shtetl more for his velvety low baritone than his awl. Sitting at his bench, he often sang to the shoes and boots worn down by the rough roads. He sang cheerful songs about rabbis and their obedient students and about strange matchmakers and pimps. Sometimes Shimon would draw out a Russian couplet from a heroic song about the powerful Volga River and the highwayman who had drowned his beloved Persian wife in it. Dudak had imported this song from Vitebsk, where the Russian tsar had resettled the Jews for being German spies at the beginning of World War One.

"What do you mean she's not here? Where is she?"

Grandmother couldn't believe that a daughter could disappear without telling her father where she was going. She would certainly find out everything from Shimon!

"Hennie set out for the army barracks," Grandpa Dovid's eternal competitor replied, concealing any worry or apprehension he may have felt.

"What? Have the Lithuanians started recruiting Jewish women into their army now? What is the world coming to?"

"Hennie, so to say, set off there of her own free will." The timid smile didn't leave his face, nor did the wrinkles smooth from his forehead as Shimon spoke. "She wanted to see your son, Shleimke." And, as if defending her actions, he added, "The daughter of the grocer, Lutsk, followed her suitor, the tinsmith Genekh, off to America. Just tell me, who in America has an urgent need for a tinsmith? And not from just anywhere, but from Jonava? I heard your Leah is looking in that direction too."

"You heard something about Leah but I, her own mother, have heard nothing? Who told you? Which eagle saw where in the world she was planning to fly?"

"People have been talking about this."

"People say that the earth revolves around the sun, Shimon. Are you rotating? Why don't I turn? Why don't you? Why doesn't Rabbi Eliezer spin with the scroll of the Torah in his arms in the synagogue, along with the worshippers there?" Shimon's words had cut Rokha, but she tried not to show it. She couldn't believe that her children would go and leave her and her taciturn husband, Dovid. It was true that Isaac had hinted he wouldn't stay in Lithuania, that he wanted to seek happiness somewhere else. But that her eldest daughter Leah would leave? And for America? Rokha simply refused to believe it.

"Shimon, it would be better for you to tell me how long Shleimke and your daughter Hennie intend to ride around together on a horse in Alytus?" Rokha drove her question like the point of a spear into the smiling face of Shimon, but he didn't grasp what she meant by their riding together.

"God only knows how long." He yawned noisily, his mouth wide. "Maybe for the rest of their lives."

Rokha was overwhelmed. But though she was unhappy, she also felt a grudging admiration for the stubborn, devoted Hennie. She decided, which was quite rare for her, to share the rumours about Leah and about Hennie's trip to Alytus with her husband.

"What do you have to say to that?"

"What is there to say?" Dovid growled. "Children are like birds; they sit on a branch, preening their feathers and singing for a while and then they fly off to another tree. The branch moves, it moves again and then it stops. As for

Hennie, she is a desperate young woman. She'll do anything to achieve her purpose."

"You shelter everyone under your warm wing, or pat them on the head and give them something, except for me, your lawful wife!" Grandma didn't miss an opportunity to upbraid him. "Now, don't get angry, but for a treasure like you I wouldn't have gone anywhere; not to Alytus, nor Shmalytus. I just pitied you, you old fool!"

"What can you do, Rokha? There's nothing sweeter than the mistakes of blind youth. You and I could have bought tickets for different trains, my dear, but instead we sat down in the same carriage and, you know, we haven't been too unhappy. Now we just have to bumble along with all our sins and baggage until God opens the heavenly gates for us. But Hennie, apparently, will get what she wants. She won't let go of our son. And, whether you want it or not, there will be a celebration in our house."

"Just look at how smart you are; *there will be a celebration*! But perhaps they'll have a good time in Alytus and then go their separate ways. Then, Dovid, there will really be a celebration in our house!"

"Rokha, my heart tells me that they won't separate." Dovid wiped his forehead with the sleeve of his shirt and, looking at his wife with timid devotion, said quietly, as if telling her a secret, "First of all, Rokha, I'll make you some new high-heeled shoes from calfskin. Then we'll go to Genekh Sharfstein, who all the women love, and order a crêpe de chine dress and, after that, Nakhum Kovalsky will fix up your hair, since it's usually a mess. And for me, Gedalya Bankvecher will sew a double-breasted jacket and trousers.

That is how we shall raise a toast to their happiness at the wedding."

"What are my ears hearing?" Rokha exclaimed angrily. "God has performed a miracle!"

"A miracle?" her husband asked, with a look of surprise.

"After sixty years of total silence, for the first time you are talking not like a cobbler but like a husband! What has happened to you, my dear?"

"Do you take me for a scarecrow without feelings? Without a heart and without a brain?" her gentle Dovid protested.

"But, Dovid, you couldn't pull such things out of you before, not even with pliers! Calfskin shoes, a crêpe de chine dress, a new hairdo! Why didn't you talk like this for so many years?" She went up to her husband and embraced him awkwardly. "Maybe, even though we're already old, you'll tell me you love me for the very first time?"

"I could do that," Grandpa said boldly. "God knows, it wouldn't cost me anything," he joked.

"Alright, alright," Grandma said, having mercy on her husband.

The merciful Shimon Dudak had given his daughter a blessing for her journey and warned her that she shouldn't stay away in a strange town for too long and worry her parents for no reason.

"Go, go. A bird that sits around on a branch all the time will forget how to fly," he said.

Shleimke, the dark-browed, well-built, sharp-eyed son of his rival Dovid Kanovich, pleased him. He was quiet, but not lazy. Who would not want such a son-in-law? All the more so since Shimon had four daughters to marry off; it would certainly bring him no joy if none of them got married. What's the use of a dried-out well from which no one can drink? In regard to his eldest daughter, Shimon was content.

3

In Alytus a slanting, heavy rain soaked Hennie to the skin. She took refuge in a dark gateway. There, like a thief, glancing in all directions, she nervously wrung out her satin blouse and skirt. When the sickly Lithuanian sun peeked out through the breaks in the clouds, which raced along with the wind, her clothes had almost dried and she left her hiding place. A little confused by the winding streets and alleys, Hennie set out at random to find her lancer. My future mother decided that if by the time the sun began to set she had not yet found the unit in which Shleimke was serving, she would try to find a place to sleep in the local synagogue. In every shtetl a Jew passing through town could always find a prayer house with a tattered couch that had a scrawny mattress, a rough pillow and bedbugs that would bite you without a twinge of conscience. She would spend the night in the house of God and in the morning ask some passing Jew how to get to the army barracks.

In all the twenty years of her life Hennie had never ventured beyond the borders of her shtetl – not counting the already long-forgotten Vitebsk, which was where, when she was a girl of fourteen, together with all the other Jews suspected of being spies, she had been expelled by the

Russian tsar, Nikolai, whose name remained long in the
memory of her people as the embodiment of hatred toward
those of the Jewish faith. When she was angry, my grandmother on my mother's side used to turn to her husband
Shimon and say, "Why are you looking at me so suspiciously,
the way Tsar Nikolai looked at *peyos* *?"

Alytus was larger than Hennie's shtetl. The streets were
broader, the houses taller and the store windows contained
greater riches. In Jonava Hennie was familiar with all the
lanes and alleys; every shop, every workshop and barber-
shop, post office and barrack, every place for holding military manoeuvres and even the police station.

If only she could bump into a policeman like Vincas
Gedraitis, who would help her so she didn't get lost, she
thought, recalling, suddenly, Jonava's guardian of law and
order who was a frequent guest in her home on Kaunas
Street – almost a member of the family.

Before the Passover holiday Gedraitis, trim and in full
uniform, usually dropped in at the house of the cobbler
Shimon, to share a bit of matza and down some honey
liqueur and, especially, to speak with him in fluent Yiddish
about the Virgin Mary, Jesus Christ and the apostles.
Gedraitis, a fervent Catholic, absolutely refused to believe
that they had all been Jews.

"It can't be, it just can't be! I don't believe it! You have
cobblers and tailors, you have usurers, but you don't have
apostles! The apostles are ours, and I ask you not to take
them for yourselves."

---

* Ear locks worn by pious Jews

"Jews. They were Jews," Shimon muttered, not wanting to get into an argument with Gedraitis. (Out of respect for his host the policeman always spoke with him not in Lithuanian, but in the *mama-loshn*.) "Jews just like us."

"A Jew could not crucify a Jew," insisted the phlegmatic and gentle Gedraitis, chewing on a piece of matza. "A Lithuanian could. A Pole maybe. A German could. A Jew – never in his life! Deceive, yes, without blinking an eye, denounce his brother to the authorities, yes- but crucify?"

"Is the ethnic origin of your God and his apostles really so important? Anyway, you tell me where Jewish villains could have bought the nails to nail poor Jesus to the cross," Shimon said ironically, watching his guest devour the matza. "Where? From Reb Yeshua Kremnitser? Or perhaps from Shmuelson in Ukmerge?" He chuckled.

"You, Shimon, are not just a master shoe-repairer, you're quite handy with your tongue too. You are. You certainly are! But be careful, even if you are a cobbler," Vincas Gedraitis said and, leaving the tasty matza until next year, he would warmly embrace the old man.

Hennie didn't know anyone in Alytus. After wandering around the strange city in vain with her cloth suitcase, she decided to turn to someone who looked like a Jew, who might tell her how she could reach her goal, the soldiers' barracks, before it became dark.

Next to a store with a huge sign of a woman's high-heeled shoe and large letters that read in Yiddish and Lithuanian, 'Meir Liberson – The best shoes in Europe' (below the word 'Europe', to attract customers, the words 'inexpensive' and 'long-lasting' appeared in smaller script) Hennie politely stopped a fair-haired man in a long black coat and asked whether he could tell her, an out-of-towner, where the lancers were quartered.

"The lancers, who are they?" the stranger asked, staring at her in total incomprehension.

"Soldiers," Hennie explained in confusion. "But not infantry. Cavalrymen."

"So why does a fine Jewish girl like you need Lithuanian cavalrymen?" The man grinned, touching his rumpled black hat with the tips of his fingers.

The fine Jewish girl took the slight gesture of his hand as a sign of dismissal and quickly added, "I'm looking for my friend. He was recently called up to the army and sent here, to Alytus, for his national service."

"Is he a Jew?"

"Yes, a Jew. A tailor."

"That's the first time I've heard that they've called up a tailor for the cavalry, and a Jewish one at that. We've never had any Jewish horsemen," the stranger repeated several times, a smile illuminating his cheeks, which were sunken and of a sickly yellow tinge. "Is he expecting you here?"

"No. It's just that I haven't seen him for so long. And I very much want to see him."

"That's understandable. Do you know at least a little bit of Lithuanian?"

"I used to hear clients from neighbouring villages speaking with my father, a cobbler. I remember something. Though actually I sound like a goat bleating when I try," Hennie admitted. "There was no one to speak with. There are more Jews than Lithuanians in our shtetl."

"So then, how do you hope to find him?"

"Perhaps I will simply run into him."

"Yes, maybe you'll be lucky. The barracks are way outside the city, on the banks of the Neman. I would like to help you get there but I can't, I'm rushing to the pharmacy for medicine. My wife is sick, very sick. She hasn't got out of bed for three weeks now. And the kids, one younger than the other, are all alone at home without supervision. Someone has to keep an eye on them."

"Thank you. I will pray for your wife. For her speedy recovery."

"And I for you. What is your name?"

"Hennie Dudak."

"Hennie, dear, it's a sin to ask God only for our own needs. We should pray for everyone and He, the One Who Sees All, will choose for himself from that multitude those who are worthy of His mercy. The others will have to stand in line." A smile spread over the sparse stubble on his cheeks like a ray of sunlight. "First walk straight ahead, turn right at the tinsmith's, then, when you cross the square, after ten metres turn left and you'll arrive at the church. From there, without turning, go straight down to the Neman. If you get lost, come to our house. Kudirkos Street, number eighteen. My name is Hillel Leizerovsky. Will you remember that?"

"Yes."

"May God protect you!"

In contrast to her fellow shtetl residents, who disturbed Him with requests from morning to evening, Hennie didn't have much faith in God and did not turn to Him. Instead she listened to her own heart for advice, guidance, and protection.

"It was love that took me to Alytus. It was my most trustworthy and best guide," Mama would tell me many years later, with tongue-in-cheek pride, when I was a student of philology. "It's true that love can take you God knows where, but it didn't deceive me – it helped me on my way and, finally, to my goal."

With her cloth bag packed with goodies, Hennie walked around the out-of-bounds area, glancing through every gap in the high fence, above which barbed wire extended all around its perimeter. The entrance to this fenced-off territory was guarded by a stocky, rosy-cheeked sentry who looked like a farmer who had just come home from ploughing and changed into a soldier's uniform. Through broad gaps in the fence it was possible to see the two-storey building of the headquarters of the cavalry regiment, an ugly row of impersonal, monotonous stone barracks, stables and a large empty square for the daily exercising of the thoroughbred army horses.

Hennie's constant wandering back and forth and her fruitless staring through the gaps in the fence alerted the sentry, who was exhausted from boredom since he really had nothing to do. The excessive curiosity of the young woman, who clearly looked Jewish, aroused the suspicions of the guard and he left his post and, with a kind of arrogant laziness, strutted toward her.

Having looked the unexpected visitor over from head to toe, as if he were trying to guess what she wanted and what she had in the mysterious bag she was holding, he asked, severely, in Lithuanian, "*Ko cia, panele, iesko?*" What are you looking for, young lady?

Hennie concentrated and with considerable difficulty managed to reply, despite her poor command of the state language, "*As ieskot chaveras Shlomo Kanovich.*" I'm looking for my friend, Shlomo Kanovich.

She succeeded in mispronouncing all the Lithuanian words except for the first person pronoun and the name of the person she was seeking.

The sentry grimaced at the girl's inability to speak the language of the state he was so dutifully protecting against its enemies. But, overcoming his disdain, he asked her a question that would remove all his doubts.

"*Jis cia tarnauja?*" Is he serving here?

Intuition told her what he was asking. Hennie quickly nodded so that her dark curls danced up and down and she hastened to open her bag, carefully removing from under the goodies a threadbare wallet with a photograph that was wrapped in newspaper. She showed it to the sentry.

Looking at the photo and recognizing the regimental steed in it, the guard spoke in a much friendlier tone. "*Palauk!*" Wait here.

Then he turned and strode over to the entrance.

Hennie waited impatiently and thought that, if Shleimke would agree, she would stay in Alytus so that she could visit him more often. She would find a place to work as a salesgirl, best would be in a haberdashery shop, or find a job as a nanny with a respectable family and rent an inexpensive room in an attic. No, a room in a cellar with a single window would be enough! And, then, together with her beloved, she would 'serve' in this foreign town for the whole period that the army required. But if he would not agree, she would earn money back in their own town of Jonava for trips to Alytus and would visit him every Saturday. Just so long as he didn't try to dissuade her! Just so long as he would agree! On Saturdays the Jewish soldiers, she assumed, were allowed to attend synagogue. Then, together, she, her chosen one and the good man Hillel Leizerovsky, with his now-healed wife and their children, would pray and ask God to ensure that Shleimke's military service was not too difficult and, God forbid, make sure he didn't fall from his horse and land on a rock. What did it matter that neither Hennie nor Shleimke knew how to pray as prescribed in the holy books? Indeed, their parents were quite ashamed about it and criticized them for being ignorant and asked bitterly whether their children were Jews at all, or whether they were converts who had abandoned the faith! This, despite the fact that each of them had explained on more than one occasion to their old folks that praying out loud, with words learned from the prayer book, wasn't the only way to pray, you could also pray silently, from the heart. Nevertheless, their parents not only made fun of them, but expected the inevitable and just divine punishment.

Time, which seemed suddenly to have stopped without promise of a positive outcome, weighed heavily on Hennie. The sentry seemed to have somehow fallen through the earth. She stood there, waiting and whispering incomprehensibly, like a village witch, attempting by fervent incantations to hasten the meeting with her beloved and extricate him, for at least an hour or two, from the barracks.

When it seemed that she could do nothing but despair after waiting so long, fortune smiled on Hennie. Accompanied by the sentry, a suntanned Shleimke emerged from the entrance in a uniform that made him look even taller and more handsome than ever. Instead of rushing toward him joyfully, Hennie could not move.

With a rapid, youthful step, Shleimke approached and embraced her, kissing her and slowly and carefully wiping the tears from her cheeks.

"Enough, enough," he said. "You don't even know how to cry properly, you just sniffle with your nose. Let's go down to the river. I'm free until evening roll call. My commander, Captain Kuolelis, asked me who that woman was that was waiting for me outside our fence and, without blinking an eye, I said, 'That is my wife. She came from Jonava.' He believed me and, for serving well, I received time off until evening. Did I say the right thing to him, Hennie?" Shleimke asked with childish insistence. "Do you really agree to become my wife?"

"I agree," Hennie replied with tears in her eyes and, dropping her bag, threw her arms around his neck.

They walked down towards the Neman, found a grassy spot and sat down facing each other. Hennie opened her bag, took out a tablecloth and set out the goodies: pie with raisins, marzipan crusts, round candies that looked like the shiny buttons on a high-school student's uniform, walnuts, two copper-nickel wine cups and an unopened bottle of Passover wine carefully wrapped in a kitchen towel. But there were more than edibles in her cloth bag. At the bottom it was possible to see some non-edible gifts: an intricately monogrammed handkerchief that Hennie had embroidered and woollen socks that she had knitted.

"You might have brought me a potato *kugel*!" Shleimke scolded her affectionately.

"I'll make you a *kugel* right here."

"Where? In the barracks?"

"I've decided to stay in Alytus. I'll find work and rent an inexpensive corner of a room in town. We'll serve together and then return home together. What difference does it make where I work?"

"You're really something! You've decided to stay to make me *kugel*? Have you gone out of your mind?"

"Yes, to make *kugel*, *kugel*! The potatoes are tastier here than in our shtetl," Hennie said, screwing up her eyes in a sly expression. Then she cut the raisin pie and poured the sweet holiday wine into the cups.

"To you!" she toasted and clinked cups with him. "And to your horse, so that he will love you and be careful with you!"

"To you, Hennie!"

Emptying his cup he began to interrogate her in detail about his parents, his brothers, and sisters and about her family. Patiently and in detail, Hennie shared the shtetl news.

"Thank God, all of them are alive and well. There haven't been any funerals or any weddings either, for that matter. However, the number of Jews has increased. My friend, you know her, Dvoira Kamenetskaya, gave birth to twins, a boy and a girl. How fortunate she is! Don't be angry, but I would also like . . ."

"What?"

"The same. To have two at the same time. Even though it's painful, as long as it is successful."

"That's what you say! But what if your future husband doesn't think two is enough?"

"Of course, I'm talking nonsense. It's better if we just sit and don't talk. It's so good here!"

Below them the waters of the Neman flowed calmly and majestically toward the Baltic Sea. From the river curious little fish jumped and fell back, seeking light from the dark depths. From the thick riverside bushes birds fluttered restlessly. After ending its day of work, the sun hastened to its resting place beyond the horizon.

Shleimke looked increasingly often in the direction to which he must return.

"When you go home, Hennie, tell my mother not to worry. No one insults me here and my horse is a calm one. I wish to God that all our Jews were as easy-going as she is. There's no reason for you to stay here for two years, giving up your home for some foreign hole. If you can, come to see me on Saturdays. We'll sit by the river, eat pie with raisins, suck sweets and go to the synagogue and ask God to forgive our sins and bless us with a long life together. And we'll try to express our gratitude by obeying him and by our deeds."

"Yes, Sir."

She didn't say another word, but wrapped up the rest of the food in the tablecloth and accompanied him back to the gate. She bowed her head to say goodbye to the sentry, kissed Shleimke on the cheek and slowly headed back to town.

4

The Dudak family eked out a living. Shimon didn't put down his hammer and awl until late at night. He repaired everything brought to him, both what was suitable for fixing and what should have been thrown out a long time before. In the shtetl people joked that Dudak was the most talkative cobber in the world. His customers were mostly his poor fellow Jews. Shimon Dudak repaired without charge the shoes of poverty-stricken Avigdor Perelman because, for more than a year, the latter had studied at the famous Telshe Yeshiva, although subsequently he had ceased being religious while retaining the tendency to instruct people how to behave in the right way and he had not lost the habit of philosophising at every opportunity. Due to this latter trait, Dr. Yitzhak Blumenfeld had awarded Perelman the nick-name Spinoza.

Avigdor would say, "May God repay you a hundred-fold. All my debts He records in His book of lenders and He is sure to repay those to whom I am in debt. Shimon, he will repay you too. My word of honour, even though one shouldn't swear in God's name! He acts the way He acts. After all, He is the main keeper of accounts. He records both our years and our debts."

"But if He does repay, then please tell me how. With money? By cheque? With abundance?" Shimon asked ironically, while with a rough index finger he stroked his luxurious moustache, which was like those of the Polish nobility.

"With long life. With good husbands for your daughters. You have so many of them – four! With grandchildren."

Shimon was proud of his daughters even though, rather than being his wealth, they were a constant and exhausting worry. Only the eldest, Hennie, added to the skimpy family income with her occasional jobs. When she traveled to Alytus to see Shleimke it was with money that she had earned at The Fireside of Itzik, a modest roadside inn, though its owner hailed his establishment as the finest restaurant in town. Hennie spent whole days cooking, cleaning and grating potatoes, frying *latkes*, baking meat and cabbage pies and pies with raisins and then washing all the vessels and cleaning the inn, which was littered with scraps and cigarette butts. And if it was not for the nocturnal insolence of the delivery men who made drunken attempts to molest her, to pinch her breasts and to touch her prominent rear, if it had not been for their lascivious looks, like tomcats in March and their proposals of a ride in the deep forest or to find some comfortable spot out in the countryside, she would have continued cooking in the restaurant even though her feet almost dropped off working there.

Itsik Berdichevsky, a tough customer, known in Jonava for his cold, firm grip, was satisfied with Hennie; she was the kind of obedient, capable cook he needed. However, despite his best efforts to convince her to stay, promising to protect her from the establishment's shameless customers and to raise her salary, nothing could have kept her from leaving.

For a long time Hennie searched for an appropriate job. But where could a girl who had not even completed elementary school and who knew only how to cook and bake, wash floors and iron laundry find appropriate work? Hennie stopped visiting Shleimke. She didn't ask her father for money. She wrote her cavalryman letters in broken Yiddish; letters full of declarations of love and complaints about her evil fate. She waited as patiently for the village postman Kazimiras, as for the Messiah. Even though she knew that Rokha had little sympathy for her and even openly disliked her, she would still rush to Rybatskaya Street to share news about Shleimke with them. After Hennie had returned from visiting her cavalryman in Alytus, she had enthusiastically told them how he had looked, not sparing superlatives, and how his army service was going. Indeed Rokha had suspected that Hennie was stretching the truth, but she didn't interrupt her. Sweet words always find their way through sensitive ears to a grateful heart.

"What does he write?" my mother would ask her future mother-in-law whenever a letter arrived.

"What does he write?" Rokha's eyes suddenly filled with tears. "He writes everything on the piece of paper that his brother Isaac reads to Dovid and me. And what, tell me, can you write to such backward old folks like us? 'I'm bored,' he writes. 'I feel alright. Only the food, oh Lord!' he writes, 'is not kosher. They give us pork sausages and the soup has mushrooms and pigs' feet in it. You can't do anything about it. Where is a Jew to go if even the air isn't kosher?' But what about you, Hennie, are you just hanging around doing nothing? Did you run away from that adventurer, Berdichevsky?"

"Yes, I ran away."

"You did the right thing. Where peasants have a good time, honest girls have a hard time preserving their purity. Do you understand what I am saying to you?"

Hennie nodded. "I know. That's why I left. Now I'm looking for other work. I keep looking but I can't find anything."

"Perhaps you could be a nanny?" Rokha said, with sudden, unexpected enthusiasm, surprising Hennie. "It's clean work, not hard physically. You would spend the whole day playing with a child from a good family, sitting with him somewhere in the shade of a tree, listening to the birds or going for walks in the park. The child would be good, not spoiled and his mother would be beautiful and educated, speaking French the way you and I speak Yiddish, but not wanting to occupy herself too much with her *karapuz*, her little toddler."

"But whose child could that be?" Hennie asked, her spirits rising. She had hardly expected that Rokha the Samurai, that cat with claws, that antagonist of prospective daughters-in-law even before she met them, would demonstrate such concern for her. Hennie reproached herself for not holding back; she should have waited until Rokha had revealed the name of the child's parents.

"They're rich, very rich." She paused a moment, breathed deeply, then continued. "Once, a very long time ago, I didn't look the way I look now, though I can hardly believe it myself, old witch that I am, but I was, people said, an attractive young woman, so good looking that men would look at me and start drooling. Now I'm wrinkled, with eyes as dull as cold coals in an oven. Don't contradict me, please! I haven't time to listen to your insincere words of consolation. It seems that all this took place not in the time of Dovid the cobbler but in the time of King Dovid himself! I was courted by the young Reb Isaiya, the brother of Yeshua Kremnitser, the grandfather of the child I have in mind. Ten years after we met, he became fabulously rich as a timber merchant, floating logs down the Neman towards the sea, from Lithuania to Russia. But he died suddenly from some mysterious disease. The timber business was taken over by his resourceful nephew Aaron, the father of the child I'm thinking about. I'm sure I have confused you with my story. Did you understanding anything I said?"

"So, is the boy the grandson of Reb Yeshua, the owner of the hardware store near the synagogue and the police station?"

"Yes, the very one. Of course he got to hear about my flirting with his brother more than once from his late wife Golda. I could well have been not Rokha Kanovich the wife of a cobbler, but Rokha Kremnitser, wife of a rich man. I'll try to put in a good word for you."

"Thank you."

"No need to thank me. I'm doing this less for you than for Shleimke, my son, who intends to marry you. But you, Hennie, what do you think? Will he marry you or not? Yes or no? Give me a straight answer, without beating around the bush?"

"I think he will marry me," she replied honestly, dark eyes shining determinedly, not turning from Rokha. Then, aware of what Rokha was thinking, she added forcefully, "If he marries me, I hope that you will not regret it."

"May that be God's will," Rokha said evasively. "I like your frankness and directness. I hate people who don't say what they mean."

From the next room came the sound of the steady blow of a cobbler's hammer against a shoe. The monotonous sound calmed Hennie.

"If I am hired by Reb Kremnitser, with my first month's pay I'll buy two tickets, one for you, Rokha, and one for me, so that we can travel by bus to Alytus to see your son. I already know the way there. You have to come with me."

"Me?" Rokha asked in confusion. "I have never travelled anywhere in my whole life. Not anywhere. I was born in Jonava and I will die here. If they had drafted young women into the army, I might have seen some other cities like Alytus, Ukmerge or Zarasai. Maybe even Kaunas. There are probably army barracks in all those cities. But the Almighty found it fitting that I spend the years allotted to me in my barracks on Rybatskaya Street, a house with holes in the roof, hungry mice and a platoon of children we had to set on their feet."

"Shleimke would be happy to see you."

"And what if they don't let him out and you and I travel there for nothing?" Rokha asked dubiously.

"They say that all gates are open for mothers."

"Maybe that only refers to the Gates of Heaven. The main thing is that Shleimke is well. The Lithuanians don't like our people very much."

"But they aren't beasts. And anyway, the head of the soldiers and the horses there treats Shleimke well," Hennie said and smiled.

"We'll see. First you have to receive your pay," my grandma Rokha noted logically. "To travel from Jonava to Alytus on foot, my dear, is not for me. But I'll tell grandfather Kremnitser that one of these days a young lady named Hennie will drop into his shop."

"Oh yes, I'll go to see him tomorrow! Perhaps I'll be lucky."

Hennie bade her goodbye and left the house, to the sound of Dovid's hammer ringing out a triumphal march.

Reb Yeshua Kremnitser, the grandfather of the child for whom they were seeking a nanny, was a religious man. He had a large head, a good-sized body and wore a velvet yarmulke and eyeglasses with horned rims. When Hennie entered, he was standing behind the counter like a statue, rocking from side to side, either to prevent himself from fall-ing asleep at such an early hour, or so that the Lord might remove the boredom that had overcome him and send him more customers than the previous day.

Seeing his first customer enter, Kremnitser rejoiced, inter-preting it as Heaven's response to his prayer.

"How can I help you, young lady?" he asked.

Hennie was confused and at first didn't know how to reply.

"Didn't Rokha, the wife of Dovid the cobbler, speak to you about me?" she asked, dismayed.

"No, she didn't. I've known Rokha for scores of years; usually she likes to wag her tongue. Just last week she dropped in and, as usual verbally demolished, in her words, 'the crazy and under-baked world God created', while at the same time mentioning that my brother Isaiya had courted her when they were young. She bought a lock for a door and I can't remember what else . . ."

"Evidently she either didn't have the time or simply forgot to tell you about me," Hennie said disconcertedly. "Well then, excuse me, please. I'd better come back after Rokha has spoken to you."

But she lingered in the doorway.

"Wait. Where are you rushing off to? You can tell me what Rokha wanted to say," the bored Reb Kremnitser said to stop her. He wiped his large, wrinkled forehead with a silk hand-kerchief. "After all, sometimes you can get as much profit from speaking with a good person as from some item you might sell. What, may I ask, did my old acquaintance, the much-respected Rokha, want to speak to me about?"

"About me. And about your grandson. Excuse me, but I don't know his name."

"Raphael."

"That's a lovely name," Hennie said.

"Why are you interested in my two-year-old grandson?" Reb Kremnitser was the model of the politeness and atten-tiveness characteristic of all successful merchants. Curious, he lowered his large glasses onto the meaty bridge of his nose and directed his short-sighted gaze at his visitor.

"Rokha told me that your son and his wife might be look-ing for a nanny for your young grandson."

"Yes, that's right. I even put up a notice on the door of my shop, but no one replied. One can't stop any young woman on the street and propose something like that to her," Reb Yeshua said and proceeded to look Hennie over from head to foot. "If I'm not mistaken, you would like to be considered for the job. Is that correct?"

"Rokha and I thought that I might be a fitting nanny for your Raphael . . ." Hennie trembled at her own temerity and bit her tongue.

"So then, do you have any experience in such work? Did you ever engage in it?"

"I did take care of all my little sisters. My mother was seriously ill and bed-ridden for a long time so I took care of the little ones; I fed them, washed them, took them for walks, put them to bed, sang them to sleep and made up stories to tell them."

"What can I say? You deserve great credit as a daughter and a sister! How many sisters do you have, my dear?"

"Three. And two brothers. I'm the oldest in the family. Mother gave birth to six daughters and four sons, but not all of them survived. Besides me there are three girls – Pesya, Hasya, and Feiga, and two boys – Motl and Shmulik."

"It would appear that you are a natural nanny. I will speak with Aaron and Ethel, my son and daughter-in-law. Drop by in a day or two and I'll let you know what they have decided."

Hennie couldn't sleep for two nights. She kept looking from her trestle-bed out the window waiting for the day to dawn.

5

On the third day Hennie was the first in the house to get out of bed. She brushed her dark curly hair, put on her best calico dress and ran to the hardware store, which was still padlocked. She recognized Reb Yeshua Kremnitser from a distance; he was walking slowly from the synagogue, his prayer items tucked under his arm in a velvet pouch embellished with an embroidered six-pointed Star of David. The pious storekeeper appeared to be continuing his prayers; he was quite content to converse with God about the important things in life with no one else around.

The closer he got, the more Hennie's heart contracted, like a piece of bread torn from a loaf that the birds were pecking at from all sides.

"You must have slept on the porch," Reb Kremnitser joked.

"Good morning," said Hennie. The fact that Reb Yeshua greeted her so warmly encouraged her.

"First I'll open the shop and then we'll discuss everything. As you see, in my advanced years I sell all kinds of small items – latches, valves, locks, nails and such junk." Pointing at the rust-covered lock on his door, he said, "I haven't even managed to replace that. I forget, you see. There's nothing to be done about it. No one has ever succeeded in escaping from old age alive, though I'll damned well be escaping soon enough. You know, of course, where one escapes to from old age? To our ancestors. Now, come in!"

After listening to his rather discouraging moralizing about old age, Hennie followed him into the shop.

"Yesterday the cobbler's wife Rokha, who did not become the wife of my brother Isaiya, came in, supposedly to buy some glue for her husband, Dovid. She swore to me that you're honest, tidy and good and that you're capable of doing many things."

"Thank you." Hennie sighed, although such a beginning frightened rather than encouraged her.

"As I promised you, I spoke with my children, Aaron and Ethel. They would like to meet you. Do you know where they live?"

"In the very centre of town, where the monument is, in the two-storey house opposite the post office."

"If you please them the way you please an old man like me, they will make an agreement with you for three months to be sure that you are right for the job and, then, perhaps for another longer period. You will have Fridays and Saturdays off as well as all the Jewish holidays. Do you understand?"

"Yes."

"Your food will be free and your salary a good one. I believe these conditions are not bad."

"They're excellent! But, tell me, will you be there too?" She choked suddenly on her words. "Will you be there too when I come?"

"Where?"

"At their house."

"Why do you need an old ruin like me for your negotiations? After all, I'm only the grandpa. My word is not decisive. I can only advise."

"For some reason I would like you to be there," Hennie said with insistent sincerity. "Please!"

"I will try."

"When would it be best to come?"

"If you want me to be present at your discussion, come on Shabbat. After morning prayers. My brother Isaiya, may he be blessed by Heaven, used to say that blessings come to the world in the morning. While all the terrible evil that exists in the world is rubbing its sleep-encrusted eyes, goodness is already rising like the sun in the haze of dawn and looking down on us in our God-forsaken Jonava."

As Reb Yeshua advised, on Shabbat, when the sun had risen above the roof tiles, Hennie approached the two-storey house, surrounded by an iron lattice fence, opposite the post office. She stood at the closed gate for some time, as if afraid that it would burn her, then cautiously rang the bell. Soon a tall, lovely woman emerged from the house wearing shoes and a flowery robe. Her thick blonde hair was beautifully fashioned, not by the local hairdresser, the 'magician' Naum Kovalsky, but by a wonder-working hairdresser from Kaunas. Her elegant coiffure had the scent of an expensive perfume.

"Hennie?"

"Yes."

"Come in, please."

The lady of the house was polite and kind. Hennie passed through the front garden with its miniature trees and into the entrance of the house. She took off her shoes, put on slippers and entered the living room.

What she saw almost blinded her. She had never seen such luxury in any house in Jonava. The floor was covered with expensive Persian carpets. On the walls hung oil paintings; there was a painting of a long-bearded, kind-looking old man in a yarmulke, Raphael's great-grandfather Reb Dov-Ber, who had almost married a rich Florentine Jewess of Spanish descent in Italy. There was a painting of the Mount of Olives and one of the Wailing Wall in Jerusalem, embraced by pilgrims, and yet another of brindled cows and a tiny herdsman in a field. The salon was furnished with mahogany furniture; a table, cupboards and bookcases.

"Sit down, dear. My name is Ethel," the mistress of the house said, pointing with a delicate hand adorned by rings to a soft chair. "My husband will soon be finished shaving and will join us right away. My father-in-law, who recommended you, will join us too. Meanwhile, can I bring you something to drink? What do you drink, my dear?"

"Water."

"Everyone drinks water. What else?"

"Sometimes carrot juice and, on Passover, sweet wine and sometimes mead," Hennie replied, blushing.

"It's a long time until Passover. How about carrot juice? Will that do?" Ethel smiled and left the room.

Hennie was left alone with the long-bearded old Dov-Ber, the fervent pilgrims embracing the holy, redemptive Wailing

Wall and the cows and the carefree herdsman in their huge frames. She suddenly felt alone and insignificant; with a lump in her throat she wanted nothing more than to leave the house as soon as possible, to disappear and return to her own home – to her sisters and brothers, to her father, who was as permanent and silent as a shadow and to her mother, who loved them all.

Just then Aaron entered the salon, elegantly dressed in a brand-new suit, looking like a mannequin from the magazine, 'Summer and Winter Clothing for All'. He was followed by Ethel, whose perfume smelled like flowering lilac, carrying the carrot juice in a carafe on a silver tray, accompanied by her father-in-law, the greatly respected Reb Yeshua.

"Here's your juice. Drink, don't be shy. Please feel at home."

In her rush to be polite Hennie almost drank from the tall carafe.

"And now, down to business," said the younger Kremnitser. "We've heard about your qualities and have no doubt that you can cope with your new responsibilities and that, in time, you will come to love Raphael."

"I hope so," Hennie said.

"Good. As for conditions, it seems that you have already been informed of them. You will receive 85 *litas* per month plus free food. Does that amount satisfy you?"

"Yes," she said, never having dreamed of earning such money.

"That means that apparently we have agreed on the main points," Aaron said, shaking her hand, as if congratulating her on her new position. "As for food, I believe that is also clear. You will eat what we eat and will join us at the table without any restrictions. After half a year of work you will have two weeks' paid holiday. You will be free on all the Jewish holidays. Furthermore, we don't exclude the possibility of other benefits. When can you begin?"

"Why, right away," Hennie murmured. Her head was spinning hearing what Aaron Kremnitser had to say. She feared that everything that she had heard was only a dream and that the dream could disappear in a moment and that the words that had been spoken would take flight like doves frightened by a hawk.

"Right away is right away. As soon as Raphael wakes up, we'll introduce you. Our boy is quite a fellow, but a sleepyhead. Meanwhile I'll tell you about his toys, which will be a great help for you. When I travel, I always bring him something. Our house is so packed with toys that there would be enough for a whole legion of his peers. When Raphael grows up, we'll ask you to give them to children from needy families. There are quite a few of those in Jonava. Will you help us?"

"Of course. I like toys myself," Hennie said, and for the first time she smiled timidly, feeling both envy and exhilaration mixed with fright.

"Well, I brought him bears, clowns, gnomes, cars, hand organs, whistles, shepherd's flutes and flocks of stuffed sheep and goats from Europe. You'll see this whole zoo for yourself soon, as well as the collection of instruments and the vehicles that belong to Raphael, but before that you should take a walk with him in the park here."

"Of course."

"Now let's go to see Raphael, Hennie," said Aaron, addressing her by name for the first time.

It should, perhaps, be noted that the local residents had given the lofty title 'park' more in jest than in full seriousness to the neglected land overgrown with weeds and thistles behind the brick building of the post office. On both sides of it there grew two rows of sickly oaks with broken branches, which, the locals joked, had provided shade to Napoleon's troops who, despite burning Moscow down, had been forced to retreat. Here and there under the oaks stood knocked-together benches on which, rather than the residents of Jonava, there shivered flocks of tiny, defenceless, eternally-hungry swallows.

Hennie had hardly begun to enjoy her unexpected success when doubts began to assail her. Would she work for the Kremnitsers for long? Wouldn't they fire her before the trial period was over? It was one thing to care for her own sisters, who were simple people like herself, but it was another thing entirely when it came to the spoiled Raphael. He had, of course, been raised speaking French not Yiddish, since his father had received his higher education in Paris. And his mother didn't work as a simple shepherd-ess, or as a cook in the kind of restaurant owned by Itsik Berdichevsky. Why didn't they hire a nanny from Paris or, in the worst case, from Kaunas? The only thing that Hennie could offer them in place of knowledge was love for the boy. Everybody understood the silent language of love, even cats and dogs.

She consoled herself with the thought that even if they ended her service after the trial period, she would have received a large amount of money just for three months' work. Hennie followed Aaron into Raphael's room.

She liked the boy very much. Like his papa, Raphael was elegantly dressed, with short velvet trousers with straps, a light blue silk shirt with very faint stripes and light little shoes with buckles. The boy's dark curly hair was parted in the middle and shone as if it had just been washed.

"Introduce yourself, Raphael," Aaron said formally, addressing his son like an adult. "Give auntie your hand, like a gentleman."

The boy didn't move. He looked at Hennie as if she were a large talking doll.

"What are you afraid of? Auntie will come every day to sing to you, to tell you stories and to take you to the park and you can feed the birds with her," Aaron said, trying to overcome his son's bashfulness.

Raphael hid behind his father's back, but from there he peeked with frightened curiosity at the unfamiliar woman.

"I promise he'll get used to you soon," Ethel assured Hennie. "At first we'll take care of him together. Please don't worry, everything will work out. Nobody turns away from those who love them, whether they're children or adults."

In fact, everything did work out. Hennie's concern that she would soon be fired turned out to be wrong and Ethel deserved much of the credit for that. The uneducated Hennie not only got along well at the Kremnitsers, but even became friends with the lady of the house, who was not much older than the new nanny and was not acquainted with many young women of her own age in Jonava. All of her peers lived either in Kaunas or abroad. Ethel did sometimes meet with her friends when she accompanied Aaron on one of his short trips to Kaunas or to Germany, where she had been born into a family of several generations of merchants. Ethel considered Jonava a place of exile. Her husband, a successful timber merchant, had long wanted to transfer his business activity to some port city, like Marseilles or Kiel, but his father, Reb Yeshua, categorically refused to part with his locks, nails and latches. As he stressed to anyone who would listen, "Nobody moves away from the graves of their parents voluntarily, not even for money."

Raphael grew accustomed to his nanny. At first, when he saw her, he would run away, hiding, as a child might, in the kind of place where he could easily be found. When Ethel and Aaron left the house and Raphael was alone with his nanny, he sulked and cried bitterly. But, at the beginning of her second week, an unexpected change took place in their relationship. Raphael dragged a doll out of the nursery; a long-legged, big-eared clown with a long drooping moustache and a funny cap with pictures of anchors on the brim. Rushing to hand her his toy, he shouted loudly, "'Ennie, 'Ennie! Peepee!"

The boy pointed down past his belly toward his little penis.

Hennie took his hand and led him to the bathroom and sat him on the potty. When a minute later a little stream came forth and the little fellow again cried, "'Ennie!" she realized that their real friendship had begun with that historic "peepee."

She spent whole days with Raphael, thinking up all kinds of games and entertainments. In order to amuse him, Hennie began to imitate a goat bleating in the garden, a frog croaking in the swamp, a rooster crowing in the neighbour's yard, or a hungry sparrow twittering in the front garden. Raphael would listen and break out into happy laughter.

After his daily nap, Hennie took him for a walk to the neglected park, where the child raced after the poor sparrows or beautiful butterflies, or to the forlorn apple orchard that had long ago stopped yielding any fruit, next to the town's Catholic church, the arrow-like spire of which somehow recalled the crucified Jesus, penetrating the deep blue sky. Sometimes they would wander down to Kaunas Street. There Hennie always stopped, pointing out the crooked house from which one could hear the continual pounding of the tireless hammer. But she never dared take the child in.

"This is where my parents live, Raphael," she told the child.

Raphael's eyes widened in amazement at the small windows and, grabbing his nanny's hand, he pulled her back towards his mother and their two-storey house.

On the way, Hennie and the toddler usually looked in at the empty shop of his grandfather and her benefactor, where there was a whole realm of locks and valves. During their short visits Raphael would receive countless hugs and kisses.

Walking around town holding the child by the hand, Hennie ran into Rokha the Samurai one day. The latter was hurrying to the *shokhet* with a white goose that rested, unconcerned, in a large basket, unaware of its imminent and merciless end.

"Any letters?" asked Hennie, after greeting her prospective mother-in-law.

"For some reason our cavalryman hasn't written for a long time," Rokha complained, shaking her head. "I thought perhaps he had written to you?"

"No. If he had written, I wouldn't have kept it from you. I would have run and told you right away. Perhaps Shleimke is on manoeuvres."

Raphael approached the basket, apparently intending to wake the goose, which continued to doze peacefully as if it was in a cradle.

"Raphael! Don't you dare touch it!" Hennie shouted. "It will peck you with its beak. Then your fingers will hurt for a long time."

"What kind of a thing are these 'manoeuvres'?" Rokha asked, intimidated by the unfamiliar word.

"Military exercises. The soldiers learn how to gallop in the saddle and, while they're galloping, they use their sabres to cut the head off a straw man who represents the enemy. And, also, they learn to shoot accurately at a target with a rifle."

"Saddles, swords, shooting." Rokha sighed. "In my opinion all this isn't Jewish *gesheft*." She patted Raphael's dark curly hair, sighed again, and said, "What a fine little fellow! He will be, or rather he already is, the heir of a hardware store and Kremnitser's other store, the grocery store and, most importantly, of the huge expanses of pine forests over in Zemaitija, beyond Raseiniai. And what, I often ask the Lord, will my grandson receive as an inheritance? Only a hammer, an awl, some cobbler's nails and glue, with a shoe tree thrown in. Oh yes, and all our troubles."

"I don't think that anyone, even God Himself, knows who will inherit what or when," Hennie replied.

The goose that was doomed to have its life taken by the *shokhet* awoke and peered haughtily at Raphael with one eye. Raphael hugged his nanny's warm hip fearfully.

"In about ten days I'll receive my first salary. Then, Rokha, you and I will get on a bus and travel to see Shleimke in Alytus," Hennie said to her future mother-in-law.

"So we'll go on manoeuvres?" Rokha remarked ironically.

"Yes!" Hennie laughed.

Then, since Raphael was bored, his nanny took him home, excusing herself to the bent Rokha and even to the arrogant goose, which had no idea of its imminent fate.

6

There was a celebration in the Dudak home on Kaunas Street: Hennie had brought home her first pay. 85 *litas*! Just imagine – 85. Almost 90! The cobbler Shimon didn't earn as much in three months! Hennie had earned three times more than her father!

"Pesya, Hasya, and Feiga, take an example from your sister!" he said.

Hennie baked her favourite pastry with raisins and *teiglekh* – honey cakes – and boiled potatoes with Greek prunes. The latter had been bought at the grocery store owned by her benefactor Reb Yeshua Kremnitser, where the shop assistant, Ruvim Birger, whose head was bald as a knee, reigned. Hennie prepared a real feast.

When the family's excitement abated a little, the fortunate young woman told them that the following day she was going with Rokha the Samurai to Alytus to see Shleimke, from whom there had been no news for so long.

"With that *baba-yaga*?" Hennie's father objected. "You're in too much of a hurry to waste your money on that witch; you're not her daughter-in-law yet."

"Rokha helped me find work as a nanny with the Kremnitsers. And what's more, she isn't a witch, she's simply worn down by life. Her whole house rests on her shoulders. Rokha is like a donkey harnessed to an overloaded cart that somebody has forgotten to unhitch. You told me yourself, Father, that her main helpers, Isaac and Leah, are planning to stretch their wings and take flight from Lithuania permanently."

"So what?" Shimon didn't relent. "She and her husband still have your Shleimke and Motl and Hava. Perhaps Leah and Isaac really will leave. Who knows? What have they got to do in our small town apart from mending and mending and mending some more, tinkering and tinkering, shaving beards, cutting hair, standing on the porch and watching the people pass by the whole day long, waiting for customers until they're blind? But in America, they say, if you go out into the street you find dollars swirling around everywhere. All you have to do is bend over and pick them up!"

"If Shleimke decides to leave here," Hennie burst out suddenly, "I'll go with him. Anywhere!"

"The question is, will he take you with him?"

"Yes. Yes he will!"

"First stand under the *chuppah* with the rabbi and Shleimke and then you can be sure."

Hennie didn't want to ruin the celebration. Her father could not be convinced anyway; for him the *chuppah* was the most dependable roof in the world.

It was even harder, however, to convince Rokha. She didn't want to travel to see her son in Alytus at someone else's expense and invented various excuses not to go.

"I'll see him, speak with him for five minutes and then I'll only get upset when it's time to leave. When you don't see someone for a long time, your love just grows stronger."

"Rokha, I'm sorry but that's nonsense! Being apart for a long time destroys love; it's like the dress hanging in the closet that mother never wears. You don't have to do anything but get on the bus! I've got everything ready; a pie and *teiglekh*, German chocolate and a pair of woollen socks for winter. They're all in my little carrying case. I knitted the socks myself. So I'll wait for you tomorrow at eight in the morning at the bus station. Just don't be late!"

"And what if Shleimke is still out on manoeuvres? We'll arrive and he won't be there," worried the thrifty Rokha, who always regretted spending her own money and was ashamed to spend that of others.

"Alright, I'll come to your house on Rybatskaya Street instead. That way there'll be less likelihood of a mistake."

The bus was, as usual, late. Hennie was afraid Rokha would run off rather than wait.

When it pulled in to the station, the future daughter-in-law helped her overweight companion into the half-empty bus and seated her in the front row next to the window so that she would be able to see the Lithuanian countryside, which she had never seen before, with its green fields and hills, streams and forests, miniature roadside crucifixes and peasant huts that seemed to grow like trees out of the clay soil.

The whole journey the old woman didn't turn her eyes from the window, outside which a poor country sped past. It was unfamiliar and incomprehensible to her, inveterate stay-at-home that she was.

"It's a beautiful country, you can't deny it," Rokha whispered, as if sharing some secret with Hennie. "But the poor people are like us."

"Yes, they're not rich," Hennie agreed.

"Then why, if they are poor like us, do the Lithuanians not like us? What harm did the Jews do to them? We sew for them, we mend their boots, we shave them and cut their hair and fix their clocks."

The bus shook and rattled along the bumpy road. Rokha bounced about on the springs and sighed mournfully. "Oy!" she repeated, grabbing Hennie with both hands.

The young woman did not have an answer to Rokha's question about the Lithuanians. She herself had often wondered where their eternal hostility came from.

"Perhaps it's because the Jews have always been foreigners," Hennie said. "Even the dove pecks at the chicks of another kind of bird. If you're foreign, it's seen as a bad thing. And anyway, in general, poverty doesn't make anyone better. Apparently that is the way the world was created and that is the way it will always be."

Rokha frowned and didn't ask Hennie anything else. The thought that, after their trip to Alytus together, the sharp-eyed daughter of Shimon was hoping to gain her consent to her marrying her King Solomon suddenly obscured all that flashed by the windows. "But perhaps Hennie is rejoicing prematurely," she thought.

They continued on to Alytus without speaking.

"Are you still alive after all that crazy bouncing?" Hennie asked finally.

"As you see, I am still alive even though all my bones have been shaken up. Is it far from the station to the barracks?"

"Not far, but not close either. We'll walk slowly and take breaks. We'll rest along the way."

Rokha had never been in such a large town before and everything attracted her attention; the three and four-storey houses, the broad concrete pavements, the colourful signs and the well-dressed people.

"Won't we get lost?" she asked Hennie.

"No, we won't."

"I wouldn't like to live here."

"Why not?"

"Back in Jonava I know everyone: the Lithuanians, the Poles and the Jews," Rokha said wistfully. "I know who is getting married and who is getting divorced, who has a cat at home and who has a fierce dog on a chain in his yard. And everyone knows me. But here? No, I wouldn't want to live here for anything."

Thus, reflecting on the advantages of their native Jonava in contrast with the alien Alytus, they made their way towards their destination.

Hennie was listening to Rokha when, from a distance, she made out the figure of the sentry. Neither in bearing nor in height did he resemble the stocky soldier who had been guarding the entrance to the military zone the previous time. Confusing cases and mangling verbs, Hennie tried to explain to the lanky, unfriendly guard what had brought them there.

"*Mes is Jonava.*" We're from Jonava.

The guard looked them over from head to toe with a disparaging glance. He didn't need any explanations; he had figured out who these women had come to see from their terrible accents and from their faces, which were unlike those of most of his own people.

"Jus pas eilini Saliamonas?" You're looking for Private Solomon?

As if on command, Hennie and Rokha nodded affirmatively.

"Atspejau. Jis cia pas mus vienintelis Zydas." I guessed so. He's the only Jew here.

Of all his words Hennie and Rokha understood only *Zydas;* that was familiar to both practically from the cradle.

"Tuojau surasime." I'll go find him, the soldier said and disappeared into the stockade.

Soon Private Solomon arrived.

"Shleimke!" Rokha cried as if her son was in mortal danger. And then she ran to him.

Hennie stood aside and took pleasure in observing how Rokha pummelled and kneaded her son with her thickly veined hands, as if he was a piece of dough.

"I swear to you, my son, that if I met you on the street I would never have recognized you! You look the same and, at the same time, so very different. You don't look like a Jew in your military uniform." Whether she was praising or teasing him wasn't clear, but her yearning for him was. "Fool that I am, I didn't want to come! I only came thanks to Hennie, who insisted on dragging me here."

Private Solomon stroked his mother's grey, untidy hair and wrinkled face, as if trying to wipe away the deep furrows there and, with a look of great warmth, thanked Hennie, who was pressing her canvas bag to her breast like a child.

The guard, who had never seen more than three Jews at one time before being drafted into the army from his native village outside Rokiškis or Kupiškis, stared at them in astonishment.

"Let's go down to the banks of the Neman. We had such a good time there together last time," Hennie suggested. "Why are we just standing here like fools?"

"To my great regret I can't go with you," Shleimke said. "I'm on duty today."

Rokha and Hennie looked at each other with consternation.

"Today I'm responsible for keeping the barracks clean and tidy; I have to get back there in five or, at the most ten minutes, otherwise I risk being locked up in the guardhouse."

"In the guardhouse? Oh, Lord!" Rokha moaned. "I barely dragged my bones here hoping to spend at least an hour with you, and now it turns out that we have to head home straight away. If we had known that, we certainly wouldn't have come! You didn't send us any letters, you didn't warn us! We just had to sit and wonder whether you were alive or not."

"Yes, I'm sorry." Shleimke bowed his head. "But anyway, you aren't able to answer my letters."

"It's true that we're illiterate, that we don't know how to write, but that is no reason to punish us with your silence," Rokha reproached him. "When you come back home, maybe you'll teach the two of us ignoramuses. Anyway, enough. We saw you, and thank God for that." She turned to Hennie, who had generously given her priority in both expressing her love and her complaints. "*Nu*, hurry," she said. "Take out all your presents for him!"

"Shleimke, take everything we brought, including the bag. When Mother and I come to see you again, we'll take it back," Hennie said guiltily, trying to in some way make up for having so thoughtlessly convinced the drooping Rokha to make the long trip.

They had to wait a long time for the bus to Jonava and the luckless pair didn't know how to spend the time. They wandered aimlessly around the unfamiliar town, looking in the store windows and at the signs of the shops, glancing through open doors into barbershops that smelled of cheap eau de cologne and had Jewish barbers equipped with scissors and razors and dressed in sparkling white aprons. They also wandered through the town market, which was packed with peasant carts, searching among the crowd for fellow Jews, who were much harder to find in Alytus than in Jonava.

Suddenly Hennie remembered Hillel Leizerovsky, his sick wife and their several children.

"The last time I was here a good person helped me find Shleimke's regiment. May God reward him equally or more richly for his good deed."

"Maybe He rewards in heaven, but not on earth. Here on earth it's not God who rules, even though He created it, but all the lords and the little lords," Rokha the Samurai commented.

Hennie was eager to stop some Jew or other and ask where Kudirkos Street was so that she could visit Hillel, but she decided not to. It would be a sin to tire Rokha even more; the sad old woman was already finding it hard to stand on her swollen feet.

At the bus station they sat on a bench and waited for the bus to Jonava. Never before had the two of them felt so close as on that little island smelling of gasoline and machine grease and littered with cigarette butts, scraps of paper and shards of glass. Even their silence drew them close because they were thinking about the same thing; they were thinking about love, love that despite everything was stronger than anger and about fate that is not kind to those who love. Who could have known that Shleimke would be on duty precisely on that day?

"Thank you, Rokha!" Hennie said, breaking the silence.

"For what?" the old woman replied hollowly.

"For introducing me to Reb Yeshua Kremnitser. If it were not for you, I'm not sure what I would be doing in our little town. Sweeping the streets? Washing floors for the miller Mendel Vasserman? Or sitting at home wearing out my dress to the sound of father's hammer? Thank you as well for agreeing to come with me here. Despite everything, I don't think that our visit was for nothing. After our visit Shleimke will be able to serve better."

"I am the one who should thank you. To tell you the truth, before this I didn't have a very high opinion of you. I won't lie or beat my breast and ask you to forgive me. In that way I am a mother. Do you understand what I am saying?"

"Yes, I understand," Hennie replied with uncharacteristic passion. "Someday I will give birth and raise a son like yours. I will also want him to have a wife who is not ignorant or impoverished, but beautiful and rich. It will hurt me too if some other woman comes along and takes him away from me forever."

At that moment the bus drove up and they had no chance to continue their conversation.

The way home seemed much shorter to both of them. Sunk in thought, they didn't notice when they arrived in Jonava.

The two women walked together as far as the synagogue.

"You, of course, will visit him again, but I don't have the strength to bounce there and back," Rokha said to Hennie before parting from her at the crossroads.

"Yes, I will visit him."

"When you go and see him the next time, come and tell us absolutely everything. Then the whole lot of us can get a close look at you and hear how our dear cavalryman is serving with the Lithuanians."

Hennie gazed for a long time at the bent back of Rokha as she walked away. All the way to Kaunas Street she pondered Rokha's words; she might not yet be totally on her side, but she was, at least, no longer her implacable opponent.

Hennie returned to work in a happy mood. Her feeling of disappointment over the unsuccessful visit to Alytus was assuaged somewhat by Rokha's invitation. Ethel and Raphael greeted her warmly.

"'Ennie!" the toddler shouted, running up to her and embracing her knees with his plump arms.

"How is your soldier doing?" asked Ethel, to whom Hennie had confided her love secrets.

"He's doing well, but he still has a year left to serve."

"The year will fly by," Ethel said and then rebuked her son. "Raphael, stop pulling Hennie by the skirt. Real men do not behave that way with ladies. When Mama finishes talking, Hennie will pay attention to you."

"The little fellow missed me," Hennie said in his defence. "And I missed him too. Now, let's go and play cat and mouse, Rafi. You be the cat and I will be the mouse. I'll run away and hide and you chase after me. When I hide you have to look for me everywhere."

"It doesn't matter how well the mouse might hide, she can never hide from the sharp-sighted Raphael," Ethel said, going along with the game. "Does your cavalryman have a civilian profession?" she asked Hennie.

"Yes, he's a tailor."

"That is wonderful, my dear. If it wasn't for tailors, kings and beggars would walk around naked or wear animal skins. In Paris tailors earn huge sums. Monsieur Jacques Levit, who sews clothes for me and comes, by the way, from Lithuania, wasn't embarrassed about taking a very substantial amount of money from me for sewing a dress and jacket last year, despite the fact that I'm the wife of his fellow countryman. Perhaps some day you might bid Jonava adieu and move to France."

"But Shleimke doesn't know a single word of French."

"His needle will teach him."

"And I don't know any language other than Yiddish either," Hennie laughed. "Why would we ignoramuses go to

Paris? God willing, we'll somehow set ourselves up in as decent a way as possible in this town."

She was ashamed to admit that she made mistakes when she was writing Yiddish and didn't have any idea about where to put full stops and commas because she hadn't even completed elementary school. Instead she had to help her worn-out mother raise her younger sisters and brothers. But, Hennie thought, how could a well-meaning, affluent woman, who had dresses and jackets sewn for her not in Jonava by old man Gedalya Bankvecher, but by Monsieur Jacques Levit in Paris, understand what it meant to live in the prison of poverty from which it was so difficult, in fact practically impossible, to escape – right to one's dying day?

Instead of arguing with her about life's difficulties, or about illiteracy, Ethel made an unexpected and attractive proposal.

"It's not a disaster that you didn't get the chance to get an elementary education; all you need is the desire to learn something. I have a tremendous amount of free time and I don't know what to do with it. I'm tired of reading romantic novels. I could teach you something. I already teach my capricious Raphael every day. I could teach the two of you."

"What are you saying? Thank you, but you would only torture yourself trying to teach me; I have such a thick head! Whenever the wind changes, it blows everything right out of it. And then, if you'll excuse me, who could I speak French with if you, Mr. Aaron and your father-in-law move away? With the *balagala*, the cart driver Peisakh Shvartsman? Or with the ladies' hairdresser, Ruvim Gertsman? Or perhaps the tinsmith Leizer Ferdsman? They all make mistakes even when they speak their native Yiddish."

Hearing Hennie's list of potential French speakers in Jonava Ethel broke into laughter and had difficulty stopping.

"It's been such a long time since I laughed so much; that really tickled me!"

"'Ennie, 'Ennie," Raphael piped up impatiently, grabbing his nanny's skirt again; for him Hennie was a large doll that could be set into motion.

So 'the doll' set about fulfilling her responsibilities. Until it was time for the boy's nap, she played the role of the persecuted mouse while he, the ferocious cat, hunted her. The next day Hennie changed into a crafty fox or a frightened rabbit. And, thus, from day to day she played the roles of all the animals in the zoo, which she had heard about but never actually seen.

Despite her objections, it turned out that the Kremnitser home became Hennie's school as well as her place of work.

The business-like Ethel hated empty words and tried, as far as was possible, to introduce a little variety into the colourless and monotonous life that she lived like a kind of prisoner. With incredible diligence and self-sacrifice she undertook to teach Hennie writing and arithmetic in both Yiddish and French. Ethel ordered educational materials from Kaunas, bought pencils and notebooks and developed a system for conducting the lessons; two hours a day just with Hennie and then, after lunch, an hour and a half with her and Raphael after his nap. Thus, with her lively conversational style, just as the teacher had hoped, they were able to learn many new words. Ethel worked hard and, unexpectedly, and to her no small delight, was transformed from an idler into a teacher.

"How will you greet your cavalryman in French when you meet him again in Alytus?" Ethel asked Hennie on one occasion.

"*Bonjour, cher ami!*"

"Bravo! You have a good ear and excellent pronunciation. With that you will manage in France."

The praise pleased Hennie, but what good was praise if the foreign language was of no use either to her or to Shleimke? Furthermore, according to rumours circulating in town, it wasn't Shleimke but his brother Isaac who was intending to move to Paris. Hennie didn't want to hurt Ethel, however, or deprive her of what obviously gave her pleasure. After all, the rich deserved pity and compassion too. No matter how different people seem to be, she thought, they all have something in common. Ethel's husband, the restless Aaron, was almost always away. He was always travelling to various ports, to Memel, to Oslo, to Copenhagen, to Marseilles or to Kiel. Ethel's father-in-law, the pious Reb Yeshua, distressed by his daughter-in-law's atheism and refusal to take Raphael to the synagogue, returned home exhausted every day from his unprofitable hardware store and remained alone in his room. In the evenings Reb Kremnitser replaced his usual spectacles with their horn-rimmed frames with a magnifying glass and took out of a bookcase that was as old as he was a gift edition of the Hebrew Bible with embossed gold binding.

Before going to sleep at midnight, he left the two-storey family house for the holy pages of the Book of Books. In the long hours until dawn he seemed to leave Lithuania's borders and travel to the Kingdom of Judea, ancient homeland of the Jews, both those dead and those still alive.

After one lesson Ethel asked, "How much longer does your soldier have to serve?"

"Less than a year."

"That's not long."

"Excuse me for disagreeing, but while for some people it may not be, for me it is," Hennie replied.

"Forgive me for asking, but I would like to know what you'll do when he returns."

"Live. If Shleimke doesn't change his mind, we will marry. He'll sew but I don't know what I will do. Raphael is growing up so you will be able to do without me." Hennie raised her head, patted down her hair and focused her eyes as if she were trying to see the future. "I will look after my husband, be his loyal servant, his cook."

"For your whole life?"

"Perhaps for my whole life. I think . . ." Hennie stopped suddenly. "I still don't know how to address you."

"Just call me Ethel, or Etya. Or Etka. Whatever you like. I'm not a lady of the upper class."

"I don't think it is so important what a person does or what language he speaks," Hennie said.

"What is important?"

"Perhaps what I'm going to say will sound silly, but it's what I believe."

"Say it! I say silly things sometimes, but no one's ever punished for being silly."

"I think that the most important thing is that someone loves you and that you love someone. There are many things in the world – there are people, languages, and money and all kinds of beautiful things, but what there is least of is love."

"That's absolutely right!" Ethel sighed.

She couldn't understand where the barely literate twenty-year-old daughter of a small-town cobbler came up with such ideas, such hard-won convictions. What had she seen in her life? Had she been to Paris, London, or Berlin? What had she read? Shakespeare, Schiller, Cervantes? Had someone managed to hurt her heart with indifference or cruelty? Ethel listened to Hennie and felt an increasing respect for her, comparing her views with her own unrealized hopes and dreams. Even in the first days of creation there had been less love on earth than enmity, hatred, envy and hypocrisy, Ethel thought. Love is still in short supply in the world today, including in this quiet and seemingly happy town where it might have seemed that she was floating like cheese in milk. "More love, more ordinary love," she repeated to herself, her lips closed and unmoving.

In the evening, when Hennie got ready to go home, Ethel tried to detain her as she usually did.

"Stay! Don't refuse me today; we could have supper together. You haven't had the chance to appreciate my culinary abilities yet."

"Oh, but I have!"

"Let's sit down and chat."

Hennie was embarrassed, since she was used to eating at home not at the Kremnitsers. This time, however, Ethel was insistent and she didn't reject the invitation; how could she turn such an honour down? After all it had been part of their agreement that she ate with her employers.

"I'm going to set the table for three; I'll call my father-in-law and we will have a feast. My father-in-law is very interesting to talk to. He has a large and generous soul."

The tablecloth was embroidered with wild flowers. Ethel set out plates with golden rims and silverware, forks and knives with ivory handles. Hennie had never seen such things before she had started working in the Kremnitsers' home.

Gently Ethel knocked on her father-in-law's door, but soon returned alone.

"Reb Yeshua hasn't been feeling well lately," she said. "He has *angina pectoris* and pains in the liver. But still, he promises to join us for a little while. Now I shall bring in the first course. I don't believe you have tried my evening dishes."

"I know you're an excellent cook, Ethel."

"Aaron says I'm the best cook in the entire Kaunas district."

"That's true," Hennie agreed, complimenting her.

While Ethel was busy in the kitchen with the Olivier salad, the first course, the bent figure of Reb Yeshua Kremnitser came out of his room in a long satin robe tied with a broad belt.

"Something's wrong with me, my child. It seems I can't manage without a doctor. I feel a pressure on my chest and something like needles in my right side," he complained. "But if I take to bed, who will take my place in the store? I can only close the shop with a calm heart on the Sabbath, only on the holy Sabbath, or on the Jewish holidays, or during *shiva* for a deceased neighbour. But as long as I myself am not deceased, thank God, I will continue to live my idle life."

"What kind of thing is that to say, Reb Yeshua? May you live to a hundred and twenty!"

"Let's settle on ninety. I'll have no objections."

"Agreed," Hennie said.

"A merchant is always ready to give a discount. I'm not greedy, my dear. You don't have to be stingy and you can leave others with at least a couple of years more than our merciful God has allotted us."

Reb Kremnitser ate little; he groaned, moaned and fidgeted in his chair and then finally got up from the table.

"Thank you, Ethel. You're a wonderful cook."

Reb Yeshua caught his breath. Looking gloomily at Hennie, who had fallen silent during the meal, and at his daughter-in-law, who was concerned about his health, he said, "But what if I were to ask our dear nanny to replace me for a week, since I recommended her and stood up for her?"

"What do you mean 'replace you'? Replace you where?" Ethel didn't grasp what he had in mind.

"You would take my place behind the counter. God knows I'm not concerned about profits and not afraid of losses. It just seems to me that I'll recover sooner if my shop stays open and someone carries on selling and trading in it. After all, who wants to catch some unknown disease from me along with a barn lock or wooden latch they've come to buy?"

"Perhaps you'll feel better tomorrow," his daughter-in-law suggested sympathetically.

"Perhaps. But, Ethel, I have never had much hope in 'tomorrow.' For Jews the future is an unreliable bank; they deposit all their hopes in it and then it turns out to be completely bankrupt."

"Could you cope with being a saleswoman?" Ethel asked Hennie. "For my part, I have no objections."

"I don't know. I never sold anything. But if I'm no good you can fire me."

"You'll learn," Reb Yeshua encouraged her. "You won't be selling land or houses or forests to build ships, just some little items: locks, latches, paint and glue. I would have sold my shop off for *kopecks* long ago but I like to talk to people. I want them to come into my shop and call out my name so that I can respond and so that my ears will hear something besides my own groaning. You're still alive and, perhaps, unlike me, you can still be useful to someone, Hennie. Don't be afraid, I'm sure you'll do well."

"That's the first thing. Secondly, you won't have to stay there forever. Reb Yeshua will get better and you'll come back to me and Raphael," said Ethel, encouragingly.

Like Ethel, Hennie hoped the old man would overcome his ailments and return to being behind the counter, but she couldn't overcome her worry that, God forbid, Reb Yeshua's health would fail completely. That would be a disaster! Aaron would bury his father in the local cemetery, erect a marble monument in his memory, then sell the hardware store, the grocery store and their house to the landlord Kapler, pack their suitcases and leave with Ethel and Raphael for his glorious Paris. And she, Hennie, would be left without a bean, as her militant younger brother Shmulik would put it, since you can't change the habits of the rich, who never think about the poor.

"In addition to what you receive for taking care of Raphael, I'll add another twenty *litas* a week and, if I become quite ill and am not able to return to my shop . . ." Reb Yeshua didn't complete his sentence.

"Agree to his proposal, Hennie. Raphael and I will wait for you," Ethel said tactfully and Hennie consented.

Every evening she went to see her benefactor Kremnitser, taking him the pitiful earnings from his shop and then, for an hour or two, she played with Raphael, took him for a walk, or swung him on the swing in the large yard of the high school. If Ethel was in the salon reading some new French novel about unhappy love, Hennie would put the child to bed, telling him stories that she had invented or singing sad lullabies to him in Yiddish. Perhaps he would still somehow grow up Jewish, not French.

Reb Yeshua was delighted with Hennie and showered her with compliments.

"You'll turn out to be a wonderful saleswoman. You could work in any large department store and make a profit for them. Maybe even in Iser Shneiderman's Rosmarin store in the capital!"

The Shneiderman network of sausage stores was the largest in Lithuania.

Reb Yeshua's joy did not make Hennie happy; on the contrary, it upset her. Of course she was thankful to him for her wages as a nanny and, in addition, for the extra pay he was offering her, but she was eager to leave the shop as soon as possible and return to her curly-haired little lamb, Raphael.

Reb Yeshua's return to the shop was delayed. His illness became worse.

The whole town, both Jews and Christians, considered Doctor Blumenfeld, who treated animals as well as people as there was no local veterinarian, to be a holy man sent by God to help the inhabitants of Jonava. For forty years, without a break and with almost no recompense, he had taken care of the ill and infirm. A confirmed bachelor, like the local priest Vaitkus, he didn't know the joys of marital bliss. He never took any money for visiting the poor when they were sick, often going so far as to pay for the medicine he prescribed himself. With his battered case, Blumenfeld visited the sick at all hours of the day or night. The doctor advised Ethel to take her father-in-law to the capital and he arranged an appointment for him with a professor at the Jewish hospital there. Ethel sent a telegram to call Aaron home from Copenhagen and they took the old man to Kaunas. Reb Yeshua was hospitalized, but it took the doctors two months to cure the acute inflammation of his pancreas. The health of Hennie's benefactor gradually improved, but he did not return to his counter in the shop. Aaron proposed selling the shop, but his father rejected the idea decisively.

"When I die, then you can sell it," he said.

Rokha the Samurai was one of the temporary saleswoman's first customers. True to her practice of looking truth straight in the face, she blurted out, practically from the threshold, "It's better to sell locks and hooks, of course, than to wipe the bum of someone else's child, but you can't mess around when you are in business. Have you gone out of your mind? You have to know how to count money! Especially other people's money! Do you want to end up in jail? That way you won't be around to wait for my son!"

"I will!" Hennie responded sharply. "Maybe I won't get to heaven, but I certainly won't end up in jail. If you want to know, Mrs Kremnitser taught me to count and write. I'm not as much of a fool as some people think!"

Wisely she didn't say anything about the French lessons she had been getting.

"From the time you became boss in this shop, you've had your nose in the air, not caring to drop in on us once, not thinking to ask us anything. Were you hoping perhaps that some bird would bring you some news and sing it into your little ear?" Rokha said, with either pity or gloating.

"What? Have the Poles occupied Alytus like they did Vilnius?"

"So you think that since you've been at the Kremnitsers you've become knowledgeable about what's going on in the world? First you might want to ask why you don't need to go to Alytus anymore and then you can come up with your wild ideas about a Polish occupation!"

"Why?" asked Hennie, feeling guilty, since it was true that she had not dropped by the house on Rybatskaya Street for quite a while to inquire about news. She had not wanted to bother anyone, since she wasn't their daughter-in-law yet.

"Shleimke's regiment has been posted closer to us," Rokha said, "to Žiežmariai, a little town near Kaunas. That's what he wrote. Why they reassigned them I have no idea. It's a secret he wrote, a military secret, as they say. And he wrote that if we met you then we should give you his greetings and his thanks for the woollen socks, which, he says, are very warm and keep his feet toasty, like a stove."

"It's good that I didn't make them too small," Hennie said guiltily.

"I expect you'll have discovered all his measurements before the wedding," Rokha teased.

"Rokha, sometimes you say things that would make a deaf person blush!"

"Don't pretend you're such a pure little thing. It's time you got used to all kinds of words, the sweet ones and the salty ones."

Rokha smiled, quite out of keeping with her habit.

"Thank God, our soldier will soon stop combing horses' tails and cleaning out their foul-smelling stables. His military service will soon be over and he'll come back home in peace for Chanukah."

8

It was still more than half a year until the joyous Chanukah holiday and Hennie intended to visit her beloved once more at his military base. All the more so since, with luck, she could travel from Jonava to Kaunas by hitching a ride on a cart and could even spend the night at the home of the leather-worker Dudak, a distant relative of her father, whose family lived not in the city itself, but in the suburb of Šančiai.

Everything had worked out for the best for Hennie; the journey to her beloved cavalryman was shorter, the health of Reb Yeshua had apparently improved and it seemed possible that he might even take up the reins in his shop again. Meanwhile her relationship with Rokha, who was as changeable as the weather, had improved – *tfu, tfu, tfu* may the evil eye not interfere.

But suddenly everything went wrong. Every day, there was some new threatening news.

"Obviously not today or tomorrow," Ethel said, "But, Hennie, it seems there will be some big changes."

Hennie held her breath.

"Aaron thinks that we can't continue to rely on Dr. Blumenfeld, despite all his worthy qualities. Reb Yeshua is seriously ill and needs treatment from more experienced physicians. My husband absolutely insists that we sell the house and the shop and move somewhere in Europe, if not to France, then to Switzerland or Italy. The medicine is better there and the air heals all by itself."

"Of course, it's fine there," Hennie muttered, concealing her concern.

"If it were my decision," continued Ethel, "I would take you with us. You're not only a wonderful nanny, you're a good person. And you already know some French." Ethel laughed mischievously.

"Thank you," said Hennie. "You praise me too much. I don't deserve it."

"However, I don't expect you will agree to abandoning everything here and leaving."

"Not for anything."

"I understand. No matter which way you look at it, the best country in the world is love; two people can live there from the beginning to the end of their lives. If you're wise you don't emigrate, so long as peace and harmony reign there." Ethel grew suddenly embarrassed at her lofty words. She took a comb out of her purse, combed her blonde hair for a long time and, as if regretting her candidness, said, "Obviously everything could change. My father-in-law is stubborn and as hard as granite. He always says, 'Please, you go wherever you like, but leave me alone with my shop and let me die here in Jonava. Let me lie in the cemetery next to my father Dov-Ber and my mother Golda, my sister Hannah and all my customers, may their memory be blessed."

"'Ennie!" A call came from the nursery.

While she was playing with Raphael, Hennie recalled what she had learned from his good but unhappy mother. In that 'eternal country of love' Ethel had lived more often in complete isolation than with her husband, who was busy with his deals, his bank accounts, checks and credit. "Everything on earth is transient," he loved to say, "except money. Money is immortal." He was always floating away somewhere far from Jonava, far from his father and from Ethel and his beloved heir, just like the tree trunks carried along the Vilija and the Neman rivers on rafts for his customers to build ships with. Hennie thought too about the old, infirm Reb Yeshua, who fell asleep at his shop counter and, when his customers woke him, would shake himself from his snoring like a hound doused with cold water.

It would be sad for her to part with such good people, but Hennie had no intention of going abroad with them. If they left, they left. May their journey be blessed! She would go to that greedy miller Wasserman, or to clean Dr. Blumenfeld's house, to wash his floors and do his laundry. Only beggars feared work, preferring to hold out their hands for alms rather than take up a needle or awl, a plane or a hammer. But what Hennie really feared was unexpected news. It's impossible to hide anything from Jews; since ancient times they have had an acute sense of hearing and a nose for both good and bad news. And, if the news is bad, it spreads like a fire through the Jewish world.

And, indeed, bad news greeted Hennie as soon as she reached home.

"You've probably already heard that the brother of your soldier-boy is leaving Lithuania for good," her father said, without lifting his eyes from the tattered sole of someone's shoe.

"Isaac?" Hennie asked.

"That's the one. What can you say? You can't deny the fellow's boldness or decisiveness," Shimon muttered. "Isaac isn't the first Jew in this shtetl to decide that it's better to be a furrier in Paris or Berlin than here in our backwater. While we have sheepskin coats, there they have fur coats made from sable. The prices for processing fur and leather are different there, the air is different, everything is different."

"But he doesn't know how to do business with anyone!"

"It doesn't matter, everything is different there and where things are different, it's already better. At first Isaac will process leather for Jews who haven't forgotten their *mame loshn* and then for Frenchmen. In contrast to an old head, a young one always has room for more ideas. Just wait, with time his head will find room even for that difficult French language."

"I doubt they will give Shleimke leave to see his brother off . . . I'll go and say goodbye to Isaac both for him and for myself."

"Soldiers only get leave from the army for their parents' funerals," Shimon said.

"But for Rokha and for Dovid this is a kind of funeral. People are saying Leah intends to leave too."

"For Paris?"

"For America."

"Yes, you can't envy Rokha and Dovid. Long ago, in my days, children were like prisoners; they couldn't move away from their parents. Not a single step! Where they were born, whether it pleased them or not, there they would live and die. And now you can't hold them back with chains. They get themselves a boat ticket and travel wherever they please. To France, to America, to Argentina. Even to Palestine; to the Turks. Maybe you and your love will also take off somewhere away from us. And after you, like cranes following the lead bird, your brothers and sisters will follow too. And only your mother and I will stay here, like moss-covered stones by the wayside, rocks destined to remain where they are."

"No," Hennie said. "We won't leave."

"Don't make promises. Man proposes but God disposes." Shimon filled his mouth full of small nails and, spitting them out one by one into his palm, started to fix a heel on a worn-out shoe. "I can imagine how poor Rokha will suffer from Isaac's departure," he whispered. "Parents don't have extra children. You can argue about money, but not about children – that's a terrible sin. Go to Rokha, you have to go and try to console her. Who knows? She may become your mother-in-law and the grandmother of your children. I expect that you'll have at least a dozen children with that cavalryman of yours; he looks like a real worker, not an idler."

Shimon chuckled, pleased with his joke.

"We'll see, but I'll do my best. A dozen isn't likely, but at least a couple, I expect. Not for America and not for Argentina, but for you," Hennie promised with a sad smile.

Near Rokha's house her resolution wavered and Hennie stopped, at a loss. The wild, fierce character of her future mother-in-law was hardly a secret in the shtetl. Rokha was sometimes unusually mild and gentle, as if she were touching a wound, but at other times, like an evil witch, she was likely to smack a person simply out of malice. It was not for nothing that, when they were both young, Dr. Blumenfeld, who had treated all her children and who in his leisure time had been attracted to the subject of ancient Japan, which he had dreamed of visiting at least once in his life, referred to Rokha as 'a samurai in a skirt'. The nickname stuck. No one knew what it meant, but everyone sensed that it suggested something uncomplimentary, even military.

Hennie hesitated, unsure whether or not go in. She knew that while Rokha valued sympathy, she could not stand being comforted in the presence of family members, whom she constantly accused of insensitivity and indifference. After some hesitation, Hennie decided to knock on the door, pretending she had come for another reason and did not know about Isaac's imminent departure.

Only Rokha and Dovid were at home. It was as if all the others had conspired to leave.

"Greetings," Hennie said.

"Greetings, greetings. Why have you come? Did you get a letter from Shleimke?"

"No."

"Then what are you doing gallivanting around the shtetl and not taking care of your little ward? After all, it's not *shabbes* or a holiday."

"Raphael has a cold. I decided to come and ask you how you treated your children when they were sick."

"With a parsley infusion."

"I'll tell Ethel that. Dr. Blumenfeld prescribed some pills for Raphael, but he still has a rash."

"Don't try to make a fool out of me. I can see from your eyes that you're lying, my dear, even though you don't blush from shame. You hardly came here because Raphael has a cold. Admit it! You'll clearly never learn how to pull the wool over people's eyes."

"Of course, I also wanted to say goodbye to Isaac. I wanted to wish him well in the name of his brother, as they won't allow him to leave his unit. Obviously a military barracks is not a prayer house; you can't come and go as you wish," Hennie murmured.

"Say goodbye to Isaac and perhaps you can find something out from him," Rokha said. "Isn't that why you came? Just don't lie, for God's sake. Trickery doesn't suit you."

"Find out what?" Hennie asked, frightened now.

"Find out what? Find out how sons and daughters can take to their heels, abandoning their mother and father. Perhaps you and my dear Shleimke have been secretly planning to flap your wings as well?"

"We have been planning no such thing! We'll never leave. We shall stay here. I promise. We will never, never leave you." Pity for Rokha suddenly overpowered Hennie, causing her to speak with an uncharacteristic lack of restraint and inhibition. "I understand, you don't believe anyone in the world. You're hurting. And, it seems to me, that pain is stronger than any faith. But if, God willing, we marry, then we will be with you to the end."

"Whose end?" asked Rokha the Samurai, as if raising a sword over her head.

"Maybe I didn't express myself very well. Forgive me. It's because I am upset . . ."

"No, you spoke right. It's a great happiness when your children are with you to the end."

Rokha began to cry. She rubbed her eyes with the corner of her apron and wiped her nose, which resembled a bird's beak. "I gave birth ten times," she said quietly. "I did so for myself, not for France or for America. Six of my ten children survived. I don't think God has any reason to be angry at me because I was fruitful and multiplied. But at least He shouldn't punish me for my words. I'm angry at Him but can't do anything with my anger, while He eats away at me like a worm. Why is He taking my children away from me? Why?"

Hennie didn't dare open her mouth. She stood to attention before Rokha like the Jewish fireman had when they stood in front of the Lithuanian high school, dressed in their brand new uniforms, as the national anthem was sung during President Smetona's visit to Jonava.

"Why, tell me please, does the Almighty not understand what you, Hennie, understand from half a word? You don't know? So then I'll tell you. Because God is a man and you are a woman who is going to give birth. Because you will carry your children under your own heart, not in a woven basket like mushrooms. And perhaps also because it sometimes seems that the Master of the World has no heart. God, forgive me, a sinner, for my blasphemy and obscenities! Forgive me! But who can prove to me that that is not how it is?"

"My father jokes that God is too high above us. How can you expect Him to hear us from such a distance? If He was a bird and could fly down and rest on our flimsy roofs with their sooty chimneys, perhaps there would be a chance our cries could reach Him. But now, no matter how loud you cry, it's no use."

"Your father is no fool. And, to tell the truth, recently you have begun to please me more and more. Before I thought that you were worthless, a flirt, but now I see you're a serious girl, who works and doesn't lie. Maybe you will be suitable to take care not only of that little 'nobleman' Raphael Kremnitser, but also of your husband. Just don't try to outwit those who are cleverer than you are! You'll simply fail. 'A cold . . . Dr. Blumenfeld . . . pills . . . infusions . . .' What nonsense you tried to put over on me."

"I understand," Hennie replied, touched. "But please, don't torture yourself. Isaac loves you. He will send you letters and packages from Paris. He will come to visit."

"The way things are going, we'll only get to see our children and our grandchildren when they come as guests. Hopefully only one will leave. But what if Isaac is followed by another two?"

Hennie was stupefied.

"Leah's thinking about going. Not to Paris, but across the ocean. And Motl too, though he and his Sarah are only thinking of going to Kaunas, thank God. Only my poor Yosef, in his Kalvarija mental hospital, isn't leaving us. Troubles don't come alone. One draws another in its embrace. Well, now we have spoken heart-to-heart. All my hopes rest on Shleimke and you."

"On me?"

"Yes, on you. Only you can hold him back."

Hennie didn't manage to reply. Dovid emerged from the adjoining room in his leather apron. His glasses, held on a thin string, had slipped down to the very end of his fleshy nose and his reddish goatee was streaked with grey. The top of his head was bald.

"Let me look at you. The truth is you're quite a good-looking girl. Lovely, well-proportioned and sweet, like a bun with poppy seeds."

"You old womaniser!" Rokha said, pouring cold water on his ardour. "Why have you put your work down? You were probably standing quietly behind the door, eavesdropping on our conversation, weren't you?"

"Rokha! Who eavesdrops on a bird? A person listens to a bird. May Hennie forgive me for my directness, but the thing that keeps a man from moving to Paris or America isn't words or pleas but the kid gloves of a wife. And her bed. That has been proved over the ages. And, Rokha, you can confirm the truth of my words since you yourself have never taken those gloves off. You wear them all year round and you don't even take them off to have them washed," Dovid said, pointing with the end of his shiny nose to the veined hands of his companion of many years.

"Just listen to this wise guy! What a connoisseur of women he suddenly turns out to be!" Rokha said in exasperation. "Go back to your awl and hammer already! Somehow we'll manage without your advice."

Dovid waved, bowed to Hennie and shuffled back to work.

"Kid gloves and a bed. That's all it takes!" he said, turning as he crossed the threshold into the next room. "They're more powerful than any argument!"

"Obviously the constant blows of his hammer on the soles of worn-out shoes have sent him completely off his rocker! But even so, sometimes, despite myself, I have to agree with him." Rokha said. "A wife has to be decisive. Men don't live long with ditherers." She got up from her chair, signalling that their conversation was over. "If you want to wish Isaac a good journey, come to the train station on Sunday at 2pm."

"I will be sure to," Hennie replied.

Only a few people saw Isaac off – his family, Hennie and the shtetl beggar, Avigdor Perelman, who was nicknamed Spinoza and who usually showed up at every wedding, funeral, meeting and parting, hoping to benefit from a large gathering of generous Jews. At weddings he danced in a lively manner with the newlyweds, at funerals he mourned with the orphaned relatives and watered the grave mound with fresh tears. When he was seeing off people who were leaving the shtetl, either to cross the ocean or to a distant land on this side of it, he would wave his long arms wildly in front of the relatives on the train platform, asking for alms.

"If everyone leaves or runs away from here, who will be left to give something to a poor man?" Avigdor repeated in his sing-song voice.

Although Rokha glared at him fiercely, like an eagle or a samurai warrior, he would not yield, asking rhetorically, "Will I really have to seek charity from the *goyim* rather than my fellow Jews? That would be shameful!"

Listening to Perelman's complaint, the complaint of Jewish beggars the world over, Hennie wondered who might give alms to unhappy parents; not *litas* but hope and sympathy.

The train remained standing in the Jonava station for only one more minute. Those who had come to see Isaac off competed with each other, rushing to embrace him and kiss him farewell.

Before half a year had passed, without waiting for her brother the cavalryman to return from military service, the determined Leah also left her parents' hearth, in search of happiness in golden America.

She was seen off from the same grassy platform of the unprepossessing railway station by the same contingent of people, only this time without Avigdor, who, it seemed, had become finally and totally disillusioned in regard to the generosity and beneficence of the Jewish people.

When the shrill whistle of the train was heard and Leah's guilty smile flashed by in the window of the departing train, Rokha could no longer endure the tension and fainted.

"Rokha! Rokha!" cried Dovid, tears glittering in his reddish beard like slivers of ice.

It was not easy to revive her. Dovid and Motl carried the poor woman home to Rybatskaya Street, which was quite some distance, and put her into bed. Rokha's head was spinning; half-crazed, she repeated the names of those that had 'seduced' her children – Paris and New York. And like her mentally ill son, Yosef, in his institution in Kalvarija, she took flight to a place where the palm trees and cypresses grew. But even more often she asked of the darkness, which hung like a threatening cloud over her bed, why and for whom had she given birth to almost a dozen children who had now become wanderers?

Motl ran for the doctor.

Dr. Blumenfeld, who out of respect was called not Yitzak, his Biblical name, but by his last name, took his marvellous stethoscope out of the bag he always carried and put its ends into his hairy ears. He listened to what was going on inside Rokha, but found nothing serious there. Then he used a medical hammer to strike his patient's wrinkled knees, and then had her follow the movements – left and right – of his index finger, checking her sight for some reason.

"Your nerves, my dear, are out of control. I'll give you a prescription for a sedative. You will have to stay in bed for a week. In no case are you to get worked up! You have to be philosophical about what is taking place in the world. There is only so much we can do, we won't change God's world for the better, we'll just ruin our own health. No matter how much we want to remake the world, we can barely control the course of our own lives. You need to remember that parents only receive their beloved offspring on credit, not forever; we always have to give them up – to another woman, to another man, to another country. Nothing will change if you pull the hair out of your head, you still won't get back those you love, but you will certainly harm yourself."

"Thank you, Doctor." Rokha had no idea what Blumenfeld meant by 'credit'. Gratefully she added, "For your care and effort Dovid will repair two pairs of your shoes without payment."

"That, Mrs Kanovich, is too high a payment for my visit. I never accept that much," Dr. Blumenfeld muttered. Carefully putting the tools of his trade back into his bag, he wished his patient good health, put on his hat and bowed in parting.

On her way home from the Kremnitsers, Hennie always visited Rokha and cooked supper, which her younger children, Hava and Motl, would heat up the following day under Dovid's supervision. She would go to the store for groceries, to the pharmacy for medicine, sit at Rokha's bedside until late in the evening comforting the patient and share the latest shtetl news and rumours with her.

"Hennie, the Lord Himself sent you!" Rokha said, by way of compliment. "But tell me, why am I so unfortunate? Why? Two of my children have already flown far away, while one, Yosef, is in a mental asylum in Kalvarija. And he was such a quiet, good, affectionate boy, but he imagined he was a bird not a human being and thought he should live in a tree not under a roof. I went to visit Yosef early in the summer. He recognized me and said, 'Really, Mama, aren't you bored with your life? Let's you and me fly south, where it's warm and palm trees grow. I fly there every autumn. As soon as the north wind starts to blow, I spread my wings and I'm up in the sky.'

" 'But, Yosele,' I said, 'I don't have wings.'

" 'If you really want to fly, Mama, you will grow them.' "

Hennie sighed deeply. "He and I were born in the same year, in fact on the very same day," she whispered.

"Lord, why do I suffer such torment?" Rokha groaned. "Why?"

"The doctor forbade you to get excited otherwise you won't get better. Lie quietly and don't think about anything bad for a week."

"The doctor forbade me to get excited! You might just as well forbid me to live!"

"Please, calm down for the sake of all your loved ones. Shleimke will be returning for Chanukah, then you will have some real help at home. The first letters will arrive from Leah and Isaac about how well they are doing and how they haven't forgotten you."

"They will probably concoct some stories about their success. They're both wonderful liars!" said Rokha with a faint smile.

"Why would they lie? Families don't usually say anything when things are going badly, but will always boast about their successes. And, you'll see, in a year or two one of them will miss you and send you an invitation to visit them. Isaac will invite you to Paris, where kings used to live and where Baron Rothschild, the richest Jew in the whole world, lives."

"I don't need Paris with its kings and its Rothschilds! My Paris is here in this shtetl, where I was born and where, despite my terrible character, someone once loved me and, perhaps, even now loves me still. And who will love him, that runaway, there? What French king or what Rothschild? But you, if I am not mistaken, promised, before witnesses, that you would love me. And I believe you."

"Yes, I did promise." Hennie nodded her head in agreement. "I don't deny it. The Dudaks don't throw their words to the wind."

"And except for love I don't need anything from life."

"Everyone needs to be loved," Hennie agreed. "But still, do you have to torture yourself so, complaining to God and cursing your fate?"

"You're like my Dovid. He, that quiet soul, once said right to my face, 'Rokha, you are a wonderful woman but you need a bridle, like a frisky horse. It's not safe to let you out of the house without a bridle.'"

There wasn't a single person in the shtetl or beyond that could make such a bridle for her. Local wiseacres joked that on the day that Dovid was born the Lord placed an awl and a waxed thread in his cradle, while in hers He put either a lance or a Cossack sword.

Whether it was because Rokha couldn't stop herself from getting excited and cursing her fate fiercely, or because of something else, she tossed and turned in bed for almost two weeks. Dr. Blumenfeld looked in on his patient occasionally, each time warning her that if she didn't follow his instructions things would end badly – perhaps with a stroke.

Even before Rokha's illness Hennie had written to her soldier, with Ethel's help, saying that Isaac and Leah were planning to leave Jonava. She then patiently waited for his reply. He wrote nothing for such a long time that Hennie, alarmed, wondered whether something bad had happened to him. Finally, right after his brother and sister had been seen off, Shleimke replied. He was very sorry that he had not been able to say goodbye to Isaac and Leah and asked how his parents were doing and how they were feeling after the departures. He described his daily life in the cavalry with humour. The letter was nothing special but, in order to encourage the heartbroken Rokha and to raise her spirits, Hennie resorted to a decent and quite forgivable ruse – she removed from the letter everything that was extraneous, and anything that related personally to Hennie herself, to whom the letter had actually been addressed. She went to the sick woman and read it to her in her own way, as an expression of her son's love not for her, Hennie, but for his self-sacrificing mother.

" 'Tell Mama not to get excited. We,' he means he and I, Rokha, 'Will never leave her, not for any money in the world.'" Hennie uttered the words, glancing at the page that had been torn from a checkered notebook.

Tears flowed from Rokha's eagle eyes, but she did not dry them. After the long period of desperation that had caused her insides to burn, they watered her suffering soul with hope.

" 'I'll finish my army service and be back home for Chanukah and Hennie and I will do all we can to help you. We'll love you enough to make up for those who have left,'" Hennie continued to improvise. " 'I embrace and kiss you and father. Hold out and wait for me!' The rest of the letter, Rokha, he writes not about you but about me," the future daughter-in-law concluded.

"Shleimke is a real son, a devoted one, not a Frenchman or an American," Rokha repeated, drying her eyes with the edge of her apron, as she was wont to do.

Meanwhile Isaac and Leah seemed to have disappeared from the face of the earth; they heard not a word from them, not a breath.

Only in the autumn, when the days became shorter and heavy, dreary rain began to pelt the town, did the postman Kazimiras bring a pink envelope to Rybatskaya Street on which there was an incomprehensible postmark and two imposing stamps – one of a general in uniform and the other of a President with a luxurious moustache. The return address was written in French, in tiny handwriting.

Isaac wrote that he was alive and well and was looking for work in his trade, but that in Paris there were far more Jews than in all the shtetls and towns of Lithuania combined. "Where there are so many Jews, there are lots of synagogues and in the synagogues Jews don't just pray, but also establish contacts and do business. So you see, some worshipper or other would not refuse to help find work for his fellow Jew who came from a distant province – perhaps as a watchman in the synagogue, or perhaps in some leather workshop. In a word, Jews won't allow a fellow Jew to die of hunger."

"I've had a good idea, Rokha," Hennie said. "I'll show Isaac's address to Ethel, the wife of my employer, Kremnitser's daughter-in-law. Her husband Aaron often goes to Paris on business. He has lots of friends and acquaintances there. Perhaps they will help Isaac find work, at least temporarily."

Rokha was taken aback by Hennie's initiative.

"Yes, do! I don't expect Isaac will be worse off if you do. It's true that we're more accustomed to helping each other with advice rather than action, but people should be thankful for useful advice too. Show the address to that prisoner in her own home, Ethel. Show it to her."

So Hennie did so.

"I know Rue Descartes," Ethel said, "It's in the Latin Quarter. There are many cheap hotels there and, I believe, a Catholic monastery and a poor house. When I was pregnant, Aaron and I often used to take walks in that area. Perhaps when he is in Paris, Aaron will go for a walk through the Latin Quarter again. He loves to look at street artists painting and, from time to time, he even buys paintings from them quite cheaply; for a bottle of Burgundy. I'll copy the address down right away and ask my husband, if Isaac hasn't moved in the meantime, to seek him out and help him somehow. After all he has many contacts." Ethel took out a pad from the drawer of a card-table, and wrote down the name of the street and the number of the house. "By the way," she said, "You look more beautiful than ever, Hennie."

Hennie raised her eyebrows coquettishly. "Really?"

"Really. You are shining. It's as if you were standing under a wedding canopy."

"I am." Hennie laughed. "I've been standing under one for quite a long time though only with one foot. Like a heron. Perhaps when Shleimke gets out of the army, I'll be able to stand under it on both feet and we'll stamp on a glass. I used to be afraid of Rokha; she wanted Zlata, the daughter of the local miller Mendel Vasserman as a daughter-in-law, not me."

Hennie laughed again and Ethel smiled.

"And now?" Ethel asked.

"It seems she's become reconciled to me and no longer thinks about the miller's daughter." Then she asked suddenly, "But what about you?"

"Me? I am married."

"But that's not what I am asking about. It's obvious that you are bored in this shtetl of ours; there's nowhere to go, no one to talk to and you're surrounded by simple people – craftsmen, if you don't count the doctor, the rabbi, and the pharmacist. No, I don't think you really have any friends here."

"I do have a friend. You!" Ethel exclaimed.

"Oh," Hennie said with both fright and joy. "What are you saying? I'm hardly a suitable friend for you."

"I don't need anyone better. As far as simple people are concerned, it's easier to relate to them than to aristocrats. A simple person lies less and is less greedy and deceitful; they're more sincere and sympathetic. But that's not the main thing. The main thing for me in life is that everything goes well under the roof of one's home. If there is some disorder in the family, then it makes you sick to live there."

With her woman's intuition, the clever Hennie detected in her mistress's words a covert complaint that her relations with Aaron were not as cloudless as they might have seemed at first glance. Perhaps that was the reason Ethel was so attached to Jonava and was so concerned about the health of her father-in-law, Reb Yeshua. As long as he was alive and going to his shop, nothing threatened her family arrangement. Boredom in a shtetl, after all, was better than divorce or having one's husband spend so much of his time abroad.

On many occasions Hennie wanted to praise Ethel for her patience and her friendliness. She wanted to say something encouraging to her, but she did not dare to out of modesty, not being able to find the right words and not wanting to appear to be a sycophant or an insincere flatterer. But suddenly, like unexpected tears, the words tumbled out of her.

"I'm happy that I live close to you," she burst out. "Not because you pay me such a good salary for taking care of Raphael and not because you're teaching me, an ignoramus, writing and arithmetic and trying to teach me French. I'm happy because you are the most ... the most ... Well, there's no one like you here in the shtetl."

"My dear, you are exaggerating. You shouldn't idealize me or think of me as a saint."

Hennie looked at Ethel, confused. Such expressions were beyond her comprehension.

"You exaggerate my qualities. I have both good and bad ones, all kinds. After all, God created humans imperfect. He made us with all kinds of faults so that we are not too proud and don't turn up our noses at others' faces and so that every day we don't forget to try to cleanse ourselves from all that is sinful and bad. I need to do something with my free time, that's why I occupy myself with such things. I try and I try but I can't feel clean. But enough about me! Instead, tell me how long you are going to be standing on one foot like a heron?"

"I would like to stand on two tomorrow, but I have to wait until my groom returns from the army. Shleimke is due to return by Chanukah. Unless some blonde Lithuanian girl has caught his eye."

"Nonsense! He won't find a wife like you anywhere!"

"Me? A find? I don't know how to do anything. I can only be a child's nanny or a servant girl."

"Well, that's something. But, actually, my father-in-law has an idea; if he's not sleeping, like our Raphael, I'll call him. Let him tell you about it himself."

Ethel left the room and soon returned with Reb Yeshua.

"Reb Yeshua, how are you feeling?" Hennie asked, a little taken aback by Ethel's words.

"Dr. Blumenfeld is satisfied with me, but I am not satisfied with myself. It suddenly popped into my head when I was in Kaunas that I didn't thank you as I should have for working in my shop."

"You thanked me, you did thank me," Hennie repeated, agitated.

"Yes, I expressed my gratitude with money, but I should have also shown my gratitude with good deeds. Good deeds are more lasting than money."

In contrast to his successful son Aaron, for whom a bank account was the primary measure in life, Reb Yeshua Kremnitser had a reputation for being someone not overly concerned with material matters, but rather one who was knowledgeable in the Torah and a pious follower of Jewish traditions. He saw the highest value in life not in enriching oneself in an exhausting chase after money, the cause of all the wars and discord in the world, but in striving to lead a good life.

"We Jews, it's not a sin to say, love to instruct and correct others rather than ourselves. Is it not for that reason that people criticize us, to put it mildly?" Reb Yeshua asked, faithful to his custom of raising any conversation from petty matters to a higher level.

"There's no need to exaggerate," Ethel said quietly, wrapping her shawl around her.

"Well, perhaps I am exaggerating," Reb Yeshua agreed. "But I believe you can improve humanity if you begin with yourself, not with your neighbour. By your own will! Not because you are threatened with a whip or a rod. I've always tried to live that way – to do good to people without expecting anything back."

Ethel and Hennie listened without interrupting.

"That's the way I am. When I got home from the Jewish hospital in Kaunas, while I was resting up, I had the idea of perhaps sending you to Kaunas for a year, Hennie, to take a course in sewing women's clothes, or something. Our Raphael is no longer a baby and Ethel can take care of him by herself now. If you agree to attend such a course, I will pay for the instruction and for your living expenses. That way you will acquire a useful profession for your life."

"Thank you for your generosity, Reb Yeshua, but I can't accept your offer."

"Why not? You will be a seamstress and your husband a tailor. That's the best family set-up one can imagine. Ethel will be happy to have you sew underwear for her and I will order jackets and a coat from your husband."

"Meanwhile I'm not a wife yet, just a long-time fiancée. After all, you know that no Jew, neither man nor woman, gets married long distance; I have to wait for my soldier to return."

"I'm sure that you'll manage the wait," Ethel calmed her. "It's not long until Chanukah. Just don't forget to invite us all to your wedding. Maybe my Aaron will manage to get here from Germany or France, even though he loves to pamper himself on the Côte d'Azur in December."

"I won't forget. We'll invite you even before we invite Rabbi Eliezer."

Hennie didn't tell anyone about Reb Yeshua Kremnitser's attractive proposal; if she had told them, then both of her siblings would have tried to convince her to accept it. And Rokha too. "Don't be a fool. Go! You won't have another chance like this. Good fortune is knocking at the door and you won't allow it to cross the threshold!"

The temptation was, in fact, great. Kaunas was a big city. There would be new acquaintances and impressions there. For a whole year she would be away from the shtetl, enjoying a life of freedom and able, for the first time in her life, to go to the Yiddish theatre, where the 'domestic prisoner' Ethel went once a month. And, most importantly, she would learn a good profession without having to pay anything. But something held her back. Something prevented her from deciding to agree, some unseen, insistent sower of doubts whispered into her ear, "Don't act in haste; consider the pros and cons. You may gain a profession, but end up losing Shleimke."

So, she made her decision: she chose her knight on horseback.

9

The Chanukah holiday was approaching. The weather was dry and windless. Snowflakes whirled around the wintry Jonava. The cold that was supposed to arrive from Finland was clearly late, apparently gathering strength and power somewhere in its native territory.

In Rokha's house everyone was preparing for Shleimke's long-awaited return from the army so they could light the first holiday candle in the cupronickel Chanukah menorah with him. Every year, in all the Jewish homes of Jonava the inhabitants marked the great miracle that had taken place in Judea during the time of the Maccabees, when in the temple in Jerusalem the lamps the barbarian Greeks and Syrians had extinguished were filled once more with pure oil and burned again with holy, blessed fire.

As had been agreed, Hennie was given time off for the Jewish holidays. So, unhindered, she concentrated on a different kind of service: rolling up her sleeves she tidied the rooms in the house on Rybatskaya Street from morning till evening, with her future mother-in-law. She cleaned the pots and pans and prepared food, as was the custom before holidays, making potato *latkes* and baking poppy pastries. At any moment they expected the door to open and Shleimke to enter wearing his uniform, to smell, finally, not *durda*, the watery barrack soup, which he had had quite enough of, but tasty home cooking.

However, Shleimke did not return for Chanukah.

Hennie and Rokha became worried and began to imagine various alarming scenarios. Perhaps, God forbid, something had happened to him.

Reb Yeshua Kremnitser was the only person in all of Jonava who subscribed to the Yiddish weekly newspaper from Kaunas. He followed attentively local and world events – the military coups, earthquakes, explosions of volcanoes, crashes on the stock exchanges and divorces and scandals involving high-society folk. When Rokha chanced to meet him in the synagogue courtyard, she asked whether something had happened in Kaunas where her Shleimke was serving, as she had not heard from him in quite some time. Reb Yeshua attempted to calm the old woman down.

"Don't get upset. It is true that a very unfortunate incident did take place in Kaunas, but not to your son the cavalryman; it related to our President and to an unlucky young Jewish baker. Thank God it didn't lead to a lot of bloodshed."

"What happened to our President?" Rokha inquired. "He seemed quite a healthy specimen. Did he suddenly fall ill and end up being laid out in a box?"

"As a president he's had it, but being a 'healthy specimen', he is still alive," joked Reb Yeshua, the enlightener of his customers and acquaintances in the shtetl. "He was simply, excuse the expression, given a boot in the rear and replaced with someone else – a professor with a beard, an expert in ancient languages. There was a military coup in Kaunas and people were arrested in the city."

"But what did the poor baker do?" Rokha insisted.

"He, along with three Lithuanian confederates, was accused of betraying the country and preparing to overthrow the government. According to the decision of a court-martial all four plotters were executed near Kaunas in the former tsarist fortress," Reb Yeshua replied sympathetically. "An emergency was declared in the capital and, just in case, the troops there were ordered to be ready for trouble. Apparently for that reason your son was delayed. When everything quietens down in the city, he'll be sent home of course."

"That's all we need to add to our woes and problems, the execution of a Jewish baker!" Rokha exclaimed, when she heard of the fatal sentence. "When a Jew is shot, the bullets fly at all of us."

"You're right, the bullets ricochet back at us." Reb Yeshua said. "That young revolutionary, my grandson's namesake Raphael Charny, was the first Jewish fanatic in Lithuania to be put up against a wall. We just have to pray to God that he will be the last. It's not right for Jews to rouse another people from their sleep, to pull the pillow from under their head and call on them to rebel. Let them sleep and then wake when they're ready!"

"Those are holy words!" Rokha exclaimed. "If that poor boy was still standing in front of his stove peacefully baking Shabbat challahs, bagels, little loaves of white bread and rolls, the Lithuanians wouldn't be sharpening their teeth to bite us. When you live in someone else's house, you don't knock the walls down if the owner of the house doesn't want you to; you don't try to reconstruct it in your style if it doesn't please you."

"Quite right! And now let's pray that God gives wisdom to those who lack it," said Reb Yeshua, as he entered the synagogue, sitting down in his place on the front row and opening his prayer book.

While the shooting of the young Jewish baker quite shook Rokha up, the arrests and the unseating of the president made no impression on her at all. Her thoughts were consumed by the affairs of the army and how they affected her son. Neither she, nor Reb Yeshua Kremnitser, nor Hennie knew when the state of emergency would end and Shleimke would return to Jonava.

Then, right after Chanukah, Motl entered the house like a bullet, breathless from running and from happiness and with a wild, victory cry, shouted, "Here he comes! Shleimke is coming! In his uniform." Then, without stopping to catch his breath, he ran back outside to be the first to fall on the neck of his older brother.

Dovid hastily followed Motl into the yard wearing the greasy leather apron it was possible to imagine he had been born in, followed by the dishevelled Rokha, legs shaking from excitement, and the quiet Hava and, finally, by Hennie, who was there because she never missed an opportunity to visit her future mother-in-law to see if there was any fresh news.

In his military uniform, riding breeches under an open overcoat, a military shirt tightly encircled with a thick iron-buckled soldier's belt and in hob-nailed cavalry boots, Shleimke looked like a traveller who had arrived at the house by mistake. His guilty smile seemed to seek forgiveness for his long absence.

"Well, greetings, my good people," he called.

"Greetings, my dear son, greetings," Rokha replied, matching his tone. Overcome with emotion, she wet the unshaven face of her smartly dressed cavalryman son with her tears and kisses, to the bemusement of her other children. "What about the horse?" she asked. "Where is your horse?"

"In the stable," Shleimke laughed, embracing in turn his father, sister and Hennie. "Mama, my black horse still has a long time to serve."

Shining, like a special Passover vessel, Rokha suggested, "They could have given you the animal for the good service you performed. And why do you have a belt with an iron buckle and riding-breeches? Where in our shtetl have you ever seen a Jew who walked around in a military shirt and such foolish-looking trousers? But a horse, a horse – that's something! If we didn't need it for ourselves, we could sell it to someone; to the water carrier Melekh Silkiner, or to the cart-driver Peisakh Shvartsman. We wouldn't ask too much for it."

There was much laughter, back slapping and cries of joy.

Hennie wisely remained on the sidelines, trying not to draw attention to herself, yielding priority to Rokha, leaving, temporarily, the returning son to her alone. Even Dovid could not compete with his wife in the outpouring of tender feelings for their son who had completed his national service. As usual, he did not waste the modest capital of his joy. Quietly he gazed at the horseless cavalryman, as if from high above. As if he were taking his measure. "Shleimke," he said, "standing before you I feel like standing to attention and saluting. However, that uniform, let me tell you, is no advertisement for its tailor. If you carry on wearing it no one will come to ask you to sew clothes for him. Uniforms, epaulettes, and officers' stripes always terrify Jews."

"I'll change my clothes, Papa. I will," the son promised, breaking into a smile.

After celebrating outside, Hennie and the family followed Rokha into the house, like chicks behind their mother.

"But we were expecting you for Chanukah! Hennie and I cooked soup. We made *latkes* and baked pastry with raisins and cinnamon, but Hava and Motl have gobbled it all down. There's nothing left, just some pea soup, a couple of pieces of chicken and the leftovers of the Sabbath *challah*. Oh yes, and half a bottle of wine."

"Enough for a glass for each of us!" exclaimed Shleimke. "The best food in the world is freedom. No barracks, no guards, no superiors with epaulettes. Freedom! What can taste sweeter than that? I want to catch up on my sleep, earn some money working for Kisin and then Hennie and I will go to Kaunas to buy a different kind of horse – an iron one. I'll buy a Singer sewing machine in installments and, with God's help, ride it until I'm successful."

"May God help you ride it to old age!" said Rokha. "A Singer is a Jew's pride; it's a faithful horse that will never rear up on its hind legs, or stamp its hooves, or gallop wildly to throw off its rider."

The family and Hennie drank the rest of the wine, embraced once more the freshly shaved Shleimke, now in civilian dress, and it was only after midnight that they said goodnight.

"I'll walk you home, Hennie," said the cause of the celebration.

He walked with her, feeling neither cold nor tired, until dawn cast its rosy glow over the snow-covered town.

"Good night," Hennie said. "Oh, what a fool I am. Night is already over!"

"Our days and nights are only beginning," Shleimke said. "May only the nights be dark in our life, not the days."

"May it be that way indeed."

Hennie kissed her beloved and they parted. When the sleepy nanny arrived at work, she was congratulated by the Kremnitsers – Reb Yeshua, Ethel and even Raphael, who was wearing a lovely outfit with a sparkling white shirt and an elegant tie. Almost immediately the boy hid in Hennie's shirt and squeaked, "Ennie, don't leave us!"

"Raphael, your 'Ennie' isn't leaving. She will always be with us," Ethel said. "Now, you can go and feed the birds with her. Hennie will tell you your favourite stories – about Snow White and the brave snail, who was tired of sliding along the ground and wanted to be a bird, so that he could fly around the earth and then settle down in our oak tree."

"So, my dear, what do you have to say to make us happy? Has your cavalryman finally come home?" Reb Yeshua asked as he was about to set off for his 'command post', the hardware store.

"Yes. He has returned."

"Thank God! I suppose that you and he have already decided when the wedding will be?" the most curious shopkeeper in all of curious Jonava asked, not satisfied with her stingy response.

"Most likely in the spring, sometime after the *Shavuos* holiday. It is said that people who marry then will never get divorced."

"Have you already been properly matched up according to our customs?"

"No."

"That's not good. The traditions of our ancestors should be followed. If you like, I will be your matchmaker. As hard as it may be to imagine, in his youth one of us Kremnitsers was not indifferent to your future mother-in-law. I imagine Rokha is biting her nails now because she rejected the courting of my younger brother Isaiya, may his memory be for a blessing."

"Thank you, thank you very much! But maybe we can do without a matchmaker; even Rokha doesn't seem opposed to my marrying Shleimke."

"Whether she is or not, a Jewish wedding without a matchmaker is a bad start. I will speak with Rokha and definitely put in a good word for you. Old bird that I am, if I Yeshua Kremnitser were half a century younger I would marry you right away myself, without the slightest hesitation."

"And when Aaron returns to Jonava in April from his beloved Paris I'll ask him not to come back empty-handed, but to buy a present for your wedding there," Ethel said. "Matchmaking is, of course, important, but gifts are even more so."

"There's no need to bother your husband. He has lots of things to do without that," Hennie replied, embarrassed.

"But we wouldn't think of coming to your wedding without bringing a present! You had just better tell us what you or your groom would like to receive. Don't be shy."

Hennie caught her breath at the idea that sprang with embarrassing suddenness into her mind. "I don't know," she said, trying hard to fight the temptation.

"You're trying to keep it secret in vain. You are concealing your wish and that way, willingly or not, you are insulting us. We are not only your employers; we are, I hope, good friends. Is that not so?"

"Yes, definitely friends. But, believe me, I don't personally need anything. Any-thing!" she repeated, breaking up the word for emphasis.

"But what about your cavalryman? Doesn't he need anything?" Ethel persisted. "You invite people to your wedding, but turn away their gifts! In my whole life I have never met a bride and groom who refused to accept gifts."

"I am not refusing. It's always nice to receive gifts, but . . ."

"But what?"

"Can I tell her or not?" she asked herself.

In the face of temptation her resolution to hold her tongue gave way and Hennie relented. She had to tell Ethel, not for herself, but for the one she loved. Shleimke wouldn't blame her. He would understand that she had acted with the best motives and would forgive her.

"Like any young tailor, Shleimke dreams of having his own sewing machine," sighed Hennie. "His own Singer." Hennie covered her face with her hands as the words came out of her mouth, ashamed at her boldness.

"For such nonsense you kept silent for so long, testing our patience? Did you think that such a gift would bankrupt us?" her sponsor Reb Kremnitser said, pretending to be insulted.

"What are you saying, Reb Yeshua? It's not a matter of buying a spool of thread!"

"Believe me, my dear, we won't be paupered from such an expense. We won't wander the world with a beggar's bowl. Your groom will have his Singer," said Reb Yeshua. "We will ask Aaron, when, God willing, he comes back from Copenhagen to Lithuania, to make a short stop in Kaunas and order the newest model of Singer to be delivered to you. Just, please, give us the exact address of your young man."

"Jonava, Rybatskaya Street, house number 8. Shlomo Kanovich," Hennie said.

Reb Yeshua took out of his jacket a leather-bound note-book and in tiny handwriting wrote down the address. Used to being precise, the experienced shop-keeper jotted down, next to the name of the groom, 'Singer sewing machine'.

"That's a gift for your future husband. What can we give you?" Ethel continued to pester Hennie. "Don't you deserve a present? Some pendant or bracelet perhaps? Jewellery doesn't do any woman harm."

"To tell the truth, I don't know what to answer. Life has already granted me the very best gift; there is no better gift than a good, loving husband."

"Very well said," Ethel responded sadly, "Fate, unfortunately, doesn't grant such gifts to all women."

Reb Yeshua looked at his daughter-in-law and, without saying anything, lowered his eyes.

With that unambiguous statement, the atmosphere in the living room grew unbearable and the old man took his leave. "See grandpa to the door," Ethel said to her son and Hennie, without looking at them.

Hennie decided not to tell Shleimke before the wedding about the gift that she had, it seemed to her, more or less extorted from the Kremnitsers. What if Aaron changed his mind and didn't go to Kaunas in April at all and didn't order the sewing machine? In that case, she, Hennie, would turn out to have deceived him and her hopes would be disappointed. But if all worked out, the gift would be a surprise for him. Meanwhile, she thought, he can work on his employer, Abram Kisin's, sewing machine.

It wouldn't be a simple matter to open his own business in Jonava; to open your own tailor's workshop was not easy. There were already quite a few tailors in the shtetl. In order to be among the best one needed not only skill and perseverance, but also the money to rent a place to work.

"The Lord himself put a needle and thread in your hands. It was as if He had leaned over your cradle and said, 'Press down the pedal, Shleimke, don't be an idler,'" Kisin had praised his worker before he was drafted into the army. "My friend, you will be better than me yet and Gedalya Bankvecher and all the rest of us. Remember what I am saying; in a year or two you will move from being an apprentice to being my competitor."

Abram Kisin knew what he was talking about. It is true that he was worried that after two years in the army Shleimke would have forgotten what he had learned, but such worries turned out to be in vain. Being a soldier did not do Shleimke any harm. On the contrary, his nostalgia for the needle helped. Shleimke cut and sewed with real inspiration and passion. Kisin viewed his production with enthusiasm and, with sorrow, realized that the day was not far off when Shleimke would part with him permanently; he would buy his own Singer and move out on his own. Wicked tongues had reason to say that the weak, partially blind Abram Kisin was now just a sign above the door and the ringer of the cash register and that Shleimke was the master, one such as the shtetl had not seen in a long time. Shleimke's earnings were not bad, but in order to become completely independent of his master, they were not enough. Since he had no one to help him he didn't turn down any work; he repaired, restyled and sewed long coats for Jews and kaftans and sheepskin coats for peasants, so that he could earn enough for a decent wedding.

As planned, the wedding took place, in a field, under the heavens, after Passover. To the joy of the bride and groom and the guests, the weather was fit for a holiday. The sun shone over Jonava like a brilliant present. Birds gone wild from the spring flowering sang hallelujahs from every tree and a whole orchestra seemed to resound from their warm, welcoming twittering and triumphant whistling.

All the members of the tailors' and shoemakers' guilds of Jonava and all the close and distant relatives of the young couple were gathered in three rows around the tables brought by the families of the bride and groom and the tables borrowed from neighbours. The couple was honoured by the presence of the synagogue *gabbai*, their landlord Kapler.

In the second row, at the end of a table loaded with food, the pauper Avigdor Perelman stood by himself, having evidently decided to submit the Jewish people to a challenge: he had become deeply disillusioned with their lack of generosity and benevolence when the brother of the groom had been seen off at the train station. Unsure how much money he would earn at the wedding, Avigdor, waiting for the feast to begin, hastened to fill his stomach from the tables, which were practically buckling under the weight of the food.

The velvet cloth of the wedding canopy wafted in the warm spring breeze, which, with its sudden gusts, played with the yarmulke of Rabbi Eliezer who, at the bride's request, had delayed the start of the wedding ceremony.

They were waiting for the Kremnitsers.

Hennie looked down the road, concerned, and strained her ears to hear a car approaching.

The guests whispered impatiently and grumbled and glanced at each other, wondering why Rabbi Eliezer, the respected native of Tilsit who was noted for his Germanic punctuality, was holding up the ceremony rather than proceeding with his duty. Why, they wondered, was he struggling fruitlessly with the 'heretical' wind, which threatened to carry off his yarmulke?

Suddenly, as the muttering rose to a roar, the sound of a motor was heard and soon a Ford pulled up in the field. Reb Yeshua emerged from the car, followed by Ethel in a long mauve dress and the 'crown prince' of the family, Raphael.

The last to emerge was Aaron Kremnitser, handsome and foppish, in a light blue shirt, velvet trousers and polished shoes, as if he were an advertisement for a fashionable men's store in the capital. He straightened the black bow-tie that covered his Adam's apple and appeared quite pleased with his own appearance. He ordered the driver to take the wedding gift he had bought from the boot of the car, the latest model Singer sewing machine.

Hennie was overjoyed at the arrival of Aaron, who had not disappointed Reb Yeshua but had indeed fulfilled his request. Unable to hide her satisfaction, she asked her brother Shmulik to help the taciturn driver. Soon the two of them had dragged the box close to one of the tables where, together with the melancholic Dr. Blumenfeld, who considered the union of marriage to be a kind of long-term imprisonment, almost all the members of the Kremnitser family were now sitting.

After Shmulik and the driver had put down the gift, Hennie and Shleimke gave a sign to Rabbi Eliezer, signifying that the rabbi could begin. Everyone was there.

According to tradition Rabbi Eliezer led Hennie, in a long snow-white dress, around her bridegroom under the *chuppah* and then, chanting in Hebrew with his stuttering German accent, he pronounced the traditional blessings. He didn't stop at that, however. After a short pause the rabbi raised his eyes heavenward and, addressing the Almighty as if he were talking to an old friend, asked God to grant the young couple patience, harmony and well-being.

While the 'reformer of sinners' was speaking fervently with God, Avigdor Perelman ceased stuffing his jowls, pushed away a plate of chopped liver and sank into melancholic memories of his own youth and wedding. The past appeared suddenly before Avigdor; he was standing under the *chuppah*, listening to the lofty words of the rabbi and then, together with his Haya, they broke a glass against the earth. He swore eternal love to his bride. Avigdor remembered how, following the popular oral tradition, to the amusement of all the guests gathered, he had tried to step on Haya's foot before she could step on his, in order to show who would be the master in the family. Yet how did it all turn out? How, good people, did it all turn out? His Haya left him for some *shmendrik*, some good-for-nothing. That worthless Haya had abandoned him and gone to Kupiškis with her lover, while he, the loving but gullible Avigdor Perelman, took to drinking and bumming around. And worse. It was better not to remember what happened.

Rabbi Eliezer stopped speaking and the guests jumped up from their places.

"*Mazel tov! Mazel tov! Mazel tov!*" they shouted joyfully.

Shleimke and Hennie were husband and wife.

Avigdor uttered a "*Mazel tov!*" too, as a large, pure tear fell upon the food-laden table. Tears were the only property that Avigdor Perelman possessed. Those he didn't have to beg from anyone.

The wedding began to liven up, flowing like the River Vilija when it's liberated from the winter ice. In honour of the newlyweds the shtetl 'orchestra', consisting of a fiddle, a flute and a drum, began to play. Shoemakers and tailors shouted to each other and clinked glasses, once again showering the table with loud toasts. "*Mazal tov! Mazal tov!* One hundred years together – without spats or woes! One hundred years!"

The rejoicing lasted until dark, when the moon shone upon the tables and the stars lit up heaven like gems in a wedding ring.

Before the guests began to depart, Aaron Kremnitser, the wealthiest man in Jonava, addressed the crowd.

"Ladies and gentlemen!"

As if on command, the guests suddenly quietened; it is always useful to listen to a rich man.

"I know that each of you brought some kind of gift for the young couple," the young Kremnitser said. "But I would like, not only in the name of my own family, but in the name of all of you, to present to the groom, now a former cavalryman, our own special gift: an 'iron horse', a Singer sewing machine that we have brought not to his home on Rybatskaya Street, but right here to the wedding ceremony."

"What a surprise! Hurray for Mr. Aaron! Hurray for his whole family!" The approving voices rose to a roar.

"I hope he will ride it for a very long time and that you all may rejoice in his successes," Aaron said.

Shouts of approval echoed from around the tables in the twilight.

"Thank you," was all the astonished Shleimke could say. "May you all be happy too!"

The wedding crowd began to dissipate. The tables had been picked clean. Only Avigdor Perelman was still working, 'by the sweat of his brow' trying, as people were departing, to squeeze out the charity he felt was owed to him. Each coin he obtained improved his doubtful opinion of the generosity and large-heartedness of the Jewish people. The tiny orchestra continued to entertain the surrounding area, and even God Himself, with music that penetrated the soul. The trees danced to the sound of the fiddle. With its fancy roulades the flute caressed the ears of the angels flying over Jonava, deep now in sleep, while with its measured beat the drum scared away the evil spirits.

Overcome with happiness and by the noise and the gifts, Shleimke and Hennie were about to rush off to the small chamber that had been prepared temporarily for their conjugal pleasures, but their way to the house was unexpectedly barred by Avigdor. Sated with the various dishes and delicacies that had been prepared by the irrepressible and tireless Rokha, he addressed his words to the groom, who was bursting with joy.

"Shleimke! I remember you as a young rascal. We Perelmans lived next to you Kanoviches on Rybatskaya Street and you ran around the yard without any pants on with, excuse the expression, your tiny little penis on show, insisting that your father was going to buy you some pigeons and would set up a dovecote on the roof for you. But I don't want to speak about your pee spout or about the dovecote at the moment. This is what I want to say. I am not a rich man. I don't own a pine forest to sell for lumber. In fact, I don't even have firewood for the winter. Therefore, as much as I would like to, I cannot give you an iron horse, as the esteemed Reb Yeshua and his family did. However, I cannot leave your wedding without giving you something. I am grateful to you for all the charity that you so regularly gave me before your wedding, or rather before that sad day when the Lithuanians took you to be a soldier. So now – are you and your dear little wife listening?"

"Yes, we're listening," Hennie replied.

"So now I want to give to you all that charity which you, Shleimke, surely intend to give to me, good soul that you are, after your wedding. You do intend to do so, don't you?"

"Of course," Shleimke said, chuckling.

"Avigdor Perelman is a fair person. He hasn't forgotten anything and he doesn't forget anything. The best memory in the world belongs not to professors and rich men, but to paupers. Until the end of their lives, poor people remember everyone who, out of the goodness of their heart, gave them a penny or two. They remember not only their faces, but also their hands, and even the way they walk."

And then Avigdor Perelman disappeared into the mist of the night like a bird frightened by a sudden shot.

"Avigdor!" Shleimke shouted after him. "I will sew a warm quilted coat for you for the winter! Without fail. Come to me and I'll do it."

That was a wedding celebration and a wedding night – in 1927.

10

Attic conditions may allow for conjugal pleasures, but they are certainly not suitable for the work of a tailor.

Shleimke took home his Singer, which still smelled strongly of grease from the factory. For lack of available space its happy master had to temporarily leave his iron horse downstairs, next to his father's lasts. He could, of course, have dragged the sewing machine up to the attic, but only a complete fool would have entertained the idea of becoming the client of someone with such a workroom.

The young couple racked their brains long and hard, seeking a way to escape from their difficult situation. They decided, finally, to rent an apartment. After a long and difficult search, they found an appropriate place – a shabby room, owned by Ephraim Kapler, that was half underground. Kapler owned not only a three-storey house in the very centre of Jonava, but also the largest store, which sold imported goods.

Shleimke and Hennie settled in their new quarters, leaving behind their attic room where, on stuffy nights, bats would fly through the wide-open windows. Their entire furniture consisted of a roughly assembled table, four much sat-upon chairs and a squeaky, termite-nibbled sofa that had been flattened by Hennie's playful sisters, who liked to jump on it. Their new residence was adorned by the shiny new Singer, the latest model, as yet 'unmounted' and a large old mirror in which, long ago, the grandfather and great-grandfather of my future father had looked at themselves. Now it would be gazed into by his customers as they wondered how they would look in their new clothes.

"It's not a very fancy set-up," Shleimke said to his new wife.

"Yes, the Kremnitsers' set-up is fancier, you have to admit," Hennie joked. "As a matter of fact, they've never set eyes on such junk. The Kremnitsers throw furniture better than ours onto the junk pile."

"There's no reason to get depressed about it. Neither of us are lazy. We know how to roll up our sleeves. We'll sweat for a year or two and then, like your Kremnitsers, we'll also throw all our junk and all the things that are falling apart into the garbage. After all, when He created the world, God left quite a bit of mess. He didn't put everything in order right away."

And as time showed, they really were not idle, but worked by the sweat of their brows, sparing neither time nor themselves.

Until midday Shleimke sewed on the old Singer belonging to Abram Kisin and then, after harnessing his own steed, he galloped at full speed in the direction of his own success, not turning down even the most menial work. He was neither picky nor proud; he even sewed shrouds. Shleimke asserted that no work was shameful. The only thing that was shameful was if one's workmanship was bad.

Nor did Hennie lag behind her husband. In the morning she took care of Raphael, who was no longer a baby, and in the evening she went to clean the homes of the Jonava shopkeeper, Rabbi Eliezer, and of the principal of the local Yiddish school, where she herself had not been able to complete her studies since her younger sisters and brothers had needed her care.

At first, as strange as it might seem, Shleimke received most of his earnings not from his own customers, but from other well-known local tailors, such as the recognized masters Abram Kisin and Gedalya Bankvecher, who never rejected work, taking orders from whoever came to them, even though they considered it degrading to drudge away sewing peasant kaftans, padded jackets, sheepskin coats and suits and jackets of cheap, tough material. Such small jobs, which were below their dignity, the local master-tailors willingly handed over to the capable novice. He might have been thinking of becoming their competitor, but at that point he was nowhere close. As for Shleimke, he was aware of his own powers and abilities. He didn't want to work anonymously, 'underground' as he put it, but under his own sign. In order to be able to do that the word about him had to circulate throughout the shtetl, hopefully in a loud and positive manner.

Spreading rumours widely was the only effective means of advertising in Jonava at that time. Without exaggeration, the influence of these rumours on customers was tremendous – they could either raise a novice tailor high above the clouds or bring about his divorce from his 'provider needle'.

In this case, the rumours helped the fortunate Shleimke. The Kremnitser family were particularly useful in facilitating their circulation from house to house.

"Do you know," people suddenly began to hear in the town, "that the old dandy, Reb Yeshua Kremnitser, has found himself a new tailor? Due to his advanced age he has stopped travelling to Zelik Slutsker in Kaunas and is giving his business to that cavalryman Kanovich. Shleimke is already sewing Kremnitser a new woollen suit. And Reb Ephraim Kapler recently ordered from his young tenant a jacket, a suit and a tweed overcoat."

Reb Yeshua also aided the talented novice directly. He was the first of the wealthy people in Jonava to order clothes from him. Those with an evil tongue claimed that the old man was less interested in the reputation of the former cavalryman than he was in trying to please the latter's young wife, the charming Hennie. As Reb Yeshua himself admitted in public, he was somewhat in love with her, remarking, "Oh, if I had not been born so long ago, if I didn't have such an off-putting birth date on my identity papers, if it were not for my cursed pancreas and that constantly nagging liver of mine, you understand, I wouldn't have missed my chance."

In fact, the elder Kremnitser came to Shleimke with a handsome piece of dark blue English Boston cloth, put it on the table covered with a simple tablecloth in the cramped apartment of the young couple and muttered something about their unprepossessing environment, to the effect that their ancestors, after they had fled from Egypt in ancient times, had lived simply in tents.

Shleimke listened to these reproaches of his distinguished customer with restraint and cautiously took his measurements, as if he was afraid of dirtying him with his grubby measuring tape. Glowing with silent gratitude to the father-in-law of her splendid friend Ethel, the bright young Hennie quickly jotted down Reb Yeshua's measurements as Shleimke dictated them – the length of his sleeve, the breadth of his shoulders, the girth of his waist – all in a school notebook that had been specially purchased for that very purpose, on the cover of which was the Lithuanian coat of arms with a helmeted knight galloping off into the bright distance.

As Kremnitser was about to leave, Hennie stopped him with a question. "Reb Yeshua, I would like to know how our ancestors lived in those drafty tents when they fled Egypt with our distant ancestor Moses and found themselves in the Sinai desert."

"Well, don't get upset but our distant ancestors who followed Moses through the burning desert were like you at first; they had nothing in their homes apart from faith and hope. They didn't have a sink or, if you'll excuse me being crude, a toilet. But anyway, with God's help they reached the Promised Land. And the two of you will also reach a better place in life."

A week later, without any supervision or instruction from Abram Kisin, Shleimke sewed a suit for the first time in his life as an independent tailor, for Mr. Kremnitser. Reb Yeshua wore it every Sabbath day, showing it off like a walking mannequin. Slowly, with an almost ceremonial step, he would traverse all of Jonava on his way to morning prayers at the synagogue. Even before he had time to sit in his place in the first row, with a roguish smile on his freshly shaven face, he would ask his distinguished neighbours, "Well, my fine fellows, what do you say?"

"Reb Yeshua, what are you referring to? The quota that the authorities have introduced for Jews who wish to enter Vytautas University?" inquired the owner of the shtetl bakery with unconcealed curiosity. Chaim-Gershom Fain was an inveterate Zionist, who dreamed that his grandsons would bake Shabbat challah not in Jonava but in Jerusalem, free from Arabs and Turks, right next to God Himself. Picking up his prayer book, he continued, "One can expect anything from our anti-Semitic rulers."

"As for the university quotas, Reb Chaim Gershon, that is without a doubt an outrage," Reb Yeshua replied with a condescending smile. "But whether the authorities in Kaunas are old or new doesn't make any difference to us Jews. Fish can either be fresh or not, Reb Chaim Gershon, but the rulers, whoever they are, will always be stale and stink. But let's leave politics aside. Today I want to boast about something new."

"Go ahead. Boast away!"

"How do you like my new suit?"

"Your suit?" the worshipper said, taken aback. "It's a fine suit. Right away one can see the hand of the master tailor Gedalya Bankvecher."

"If you please, Reb Chaim Gershon, what does Gedalya Bankvecher have to do with it? It was sewn by a different master – the young Shleimke Kanovich."

"Do you mean the first Jewish cavalryman in Jonava and, who knows, not only in Jonava but in all of Lithuania? Is he the one who sews so well?"

"Yes, he is the very one," Reb Yeshua confirmed.

"It can't be! Is that what he learned in the most ferocious and battle-ready cavalry in Europe?" Chaim Gershon Fain asked ironically.

"Shleimke received his gift from God. The cavalry can't give you the kind of gifts given by God."

"I'm amazed."

"There's nothing to be amazed at. Doesn't God give each of us some special gift when we are born? You're a baker, for example. God gave you the gift of baking better than anyone else; from formless dough you bake the tastiest *baranki* and *bulochki*, *pirogi* and *pirozhki* in our shtetl. To him, a tailor, God gave the gift of being able to sew a beautiful garment from a formless piece of material, to the envy of all. I very much recommend, dear Reb Chaim Gershon, that you take the opportunity to make use of Shleimke's services. You won't regret it, I swear! He sews as well as you, my esteemed friend, bake rolls."

The first thing the young couple bought was the thing that is most necessary for the continuation of the human race: a double bed that did not squeak and a new mattress. Then, from the local furniture factory, they obtained at a discount a broad oak table and six chairs with high backs, strong legs and solid seats, for visitors and clients, no matter how heavy. Then they commissioned the lame painter Yevel, a distant relative of Rokha, to whitewash the ceiling and walls. Yevel didn't make them wait. The very next day he arrived with a ladder, a bucket, paint and a brush.

He worked slowly and carefully, singing popular songs as he worked in a pleasant bass voice. He sang about wild daisies and about an anonymous young woman whose beauty could not be compared to that of anyone else in the world and about a mischievous dancing rabbi who not only pored over the Torah, but also cut various capers with his students.

Yevel's brush moved, as if in obedience to his pleasant melodies. Sometimes it swept along smoothly; at other times it jumped around in unexpected sweeps and swirls. The painter was not only lame, but also near-sighted. He wore glasses, behind which there shone sparkling, perky, penetratingly dark eyes that appeared unexpectedly brilliant in his sad face. He spoke only during the breaks when he got down from his ladder, took a satin tobacco pouch from his pocket, rolled himself a homemade cigarette and puffed away at it with pleasure.

"So, Shleimke, how was it in that famous Lithuanian cavalry? The horses there don't like Jews very much, do they?" asked the painter, sucking away at his cigarette. "Do they kick?"

"Horses are horses; they don't have any interest in Jews. Most of all, Yevel, they love oats and so the important thing is that their feedbag is filled with oats. As for who fills the bag, whether it's a Jew or a Gypsy horse-thief, what do they care?"

"What do you mean? Do horses have a kind of conscience?"

"They do, they do," Shleimke assured the eternally gloomy Yevel.

"I always thought that domestic animals, cats, goats, dogs and so on, have more of a conscience than people do. You just tell me what a person needs a conscience for? It's an unnecessary burden. It's hard enough to live even without one. It won't be long before I will have been painting walls for a quarter of a century. Can you imagine that?"

"Really! So?"

"So, even if you threatened to kill me, I couldn't remember how many walls I've painted in that time. But I am sure of one thing."

"What's that?"

"You can whitewash wood and stone, but a person – there's no way. Unfortunately! Apparently when our Father in heaven was creating the world there was not enough whitewash. But, Shleimke, I see that you take care of your health and don't smoke."

"No, I don't."

"So you want to live a long life, then?"

"I want to sew for a long time," Shleimke joked. "And smoke, Yevel, fogs over the eye of the needle so you can't see the thread."

"You have a way with words. Fine, I've had my smoke, so now back to work. By evening you and your wife will not recognize this miserable doghouse, which I am going to transform into a thing of beauty."

Indeed, after being whitewashed, the room was unrecognizable. It appeared more spacious and it felt easier to breathe.

"Yevel has golden hands!" exclaimed Rokha, who came to look at the new walls and ceiling. "We should have our place redone too, but for whom should we be doing it now? Isaac has left and Leah has flown off too. Any day now Motl and his Sarah will move to Kaunas, where his future father-in-law has promised to buy a hairdresser's shop for his daughter. Yes, who should we redo it for? For the mice and the spiders? Let everything remain as it is. What does it matter, in the end, if you're carted out from a luxurious palace or from a pitiful hut?"

"That's not right, Mama," Shleimke said, trying to cheer her up. "As long as a person is alive, they should do something to make their life more beautiful."

"That's true, son, but in my opinion it's not painters or cobblers that make life beautiful, nor tailors or hairdressers – but children. You know how many I brought into the world? How many I nursed with my own milk?"

"Eleven, I believe."

"Ten. But how many do I have left?"

A heavy silence loomed over the room.

"Will you have some tea with us? Yesterday I bought fresh lime honey from a bearded Old Believer at the market," Hennie said, resorting to an obvious ploy, hoping to distract her mother-in-law from her dismal thoughts.

"I have four left. Three are still with me, at least for the moment, and Yosele is in a mental institution in Kalvarija. He thinks he's a bird: sometimes a goldfinch, sometimes a crow." Rokha took out a handkerchief and wiped her eyes. "Hennie, I will have some tea. Why not? Yes, I'll have some. But first let Shleimke read me a letter. Then we'll look at a photograph together."

"Is the letter from Leah?" Hennie rejoiced.

"No, it's from Isaac, from Paris."

Shleimke took the letter from his mother and, without wasting any time, began reading.

"Isaac writes that, thank God, he is alive and well. He is working in the crowded Latin Quarter in a large leather-goods workshop that belongs to Monsieur Kushner, a Bessarabian Jew, who treats him very well and appreciates his abilities. Furthermore Isaac wishes to inform all his dear ones that his salary is fine, in fact more than fine and that soon he will be saying goodbye to his bachelor life and marrying his beloved Sarah Melamed from Kedainiai."

"*Mazel tov!*" exclaimed Rokha. "Only I don't understand why one has to travel to Paris in order to marry a girl from a nearby shtetl."

"Don't interrupt, Mama. Let me read the letter to the end," said the imperturbable Shleimke.

"'Dear Mama, dear Papa, along with my brothers Motl and Shleimke and dear sister Hava, in this picture, taken for two francs by a street photographer, you can see me and my future wife Sarah. We are standing next to the tallest tower in the world, built by the engineer Eiffel. The photo turned out so-so. In fact, it is not very good, but I don't have enough money for a camera of my own yet. Write and tell me how you are, what is new with you and ask Ethel Kremnitser to write our address in Paris in French on your envelope; that way your letter will arrive sooner. Your loving son and brother Isaac and his chosen one Sarah.'"

He read hesitantly, since Isaac's handwriting resembled thistles and it wasn't easy to decipher all the squiggles and twirls. After Shleimke had finished reading, the three of them examined the photograph.

"Isaac looks like a real foreigner!" Hennie couldn't help exclaiming. "With his cap on sideways and with a cape to his heels! You can only see his shoes. His Sarah is lovely; what a good figure! But she has her hair cut short like a man. Look at her high heels and the scarf around her neck. You can't buy anything like that here!"

"I've had enough time to look at them," said Rokha with pronounced indifference. "I like Isaac better as he used to look, in a cap with a broken peak, a wool shirt not tucked into his belt and leather shoes with a thick sole made in his masterly way by Dovid for our son's birthday. In any case, I would like to see him alive, not in a photograph."

"What are you saying? Don't commit a sin! He is alive now!" Shleimke said to his mother.

"Yes, alive," Rokha said, "but not for me. He's alive for his Sarah. May they both be happy for a very long time! I wish them that with all my heart. But I'm a mother and you have to agree that it is a bitter thing for mothers to learn about the happiness of their children only via the postman."

"We should put the kettle on," Hennie interjected. "Our discussions and disagreements won't bring the water to the boil."

Rokha nodded her head. "I'll help you," she said, following Hennie into the kitchen.

Hennie put the water on the primus stove, made some chamomile tea and was about to go back into the room to pour it into the porcelain cups Ethel had bought from Germany as her wedding gift, but her mother-in-law stopped her.

"Wait a minute, Hennie. I need to speak with you about a serious matter," Rokha whispered, hinting that the matter should not be put off. "Hennie," Rokha said emphatically, "Just don't be in a hurry!"

"With what?"

"Not with what, with whom? How slow you are to figure things out! Were you born only yesterday?" her mother-in-law said. "First, get on your feet and start making a living, then provide for your offspring so that they won't be running around the shtetl barefoot and naked."

"I can't promise, but we'll try, Rokha. But it may not turn out that way. You yourself know, you try to be careful, you do try, but it only takes a moment to make a mistake and it happens, like a worm on a fish hook."

Rokha laughed aloud. "What's true is true. I know from my own experience. Otherwise I wouldn't have been caught on that hook ten times in a row, as they say. My energetic 'fisherman' would cast his line almost every night, so it wasn't easy to agree on things. But, be careful. Anyway, forgive me for my tiresome advice. As for me, I would like to be a grandmother soon, to have grandchildren. And not in wonderful America or in France, with its tower that sticks up like a cornstalk, but here, where I was born and will die."

"You will have grandchildren, both here and there. With 'fishermen' like your industrious sons, you'll have a hard time counting them."

"Hennie, from your lips right into the ears of the all-merciful-but-somewhat-hard-of-hearing One. Still, don't be in a hurry."

They drank the tea and lamented that Leah had not written to them. They were afraid that she was sick, because even in happy America people became sick and, Heaven forbid, died.

"She will write, she will, as soon as she starts getting by. As soon as she manages to find a rich Jewish husband," Shleimke said to calm his mother.

"I don't mind if he's poor, as long as he is good," Rokha mumbled. "A good man can grow rich, but a rich man can never grow good, they can only pretend to be so. But how are things with you?" she turned to Shleimke. "Are customers coming to you or are they passing you by and going to Gedalya Bankvecher? You don't even have a sign out, although, to tell you the truth, you don't have the room to hang one."

"A tailor needs a name, not a sign," her son replied. "Things aren't bad. I'm getting more orders, and it's not just the Jews and Lithuanians that are coming to me, but even Old Believers. And not only people from Jonava, but also from the nearby villages. They have found out that I take less for my sewing and that my sewing is just as good as that of others."

As the tea-drinking was coming to an end the doorbell rang and Kapler, the owner of the house, entered the newly painted room. Kapler was portly and smooth-shaven, with a well-groomed moustache.

"I've come for an inspection," he announced.

"Of course!" Hennie said, rising and offering him a seat. "Perhaps, Reb Ephraim, you will have some tea with us and taste our fresh lime honey?"

"Thank you sincerely but, if you don't mind, I'll have tea with you another time. I have an important meeting with the mayor and he is very punctilious. He doesn't like people to be late. I must admit that I'm a real lover of lime honey.

I can smell it a mile away. Its smell drives me out of my mind!"

With his sharp, observant eyes Ephraim Kapler scrutinized the room.

"Beautiful!" he said. "That cripple Yevel does wonders, even if he does hit the bottle sometimes. God didn't short-change my tenants when it came to parcelling out intelligence. I must say, it's quite an advantage to have my own tailor in my house. Perhaps I no longer need to drag myself more than 30 kilometres to be measured by Zelik Slutsker in Kaunas and can have my sartorial needs taken care of locally? What do you say?"

Shleimke, wisely, remained silent. It wasn't in his character to force himself on others.

"Young eyes see much better than old ones," Kapler said, stroking the moustache to which he devoted the same care others would to a rare plant.

"Just try him, Reb Ephraim! My husband is neither an imposter nor a bungler. Believe me, he will sew for you as well as Abram Kisin or Gedalya Bankvecher," the loyal Hennie interjected.

"Gedalya Bankvecher is old and seriously ill, while Kisin, unfortunately, cannot sew for anyone anymore."

"How is that? Why can't he sew for anyone anymore?" Rokha asked.

"That's the way it is on this earth of ours. While some sit quietly in a warm room drinking tea with lime honey, in the same town and at the same time others get ready to accompany someone on his last journey. But, from your faces, I see you didn't know anything."

"Do you mean that Kisin has died?" exclaimed Shleimke fearfully, startled by the idea.

"Yes. He had been sitting at his Singer from early in the morning, as usual, pressing on the pedal. But he didn't make it to lunch, only to his end. Not for nothing is it said in scripture, 'a person knows neither his place nor his hour'. Sooner or later we all go to the same destination. Now there are only two master tailors in our shtetl, Gedalya Bankvecher and you, Shleimke. There are no other good tailors."

"And there won't be any others like Reb Abram, may he rest in peace," Shleimke replied.

At the cemetery, where from time immemorial the Jews of Jonava had found their resting place, Abram Kisin was honoured by just a handful of former customers and neighbours.

Reb Abram had bought a plot for himself before he died, on a hill next to the grave of his wife, Hava, who had died the previous autumn from a cerebral haemorrhage. The Kisins did not have any children, so there was no one to mourn him besides a Lithuanian woman called Antanina who had helped Abram around the house. She was a God-fearing woman, as quiet as a dream, and spoke Yiddish as well as Rabbi Eliezer. The only relative of the deceased, and a distant one at that, was Avigdor Perelman. Normally he never entered the Jewish cemetery itself, but remained outside the gate. This time he stood at the grave and gazed into the yawning void with frightened curiosity, as if he were trying it out for size or estimating its depth. His eyes were dry. Avigdor claimed that you didn't have enough tears for everyone, so one should weep for the living first, rather than the dead, since the living still had to suffer. And anyway the same unavoidable fate awaited everyone.

Rabbi Eliezer, who in his free time wrote poetry in a lofty Hebrew style about Joseph and his brothers, the heroism of the Maccabees and the wisdom of King Solomon, recited the *kaddish* prayer and, after a pause, as a former faithful customer of Abram Kisin, allowed himself to deliver a somewhat abstract speech, adorned with lyrical digressions and quotations from the Five Books. Loftily, the Rabbi explained how, when the Messiah came, the first to rise from the dead would be the old master craftsmen and that Reb Abram Kisin would definitely be one of the first to return from Heaven to his home, his native Jonava. The gifted master would once again, as he had after a vacation in Palanga, enter his home on Kostelnaya Street, sit down at his sewing machine, wipe off the dust that had settled there and, to the joy of all his living fellow shtetl residents, resume sewing with his previous enthusiasm and energy.

At this point, the sharp-tongued Avigdor Perelman could not help interrupting the lofty, life-affirming rhetoric of the local shepherd of the flock with his own modest contribution.

"Amen! All the more so since the way from heaven to Jonava is not so long. It would be much more difficult for Reb Abram to reach America or some such place."

Those who had accompanied the deceased on his last journey let the poor joke of the impoverished man sail past their ears and began to depart.

Cautiously Antanina approached the cemetery gate, which was adorned with shaggy-maned wooden lions holding in their paws chalices, full of the blessings of the other world. Wanting to make a request or ask a piece of advice, she turned to the favourite apprentice of the deceased.

"Shleimke, perhaps you will help me. Berel, your teacher's nephew, is a tinsmith not a tailor and he lives in Jelgava in Latvia. Berel didn't manage to get to his uncle's funeral and it will be quite some time until he is able to come and take care of everything. I can't figure out what to do with the work that the deceased didn't have time to finish. Shall I return it to his customers? The trouble is, I have no idea what belongs to whom if they suddenly turn up and ask me for their items back."

Without giving her husband the opportunity to open his mouth, the practical Hennie came up with an idea of her own.

"Why give them back, *Ponia* Antanina? As everyone knows, Shleimele was his apprentice. My husband can finish sewing them. He will figure out whose jacket is whose and which overcoat belongs to which person. There won't be any mix-up. Don't worry! Everyone will receive everything that belongs to him and the money paid for the sewing will go to buy a gravestone for Abram Kisin. With your permission, we will take all the items which haven't been finished. If someone wants to take his material back and go to Gedalya Bankvecher, let him do so, and may he be healthy. You've done the right thing, *Ponia* Antanina! After all, when we needed help, good people came to our aid. Why shouldn't we help others? Right, Shleimke?"

"Right." Shleimke nodded, amazed at Hennie's shrewdness.

He hadn't expected such an initiative from her, although he immediately grasped that she was less concerned about a monument to the late Kisin than about her husband and his good name, since there is no better advertisement than selflessness and good deeds. The whole shtetl would be talking about Shleimke Kanovich. "Did you hear, he's not taking a penny for himself? He's giving all the money to Antanina, who will look for the right stone for a gravestone. Her relatives will bring it on a cart to the cemetery while the stonecutter Yona will inscribe a few appropriate words in Reb Kisin's memory."

"Thank you," Antanina replied gratefully. "My master, may his memory be blessed, always said that Shleimke would go far and very much regretted that the Lord God had not given him such a son."

The next morning, with Antanina's help, Hennie carried all the unfinished items to the house that she and Shleimke shared.

After that summer morning, an unexpected and favourable turn took place in Shleimke's life. Not a single one of Kisin's former customers turned down the former apprentice's services. Unanimously they agreed that Shleimke should finish sewing their overcoats or the suits that the late Reb Abram had not completed. Things turned out just as the far-sighted Hennie had hoped. The customers praised the young master tailor and, as a result, brought him a flood of new work.

Shleimke worked with joyful inspiration. His Singer rarely stopped singing. Kapler, however, was far from enthusiastic about the industriousness of his tenant. On more than one occasion the landlord descended from the second floor, of which he was the sole occupant, and began to angrily upbraid Shleimke. The unceasing machinegun-like stutter of the Singer would awaken him in the night and he wouldn't be able to close his eyes again until dawn.

"My friend," the landlord said, "Do you have to sew at night? Don't you have enough time during the day? You shouldn't sacrifice your rest and sleep for the sake of more work – God gave it to us as a reward for working in the daytime. He himself rested on the seventh day and commanded us to take care of our strength during our miserable lives. And, what's more, He created the world during the day and not at night."

"There's nothing I can do. I have many orders. I have to sew both day and night. My customers are impatient and I'm working alone. Sometimes, it's true, my wife gives me a hand; she gives me advice, heats the iron on the stove and jots measurements down in her notebook. I'd like to teach the trade to her brother the hunchback, as Hennie has suggested. If there were two of us things would be easier."

"In my opinion, my friend, sewing every night just lowers your dignity as a man," Ephraim Kapler said, pulling a sour face with the aid of his handsome moustache. "Jews don't sew at night, they do you–know–what. How does your wife view this strange behaviour?"

"Well, it's normal."

"Normal?" Reb Ephraim's cheeks puffed out with surprise and pique. His thick, silver eyebrows rose. "But what about God's commandment, *pru urvu*? Do you get what I am saying?"

"Unfortunately, no Reb Ephraim. You'll have to translate God's commandment into Yiddish so I can understand. Unfortunately, I've forgotten the bit of Hebrew I once knew."

"It means, be fruitful and multiply."

"Oh, so that's what you're talking about. Well, in that regard I hope, everything will work out. Forgive me for my frankness, Reb Ephraim, but only the cuckoo sticks its eggs into another bird's nest."

"Fine. That's your business. But if you continue to be stubborn and insist on sewing at night, then you'll have to find somewhere else to live," the moustachioed Ephraim Kapler warned. Reb Ephraim was worn out from lack of sleep and wasn't used to trouble from his tenants.

After this warning, he left without saying goodbye.

Shleimke, being cautious by nature, and preferring not to get into a fight with anyone, heeded his landlord's warning and stopped applying his spurs to his Singer at night. He was loath to leave the apartment they had just fixed up, to live back in that narrow, stifling, bat-infested attic.

Continuing to work with his previous enthusiasm, he 'stabled' his 'steed', as he referred to his sewing machine, before midnight so that, God forbid, he might not disturb the precious sleep of Reb Kapler. He would not take the Singer 'out of its stall' on the Sabbath either. Shleimke succeeded in taking care of all of Kisin's customers in time and, according to the agreement, all the money he received he handed over, via Antanina, to the nephew of the deceased, a bony, stuttering tinsmith namedBerel, who came from Jelgava to dedicate his uncle's gravestone.

On the smooth oval stone Yona, the stonecutter, engraved the traditional Jewish letters signifying 'Here is buried', followed by the first and last name of the deceased. But then he allowed himself some liberty, engraving below the image of a thin thread cut off in the middle and, under that, a needle, as if it had fallen from the hands of the deceased onto the grave mound.

Rokha could not help but rejoice at her son's success and praised him and his bride to everyone she met. "He won't betray me by running off to France or America, or to Palestine. He's sure to be here to close my eyes and those of Dovid," she told herself fervently.

The Kremnitser family also rejoiced in the fact that the number of customers of the young tailor was increasing. "And just who was his Columbus?" Reb Yeshua asked, stressing his own role in the matter. "Who discovered him first for the world?"

Few people in the shtetl had any idea who Columbus was. It was likely that even the mayor of Jonava, who was the son of a peasant, had never heard his name.

Meanwhile, time passed like a quiet stream into a river, without either whirlpools or splashing. No one else was executed in Lithuania. The new president gave professorial speeches, as he was supposed to do, and sometimes even deigned to visit the provinces. On one occasion, he visited Jonava. In the town square, he listened as a mixed choir from the local Lithuanian high school and the local Tarbut Hebrew-language school sang the national anthem, 'O Lithuania, our homeland, country of heroes'. Then, convinced of the love of his young subjects for their native country, he returned to his presidential palace in the capital.

Life in Jonava flowed smoothly on without any shocks or earthquakes.

Hennie continued to work for her benefactors, the Kremnitsers, even though Raphael, who was growing in both age and height, no longer needed her games and stories.

"You're not telling it right," Raphael complained, listening yet one more time to her story about the snail that had learned to fly like the swallows and the bluebirds and to live in trees. Snails don't fly."

"But this is a fairytale, Raphael, and in a fairytale, darling, everything is possible."

"I asked Grandpa Yeshua and he told me that only birds, flies, mosquitoes, bees, wasps and chickens from the chicken coop fly, though chickens not so very well. Snails don't have wings. You're just fooling me and Mama says it's not good to fool people."

Raphael had not needed a nanny for quite some time. He turned the handle of a hand organ and listened to some simple songs, built houses out of blocks, constructed a railroad with tracks, along which moved an express train with cars of different colours. On the doors of the cars, along with numbers, the French alphabet was drawn in large letters. When the boy became bored listening to songs about being a builder or a railwayman, he took up a book about animals from all the continents: elephants, bears, giraffes and kangaroos, deer and elk, whose images he could colour in with his coloured pencils. Hennie's flying snail could not compete with those marvellous pictures and the colourful alphabet that Aaron Kremnitser had brought his son from the wonderful but hopelessly distant Paris.

Hennie was tortured by pangs of conscience. She caught herself reflecting that she had been receiving a respectable salary undeservedly for being Ethel's confidante rather than for taking care of Raphael. She was being paid to listen to the sad and heartfelt confessions of her mistress. Hennie did not want, of course, to be deprived of this salary, but she didn't want to receive it for doing nothing. God does not commend us for accepting payment, either small or large, for sympathizing with the suffering of one's neighbour.

Nor did Hennie forget the instructions given long ago by her parents that lying was a sin and that one should not speak the truth hastily, but rather with good sense and caution because, although truth adorns a person, unfortunately it doesn't feed them. If you want to eat, then you have to find some way to provide for yourself, whatever that might be. Such, indeed, had always been the Jewish fate. However, Hennie didn't want to accept such a degrading fate.

"I am happy to be with you," she said to Ethel, but was reluctant to continue.

"And we are to have you with us," Ethel responded.

"But Raphael doesn't need me anymore."

"We all need you: Raphael and I, and Reb Yeshua," Ethel replied.

"Raphael is bored with me. What can I give him? After all I only completed three years of elementary school. I'm an uneducated village girl and Raphael no longer wants to hear about flying snails, or mice that became the friends of cats and other such nonsense."

"The main thing, Hennie, is the soul. What good is it if someone knows everything in the world, knows about everyone, but his soul has long turned to stone?"

"But what kind of thing is it, the soul? Isn't it just the same thing as the heart?"

"Not quite. Everyone has a heart, but unfortunately not everyone has a soul. You are posing questions to me to which even our sages were hard pressed to give intelligent answers to, my dear. I break my head on them too. What kind of a thing is the soul? Maybe I'm talking nonsense, but I believe that the soul is what distinguishes a human being from a two-legged mammal. It can't be buried in the grave because the soul is immortal. After death it resists decay and flies up to heaven since death has no power over it."

"Such explanations are beyond me."

"Beyond me too. So let's rather return to our affairs. Where did you get the idea that we don't need you? No one is complaining about you. You are not earning your bread by idleness. You might not believe it, but I can no longer imagine how we could get along without you. So even if you want to leave us, we won't let you go. As for Raphael, you're right, he needs less looking after now, but it's my father-in-law that I am concerned about."

"What's the matter with him?"

"He's taken to bed again. Dr. Blumenfeld prescribed him some powders for the pains in his liver and some pills to lower his blood pressure. He ordered him to stay in bed for at least a week, but Reb Yeshua is constantly eager to get up, get dressed and go to his shop. He doesn't pay any attention when I urge him to follow the doctor's orders. He just waves me off as if there were no problem and replies, 'I want to die standing behind my counter.' I feel that I can't deal with him by myself. If only Aaron would come back from Paris. Whoever heard of a man in his right mind having the idea of dying while standing behind his counter?"

"How many years has he been working there?"

"As long as I've been here, at least ten, probably many more – from the time when Aaron was engaged in selling lumber. All the doors of the houses and storehouses in Jonava, all the barns and huts and all the mills in the area are secured with locks and bolts bought in Reb Yeshua's shop. In fun the peasants call him to his face 'Peter of the Keys'. He knows their children and grandchildren and the names of every customer. For them he is the very best Jew in the world. He sells at reasonable prices and gives credit without rushing people to repay their debts. When Reb Yeshua was younger, he would visit them as a guest and even drank moonshine with them."

"He really is the best," Hennie said, confirming the opinion of the peasants. "May God grant him good health!"

"Amen," his daughter-in-law concurred, but for some reason she did not repeat the statement that Reb Yeshua was the best Jew in the world.

"Maybe I could work behind the counter for a week?" Hennie proposed.

"Speak with him. Who knows, maybe he will agree. He is not sleeping now, he's reading the Torah. Knock on his door," Ethel said.

Hennie knocked and a moment later heard the words, "Come in whenever you want."

Quietly, almost on tiptoes, she entered the room.

"Hello," she said.

"Oh, who do I see?" Reb Yeshua perked up. "Not that nudnik Blumenfeld or Ethel with her pills and powders, but a lovely woman! Don't stand there. Sit down!"

"Reb Yeshua, you shouldn't talk too much." Hennie moved a woven chair near the bed of the patient and sat down.

Yeshua Kremnitser lay on a sofa in coloured pyjamas, covered to the waist with a quilt cover and breathing with difficulty.

"I can still talk, my dear, but I can't live. I can't! What kind of joy is it to ruin the life of another person for my own worthless life?"

"That's not true! You aren't spoiling the life of anyone. Don't let your imagination run away with you or speak ill of yourself."

"What I said is true. If I joined our ancestors, as my contemporary Abram Kisin has, it would be better for everyone." Reb Yeshua coughed, drank some carrot juice and, after a long silence and without looking at Hennie, continued, as if speaking with himself. "Then Ethel wouldn't suffer years of boredom in this hole, as if she were in prison. In the blink of an eye they would pack up their suitcases and be out of here."

Despite his shortness of breath, he whistled energetically like a boy. "Nothing holds them here," he added.

"But this is their native home," Hennie said.

"Home? They spit on this home. Furthermore, Ethel was born in Germany, not Lithuania."

"But she has lived here for so many years . . ."

"They will leave without any qualms and forget everything and everyone. After all, what do they have to remember? Lithuanian rain and the blizzards? Drunken peasants at the village market? The shop which gave me, an old man, as much pleasure as Raphael used to get from his rocking horse? At least I didn't bother them, didn't get in his parents' way."

"Reb Yeshua, the doctor ordered you not to get excited. Get such harmful ideas out of your head and, please, try to get well soon."

"I can't reject that." Reb Kremnitser sighed. "But the problem is that no matter how much I try to get rid of the rubbish in my head, I don't have the strength. It's been there for years and already smells of rot."

"There, now you've really gone too far."

"You just live and you will see. It's a sin to blame God, of course, but not a single rabbi says you can't complain to the Master of the Universe about your pains and troubles. God didn't bypass me when it came to blessings. I thank him for giving me a successful son. But I can only blame myself that I didn't have a daughter like you. My dear Golda and I were too slow. If, with God's help, I get on my feet, the first thing I'll do is go to Kaunas to my notary."

Reb Yeshua fell silent again, waiting until he had recovered a bit from his accumulated bitterness so that he could utter the words he needed to say.

"The time has come for me to do something about my will," he said quietly. "Anything can happen to an infirm old man. I don't care who buys our house, I don't care where Aaron takes his family either. But about the shop . . . I don't want it to go to just anyone. Maybe, while I am still alive I will surprise my friends, as well as those who wish me ill, with a last act of will. You'll never guess who I intend to leave the shop to."

"You're right. I can't guess."

"I'm going to leave it to you. What do you have to say to that?"

"What are you saying?" Hennie replied with a start. "Where did you get such an idea? You have already spoiled me so much with your generosity. Don't even express such a thought! While you are ill I can, if you like, replace you again behind the counter until you're fit to return to your shop. But not as the owner! May you live until a hundred and twenty and be the proprietor as long as you can! To such a good person as you God should only add, not subtract, years."

"Our God can do anything, but for some reason He is not in a hurry to do so. Why? Because people are people. Otherwise they would never moderate their appetites or overcome their pride."

"Please, lie quietly. You've got yourself worked up from talking. That will make you worse, God forbid."

"Thank you for dropping in. You help me much more than Dr. Blumenfeld's pills," Reb Yeshua said after a short pause. Then he began to look under the cover for his handkerchief to wipe away the tears that had betrayed his emotions.

"Reb Yeshua, don't be angry at me for my frankness, but in the future I have no intention of taking care of or being a nanny for the children of others. I want to have children of my own. Evidently I am not capable of anything else. My mother always used to repeat to her flock of daughters that we shouldn't forget that every Jewish woman, rich or poor, has no more important duty in the world than making more Jews with her good husband."

"With you, Hennie, a person can't help feeling better. I should pay you and not that old crusty Blumenfeld for every visit," Reb Yeshua exclaimed.

She bowed in parting and left the room as quietly as she had entered.

11

The flow of customers into the semi-underground workshop continued and Shleimke, who never refused a job, worked industriously until he was exhausted. Worried about his health, Hennie suggested he took on her mischievous, militant brother Shmulik as apprentice-assistant. It was not without reason that Grandfather Shimon called his son Shmuel a 'Bolshevik', as people in those regions referred to the revolutionaries who were trying to topple Tsar Nikolai from his throne. Grandfather Shimon had been exiled to Vitebsk at the age of fourteen, becoming an involuntary witness to the Russian revolution. The nickname stuck with him for quite some time.

While Shmulik didn't call for the overthrow of President Smetona, he did vehemently condemn the existing order in Lithuania while praising his idol, Vladimir Lenin, the late leader of the workers of the world.

"Someday you'll end up like that unfortunate baker who gave up baking bagels and began to call on the poor to revolt; the fool tried to convince everyone that it was time to follow the example of the Russians and replace the bourgeois rulers in Kaunas with the kind of rule they have in Russia. The only reward for that kind of nonsense from a trouble-maker like you is a bullet," his father grumbled, foreseeing a sorry future for his son. The old man could simply not grasp how a bald Russian, now deceased, could be the leader of all the workers of the world.

The industrious Shleimke didn't need a warrior against the bourgeoisie, or an ardent follower of the dead Lenin, about whom he had not even heard, but a diligent workman. Shleimke was not interested in discussions about liberty, equality and fraternity; he knew that you only found equality in the grave in the activity of the worms. Inequality had existed from time immemorial, in any kind of regime in the world. The rich and the poor would always exist. There would never be a lack of jailers and as for fraternity, sometimes even blood brothers don't get along all the time, fighting over a couple of hundred dried-up acres of land they inherited.

However, a refusal on Shleimke's part would have meant a fight with Hennie, so he gave in.

At first Shmulik refrained from criticizing the local authorities and praising the new Soviet regime in Russia. He worked in concentrated silence, not drawing Shleimke into discussion. He soon became an excellent tailor of trousers, beginning by ironing cuffs, mending holes and occasionally sitting down at the sewing machine and, under Shleimke's supervision, learning to sew a straight seam.

Shleimke was surprised not only at the sewing skills of his brother-in-law, but also by how well read he was and how much he knew. In Kaunas Shmulik had obtained an old tinny Philips radio, which he had repaired. In the evening he would listen to the news in Lithuanian, Russian and German, even though he really didn't have a mastery of any of those languages.

"It's not enough to only know about what takes place right under your nose, or under your window," he said once to his master.

"Why?" Shleimke replied.

"We're not living on the moon or like cattle in a pen only needing to know that there is a fence and a bale of hay."

"Shmulik, first of all one needs to know not what is going on outside our windows or beyond the fence, but what is going on in our own souls and heads. That is where one has to create order rather than carrying out revolts," the ever-cautious Shleimke said.

"That's true, but what happens to us and our homes depends on all the things that happen in the world. But what do you and I, tell me please, get to see and hear about in this run-down 'hen-house' where we live? What if tomorrow, for example, war breaks out or pogroms begin? Have you even heard about the evil plans of that nutcase Adolph Hitler and his accomplices? Evidently, you haven't!"

"So who is he that I should have heard about him and his plans?"

"He's a downright scoundrel and hates the Jews! That is for one thing. Secondly, Hitler's accomplices threaten to eliminate 'bloodsuckers' from the world, to destroy every single one of us. How does that perspective suit you?"

"There are some madmen in the world . . ."

"At the moment, thank God, they are only a few, but there are more and more of them every day."

"If you start calculating the number of madmen and scoundrels, Shmulik, you and I won't get any useful sewing done. You need to listen less to your lousy Philips radio and let the doctors take care of the madmen," Shleimke said calmly. And then he repeated, "You have to sew. Only an idle person wags his tongue without a break. Chatter never brings any benefit, but it might land a person in jail. Do you want to be eating prisoner's gruel?"

The attitude of his brother-in-law to the revolutionaries like the poor baker, who had been executed to dissuade any similarly inclined Jews and their benighted followers, did not prevent Shleimke and Shmulik from working together and even from becoming friends.

Shmulik grasped things quickly and, though he was often ironic, he was neither nasty nor hurtful. For his part, Shleimke got along with Shmulik easily; he found it interesting to talk to the inveterate disputer and enemy of the bourgeois oppressors like his landlord Kapler.

Furthermore, the overworked young couple were pleased to enjoy the talented Shmulik's culinary skills. Hennie was busy in the shop until noon. After lunch, she helped Ethel around the house since her mistress spent a lot of time reading novels, tormented by the absence of her husband. She was always trying to predict the future by means of cards. Hennie also managed to sit by Reb Yeshua's bedside, giving him his daily medicines and passing on to him the regards and good wishes of his customers.

"We're thinking of you, Reb Yeshua," they said, "and awaiting your recovery."

Often Shmulik had to cook, roast, or bake something for

Shleimke and himself. They ate together and, after eating, washed the dishes, halting temporarily their disputes about the ills of the world and putting off the end of the world for another day.

When Shmulik learned about the intention of the eccentric ailing philanthropist Kremnitser to leave his shop to Hennie as an inheritance, he began to interrogate her as soon as she returned home that evening.

"So?"

"What?"

"I hope you're not about to imagine you're some kind of noblewoman of the house of Count Potocki or a niece of President Smetona and reject the old man's inheritance."

"I did reject it. Would you have wanted me to accept him and rush to kiss his hands?"

"Just look at this proud one!" Shmulik raised his eyes to the ceiling. "Anybody might think that you owned a shop of imported goods on Svoboda Street in Kaunas and a second shop selling expensive perfumes and cosmetics for women in the very heart of Paris!"

"Don't be a fool, Shmulik," Hennie said apologetically and sadly. "Whoever covets someone else's property will never have any of his own."

"Do the Kremnitsers not have property of their own? No, they don't! The forests beyond Rietavas are not theirs, nor are the shops theirs either, they were bought with money paid to them for the trees cut down and shipped abroad to the Germans! All that property belongs to the people!"

"So, Shmulik, what do you think?" Shleimke interjected, rising to Hennie's defence against her brother, the advocate of equality and fraternity. "Does the Singer sewing machine that was given me as a present at our wedding not belong to me either, but to this 'people' of yours?"

His wife's brother didn't have an answer.

"It is not the people, Shmulik, who are sitting at that Singer. If you want to know, the people are a bad master; they don't know how to take care of property. Property is only increased by individuals, the so-called owners of private property," Shleimke said, condescending to the logic of his assistant. "Just think, no one creates a baby collectively, thank God. Everyone, according to his strength and abilities, does his best to bring a human being into the world without outside help. I believe that you get better results doing things individually rather than 'with the full support of the people.'" Shleimke smiled, satisfied with his speech.

Hennie gave him a grateful glance, all the more so since she was concealing her big secret – for two months she had been carrying her first child, certain that it would be a boy.

Hennie had firmly resolved not to reveal her secret to anyone, even her husband, until it became obvious. She understood, of course, that pregnancy was the kind of secret that became increasingly hard to keep with each passing moment, and that no amount of tricks would allow her to conceal it forever, but still she kept silent to avoid the reproaches and grumbling of her mother-in-law.

The first to suspect that Hennie was pregnant was Ethel Kremnitser.

They were alone in the living room. Raphael was sleeping and Reb Yeshua was deep in his thoughts, in his room.

"Recently, my dear, you appear to have become a bit broader," her mistress commented with friendly irony. "It seems that you're also walking more carefully, as if you're afraid to slip on our parquet floor. Is it possible that you have caught a little fish? Tell me the truth. You can trust me, I won't blab."

She might have been able to lie to someone else, but not to Ethel. After all, on more than one occasion Ethel had shared her own secrets, things she did not confide to anyone else.

"Yes," Hennie admitted.

"Good luck! You won't believe it, but I, spoiled young lady that I am, always dreamed of having lots of children, but Aaron was always opposed; he said that families with lots of children were outmoded. They're no longer the style in Europe and America apparently. Of course, you can find families in the underdeveloped wilds of Africa and deep in the sticks, where the provincial locals have no other form of entertainment than that tiresome, if pleasant, way of spending time. But I believe children have never gone out of style and never will."

Ethel sighed. She was silent for a while, and then said quietly, as if to herself, "Whatever you say, you're quite some person. It's much easier to give birth when you're young. God willing, our Raphael will have a little boy or girl friend. Or even, perhaps both a boyfriend and a girlfriend!"

"Oy!" exclaimed Hennie. "So you're predicting twins for me! It'll be hard enough to feed and provide for one. Whatever God sends, we will receive with gratitude."

"The main thing is that it all goes well. I gave birth to just one, unfortunately. My mother, though, had twins. Our family was living in Germany then, in Berlin, on Friedrich Schiller Street. My sister Esther, who arrived in this world a quarter of an hour before me, didn't live to reach the age of three."

"What was wrong with her?"

"She had an inherited heart defect. Sometimes I think it would have been much better if I had died instead of her."

"It's a sin to talk like that; God hears our every word! The Master of Life could become angry at us and even punish us for saying such things."

"He punished me long ago. Just tell me what kind of life I have?" Ethel exclaimed and, unable to stop herself, added, "I live like a nun, along with a father-in-law with a host of illnesses and wise sayings, while my husband is always off somewhere on business. My only joy and consolation is Raphael."

Hennie didn't dare interrupt her. It often happened with Ethel that something suddenly overcame her and she just opened up.

But then, her mistress turned things unexpectedly in quite a different direction.

"I'm very happy for you. Aaron was always worried about who would inherit the toys that he brought for his beloved son from all over Europe. If you have a boy, all the toys can be his. And I hope you will not refuse the wardrobe of clothes that Raphael has outgrown. I didn't throw anything out, but not from greed. I carefully put everything aside for a future brother: summer and winter trousers, little embroidered shirts, kid gloves, hats with pompoms, little leather boots. But in vain; it's clear now that it was not my fate to become a mother a second time. Why should all these good things go to waste?"

"Let's just wait till the happy day comes," Hennie replied evasively. "Maybe I will have a girl not a boy. But I wanted to talk to you about something else entirely, not about toys."

"You can talk to me about whatever you like."

"When I grow as round as a barrel, I don't think it will be appropriate for me to stand at the store counter. It will be necessary to find a replacement for me. To my great sorrow, Reb Yeshua is hardly going to return there."

"That's most likely. His condition doesn't induce optimism. I have become his permanent nurse. I jump up in the middle of the night and run to his room to find out whether he is still breathing." After a short silence, Ethel continued sadly, "Aaron has made up his mind to sell all his property in Lithuania and, despite all of his father's objections, he wants to move to Paris. In his last letter Aaron wrote that shtetls are an absurdity and that, even though they don't have barred windows and wardens, they are self-imposed jails where Jews languish by their thousands. 'Within half a century,' he says, 'all such places of poverty, limitation and naive faith in the might of the Lord God will disappear from the face of the earth, together with all their inhabitants. The Jews, after all, need room where they can develop, not a cage.'"

"Oh! Then just where, in his opinion, will we all go? Are we going to fly off to some warmer country like the storks do? Or will we all perish from the plague? I'm not sure that I agree with Mr. Aaron," Hennie said thoughtfully.

"He's so impetuous. He's always shooting his mouth off.

If you keep on shooting off like that, you might end up shooting something down unintentionally."

"It will be a pity to part with you," lamented Hennie. "There's no one in Jonava who could replace you."

"It won't be any time soon. Aaron is like the wind, he's full of air and changeable. You will have time to give birth before anything is finally settled about our move," Ethel encouraged her. "Meanwhile you can continue to work without worrying."

Hennie returned home with a heavy heart. Aaron would take his father away from the shtetl and she, being in 'an interesting situation', would be deprived not only of an excellent salary, but also of a true friend. In her mind Hennie put off the time of the inevitable parting, but she had no doubt that it would soon come, even though, despite all his travails, her benefactor Reb Yeshua was still alive.

At home Hennie discovered, not for the first time, that bad news doesn't travel alone; en route some awful companion always joins the first.

Shleimke's father had taken to his bed. Dovid had untreated consumption. From time to time, this was indicated by a thunderous cough that brought up blood.

"From the day we got married he has just coughed and coughed," Rokha said. "When we got married I had the impression he had a fish bone stuck in his throat. I will never forget how my poor chosen one coughed so loudly under the *chuppah* that no one could hear a single word of the rabbi." Rokha always repeated the same story to Dr. Blumenfeld, whom Hennie had managed to bring from the other end of the shtetl.

The doctor bent over the drowsy Dovid and, without asking his family any extraneous questions, said somberly, "As my teacher in Zurich, Professor Ludwig Sezeman, used to say, 'Even without an autopsy the picture is absolutely clear.' I've brought some pills from Switzerland. One should be taken every four hours after eating, for five days. And you must stay in bed – lie in a warm bed, just lie there and rest and don't try to talk."

"I have a lot of work to do," groaned Dovid. "How can I rest?"

"I will do the work for you," Rokha said and then added, "It won't be the first time I picked up the hammer and awl."

"Do you know how to do a cobbler's work?"

"I could shoe a horse if I had to," Rokha boasted. Then she turned to the doctor. "My daughter-in-law Hennie and my daughter Hava will cook for all of us for five days while I take to the cobbler's last. While Dovid is sick, I will take his place, with hammer and awl in hand and tacks in my mouth, with God's help!"

"That's the attitude!" Blumenfeld exclaimed.

"You have to learn everything," Rokha said. Then, in a rare burst of emotion, she added, "What good fortune it is that we have you, Doctor! What would we have done if you had remained with that Ludwig of yours in Rurich?"

"Not Rurich, Mrs Kanovich, but Zurich," Blumenfeld corrected her. "I didn't stay there because, in my opinion, here we are a bit closer to God and, also, He seems to be closer to us," the Doctor joked. "As people say, water is purer at the source of a river, at its mouth. And our source is here."

"For some reason, Doctor," Rokha cut in, "I have never

encountered the Lord God even once here in the shtetl, perhaps because of my inborn near-sightedness or, perhaps because He and I simply travel along different paths. While I ride along Rybatskaya, he strolls along Kaunas Street. And the other way around!"

Rokha burst out laughing and, then catching her breath, she said, "Hennie, please pull up a chair for the doctor."

"You had better give the patient his first pill while I stay with you for a couple more minutes."

"Right away!" said Hennie. Relieved that at least for the moment she could hide her still unnoticed stomach, she ran to take the medicine to her now quiet father-in-law.

"If, as you say, the One on High is a bit closer to us sinners here in Jonava than to those who live in big cities abroad, why are things so hard for us here?"

"Why? Because here we still believe that He follows our every step and that He cares less about our wallets than about our souls."

"Well," grumbled Rokha with unconcealed anger, "Our Heavenly Father could also care about the wallets of the poor."

"You can't prescribe anything – real faith is not rewarded with banknotes. You yourself know what the problem is."

"No, I don't know."

"The problem is that the golden calf has butted its horns into our faith almost everywhere we go. But no matter how a person bows down before money, no one ever has enough to last for eternity."

"We don't have enough for tomorrow, never mind eternity!" Rokha said.

Dr. Blumenfeld didn't respond, but glanced sympathetically at the walls, long unpainted and peeling. On one of
them, in a glass frame, the distant ancestors of either Rokha
or of the industrious Dovid were squeezed together in an old
daguerreotype.

"As for myself, I stayed in Jonava because of my late
father," sighed the doctor, "the intercessor Genekh
Blumenfeld. People here must remember him."

"Of course, of course. Your father wrote all kinds of requests
and appeals for his fellow Jews to the highest authorities. He
wrote to our mayor and even to the customs authorities in
Kaunas," Rokha said, rushing to confirm the doctor's remarks.

"My father wrote to me in Zurich demanding that I come
home at least for vacation. 'I'm old,' he wrote once. 'Who
knows, it might be that your vacation will coincide with my
funeral.' He complained about his illnesses and loneliness. It
might be hard to believe, but my last student vacation did
indeed coincide with his passing. Since then I haven't left
Zlata my mother and Genekh my father, may their memories be blessed, and I'll never part from them."

Dr. Blumenfeld buttoned his jacket, closed his medical
bag. "If Reb Dovid gets worse and, God forbid, spits up
blood again, let me know immediately," he said from the
threshold.

"We will." Rokha nodded. "Everyone knows that when
you need help your house is much nearer, Doctor, than
God's," the cobbler's wife remarked, unable to refrain from
criticizing the One on High.

For a whole week, Rokha sat at the cobbler's last and
pounded it in a frenzy, as if she were hammering away her

accumulated anger at her unenviable fate. From his sick bed, Dovid informed her hoarsely which shoes to repair first, and which could await his recovery.

"Start by heeling the shoes of the priest," he said. "I promised his housekeeper, *Ponia* Magdalena, that they would be ready on Monday. On the shoe tree are the canvas boots of the wagon-driver Shvartsman, who swears his foot size was a thirty-six when he was still in the cradle and that it's a forty-seven now. He's lying, of course. Though to tell you the truth, I've never seen such huge paws as he has on anyone else in our shtetl. But not a forty-seven! To hear him talk, everything of his is the biggest – from top to bottom," Dovid remarked, chuckling.

"You dirty old man, you miserable and obscene creature! I can manage quite well without your advice. I'm not blind. And don't babble away so much; just lie still and get better. You're crowing too much!"

Whilst not ceasing to be amazed at her mother-in-law's ability to cobble, Hennie still tried to avoid being seen by her and kept her distance from the shoe tree. Sometimes she whirled around in the tiny kitchen and sometimes she went down to the cellar for potatoes. Then she went out into the yard, where she fed the few animals: the handsome rooster with his hussar-like bearing and the three seductive hens who, on both weekdays and holidays, delivered large, yellow eggs as if on schedule.

After she had prepared the food and cleaned up the home of her sick father-in-law, Hennie set out to see the distraught Ethel, who lived in constant expectation of an order from Paris to pack her suitcases and get ready, along with Raphael and the infirm Reb Yeshua, for the long trip. Hennie returned home to Shleimke late in the evening so as not to have to rush across the sleepy shtetl to Rybatskaya Street when it was quite dark.

Caught up in the first days of work, Rokha paid no attention to her daughter-in-law. Putting on a man's leather apron, she laboured away with hammer and awl.

On Monday, as Dovid had said, the priest's housekeeper Magdalena came for his shoes. She was a thin, round-faced woman with thoughtful eyes, looking as if she had just stepped out of some old painting. She paid Rokha, turning down the change. Carefully putting the pastor's shoes in her bag she chirped, "The holy father asked me to tell you he will pray for the health of your husband. He says one should pray for all good craftsmen, both Jewish and Christian." Magdalena crossed herself and added unintelligibly, "*Laudator Jezus Kristus*!" Praise be to Jesus Christ.

After Magdalena had left, Rokha took up the wagonner's canvas boots, muttering the whole time under her breath, wondering how Peisakh Shvartsman had worn out the soles of his shoes so quickly, since he didn't have to walk day after day along the gap-toothed sidewalks of the shtetl, but sat rather on the back of his cart, or in the driver's seat cracking his whip, enjoying his view of the fields and the forests.

Hennie rushed from one house to the other, playing a futile game of hide-and-seek with Rokha until, one fine morning, she grew tired of it. In any case, with each passing day her secret stuck out more visibly from under her chintzy dress. What did she have to be ashamed of? She wasn't carrying the child of a wandering gypsy, or of the womanizer Berdichevsky, who owned the roadside pub, but the child of her husband, the child of Rokha's own son!

"I have something very important to tell you," she began. But then suddenly she fell silent, not knowing how to address her mother-in-law; it would be hard to utter the unaccustomed 'Mama', but nor could she address her disrespectfully as 'Rokha'.

"Why are you speaking in such a funeral tone? If you want to tell me something important, then speak directly, don't beat around the bush! No one will bite your head off!" Rokha snapped, raising her finger in a didactic manner. "What kind of foolishness-shmoolishness can there be between us?"

"I am expecting, I am waiting for . . ."

Agitated, that was all that Hennie could manage. She was hoping her mother-in-law would guess what she was trying to say.

"The Jews have been waiting for something for all ages. Some await the Messiah, some a fortune from the lottery, some an inheritance from America. What are you waiting for, Hennie?"

"I'm expecting a baby," her daughter-in-law said, finally giving up her secret, as she patted her stomach.

"That is some news!" exclaimed Rokha. Jumping up from the shoe tree, which was covered with bits of leather and unused tacks, she approached Hennie and stared at her as if seeing her for the first time in her life. "That means you weren't careful!" her mother-in-law said, but with an air of joy rather than of criticism.

"No, I wasn't careful. Can one be careful when one is dealing with your son? Will you forgive me for being such a bungler?" Hennie sighed.

"For what?" Rokha asked, surprised, forgetting, in her joy, about her admonition to not rush into getting pregnant. "Does one need to ask forgiveness for bringing another Jewish boy into the world?"

"It might be a Jewish girl."

"So, then let it be a girl! Come let's give Dovid a reason to rejoice. Joy is the best medicine in the world. It's a shame that God gives it to us, unfortunates, in such small doses. And so rarely." Rokha's eyes suddenly filled with tears. "*Mazal tov*! Now, Hennie, we will wait with you."

Hennie was amazed; up until that moment only her mother had called her by such a loving name.

Rokha took off the apron she was wearing and both of them entered the next room where, under a quilted cotton cover, Dovid lay staring at the ceiling.

"Enough of being sick, you lazy bones!" Rokha shouted. "It's time to get to work to earn some money for a present for a grandson!"

"A grandson? What grandson? What present? What are you talking about? As far as I'm aware no one has produced a grandson for the two of us yet."

"You used to brag to everyone in the shtetl about how you produced little boys. It turns out that your son Shleimke is also a cracker-jack when it comes to that. Well, aren't you happy?"

"Happy? Of course, I am. Grandchildren are the riches of our old age, so to speak. You don't invest anything, yet still your account grows! Ha ha ha!" Dovid laughed uproariously before his wife and daughter-in-law.

"Just look at him! What ideas enter the head of an old fool!" Rokha quipped.

"As you see, ideas come. I don't lock my head up at night like a door. I lie and look at the ceiling and think about all kinds of things; life and death, for example."

"Really?"

"About why we are living on this earth. About what will remain of us after we part forever from our hammer and awl, from the broom and the brush. What if the answer is absolutely nothing? What if all that remains is dust? Then would it be worth being born into this world at all? For what? For only a stone on your grave with the rubbed-out name 'Dovid' and the last name 'Kanovich'? That is what I am thinking about when I am not coughing."

"Think as much as you want, just don't cough," Rokha said, not wanting to disagree with her husband in the presence of their daughter-in-law, or make fun of his intellectual abilities. "Winter is coming soon," she added. "Then there will be hell to pay with your cough!"

12

The winter of 1928 was one of the most ferocious ever in Lithuania. The mischievous Vilija, whose waves sparkled in the sun, encircled Jonava with its tributaries like a precious necklace. But in the winter the necklace turned into icy convict-chains. Bitter, impenetrable storms blew in without pause and each day the snowdrifts snuck closer and closer to the windows of the sunken huts, peering in and embracing the residents in their deadly grasp. Fortunately, not a single person in the shtetl died the whole winter. The burial society was idle and both the Jewish and the Catholic cemeteries were covered for a long period by the same thick shroud.

As it grew colder, Shleimke tried to convince Hennie, who was already in her sixth month, not to leave the house for any reason, but rather to sit in the warmth and temporarily give up her work at the Kremnitsers.

"You'll get a cold and it won't be *litas* you'll be getting paid in, but pneumonia."

"Ethel gave me four days off because of the cold and also she lent me her squirrel-fur coat. She wore it in this kind of cold when she was carrying Raphael and didn't get sick once. And she also gave me a wool scarf. Don't worry. Nothing will happen to me."

"In your condition why should you take a chance with your health? We can get along without their salary."

"I'm not doing it for the money."

"Then for what?" Shleimke demanded to know.

"If I tell you, you'll call me a half-wit," Hennie said.

Could he really understand that during the time she had worked at the Kremnitsers' she had been transformed from being a nanny and a servant to being almost a full member of the family? Before their marriage, Ethel had even said that if Aaron insisted on carrying out his decision and they moved to France, she would gladly take Hennie with her.

Despite all Shleimke's efforts and even with Shmulik's support, he rarely succeeded in convincing her to do anything. This time too, the men had to admit defeat. Covered with snow and scrunched over against the cold, Hennie set off once more to see those she took care of.

She felt the inescapable gloom in every corner of the Kremnitser house. Ethel was almost unrecognizable. She had suddenly aged, appearing shrunken, sometimes hastily wrapped up in a fluffy jacket, as if trying to ward off the cold, despite the fact that it was warm in the living room. Reb Yeshua had grown so thin he too was unrecognizable and moved from room to room with difficulty. He leaned upon his beloved cane with its knob in the shape of either a miniature crocodile with wide open jaws, or some antediluvian lizard. Old Kremnitser sat in a plush armchair and gazed without blinking at the luxurious chandelier as if it were a distant planet on which he would soon settle. Sometimes, his words slurring, he would call out to Ethel or Hennie like his little grandson Raphael had not long before, "Pee-pee, pee-pee!"

One of them, usually Hennie rather than Ethel, would take Reb Yeshua to the toilet. But sometimes, it's no sin to say, they would not be in time.

When Reb Yeshua was still making sense he often said that he very much wanted to die at home in Jonava, not somewhere abroad, and to lie in the cemetery there. That was where, he devoutly believed, the dead led an invisible life. That was where, after death, he would be together with those who had been close to him – his mother Golda, his father Dov-Ber, his brother Isaiya and his many friends and grateful customers. "And who," asked Reb Yeshua, "would be my companions in a cemetery in Paris or Berlin? A crafty real estate agent who has long ago forgotten his native Yiddish, or a stuck-up banker who wouldn't even greet anyone in the morning? Don't try to tell me," stated Reb Yeshua, "that we come from dust and will return to dust! A human being, if he is not just a bag of bones with a layer of meat on them, will never completely die. Even after death he needs the company of people close to his heart."

Reb Yeshua's helplessness and the failure of his memory upset Ethel. Fearing that her father-in-law would die and that all the funeral arrangements would fall on her shoulders, she sent alarming telegrams to Aaron in Paris with insistent requests that he return to Jonava immediately. He, for his part, promised to do so, even going so far as to give specific dates, but he always found some important reason to delay his arrival.

"He's obviously delayed by business," Hennie remarked, defending him. "And Reb Yeshua isn't about to leave us just yet."

"Business, business!" Ethel repeated. "What kind of business can there be when your father is in such bad shape?" Then she suddenly blurted out painfully, "He must have another woman there".

"My mother says that being apart is like going to see a gypsy fortune-teller. You never know what the future might hold; don't rush to believe dubious prophesies," Hennie said, embracing Ethel.

Reb Yeshua sat quietly in his armchair, turning his cane with its strange knob. With his half-blind eyes he looked at the extinct planet above the table and smiled foolishly. Seeing his smile, Ethel retreated even further into herself. Only Raphael was content, skipping around the living room with his skipping rope and learning, as he lost count, to deal with the first frustrations of life.

Towards the end of winter, Aaron finally gave in to his wife's pleas and returned to Lithuania. When he arrived home, he kissed everyone noisily and handed out the gifts he had brought back from Paris. To Raphael he triumphantly presented a huge stuffed teddy bear, to Ethel an expensive pearl brooch. For his father he had brought a box of new medication, while he presented Hennie with a silk summer dress with a pattern of dots and waves and a belt. Without wasting any time, Aaron announced that the long exile of the Kremnitser family, who had wandered from their native Dusseldorf in Germany to Lithuania, where they had settled in Jonava two and a half centuries before, would soon be drawing to its natural historical conclusion.

"I will take Papa and get him a place in a prestigious old folks' home with round-the-clock medical services. Until we sell the house and the shop, you Ethel, will have to wait and be patient. I'll take you too." Aaron looked at Hennie and, smiling, added, "I would take Hennie too, but her husband would hardly let her leave with the important new 'burden' she is carrying."

"No, he certainly wouldn't," Hennie said.

With his jokes, his smiles and patter, Aaron attempted to moderate his usual dryness and businesslike manner.

"Dr. Blumenfeld is a good specialist and I'm grateful to him, but in Paris, I'm sure, the doctors have more experience. I don't think we should hope for a miracle in our case, I'm afraid. But, perhaps, under the supervision of more than one renowned French Aesculapius, Papa will hold out for some time."

"Papa wants to remain here at home," Ethel interjected cautiously. "With Mama."

"Home?" Aaron repeated. "Where do you think our home is? Where we were born and where our sole privilege is to be buried by the *hevra kaddisha*, the Jewish burial society chanting ancient prayers? Or where we are not outcasts, pariahs, cannibals or parasites accused of undermining all kinds of social norms and mortal sins? No! Our home is not where we are deprived of the possibility of living without being stigmatized, where we live and flourish only at the short-term mercy of the local nobleman, but somewhere we can live according to our inherent right to be equal to everyone else!"

"There is no such place," said Ethel with equanimity. "Not anywhere. Neither in Lithuania, nor in France."

"I won't argue with you, but as for Father, I don't see any other possibility. I cannot leave him in such a state under the care of our fine Dr. Blumenfeld who, though, I must admit, cured me of measles and scarlet fever when I was small."

"Do what your heart tells you. It's your father, Aaron. Unfortunately, you can no longer ask him whether he wants to go to Paris or not."

"I assure you that you won't have to wait long! I have my eye on a good, amenable buyer. As soon as we finally sign a contract, I will come for you. You probably think that I'm happier in Paris without you than with you. If so, you are greatly mistaken!"

At that moment, the thought of her husband's infidelity flashed into Ethel's mind. Although she did not completely reject the suspicion, she doubted it now for the first time.

While he was in Jonava, Aaron Kremnitser spent the whole week being affectionate and attentive to everyone. He visited the Jewish cemetery with Ethel and bowed down at the snow-covered gravestones of his mother and of his uncle Isaiya. After returning home and warming up from the cold in front of the warm fire, he tried for the umpteenth time to speak with his father. But once again the latter did not recognize him. It was as if it was not his son facing him, but some itinerant beggar. The old man was silent and stared, as before, at the distant, beckoning chandelier-planet.

Before leaving Jonava for Paris with his father, who had regressed into a second childhood, Aaron decided to meet with Dr. Blumenfeld, who was well acquainted with all the illnesses of his longtime patient and Sunday bridge partner, Reb Yeshua.

"Unfortunately," the doctor said, "there are no medicines to heal the loss of memory. None have yet been invented.

Take with you a preparation for improving the action of his heart. An envelope with sleeping pills wouldn't be a bad idea either; it's a long way to France."

The departure was a modest one. Reb Yeshua, wrapped up in seven covers, was carried out of the house and seated in the vehicle that Aaron had ordered from Kaunas. Ethel and her father-in-law were seated in the back seat, while the timber-salesman Aaron sat next to the driver, the same sullen Lithuanian who had brought the latest model Singer sewing machine to Hennie's wedding.

Raphael, who had been smothered with kisses by his parents, stood with Hennie next to the car and watched sadly as Aaron and Ethel settled in. Hennie sniffed, wiped her eyes and then had to hold back the boy, who wanted to rush to the car.

"Your mother will be back soon! She's only accompanying your grandpa to the train and then will come home," Hennie said to calm him, even though she herself was weeping openly.

Raphael squinted at her and began to wave his mittens. The car rumbled, as if involuntarily, covered the passengers with a blue cloud of gas and then suddenly lurched forward.

"Why are you crying, 'Ennie'?" asked Raphael who, from the time she had put him to sleep in the nursery, had still not learned how to pronounce her name correctly.

"I'm not crying. It's the snowflakes that are falling in my eyes and melting."

"And why did Mama and Papa kiss me but Grandpa didn't? He always kisses me."

"The doctor forbade Grandpa to kiss anyone. His throat hurts," Hennie said, lamely.

"But why doesn't he talk to me? He doesn't say anything," the child insisted stubbornly.

"Because your grandpa has already said all that he had to say. Raphael, when we are old and have said everything to each other, you and I also will also be silent like Grandpa. Now, my dear, it's time for you to sleep," Hennie murmured through her tears, not believing the boy understood any of her clever explanations.

After putting Raphael to bed and hearing his loud snores, Hennie lay down on the small sofa nearby and began to pray for her benefactor, Reb Yeshua. It was not a prayer in the usual sense of the word, but a soundless, direct conversation with God.

"God! Reb Yeshua Kremnitser lived with us in our shtetl as Your faithful servant and he deserves Your great mercy," Hennie whispered in the darkness. She was certain that her thoughts were being transmitted through the night air straight to the Almighty in heaven. Listening in silence and waiting for a clear response to her words, Hennie began to enumerate all the fine qualities and good deeds of Reb Yeshua Kremnitser. But her conversation was suddenly interrupted; Raphael turned and sneezed loudly a couple times. Hennie jumped up from her warm place, threw a woolen plaid blanket over the boy's legs and then returned to God, the only one in the whole shtetl who never contradicted the person speaking to Him.

"Why, Almighty One, did You not show Your great mercy to Reb Yeshua?" She rebuked the Ruler of the World the way a woman rebukes a guilty neighbour. "Perhaps you forgot because You're being pestered from all sides with endless requests? But this time, I beg You, remember him and alleviate his suffering. Heavenly Father, don't be angry at me; explain to me, please, why You chastise those who serve You truly, weakening them so they are unable to speak, rather than punishing those who deny You with their hypocrisy and lies despite the fact that they swear that they love and respect You?"

The boy was sleeping quietly now and, as if in a delirium, his nanny muttered something, falling asleep herself to the tune of Raphael's quiet snores.

But the Lord, about whom Hennie thought more often now than she ever had before, perhaps because she was expecting a child or perhaps simply due to her pity for the sick Reb Yeshua, appeared to her in a dream. For some reason He was waving to Dr. Blumenfeld. Blumenfeld wasn't carrying his medical bag or wearing his eyeglasses with their horn-rimmed frames, and was dressed completely differently than usual. He wore a velvet jacket well worn at the elbows, which had been sewn for him many years before by Abram Kisin, while God was wearing a snow-white tunic made of beautiful Lithuanian wool. Hennie dreamed that God and Blumenfeld were in the small front garden of the synagogue. The three of them were standing together – she, God and Dr. Blumenfeld, who interceded before their Father in Heaven for Reb Yeshua, praising him for his good deeds and virtues, not forgetting to mention the imported Singer sewing machine that the family had presented to Shleimke at his wedding.

"So who told you, Hennie, that I have been punishing Reb Yeshua Kremnitser?" God asked, looking down at her graciously. "Nothing of the kind! During his most difficult moments, I encouraged and supported the most worthy Reb Yeshua. Evidently, you want to ask me to help him. Don't be shy – ask!"

"I beg You, please let Reb Yeshua reach Paris alive," Hennie pleaded.

"He will reach Paris," God replied. "He will certainly reach there."

Shleimke and Shmulik were always dubious about the bizarre dreams that Hennie relayed to them, believing she must have made them up like the stories she told when she was putting Raphael to bed, inventing fairy tales that would liven up their grey days. However, this time her dream proved prophetic and everything turned out happily – with God's help Reb Yeshua was still alive when they reached Paris.

A week after Reb Yeshua's departure, encouraged by the promises of her husband, Ethel hastened to share with Hennie good news from Aaron in Paris.

"Immediately after their arrival Reb Yeshua was placed in one of the best care homes there," she said. "His situation is still very serious, but not hopeless."

"May the evil eye not be aroused by our hope!"

"And the negotiations about the sale of our property, except for the forests, seem to be proceeding quite success-fully. The deal should be completed by the spring. Soon, Aaron assures me, we will all be together and Raphael will start school, not with that fervent Yiddish teacher Balser in Jonava, but at a French school in Paris."

"I will be sad to part with you," said Hennie.

"I am already sad," admitted Ethel. "If Aaron has advised me to start getting rid of things we won't need, that means our parting will be quite soon. He used to ask to whom we should give all our little rascal's toys when he grew up . . . Well, as far as the toys are concerned, I believe it is quite clear. Of course, you will take them."

"First I have to give birth. My mother-in-law says that it's a sin to count your chickens before they are hatched. She is superstitious. When a black cat crosses her path, Rokha freezes like a snowman and then, quaking with fear, turns down a side street."

"How much longer do you have to wait?" Ethel asked, not interested in Rokha.

"By my calculation it should be in the spring – in mid-March or April. That's what our famous midwife, Mina the redhead, says. Half of the Jewish women in the shtetl have gone through her hands. We have no one else to turn to. Dr. Blumenfeld treats women only down to the waist," Hennie added with a burst of laughter.

It was still two or three weeks until spring, but winter had already weakened. At night there was still a bit of snow, but during the day people began to feel the effect of the happy, carefree sun.

For the old-timers of Jonava the beggar Avigdor Perelman was the only real herald of the approaching spring.

"For the poor, winter is a disaster," Avigdor once said on a freezing January day to that 'good fellow' Shleimke, whom he refused to let go of for some time. The young master craftsman had always given him some money. He never passed Perelman without giving him a coin and, for that reason, had gained considerable respect from the old man. "Frosts, blizzards, snowdrifts up to your knees – all that, excuse me, is not for my brothers in poverty. For us they always lead to great losses," Avigdor continued. "You have to sit, damn it, for whole days at home. Instead of chewing on French rolls, you chew your nails and wait for the birds to begin to chirp and the rivers to start to flow and the trees to turn green. But in spring, anyway, our people are generous. In spring, Jews open their purses much more willingly. In spring, Shleimke, even the dogs bark more quietly at us poor people. When you go out on the street you feel thankful, you breathe with a full chest, and you extend your hand at every step. Even if your fellow Jews don't give you a damn thing, your fingers don't freeze the way they do in winter."

However, the waning winter did not surrender without a fight, striking at Jonava with freezing northern winds and beating down on it with hail. With their whistles and calls, flocks of birds began to fly over the shtetl, which was beginning to awaken from the slumber of winter.

And soon, from everywhere, not only birds, but also good tidings of spring flew to Jonava. The mailman Kazimiras, a dedicated collector of foreign stamps, brought two letters at the same time to Rokha's house: one from France, the other, with a strange piece of paper inside, from America.

"Kazis, what kind of paper is this?" asked Rokha, opening the letter in the postman's presence and looking at the incomprehensible words. "What language do you think this is written in?"

"In the language of money. They sent you a cheque from America for fifty dollars," Kazimiras explained and, glancing at the return address on the envelope, continued, "It was sent by some man named Leah Fisher."

"Leah Fisher! That's not a man, that's our dear daughter! If she has a new last name, that means she has married!"

"Whatever you say, Jewish children are good. They write to their parents from wherever they are and, sometimes, even send money. They're not like our blockheads."

"Yes, but you can't expect help from all of ours."

"My God, how many of yours have already galloped off to America, to Uruguay, Argentina, or Brazil?" Kazimiras sighed. "But still they don't forget their own home. Maybe I'm wrong, but if there hadn't been so many who emigrated, our post office would probably have closed down long ago. I would have nothing to deliver and wouldn't have a crust of bread to eat. Your sons and daughters will do well there and then will take you to join them. Jonava, perhaps even all of Lithuania, will be left without any Jews."

"Jonava will never be left without any Jews. Whatever happens in the world, one Jew will always remain," Rokha said. "That is, God himself! So, don't worry your head in vain, Kazis. Take it easy. They won't lock up your post office. Furthermore, come for the stamps after *Shabbos*. I'll save them for you, but you'll have to steam them off yourself."

13

Every time the fleet-footed Kazimiras brought a letter from America or France to Rybatskaya Street, Rokha baked her famous raisin pies and had a meal in her house to celebrate with those relatives who were still left in the shtetl. Shleimke was the most literate of her children; he knew how to read and write passably well in Yiddish. When he was in *cheder*, the Jewish elementary school, he scooped up knowledge 'with a ladle, if not with a bucket' from the stern teacher, the *melamed*, Reb Zusman. Reb Zusman often rewarded his students with a blow on the hand for gazing not at the *Tanakh*, open on the Ten Commandments, which the teacher demanded the pupils learned by heart, but through the window at the hungry sparrows fighting frantically for crumbs. In the army, Shleimke learned some Lithuanian from his fellow soldiers and could make himself understood, even though he spoke with a strong accent and made grammatical mistakes. For this reason he usually had the honour of being the first in the family to look over any official papers and to read any letters that came from abroad.

Shleimke left out any details he considered insignificant in the letters, not dragging the reading out, trying to hasten the moment when they could all sit back and enjoy his mother's pie. Usually he limited himself to a short paraphrase of what his brother or sister had written in their letters.

"So, listen," he announced, glancing at the tempting pie that had not yet been served. "Our dear, irreproachable Leah has not only made a successful marriage, but, together with her husband Philip, has opened a store in the Bronx. They decided to sell things like almonds, figs, raisins, Greek nuts, plums, dates, candied orange peel and spices, which are all in demand. And, thank God, they've done the right thing. The demand for dried fruit and spices exceeded their expectations. There has been no end of customers – Poles, Romanians and Russian Jews. The Fisher couple have also bought a two-room apartment with a lovely little kitchen. Unfortunately it is in a rough neighbourhood."

At the end of the letter, Leah asked everyone's forgiveness for sending only fifty American dollars for the Passover holiday. Next year, she solemnly promised, if their hoodlum neighbours, who were consumed with jealousy, hadn't rioted and burned down the store, and if their income, to their shared joy, grew, she would increase her Passover gift twofold. Shleimke ended his recitation and paused.

"What else is there?" asked Rokha.

"What else? Our generous Leah sends each of us, in age order, starting with her beloved father and ending with her little sister Hava, not just dollars but warm greetings from the Bronx, her best wishes and she tenderly embraces and kisses us all."

The embraces and kisses, however, did not evoke the same delight and gratitude as the cheque for fifty dollars. After that, in high spirits, everyone then travelled vicariously to France, to hear the good news Isaac had sent them.

After consuming a piece of pie, Shleimke took up his brother's letter. To the everyone's great sorrow he did not find a cheque, but instead, drew from the envelope a postcard with a photograph of a tall arch, decorated with sculptures and bas reliefs. Shleimke immediately passed it around.

"Those Frenchmen don't know what to do with their wealth. They build God knows what in their cities. Is such a structure really useful to those living there? Perhaps it's to protect people from a downpour when it's raining," Rokha said, looking at the postcard and then handing it to her husband. "Tell me, who needs such ridiculously ornamented gates?"

"Just hold on a minute and you'll find out everything," said Shleimke. After a short reconnaissance, he announced amiably, "On the other side of the postcard Isaac has written a note in Yiddish. 'This marvellous arch was erected in honour of the famous French emperor Napoleon.'"

None of those sitting around the table knew anything about Napoleon. What interested them was not arches, or '*shmarches*', as the sharp-tongued Rokha called them, nor emperors, but how Isaac and Sarah were living and what they were doing in Paris.

"And, Shleimke, is that all that your older brother could write to us after such a long time?" retorted Rokha.

"He also wrote that his work, may it not suffer from the evil eye, isn't going badly. His boss in the leather workshop, the stingy Monsieur Kushner, didn't turn out to be so greedy after all. He's raised Isaac's salary by a third. Our brother writes that he and Sarah plan to put together some francs and come on holiday for a week to their native Jonava or spend their summer vacation at a lake somewhere near our shtetl." Shmulik concluded. "Until then, may God preserve the health of all our relatives and allow that they enjoy the marvellous beauties of the inimitable Paris."

"They will come to visit only when we are no longer in this world. They will place stones on our graves and then just go back to Paris with all its marvellous beauty," said Rokha with unconcealed bitterness.

"At the end of his letter Isaac wrote that he and Sarah are seriously considering bringing an heir into the world," noted Shleimke, trying to console his mother, who was in no mood to be pacified.

"What is there to consider?" the taciturn Dovid asked. "There is nothing to think about, the man should just do what is needed. He should take an example from you two and get on with it!"

The reading of letters in the family home was often accompanied by Rokha's complaints and bitter tears. However strange it might seem, Isaac and Leah's letters induced in her an acute sense of irretrievable loss rather than the joy one might have expected. She was suddenly overcome by an overwhelming grief, mixed with anger and an irrepressible desire to pour out this anger on those who had abandoned her.

"What good to me are their tenderness and embraces via ink, all those virtual kisses and their postcards?" Rokha burst out. "What good to me are these emperors and those beautiful buildings that I will never see in my life? What good to me are their dollars? What I want more than anything cannot be bought with money anywhere – not in America, not in Paris, not in Jonava!" She took a deep breath, gasping for air, and then said hoarsely, "If you are so smart, tell me what kind of children every Jewish mama dreams about? About ones on paper? Ones written about in letters with foreign stamps? With two-franc photos? Or does a Jewish mama need children of her own flesh and blood?"

After she had spoken a silence as thick as ice fell upon the table. Then, like warm smoke lifting from a chimney on a cold winter morning, the quiet voice of her daughter-in-law broke the silence. "Excuse me, Mama, but you are not being fair to them."

For the first time Hennie addressed her in a way which, until that very moment, she had used only to her own mother. "Don't insult them for nothing! Now, when I myself am expecting a child, I understand how very hurt you are. There is nothing you can do, that's life! It gives and it takes away what it gives. What is important is that, wherever they live, whether on Rybatskaya Street or a thousand miles from here, your children love you. The main thing, I believe, is that they are happy wherever they are."

"Let's see what tune you sing, Hennie, when they take away what is dearest to you," Rokha said, giving as good as she got.

"I think," Hennie replied, "that for mothers, suffering from being separated from their children, there is no greater reward than their well-being and happiness."

Although the raisin pie had not been finished off, the family members left, without arguing, but without settling their differences either.

"Good for you!" Shleimke praised his wife on the way home. "You said the right thing to her – the main thing is that one's children are happy regardless of whether they are in Jonava or New York." Then, after a short silence, he glanced at Hennie's expanding waist and asked, "How much time is left?"

"Not much. Not much at all."

"Are you going to go to see that redheaded witch Mina again? She knows what she is doing. You know that anything can happen when you give birth. Sometimes women have to go to Kaunas. Just in case, I spoke to Faibush Gorodetsky, who is the same age as me. He has a car and, if necessary, he will drive us to the Jewish hospital in Kaunas. He's a friend of mine. We used to play football in the empty field behind the barracks."

"Yes, I'll visit Mina. At night the baby kicks as if he wants to come out soon," said Hennie.

By profession, the redheaded Mina was a seamstress; she earned her daily bread by sewing lace dresses rather than helping women give birth. She helped women to become mothers simply out of altruism, not for any material benefit. Mina herself had never given birth. She had been widowed at a young age. Her husband, the stove-maker Gershon Teplitsky, had drowned in the Vilija River early in their marriage and, from then on, the unfortunate Mina had grown old by herself.

"I have innumerable children in Jonava," Mina joked sadly, "even though they have other mothers."

Stout, with muscular, manly arms, a shock of reddish hair and insistent on standing rather than sitting when she was called, Mina rushed to help not only the Jewish women, but also the local Lithuanian women and even the wives of Old Believers who lived in nearby villages. There was no other Jewess in Jonava whom the grateful Christian women unfailingly invited to the christening of their little ones.

Mina lived across from the synagogue in a one-storey brick house, inherited from the wealthy parents of her late husband. She and her husband Gershon, Shimon Dudak's second cousin once removed, had known her latest visitor from the day Hennie was born. She had helped Hennie's mother with all of her births.

When she arrived, out of breath, Mina asked, "Have you been waiting here for me long?" Hennie had been circling her house for a long time, looking in through the curtained windows to see whether someone was moving behind them.

"No, I haven't," replied Hennie.

"Whether it's pouring with rain or there's a snow storm howling, my dear, I have to go to the synagogue for the morning prayer service. In the morning the Lord is still in a good mood and attentive to those who pray to Him. By evening, He gets very tired, like all old people, and I, old woman that I am, want Him to listen to me first, not to the wife of the miller Vasserman. After all, as you know, there is no one to speak to in our shtetl. All anybody talks about is either money or illness. Everyone has many illnesses and little money. But that's enough jabbering, let's go inside! Only hens and roosters talk outside."

Hennie entered a clean, orderly room with little vases of geraniums on the windowsills, a table covered with a colourful tablecloth and a massive wardrobe of solid wood. On the recently whitewashed wall, there hung a single photograph of a young, laughing Gershon in a gold-leaf frame.

"Sit down," Mina suggested and moved a chair up for her visitor. "I see that it's not our Father in heaven you speak to in the mornings, but your husband in bed."

Hennie didn't say anything. She was not happy at the direction the meeting had taken; she had come for a conversation, but Mina had turned the discussion in a spiritual direction.

"I didn't speak with Him either until that terrible day when my Gershon drowned. Don't bother Him with your petty complaints if you haven't lost someone you love. Even so, His hearing hasn't been up to standard for a long time."

Hennie felt uneasy. She wanted Mina to talk to her about how to get through the final weeks of pregnancy, to give her some advice, and she hoped she would agree to help her give birth, but she didn't feel that she could interrupt her.

As if reading Hennie's mind, the stern Mina, who would never ingratiate herself with any of her mothers-to-be, finally relented. "Now, I'll examine you and see if I can tell you, dear, whether the birth will be an easy one or difficult, as fate will soon determine."

The midwife placed her horn-rimmed glasses on her nose and began to meticulously examine the body of the now disconcerted Hennie.

"Please stand by the window; it's lighter and I can see better there. Turn sideways. That's the way, yes," Mina said. "Now I can see you clearly. Your pelvis, to put it bluntly, will not be helpful when you give birth. However, my dear, you can't argue with Mother Nature. The way that your mama and papa made you is the way that you will live out the days allotted to you in this world. Meanwhile, from all that I can see, your little 'prisoner' is getting bored already, all by himself. He's already trying to escape, the little rebel. He's already kicking and raising his fists, as if to say, 'Let me out of here quickly, just get on with it, please!' Isn't that how it is?"

Hennie was taken aback by Mina's tirade.

"Yes, it's true. He is ready to burst out, kicking."

"That's how it is supposed to be. A prisoner's term is ending and, it turns out, he is not ready to be released yet."

"It is almost ending."

"That's right," agreed Mina. "Judging by your belly, your prisoner is already pretty big, while your pelvis, I repeat, excuse my frankness, is disappointing."

"Disappointing? My pelvis?"

"Yes, your pelvis. It could be a little broader, my dear. The wider the opening the easier it is for a full cart to be emptied. I'm afraid I'm not the right one to help you. After all, my dear, I am not an obstetrician; I work according to the old tradition – press here, press there, cut the umbilical cord and tie it off. Sweetie, think about this: if, God forbid, you need real help during your birthing, then what good would I be to you?"

"Real help? What kind of help?"

"The help of a doctor, not of a midwife. Where can you find such a doctor in our town? Why don't you and your active little fellow go to the Jewish Hospital in Kaunas? I'll feel easier about it and it'll allay at least some of your fears, my dear."

"I'll think about it, Mina."

"Do that and I, my golden one, won't load upon my soul responsibility for three lives. It doesn't make sense to take chances when giving birth. You can take risks with a little one, if it's the size of a pimple, but with a good-sized one like your first born, it will be hard to force him out. My heart senses that his arrival will not be easy for you."

"Thank you." The visitor indicated with a gesture of her head that she understood.

Frightened now, Hennie decided not to hide the news from her husband.

"Mina doesn't wag her tongue over nothing," said Shleimke, when Hennie had shared her fears with him. "She really has lots of experience. We should listen to what she says. Of course, it is less expensive to give birth in our shtetl, but it is safer in Kaunas. Don't worry; I've already made arrangements with Faivush Gorodetsky. He won't let us down. You should stay at home for now and not go anywhere. I will inform Ethel."

"No, I'll go to her myself."

"Look at me!" her husband said with a severe expression. "Don't you dare wash her floors!"

Although Ethel and Raphael greeted her with their customary warmth, their behaviour already hinted at the distance that would inevitably grow between them. Both the mother and the son were like weary travellers sitting at a train station waiting for a train that had been delayed.

"I didn't come to say goodbye. I hope we'll see each other again before you leave for Paris. I hope that I'll manage to come again before Mr. Aaron comes for you, even though I know you two are eager for him to arrive."

"He'll come in April," Ethel stated. "Fortunately everything has been sold now – both the shop and the house. We just need to pack our things and send them off, except for the furniture. That's not so simple."

"The main thing is that finally you will no longer be living in two different houses but will be together with Mr. Aaron."

"If not together, at least close – under the same roof." Ethel smiled sadly and added, "That would be more accurate."

Hennie nodded mechanically. She was not paying attention. She was thinking about the Jewish Hospital in Kaunas and the approaching ordeal she would have to face. Then, glancing at the empty plush armchair in which the fading Yeshua Kremnitser used to sit, Hennie returned suddenly to the present.

"How is our Reb Yeshua doing?"

"Not well. He seems neither alive nor dead. Aaron has hired someone to look after him around the clock. She dresses and undresses him, feeds him with a spoon, puts him to bed, and sometimes takes him out in a carriage along a boulevard shaded with chestnut trees." Ethel took a deep breath, as if choking on her words. "Everyone fears death, but for some it is God's last great mercy. But let's not speak of sad things."

"Let's not," Hennie agreed, even though she had no idea what she could continue to talk about with Ethel.

"I am sure we will meet once more. Life is like a circus acrobat, there's no knowing what somersault it will perform tomorrow. By the way, I have decided to pay your salary for two more months," said Ethel. "Please don't object. Money is always useful. I have also put together Raphael's toys and his things. In the event that we don't see each other, I will leave everything with Antanina, who used to help the late Abram Kisin around the house. She also worked in our house once. If only all the members of her tribe were as fine as she is!"

"As far as fellow tribe members are concerned, they vary. Our brother Jews are no exception. Not all of them are worthy of praise," Hennie said. "And also, finally, I hope that you will forgive me if I ever did or said something wrong while I was working for you."

"What do you mean? I have no better friend than you! I will never forget you." Ethel embraced Hennie. "Raphael, come, kiss 'Ennie'!" she said.

Immediately Raphael ran to his nanny and, when she bent down, kissed her awkwardly on the cheek.

The tears in Hennie's eyes betrayed her feelings.

"Don't be afraid!" Ethel said. "The first time it's terrifying to give birth, but don't worry. Everything will be fine," she repeated. "I will pray for you."

Hennie bowed and headed towards the door.

"Wait. What about the money?"

"But I haven't earned it."

"You certainly have." Ethel laughed. "Take it. No one gives birth in the Jewish Hospital without paying." She pushed an envelope into Hennie's coat pocket. "God be with you!"

Near the entrance to the synagogue, Hennie met Avigdor Perelman, who, like God, was omnipresent. Having noticed the young woman from a distance, Avigdor stopped, smoothed down his grey, shaggy hair with a rough palm and, when she came closer, bowed in a picturesque manner.

Hennie responded politely, wanting to avoid a long conversation, and took out a coin and gave it to the beggar.

"Extremely grateful!" Avigdor boomed. "Pregnant women are generous. Furthermore, when you take money from a pregnant woman, it's like you are receiving from two people at the same time!" He grinned a toothless grin. "I won't hold you back, Shleimke must be waiting for you. I have only one small request; give birth, please, to a good, generous person. The world already has plenty of poor people and it's certainly got enough rich, unkind, greedy ones."

"I'll try."

Her brother Shmulik didn't have any requests. Trying not to think about any possible problems, he endeavored to encourage his pregnant sister by reminding her of the example of their self-sacrificing mother.

"Hennie, I want you to remember that our mother gave birth to ten children," he stated in such a triumphant way that you would think she didn't know it.

"So, what conclusion do you draw from that?" asked Hennie.

"It's the only way we can increase the ranks of the workers. If we members of the proletariat bring into the world nine or ten healthy offspring for every lordly son or daughter, the oppressors and capitalist pigs won't be happy."

"You and your future wife, Shmulik, can increase the ranks of the workers with your own strong, healthy offspring."

"I am joking, Sis. I am not asking you to bear ten children."

"I know you aren't serious. I do. But if you had to give birth today or tomorrow, you wouldn't make such jokes."

Her labour pains began that night.

Shleimke rushed to awaken his friend, Faivush Gorodetsky, who was one of the first in Jonava to exchange his cart for a used American Ford. Fortunately, Faivush was still awake and he and Shleimke immediately went to get the car.

On the way to pick up Hennie, they stopped at Rybatskaya Street. Rokha wanted to accompany Hennie to the hospital, but the men convinced her to stay home. "Perhaps, while you're gone, some customer might knock on the door of the empty workshop and ask for the master-craftsman who had told him to come to be measured," they suggested.

While the subdued Hennie sat scrunched over in pain, Shleimke hurriedly collected the documents needed. Faivush turned on the ignition of the asthmatic car, disturbing Ephraim Kapler's sleep. Meanwhile Rokha got together some warm clothes for her daughter-in-law so that she wouldn't catch a cold on the way.

The nights at the end of March were still raw and white flakes of snow glistened in the ravines and ditches.

It was a long way to Kaunas. Faivush drove his battered Ford cautiously along the cobblestone road, afraid of shaking the precious load entrusted to him. Silently he peered into the thick darkness, which was only dimly illuminated by the headlights. Shleimke was also silent.

"Why are you both as silent as the grave?" Hennie suddenly asked from the back seat.

"We thought you were sleeping," replied Shleimke. "We didn't want to bother you."

"As if one could sleep with my impatient little 'prisoner' as a fellow passenger." Hennie sighed. "May God bring us safely to the hospital. Is it still far to Kaunas?"

"We've already covered half the distance," the uncommunicative Faivush said. "In a quarter of an hour we'll be in the city."

"Just be patient a bit longer," Shleimke urged Hennie.

Just then the car drove into the deeply slumbering suburbs of Kaunas, where little old wooden houses were scattered in disorderly fashion. Winding its way through streets and alleys, the Ford slowly approached the hospital that was renowned throughout Europe. From time to time, from around the bend, as if scalded, a homeless dog jumped out and Gorodetsky slammed on the brakes while Hennie screamed in fright.

Finally, as they drove into the old town, the bright shining windows of the Jewish Hospital emerged out of the thick, hostile twilight.

Faivush unloaded his passengers, wished Hennie well, and turned the car around. Then, encouraged by what he took to be the good wishes of the prolonged tooting of other cars, he headed home.

The first thing that struck Hennie and Shleimke was not the hospital building, as impressive as it was, but the reception room, where the nurses, the doctors and the cleaners all spoke Yiddish, just as they did in the shtetl of Jonava.

"Good day," said a thick-set man in a white robe and a round white hat. He took the documents from Shleimke and perused them carefully. "Happy to make your acquaintance," he boomed. "I'm Dr. Ben-Zion Lipsky, head of the maternity ward," he said to the expectant mother. "Please come up with me to the second floor for an initial examination. Unfortunately, I will have to part you and your wife until she is released from the hospital," he said to Shleimke. "It's strictly forbidden for non-patients to be in our hospital. Is there some place where you can spend the night in Kaunas?"

"Yes. I have a brother here."

"Good. Come back in the morning. Ask downstairs for Dr. Lipsky. I will come and tell you everything in detail. Now you can give her a kiss. See you tomorrow."

Dumbfounded, the husband did as he was told. He embraced Hennie awkwardly, kissed her, and wished her a successful birth. The doctor nodded to him and disappeared with Hennie down a long corridor that smelled strongly of medicine.

Shleimke did not go to sleep at his brother Motl's house. He wasn't familiar with the city and was afraid of getting lost before the light of dawn. He decided to await the morning under the shining windows of the hospital. In any case he wouldn't be able to sleep.

Shleimke had never felt so alone and helpless as he did that night. He circled the three-storey building, trying to guess behind which illuminated, yellow window Hennie was writhing in pain. The sky was covered with thick clouds that wandered off like sheep in different directions, while some lingered like shrubbery from behind which the sparkling, dying stars seemed to peek out. Shleimke gazed up at them and, for the first time in his life, engaged the stars in silent conversation. All at once, he recalled his mother saying that stars were the innocent eyes of prematurely dead children. He was overcome by a tremendous confusion. He made an effort to stop looking, but, as if pursuing him, the stars continued to appear before his eyes in all their clear brilliance.

He decided that after the doctor came out to him with the good news in the morning, he would go to his brother's, wash, shave, buy the largest bouquet of roses in the flower shop and rush back to the Jewish Hospital to Hennie and his newborn son. He very much wanted a boy and had decided on the name Borukh, meaning blessed. Thoughts about his son drove out all the fears the midwife Mina had planted in his head.

The light of dawn began to emerge. The sickly yellow light gradually faded in the windows of the hospital. Only from the operating room did the blinding light of the lamps hanging low from the ceiling continue to be visible. The fateful night was drawing to a close and there followed, as it said in the holy Bible, the first day.

The worried Shleimke asked the pretty young woman at the reception desk several times about Dr. Ben-Zion Lipsky, and each time received from her a polite but inconclusive answer. "Dr. Lipsky is either making the rounds or taking part in an operation at the moment. Ask me, please, a bit later."

When he asked when the doctor might be available, the polite young woman merely shrugged her shoulders perplexedly and looked at the visitor coquettishly.

Hungry, tormented by dark premonitions, Shleimke's eyes followed every person wearing a white coat and cap who came into the reception room, but Dr. Lipsky seemed to have disappeared from the face of the earth.

Only two hours later did Shleimke see him slowly descending the stairs. In violation of all hospital rules, Shleimke rushed towards the doctor.

"It looks like you spent the whole night under our windows and didn't go to your brother at all."

"No, I didn't."

"It won't be any better for the patient if you stand under the windows. Have you been waiting for me long?" Lipsky asked in the even, colourless tone that he used to communicate both good and bad news.

"Yes, for quite some time."

"Most likely, you are quite worked up from waiting so long?"

"Yes."

"We have to have a serious conversation."

From the solemn but impenetrable expression on the doctor's face, Shleimke realized something serious had happened.

They walked down the hall and sat opposite each other across a low coffee table. Without waiting for Lipsky to start, Shleimke suddenly blurted out, "Tell me, Doctor, is my wife alive?"

"Your wife is alive," Ben-Zion Lipsky replied in a markedly calm manner.

"That's the main thing," sighed Shleimke.

"The birth was difficult. Also, we had to take an extreme

measure – a caesarean section, that is, to cut open her abdomen."

Even though the ensuing pause did not last long, the hall became intolerably stuffy.

"In all the hospitals in the world such an operation entails great risk," Lipsky continued, "endangering both mother and child. But in certain cases doctors have no other choice and have to resort to the scalpel." The doctor delayed giving the news for a moment. "Thank God, we saved the life of your wife, but, despite all of our efforts, we were not able to save the child."

"Was it a boy?" Shleimke found the courage to ask, his voice stifled with grief.

"Yes. Believe me, we did everything we could, but doctors are not gods."

Shleimke listened gloomily and grew increasingly depressed.

"I sympathize with you with all my heart," Ben-Zion Lipsky said sorrowfully. "No matter how bitter the truth, doctors cannot, despite the desire of the patient or close relatives, either delay or refuse to divulge it."

"When can I see my wife?" whispered Shleimke, his lips frozen.

"I believe tomorrow or the next day."

"When will I be able to take them home . . . to Jonava?"

The ensuing silence was as thick as a swamp. It seemed possible to hear the beating of the heart of the recently demobbed soldier Shleimke under his cloth shirt.

"When?" The simple question caught Ben-Zion Lipsky, who had become somewhat inured to others' misfortunes, by surprise. He didn't know how to respond. "I will ask Professor Rivlin. Your wife, perhaps in a week, perhaps earlier, depending on how the recovery proceeds." The doctor was silent for a moment, avoiding the most painful topic – the child who had died during his mother's labour. "As for you, Mr. Kanovich, you should go home. People who are suffering shouldn't stay on their own for a long period of time."

"No," Shleimke cut him off. "No."

"Here you will only suffer more. You will only end up needing medical help yourself. Well, have it your way. As an exception, I will allow you to see your wife. But on one condition – it can only be for five minutes, not one minute longer! I will be counting the time. Otherwise, they will fire me from the hospital for breaking the rules. Let's go."

Hennie was lying in a large ward propped up on high white pillows. Her thick hair seemed to have been messed up by the wind; it covered her closed eyes like a black veil of mourning, but she did not push it away.

"It's you," Hennie said, recognizing her husband by his bear-like gait and his breathing.

"Yes, it's me." He leaned over the bed and carefully touched Hennie's cheek with his unshaven face. She suddenly burst out sobbing uncontrollably.

"Don't cry. Be clever, don't cry. I love you very, very much. You know that," he repeated deliriously, himself about to wail from grief and anger at their fate. "No one can possibly take that away from us. Do you hear me? No one. Ever. As long as we live we shall . . . each other . . ." He couldn't finish the sentence, gulping from his helpless profession of love.

"Shleimke, how can we go on living? How?" Hennie asked. She could say no more as she was overcome by convulsive sobbing.

"We'll live. It's not a crime to grieve, Hennie. It's not a shame."

He heard the creaking of the door.

"I will return soon . . . very soon," he rushed to add.

The firm Doctor Lipsky took pity on him and allowed another minute for a goodbye kiss. Shleimke leaned toward his wife and two large tears fell on the cover, which was as white as a shroud.

Word of the unsuccessful birth reached everyone in town. As Rokha used to say, for Jews misfortune always outruns the 'tortoise of joy' which, in general, was more of a rarity.

As soon as he got back to Jonava, Shleimke went to see Rabbi Eliezer. Out of respect for his great sadness, the rabbi was silent for a long time. He moaned in a restrained way, as the leader of his flock should, and he sighed and stroked his greyish beard.

"May God give you strength, *mayn kind*," he said then, sadly.

"I have come to you for advice, Rabbi. What should be done when I bring him here?"

"It is a good question, my son." Rabbi Eliezer again stroked his beard. "According to our Torah, male children who are born dead are not circumcised and are not given a name. It is forbidden to sit *shiva* or to erect a gravestone for them. Furthermore, when they are buried the *kaddish* prayer is not recited."

"Do you mean that we just bury him?"

"Yes. But parents and relatives are not forbidden from visiting the stillborn's burial place, or taking care of it as is appropriate. Speak to Hatzkel, the head of the burial society. He will explain everything to you and will see everything is done as it should be."

"That German Rabbi doesn't know anything," Rokha said indignantly. "No one can prevent us from sitting *shiva*. What does it matter if Rabbi Eliezer doesn't write his name in the registry book? We will get along without his recording it. There is no memory without a name."

"Perhaps we should wait for Hennie," suggested Dovid. "Somehow it doesn't seem right without her."

"We shouldn't cause her suffering soul more pain. Just imagine how it would be – first the funeral, then the period of mourning! Hennie might not survive that," said Rokha. "No one can heal such pain."

They listened to Rokha and not to Dovid or Rabbi Eliezer, 'the German' from Tilsit. For the seven days of mourning neither family left their house.

Even the blasphemous Shmulik, despite his firm conviction that God had been invented by the exploiting class in order to deceive the working masses, grieved together with the others.

"In grief we need to demonstrate proletarian solidarity," he said, sitting alongside his brother in-law. "Right now my sister is dearer to me than justice."

The owner of the house, Ephraim Kapler, with his velvet yarmulke and a black ribbon in his buttonhole, also attended the funeral ceremony. So did the drunkard Yevel, with his bucket of paint and his brush, which was his constant companion. The home on Rybatskaya Street was also visited by Dr. Blumenfeld and the midwife Mina.

Nor did Avigdor Perelman fail to show up to express his sincere, unselfish sympathy for the mourners.

"No one can understand how hard it is for you," he said, sitting at the table opposite Shleimke. "I never had it this hard, even though I have been hungry, cold and alone. More than once I have wanted to say adieu to the world and lay hands on myself but, dog that I am, I never had the will-power to do so. Still, I never experienced such a sorrow. Be like a soldier, Shleimke, stand strong and do not despair. You still have everything ahead of you. It's not the same as for me, a nonentity. I have already lived through all possible times – the past, the present and even the future. Thank God, there is no fourth time."

"Thank you, Avigdor, thank you," replied Shleimke, hoping he would stop there. But his suspicion that he wouldn't was confirmed.

"If I may, a few more words," continued Avigdor.

"You may."

Although he too, like everyone else in the shtetl, was irritated by Avigdor's tendency for long-winded philosophising, to which he had become accustomed in the Telshe Yeshiva, Shleimke didn't feel able to deny him his request.

"Of course, it would have been better if your son had been born alive and healthy. But, don't be angry at me, insignificant worm that I am, for my words. I always say what I think, because I no longer fear anyone or anything."

"We know. We know," agreed Shleimke, attempting to stop Avigdor's rambling.

"Perhaps, at the last moment, your son reconsidered and decided not to enter this lousy, thrice-cursed world, but wanted to remain in his mother's womb where it was warm and comfortable. Once again, Shleimke, don't be angry at me. If our pitiless God punishes such good people as you and your Hennie, do we really need such a master? If the One on High could have given all of my seventy-four years to someone else, such a person might well have lived a more worthy life than I did."

Avigdor sat there a while longer, ate a poppy roll, drank some seltzer water and dozed for a while on his chair. Then he stood up, preparing to leave.

"It's time to return to my work place, the pavement," he said and left as if in mourning.

"I thought he was nuts, but his mind is all there and he has quite a developed class consciousness," Shmulik noted, praising Perelman.

"With a mind like his he could have been a rabbi," Shleimke replied. "But Avigdor had no luck. His wife Haya ran off with some salesman and, instead of getting himself another wife, he hooked up with some loose woman and then everything went to hell for him. When that whore also left him, Avigdor's life grew even worse. It began with moonshine and ended in poverty."

Soon after Perelman left, the other visitors gradually departed.

The last to leave the house of Rokha the Samurai, filled now with a sense of sorrow and irreparable loss, was the midwife Mina.

"Take care of Hennie," she said to Shleimke. "She needs to learn how to be born again herself."

The day before the end of the seven-day mourning period, Shleimke set out for Kaunas. Once there, he walked quickly, at a soldier's pace, from the bus stop to the Jewish Hospital.

In the reception room Shleimke turned to the pretty, coquettish young woman he already knew and asked to speak with Dr. Lipsky. Quietly she picked up the phone and called the maternity ward.

"Doctor," she said, "a visitor wants to meet with you right away. He says that you already know him and that he previously visited his wife here."

"Who is he and where is he from?" Lipsky asked on the other end of the line.

"Just a minute!" said the young woman and passed on the doctor's questions to Shleimke.

"Kanovich from Jonava," Shleimke replied.

"Thank you," the young woman said to the visitor, turning her finely sculptured head toward him and reporting over the telephone precisely what she had been told. After getting an answer, she blinked her eyes, as round as cherries, and informed Shleimke that Dr. Lipsky would be available in fifteen minutes.

"The doctor is very sorry that he can't meet with you sooner," she added.

Lipsky kept his word. He arrived exactly a quarter of an hour later, greeted Shleimke and proposed that they go out into the courtyard where they wouldn't be bothered and could talk face to face, in the fresh air. When they were both seated on a wooden bench, Lipsky turned to Shleimke.

"Do you smoke?"

"No," Shleimke replied.

"Just imagine, until this very day I haven't been able to stop. I gave it up several times but, after a day or two, I began to pollute the environment once again. Do you object if I smoke in your presence?"

"No, I don't."

"Now, down to business. There is a cabby stand near the Catholic Church. Choose a cabby and have him drive up to the hospital. Take it easy to begin with; your wife should avoid extra effort so her stitches don't come out." The doctor reached into his pocket, took a cigarette out of a monogrammed cigarette case and lit it. "As you'll understand," he continued, "you can't possibly go travelling around the city with that terrible package from the hospital morgue. In such unfortunate situations, the parents normally give consent to bury the little ones in some nearby Jewish cemetery." Ben-Zion Lipsky inhaled deeply and then blew a ring of blue smoke upwards. "I hope you won't consider me a monster or a butcher. I'm a father too and understand all too well what a price your nerves are paying for what has happened. Believe me, I feel it too. The price is, of course, incomparably less for me than you, but, I assure you, I have to pay too. However, I'm a physician and it's my duty to warn you of the dangers."

"Of course, I will hire a wagon driver. I myself thought of doing that," Shleimke said.

"You appear to be sensible, not a coward or overly sentimental."

"Yes, a man shouldn't take risks, but there is a limit to everything," Shleimke said. "With your permission I'll go now and get a cabby."

"Yes, go now, my dear fellow! It's quite close; you can see

the church from here. However, as a doctor, there is something else I must tell you."

"I'm listening."

"Unfortunately, it is better that your wife does not become pregnant again. Another pregnancy might turn out to be catastrophic for her. That is not only my view, but also the view of the *consilium*."

"What's a *consilium*?"

"A council of doctors. But, for God's sake, please do not speak to her about this for as long as possible. I hope that I don't need to explain to you that among all living creatures there are no more self-sacrificing creatures than loving women. Due to their love, they will not stop at anything. They absolutely refuse to take into consideration any medical advice or prohibitions."

"But until now I have kept no secrets from my wife."

"Nevertheless . . . In a word, be careful. Caution never hurt anyone."

"Thank you for the warning."

Shleimke got up and headed towards the church.

At the church square cab drivers idled away their time waiting for customers. Shleimke chose the first one his eyes alighted upon – a sturdy, large-nosed man who looked morose from idleness or boredom and resembled either a gypsy or a fellow Jew.

"Are you free?"

"*Yo,*" the driver replied in Yiddish. "Hop in!"

"I'm not alone. We have to drive up to the Jewish Hospital. From there I want to take my wife to the bus station with my . . ."

"I'll go anywhere for money, right to the end of the world, even to Palestine. Why not? Ho ho!" he roared. "Hop in, hop in! I give a discount to Jews – 10% off, for long distances even fifteen or twenty."

They drove up to the gate of the Jewish Hospital. Accompanied by Dr Lipsky, Shleimke went up to the second floor and took Hennie, who was more dead than alive, by the arm.

Downstairs, according to the arrangement made by Lipsky, a tall orderly was waiting with my brother who had died at birth. He was wrapped up in a sheet like a baby calf.

Shleimke said goodbye to the doctor and helped Hennie into the cab.

It was March 1928. Lithuania had just triumphantly celebrated the tenth anniversary of its independence. On all the houses, both Jewish and Lithuanian, rumpled tricolour flags fluttered victoriously in the wind.

"Whoa, Pesele!" shouted the cabby. "My horse knows every place in this city. Just say to her 'Pesele, to the Metropol Restaurant, to the officers' club, or to the residence of President Smetona where our rich Jews play cards in the evening,' and, without any prodding, my horse will take you right there. After all it's hardly the first year that she and I have been traversing these streets. She may be a four-legged animal but she has a Jewish head."

"Could we ask your gifted Pesele to trot a little more gently, so she doesn't knock the stuffing out of us? My wife has just had a serious operation and we have plenty of time to catch the bus."

"Of course! Usually my Pesele shakes up our enemies. Believe me, she can smell an anti-Semite from a distance, but she just has to hear the *mama-loshn* from a customer and she shifts from a gallop to an easy trot," the driver joked. "My horse is a real lover of Yiddish, she just doesn't know how to speak it. Which is a pity!"

Hennie sat immobile, cut off from everything that surrounded her. It seemed that nothing existed except for the keen pain of her loss. She didn't notice her husband or the driver and paid no attention either to the white bundle resting on the knees of the silent Shleimke.

Shleimke could not bring himself to speak to his wife to try to distract her from her dark thoughts. Although he too was devastated, he concealed his despair and confusion as if in a deep cellar, blocked behind an iron door of silence.

The clatter of the obedient Pesya's hoofs was accompanied by an inharmonious tune from the driver and the city floated past them like a mass of gravestones in a nightmare.

"We're here!" said the driver, politely calling for Pesya to stop.

Shleimke paid him with what was left of Hennie's earnings and they quickly took their places on the bus out of town.

You could count the number of passengers on your fingers. Unlike Pesya, the driver, a broad-shouldered, uncommunicative Lithuanian, spared no one; he didn't miss a single bump or pothole. The bus shook and jumped like a huge frog. Hennie put her hand over her thumping heart, which felt as if it were going to jump out of her dress. At the same time Shleimke grasped the bundle, pressing it to his chest so that, God forbid, it wouldn't fall on the floor from the sudden jolts, revealing its contents to the small number of fellow passengers.

Shleimke had asked that no one meet them at the station; if they did, they would ask, "So how did it happen and why?" The Lord God did not create Jews lacking in curiosity; constantly and for any reason they bothered each other with endless questions. And not only each other; even God in heaven!

As Shmulik would say, "Jews were made not of flesh and blood, but of a multitude of question marks."

Members of both sides of the family gathered in the small rented apartment. Rokha had also invited Dr. Blumenfeld, just in case something happened to Hennie, who had not recovered from her misfortune.

"How good it is that you are with us now," my grandmother said to her daughter-in-law. "May God protect us, always and everywhere."

"Amen," Grandpa Dovid responded.

"Amen," echoed my mother's parents.

"We all wish you a most speedy recovery," said Dr. Blumenfeld, who could not resist giving some advice. "Hennie, dear, you must forget everything that has happened and think about the future. Please, do not imagine that the sun has set forever. Morning will come and it will rise."

Hennie did not utter a word in response. She glanced at everyone blankly and smiled in a way that made her family shiver. Her expression seemed that of someone who felt she was doomed.

"My dear, it doesn't make any sense to extinguish a fire by throwing dry wood on it," Isaac Blumenfeld said, almost in a whisper. Before leaving he added, "I am leaving you this packet with some pills. They are a sedative. Take one every night and you will wake up more cheerful in the morning."

Hennie did not take one and fell asleep only close to morning.

"Shleimke has gone out. He'll be back soon," Shmulik told his sister when she awoke.

"Where did he go?" Hennie asked.

"I don't know."

Although he was usually quite talkative, that day Shmulik hardly said anything. He knew that Shleimke had gone to make arrangements with the head of the burial society, Hatzkel Berman, about the day their son would be buried.

On the way home Shleimke stopped in at Rybatskaya Street to see his mother.

"Is there a reason you've dropped by in the middle of the day?" Rokha asked.

"I was at Hatzkel's."

In Jonava the name of the unsociable grave digger Berman was a kind of watchword.

"I see. When will the funeral be?" my future grandmother asked.

"Tomorrow. I came to ask your advice, should we take Hennie or not?"

"Are you out of your mind? Do you want to finish her off? Of course not! When she gets stronger, then we will all go to the cemetery together. We won't be able to keep the truth from her forever. You can't conceal anything from the living. Hatzkel Berman is the first person who will talk about those he has buried."

They buried my older brother Borukh (may his memory be blessed), who hadn't once been wrapped in a nappy, or fed with his mother's milk, and whose name was never recorded in any book, on a slope between two young, graceful pine trees to the sound of chattering ravens who thought nothing of the dead. The last golden rays of the sun gently tinged the sides of the deep grave, which was too large for such a little mite. At the open grave stood both of my grandfathers in satin yarmulkes, both my grandmothers in black kerchiefs and dresses down to their heels, my unbelieving father in a cap with a hard canvas peak and Uncle Shmulik, infamous for haranguing his fellow townsmen with militant calls for freedom and universal equality. They shuddered as each shovelful of the wet, frozen clay fell. In a barely audible voice, my superstitious Uncle Shimon recited the *kaddish* prayer that Rabbi Eliezer had said should not be recited. The gravediggers wiped the sweat from their brows.

The sun set and the relatives left in silence for their homes.

For two weeks Shleimke did not touch his needle or saddle his iron horse. Impatient customers harried him, threatening to go over to Gedalya Bankvecher, but he held on to them with promises. He devoted himself solely to Hennie.

Shmulik sewed away on the Singer, fighting his innate laziness with couplets of Russian revolutionary songs about hostile storms that threatened the poor.

In the presence of his sister, Shmulik lowered his voice to a whisper. As a result the whole apartment echoed, not to the sound of anger and hatred, but to depression and sadness. With all their might he and Shleimke tried to extricate

Hennie from the frightening state of indifference she had fallen into. She avoided those close to her, including her parents, and pressed her lips closed when she heard words of consolation or sympathy. She did not respond to questions and simply ignored strained jokes. From morning to evening Hennie sat at the window watching the passers-by, the fussy sparrows jumping about in puddles and the doves engaged in mating dances.

If, from the street, she happened to hear the crying or screaming of a child, Hennie immediately closed the curtains and covered her ears with her hands. Following the example of Mina the midwife, she began to attend synagogue regularly and to pray fervently, though awkwardly, for a long time.

Once, when she seemed to have lost control of herself, Rabbi Eliezer, more sensitive by now, came to her.

"In life there are some circumstances," he said, "when the omnipotent God Himself, like a simple mortal, requires help. Sometimes even more than we sinners do. My dear, help Him now; try to overcome your despair and transform your weakness into strength. The One Above pities the weak, but supports those who are strong."

Although she didn't understand what the rabbi was saying, she cried tears of gratitude.

At home, Hennie didn't touch anything. Her mother-in-law took charge of the kitchen, cleaned the room and did the ironing. Shmulik, who had learned from his mother how to prepare food as a child, helped Rokha. He would put aside his needle, roll up his sleeves and peel the potatoes and chop up the cabbage.

Things continued in this way until one memorable day in early summer when Hennie suddenly, quietly but distinctly, not apparently directing her words to anyone in particular, asked, "So where is our little boy?"

By this time, Shleimke no longer left the Singer idle; from morning to evening its noise drove his dark thoughts away. Though surprised by his wife's question, he recovered quickly. Shleimke did not know how to lie.

"We buried him."

"We? Where?"

"Here, in the cemetery on the hill." Every word stuck like a bone in his throat.

"Why did you do it without me?"

"You were very weak then. We discussed it as a family and decided, after what you had already suffered, not to subject you to yet another heavy blow. Hennie, you wouldn't have been able to stand it. It would have destroyed you."

"I want to see him," she said, as if they were speaking about someone who was alive, not dead.

"Alright, alright," Shleimke agreed, not understanding the hopeless meaning of her involuntary and terrible slip of the tongue. "Whenever you say."

"Tomorrow."

"If you say tomorrow, then it's tomorrow."

He very much wanted Hennie to ask about something else; he wanted her to question him, to reproach him even. Shleimke was ready to defend himself, or to blame himself and express repentance. But his wife kept stubbornly silent. He didn't dare open his mouth again.

Making their way between the gravestones, they arrived at the anonymous hill where rested their anonymous child, who had not uttered even a single cry.

The sun illuminated the clay hillock with crimson rays.

Bees buzzed busily. Butterflies, which had just emerged from their cocoons, flaunted their fleeting, blinding splendour with fragile wings of divine, unbelievable colours. Jays cawed noisily in the juniper bushes, while in the thick, succulent grass field mice darted and intrepid ants scurried in a business-like manner from one gravestone to another. And languishing in the sun, the crows, those harbingers of death, preened their feathers in the trees.

As if to spite the mourning couple, everything was alive, moving, illumined with all the colours of the rainbow; nature rejoiced and its creatures multiplied.

Bending down, Hennie took a handful of earth from the grave and began to pour it from one hand to the other. Shleimke was sure that she was about to sprinkle the earth, like ashes, on her head and begin sobbing. However, with an enigmatic expression, Hennie stood immobile next to the hill and slowly, as if performing some rite, sifted the small bits of earth through her fingers onto the forlorn grave.

Hennie and Shleimke bade farewell to their son and, in mournful silence, approached the graves of their grandfathers and grandmothers. Their grandmothers had had ten children, not in the Jewish Hospital in Kaunas, not in Paris, nor in the New York borough of the Bronx, but under the shingled roof of their own home in the backwoods of Jonava. Hennie and Shleimke bowed to the graves respectfully and silently, pulling up unseemly roots that had grown up around the gravestones. After venting their grief and anger on the weeds, the unhappy grandchildren headed back toward the crumbling gates of the cemetery, which had been erected by the first Jewish settlers in the area in the distant past, even before the Emperor Napoleon had led his victorious troops along the impassible Lithuanian roads into Russia.

It was not possible to stay silent. Something remained unspoken between them and needed to be said.

While they were still among the gravestones, a new wave of despair overwhelmed Hennie. With a rush she began to speak about what had been tormenting her in her heavy-hearted silence.

"Tell me, please," she said. "Don't avoid answering; why do you need me the way I am now?"

Following the unsuccessful birth, while she was still in the hospital, Hennie had convinced herself that Shleimke would leave her for another woman, one who would bear him lots of children and on whose young body there would be no scar or flaw.

"What are you talking about?" Shleimke asked, perplexed.

"Who needs a dried-up apple tree that will produce no fruit?"

"Where did you get such a foolish idea?"

"Where? When Dr. Lipsky released me from the hospital, he said that I should not get pregnant again. He warned that the next time it could lead to a catastrophe, not only for the child, but for me as well, and that not a single hospital in the world could guarantee a positive outcome in such a case. So I am asking you directly, tell me, why do you need such a failure for a wife?"

"Dr. Lipsky told me the same thing. And so what? God gave our ancestor Moses the Ten Commandments on Mount Sinai, which say, 'Do not murder', but how many people kill each other in war without any qualms or pity? They also say, 'Do not steal', but how many people steal from other people without a thought, from people they don't know and even from their neighbours whom the Lord God commanded them to love as themselves?" Shleimke simply could not stop himself. The words tumbled from him. His face was flushed and his eyes sparkled with an anger that was quite untypical of him.

"I'm not trying to fight for myself," Hennie replied. "People don't die twice. But I am sure you won't contradict Dr. Lipsky. Listen to him."

"I don't understand."

"Are you going to accept the ban on having sexual relations that has been placed on you and fast the whole year long? You don't wish me ill. You don't want me to die, do you?"

"No. I don't wish you ill and I don't want you to die."

"Understand me, please! The destiny of any woman is to defy the prohibition for the sake of motherhood, for the sake of continuing the human race. What if I am an apple tree that has a strong trunk and a lush crown but which is shrivelling and bears no fruit? You will get tired of nestling in its shade, not enjoying the sweetness of its fruit, just listening to the rustling of its yellowing, falling leaves."

"Hennie, enough of your ridiculous analogies. What's going on? Have you forgotten how to speak to me in a straightforward manner without any of these fancy expressions?"

"Are you sure that one fine day you won't grab hold of an axe and cut down this apple tree in order to plant a new, fruitful one?" she pressed him.

"Can't you stop your fancy talk? I will neither plant anything, nor will I cut anything down. Explain to me briefly and clearly what it is that is upsetting you so."

"You mean you won't get rid of me?" she finally asked directly.

"At least now we're having a comprehensible conversation. I will only get rid of you, if you want to get rid of me or, as you put it, if you want to cut me down and plant something or someone else in your garden, instead of me."

"Then it won't be so terrible to die."

Desperate and exhausted by grief, Hennie fell on her husband's chest, knocking him to the ground. Suddenly, she began to kiss him feverishly on the lips, on his cheeks and his forehead. From the tall pine trees the crows looked down at them and tried to frighten the shameless couple with a loud, scornful cawing, for not having found a better place for their lovemaking than the high grass of the cemetery.

"You're out of your mind!" Shleimke said, unsuccessfully attempting to free himself from her hungry embrace and to get to his feet.

When they got home they found the radical Shmulik being lectured in Yiddish by the policeman Gedraitis, who had acquired the language during his long years of service in the shtetl.

"*Sholem aleichem, Ponas* Vincas," my father greeted him, not smiling.

"*Aleichem sholem*," the policeman replied politely and, as if there were no problem, continued his serious conversation with Shmulik.

The issue, perhaps unsurprisingly, was not the sewing of a new suit, but the hostile winds that threatened Hennie's unfortunate brother along with all the other honest workers of the world. It turned out that Shmulik Dudak had managed to gain a reputation in the shtetl, less as a tailor than as a virulent enemy of the rich. The mild-mannered Gedraitis had dropped by to present, in the name of the authorities, the first serious warning to Shmulik about his incitement of the Jewish youth with his inflammatory words.

"Mr. Dudak, I have long known your father, the worthy cobbler Shimon, whom I always turn to to mend my shoes and boots," the guardian of law and order said. He coughed. "I also knew your grandfather, Rakhmiel, and Shleimke's grandfather, the stonecutter Berel." He tried to flatter his host. "Both of them were really masters of their craft."

"Why are you telling me all this?"

"Why? As an old friend of your family I want to tell you with total frankness, before it's too late, that it would be much better to mind your own business and earn a good living rather than shouting, 'Down with the dictator Smetona!' in front of some blockheads in the market square on Sundays. There's nothing more just in the world than work. It won't do you any good trying to incite people. It's dangerous. You won't feed a family like that."

Shmulik didn't allow himself to be drawn. He stood there, biting a thread between his teeth.

"My advice, Mr. Dudak, is this: take an example from your relatives, not from those revolutionaries whom it's occasionally necessary to silence with bullets. However, I won't bother you further. Sew away," Gedraitis boomed and, clicking his heels, he departed.

"If you carry on playing games like this, Shmulik," Hennie sighed, "we'll have to bring you food parcels in prison."

"I agree. You are a fine cook and you well know that I love goose neck, chopped herring and potatos with prunes," Shmulik said, delighted that Hennie had apparently returned to life.

It had become easier to breathe in the house, as if the walls had moved to allow in more air. Rokha was overjoyed at the rejuvenated Hennie. In order to free her from the daily chores, Rokha continued to bake, fry, cook and store all the food in heavy pots or a large basket in their tiny apartment. After all, it wasn't a simple matter to fill the bellies of two healthy fellows who didn't lack an appetite or suffer from ulcers! No matter how much you put on their plates, they ate it all!

"You should eat too," she said, keeping a close eye on Hennie. "You need to eat a lot. Twice the amount that the rest of us eat. In the hospital, my dear, you really got thin. You look like a walking skeleton! You need put some meat on your bones."

Shleimke worked day and night, not allowing his hands to stay idle, as they say. And even Ephraim Kapler maintained control of himself, not complaining about how the noise of the sewing machine prevented him from sleeping according to his usual schedule. "After all," he said of the couple renting from him, "they had the kind of misfortune you wouldn't wish even on your enemies."

After Yom Kippur, Hennie and Shleimke had an unexpected guest. Antanina, the former housekeeper of the late Abram Kisin, was carrying a bulging bag tied with string.

"Greetings," she said in a falsetto voice that betrayed her age. "I've been meaning to visit you for a long time and now I'm finally doing so. Many times I said to myself, 'Antanina, aren't you ashamed? So much time has passed and you still haven't given them the things that Mrs Ethel left for them.' It's been a long time of course, but everything just flies out of my old head."

"What is it that you failed to give us?" Shleimke asked warily.

"Your wife knows. Before she went away Mrs Ethel left two sacks for you. There are toys in the bigger one. The smaller one has other things in it."

"A sack with toys," said Shleimke, staring at Antanina.

"Yes, toys. The other sack has suits, little trousers and shirts that belonged to Raphael. I'll bring the other sack next week when I go to morning prayers."

The partially blind Antanina began to slowly untie the string.

"There are all kinds of things here!" the old woman said, pulling the gifts out of the bag with delight. "A whole store of toys from France, Spain, Germany, and Latvia."

Shleimke and Hennie looked at each other in dismay. It was clear that in her isolation Antanina had not heard about their misfortune.

"Shall we take them?" Shleimke asked, almost inaudibly, his voice shaking.

"Let's take the toys. Why not? I'm not superstitious, I don't believe in bad omens," Hennie said, surprisingly quickly and firmly. She turned to Abram Kisin's hard-of-hearing former housekeeper. "Thank you, *Ponia* Antanina! We should have come to take them ourselves; you've dragged quite too many heavy burdens in your life."

"What?" she asked. "Recently I don't hear so well and I forget a lot. Oh, the years, the years fly by! What they do to a person! They ruin your hearing, they fill your eyes with ooze, they hobble your feet with chains. You take a step and right away you have to find a place to sit down. In old age woe comes to your house, not as a guest and not for an hour or two, but like the mistress of the house and for a long time. Oh what a long time! She won't leave whether you try to chase her away or not."

"I don't know how to thank you," Hennie said, bringing the conversation back on track.

"It's not me you should thank, but Mrs Ethel. She is an angel. May God protect her."

"Thanks are due to you too," Hennie said. "I hope that these toys will be of use to us."

What was Shleimke hearing? That the toys might yet be of use to them? Did that mean that, despite the prohibition, Hennie had decided to get pregnant again? Despite the risk to her life! Dr. Lipsky had turned out to be a prophet when he said that loving women can be self-sacrificing to the point of madness. They are ready to do anything. They can't be stopped.

In less than half a year my mother did indeed become pregnant for the second time and in that same Jewish Hospital, once more by Caesarean section, she gave birth, thank God, to a little boy and both mother and child survived.

That boy was me.

The sharp-tongued Grandma Rokha named me the 'forbidden fruit', but in mid-June 1929 the 'German' Rabbi Eliezer, from Tilsit, wrote down in the Book of Fates, the community record book, not my nickname Hirshke, but my two official names – Hirsh Yankl, or, in Russian, Grigory Yakov. The second name was evidently intended to serve as a kind of 'insurance' for the first one and to drive all illness and misfortune away from me. As it turned out, it didn't succeed in averting all illness and misfortune, as had been hoped.

Unfortunately, my poor memory does not recall which of the foreign toys that had been given to my older brother Borukh were in fact handed down to me by the hand of fate. I can clearly visualize only the most attractive one, a fancy hurdy-gurdy that Aaron Kremnitser had bought for his heir either from Paris or Berlin. The hand organ was varnished and decorated with amusing animals – foxes, rabbits, bear cubs, exotic kangaroos and ponies. The handle was on the side. If you turned it, twice I think, there would suddenly emerge from inside a touching melody that sounded like a lullaby.

As strange as it seems, even today I can see in my mind's eye that wonderful hurdy-gurdy and hear its tunes. The sound of it, rustling like leaves, wafts over my grey head and carries me back to Rybatskaya Street and the distant Jewish Jonava. Sitting at my computer now, I feel as if I am not typing letter after letter but, as in my irretrievably distant childhood, turning the handle of that wonderful hurdy-gurdy. Slowly, close-up, like in a silent movie, one by one my unforgettable fellow shtetl dwellers stream past my eyes. I listen to a simple tune and they come alive again, lined up in one friendly row; the philosophising beggars and industrious tailors, the rich philanthropists and home-grown transformers of the world, like my Uncle Shmulik, who dreamed about a freedom that turned out to be an illusion, an unattainable equality and a mythical fraternity. This company was followed by 'the German', Rabbi Eliezer, the unfriendly gravedigger, Hatzkel, and the gentle, matza-loving guardian of law and order, Vincas Gedraitis. It was the very same Gedraitis who, on more than one occasion, advised the ardent, educated, aspiring revolutionaries from the poor Jewish families not to mislead their fellow Jews with illusions of a paradise on earth on the Russian model, but asked them in Yiddish, "My fellow Jewish citizens, why waste your time and energy trying to improve the lives of others when you will only end up taking a short walk in leg-irons around the inner courtyards of jail? Wouldn't it be better to mend footwear, to sew suits and *lapserdaks*, the long coats you Jews wear, and rough kaftans for Christians, to shave and to tinker, to construct home stoves, or to roof houses with tiles? For that Lithuania would only thank you!"

But, alas, Lithuania did not thank them, even though the majority of its Jewish citizens did follow the wise advice of the village policeman. His advice, however, didn't alter the terrible fate of those who, in their simple faith, believed him.

Tell me, you magic hurdy-gurdy, where will you yet take me with your simple melody? Where? To my school, which no longer exists? To my teacher, Balser, the enthusiastic promoter of Yiddish? To the synagogue of my shtetl, which was transformed into an ordinary bakery? Or to that bare hillock, to the nameless grave where my older brother Borukh was buried and of which not a trace remains?

In that eternal habitation of the dead you can hear now only the rustling of old shrivelled pines and see the black and tattered nests of noisy ravens and feel the memories that surround you. I stand beneath the scalding heat of these memories and in my agitation whisper something to the toy hand organ and continue to turn its tin handle, while the bears and rabbits and the foxes, the ponies and the kangaroos echo my sorrow as a choir.

Memories, memories! Are they not the most long-lasting cemetery in the world?

Though it is protected by no one, that burial place is indestructible and imperishable. No one will desecrate it, or pilfer its stones to build a house for himself. Its walls are built not of brick, but of gravestones inscribed with ancient letters, which no one would dare to trample with soldiers' boots, since there the earth burns with an undying flame under the feet of the wicked.

Blessed be the memory of all those who peacefully lie in these comfortable (how terrible it is to call them that) burial places that have been watered so freely with bitter Jewish tears. To this very day the voices of my eternally departed fellow shtetl dwellers rise from under the silent cemetery turf, trying to grab the attention of the Lord God with their disembodied voices. With His help they try to touch the callous hearts of the living, appealing for the care of the defenceless and for justice, which every day recedes further from the world.

BOOK TWO

1

I remember one bright Passover morning in 1934 when Grandma Rokha leaned over my bed and, with uncharacteristic playfulness, woke me tenderly, whispering in my ear. I was five. My parents, busy earning our daily bread, had given their dearly beloved offspring over to the care of Grandma Rokha from the beginning of spring until the end of the short Lithuanian summer.

"Wake up, Hirshele! Wake up, my golden one! Today it's an important holiday. Pesach! Passover! I'm going to take you today, my little dove, to the synagogue for the first time. To the *Beit Knesset hagadol*."

"Where?" My eyes, still not unstuck from my sweet sleep, expressed nothing but fear.

"To the Great Synagogue. You've never been before. Each day *Gotenu*, our dear God, descends from heaven to there. We will pray together and thank our Protector and Benefactor for delivering us from Egypt thousands of years ago and liberating us from the Pharoahs."

I listened and yawned, trying to shake off my sleepiness.

"Hirshele, you are still small and, of course, don't know what pharoahs are and what we mean by the terrible slavery of Egypt, but, when you grow up, you'll read the Passover

Haggadah and then you will know everything; how Moses led us for forty years in the desert, how our ancestors lived in tents, and how they baked matza on their camp fires."

She polished my light, laced summer shoes to a shine, decked me out in an almost new woollen suit, the one in which, not long before, Raphael Kremnitser had used to dandy his way around the shtetl before he moved to France. Then she put Uncle Yosef's yarmulke, which had been packed in naphthalene and still smelled of it, on my head. Yosef was sick and imagined he was a blackbird or a sparrow. He did not fly heavenward, but around the hospital ward for mental patients in Kalvari, far from home.

After carefully inspecting me from head to foot and expressing her satisfaction by smacking her lips, Grandma took me by the hand. We set out at a leisurely pace through the still-sleeping shtetl toward the Great Synagogue of Jonava in Sadovaya Street, where, as Grandma Rokha put it, our *Gotenu* 'lived', descending from heaven each day.

At that time I had no idea about either God the Liberator or the Egyptian pharoahs. I didn't worry my head back then, of course, about such ideas as freedom and slavery. However, that Passover morning of long ago has never left my memory. Sometimes it sank to its depths, sometimes it rose to the surface, as if floating on the surface of a river.

When a little more than a year later I went to school and was, perhaps, a bit smarter, I suddenly realised that my wise grandmother Rokha didn't understand everything either, although on no occasion did she ever, even briefly, admit that someone else was right, nor was she ever shamed into silence by her interlocutor. Whether lying down, standing up or sitting in her seat, she never stopped instructing others with a certainty that was enviable, or advising, arguing, or just constantly talking and talking. Words were her defence and, evidently, gave her strength, just like the powders and tablets that were prescribed by Dr. Blumenfeld. Even the positive words that occasionally emerged from her lips had the imperious tone of an order. Grandma Rokha (may her humble name forever have its place on the list of self-sacrificing Jews) nourished me, first as a child and then as a lad, with her endless conversation. Even today, in the twilight of my life, many of her words still echo, either irritating or caressing my heart.

"Hirshele, I look at you and you can never guess what I'm thinking about." What Grandma was thinking about not a single clairvoyant in the world could or would dare guess. "What I am wondering, Hirshele, is whether you will be like the other members of your family."

"I don't know. Papa says that I am like him, but Mama doesn't agree."

Noting my puzzled expression, Grandma concluded, "No! You won't be like either your father or your grandpa, or like your uncles either. They are all atheists and blasphemers. They don't go to synagogue and mock anyone who believes in our Lord God. Because of their lack of faith and their mockery they will never ever deserve His mercy!"

I listened without understanding what she was talking about, but I didn't dare object. Any contradiction drove Grandma crazy.

"Just take your father," she continued. "What does he believe in? He only believes in his Singer sewing machine.

And your grandpa? He believes in his awl and waxed thread. And as for your uncle Shmulik, that good-for-nothing believes in some bald Russian with a goat's beard. He even clipped a photograph of that baldy out of a Yiddish newspaper and framed it. There his god stands in a poorly tailored wide-open overcoat, on the front of an armoured train and extends his arm to the people! But not a single one of your relatives – Hirshele, please, pay attention and listen when I am talking to you! As I was saying, not one of them believes in our All-powerful God. But I want you to believe in Him."

"All right, all right," I repeated mechanically, without grasping the meaning of her words. I had no idea what it meant to believe; nevertheless, I suspected that it probably wasn't particularly hard work from which you were likely to get tired or sweaty. In other words, it wasn't worth upsetting Grandma. If she asked me whether I wouldn't disappoint her I would nod as a sign of agreement.

However, to my misfortune, Grandma Rokhl couldn't stand nodders.

"You must have learned how to nod from your father. It's not for nothing that the Lord God provided us with words to distinguish us from cats and dogs. Nodding, Hirshele, is a disgusting habit. The earlier you stop the better. The person who nods his noggin instead of answering is either a coward or a scoundrel," she informed me. "A normal person doesn't spare his words, as if he were saving them up for old age, but dispenses them generously among his friends and relatives. Do you understand me? Yes or no?"

"Yes," I replied.

On that distant April day in 1934, we continued calmly on our way along the still empty cobblestone streets of Jonava, to the main prayer house where, my teacher and guide assured me, our merciful *Gotenu*, our God, lived.

The brick *Beit Knesset hagadol* was not the only synagogue in our God-fearing shtetl, which from ages past had been thickly settled with Jews. Other than this one, which was ceremoniously referred to in Hebrew, Jonava had other prayer houses named after the butchers, tailors, carpenters, cobblers and furriers who attended them. The tailors would not address the One on High in the prayer house of the butchers, and the carpenters were hardly enthusiastic about the fact that cobblers now prayed on the benches worn down by the rear ends of their predecessors – masters of making furniture from mahogany, who were inclined to indulge in the sin of drinking. However, when even a not-so-famous cantor came to town from Poland or from Riga, all their differences were immediately forgotten and they gathered to hear the singer in the Great Synagogue on Sadovaya Street, pious craftsmen with their wives and children from all of the shtetl's tiny prayer houses. As my sharp-tongued uncle Shmulikk (who was under constant police surveillance) said ironically, any traveling tenor with some kind of reputation united them more than God Himself.

While we were still quite a way from the Great Synagogue, I turned to Grandma. "Tell me, does our good *Gotenu* also live in the prayer house of those fat butchers with their blood-stained aprons?"

"Yes," the old woman replied with some pride. "If they don't sell non-kosher meat and don't cheat on their customers, our Lord God also lives with them."

"And does he also live in the prayer houses of the tailors and the barbers?"

"Yes," replied Grandma, whose heart simply melted from my questions. Questions always pleased her more than answers. Inappropriate answers would make her shrivel up, become bent and grow old before your eyes.

"But, Grandma, can that be? On one and the same day, here and there? In different places?"

"Hirshele, you are not a fool. You will amount to something if you listen to me and not to Uncle Shmulik, who prays to that bald Russian fellow with the goat's beard, or to your Grandpa who says that the best job in the world is mending boots and tacking on soles."

"I will listen to you, Grandma," I said, after a bit of consideration.

"Let's live and see. I never believe men's promises. All men are liars and deceivers. They imbibe deceit with their mother's milk."

"I will listen!" I insisted.

"All right, all right. I had better answer your question about our dear God. A human being, Hirshele, lives in one place until he dies – like on Rybatskaya Street, for example, like your Grandpa and me and Hava, or on Kovno Street like your other grandma, Sheyne, and Grandpa Shimon. But our *Gotenu* lives everywhere! There is no place in the whole world where He doesn't live."

On that memorable holiday morning I was very impatient to arrive at the place where our merciful *Gotenu* lived.

Of course, I was impatient. With Grandma it was never possible to get anywhere quickly. She stopped often, not to rest – even though like Grandpa Dovid she was short of breath – but because she was not prepared to forgo any opportunity to talk with one of her old acquaintances. She greeted everyone and unfailingly exchanged a few words about this or that, completely forgetting about God and his residence – the *Beit Knesset hagadol*.

"Every passerby in the shtetl knows you better than our mayor," Grandpa would joke.

He himself would rarely go with her to pray, complaining either about his infirm legs, his consumption or about a rush job for an important customer for whom the work had to be ready by Monday.

"I think God listens to women more than to men, that's the thing," Grandpa said, attempting unsuccessfully to defend his modest free-thinking. "What if I do go with you? Then what? I don't have anything interesting to say either to Him or to the people there. The second thing is I don't have the right abilities," he continued, referring to Grandma's habit of stopping to have a brief conversation with everyone she met on the way to synagogue. "If you should happen to hear some good news from the One on High, you wouldn't keep that from me, would you? You would come home and tell me right away. So what would be the sense of my going with you?"

"Your Grandpa's children are all the same," Grandma said. "Your father, your Aunt Chava, your Aunt Leah who ran off to America and also your Uncle Isaac who left to be with the Frenchies, they all stayed away from the synagogue," she complained, as if Grandpa's children were not her children too. "We members of the Mines family don't pass a single day without our prayer books. But I have been praying for all those disobedient ones and I am praying for them now. I pray to the Almighty One that He doesn't punish the fools, but leads them to see reason before it's too late," Grandma said, raising her teary eyes to the gloomy Lithuanian sky and whispering something mysterious.

We walked on in silence. The warmth of Grandma's hand flowed into my body like a river in spring. From the trees, the green branches of which framed the cottages along the way, we could hear the singing of birds whose names I didn't know. "Birds," I was told in my parents home, "are just birds, Hirshele. And flowers are just flowers. Just because you don't know what their names are," I was assured, "it won't stop the birds from singing or the trees turning green in the spring and casting off their leaves in the autumn, just as they have always done."

"Why do you need to know something that won't make a poor Jew either happier or richer?" Grandmother said, attempting to comfort me.

The first acquaintance she stopped to unburden her soul to on the way to the Great Synagogue after a week of complete seclusion was the policeman Vincas Gedraitis, who was wearing his uniform jacket and matching trousers tucked into shining military boots.

"*Gut yontof,* Rokha!" he greeted her in Yiddish. Happy holiday! He straightened his policeman's cap and smiled broadly.

"*Gut yomtof, Ponas* Vincas," Grandma replied, responding to the policeman with a grateful smile marked with deep wrinkles.

"*A likhtikn un freilikh Peisakh* – A bright and joyful Passover," Gedraitis said, holding his smile and sticking out his chest as a sign of friendship and of his good mood. "For the festive meal . . . how do you call it? The word has totally slipped out of my head."

"The *seder*."

"I know I missed the first *seder*, but tonight, if you'll allow me, I would like to drop in for your matza balls. Every Lithuanian should have his Jew and every Jew – his Lithuanian. As for me, I am fortunate; I don't have just one Jew, but two – Shimon Dudak and your Dovid. I feast with both on Passover."

"Please do come," Grandma muttered without enthusiasm, saving her next smile for another, more worthy, acquaintance.

"That Gedraitis is not a harmful person. What's true is true. But policemen, like bedbugs, are not the favourite guests in a Jewish home," she whispered to me.

"I love matza balls!" repeated the genial Gedraitis. "Do you remember, Rokha, when I first tasted them at your house? I wasn't a policeman then; I was working for Mendelson at his sawmill. And you and Dovid were so young!"

"I remember. We went to get boards from you to lay a new floor for our house."

"Do you recall how I asked Dovid if there was a lot of our Christian blood in the matza? Your dear husband just stayed calm and said, 'Just a bit.' And I said, 'If there's just a bit, Dovid, then I'll have some.' Everyone laughed! I never laughed so hard in all my life. A lot of water has flowed by in the Vilija River since then. What do you think? How much matza have I consumed over all these years at your house and at the house of your in-law Shimon? Maybe, half a *pud*, maybe more." Gedraitis wheezed, touched his fingers to his cap, and walked on.

"Grandma, Grandma," I asked, pulling at her holiday calico dress. "Is it much farther?"

"To where, my dear?" Grandma asked.

"To the . . . to the synagogue where our *Gotenu* lives."

"It's not far, Hirshele," she replied, looking around to see if, perhaps, she might see any other acquaintants nearby with whom she might chatter in the fresh air. "It's not a sin to have a little chat if you've had to stay at home all day, sentenced to eternal imprisonment, listening to your faithful one banging away without pause with his cobbler's hammer, giving you a tremendous headache made worse by the insistent flies, who never stop their incessant buzzing."

At the entrance to the *Beit Knesset hagadol*, in the yard where chestnut trees were blooming profusely and agile swallows manoeuvred, Grandma caught sight of the hunchbacked beggar Avigdor Perelman. She tried to rush past him in order to get a good place in the balcony, but Avigdor Perelman would not have been Avigdor Perelman if he had not stopped her to greet her with a laugh. You see, good manners and grace are not only the preserve of the wealthy, but also of the poor.

"Thank you, Rokha. May God reward you a hundred times for your goodness. For someone like you He should make an exception."

"And you, Avigdor, instead of just standing and collecting alms on every corner, it would be better if you would drop in at the synagogue once in a while and pray. Think about it! He might forgive you for all your sins and provide you with something."

"No, my dear, my relations with Him have been spoiled for ever. If I pray or if I don't, it won't change a thing. If you are a hunchback, you will remain a hunchback. After all, Rokha, even your life hasn't changed so much for the better by praying."

Avigdor Perelman's eyes filled with tears; it seemed that he was always crying. I was sorry for him, but I didn't say anything to Grandma. She never pitied those who didn't work. She called them parasites and good-for-nothings.

"Hands, Hirshele, aren't given to people to hold out asking for charity, but to raise calluses on them," she instructed me.

We entered the synagogue and slowly ascended the stairs to the balcony for women, holding onto the wooden rail that was polished by decades of use. The women were all wearing their holiday outfits, coloured dresses and silk scarves. Among them was my other grandma, Sheyne. She was sitting in the highest row, small, hardly noticeable and as quiet as an old tree by the roadside, denuded of leaves and birds. Although Grandma Rokha was not close to her, she still immediately told me to wish her a Happy Passover and to give her a kiss.

Bumping against the sharp knees of the surprised women worshippers, I went up to the top row.

Before I had the chance to greet Grandma Sheyne, she kissed me and patted me several times on my yarmulke, the one worn by my unfortunate Uncle Yosef before he became insane. She showered me with compliments like wild flowers, while I kissed her warm, flabby cheek and blushed with embarrassment.

"My handsome one, my smart one, oh how you have grown!" Grandma Sheyne repeated quietly. "Why do you come to see me and Grandpa Shimon so rarely? Come visit us! You are already big! You can find the way yourself without any help. You won't get lost." She wanted to say more, but just then the respected Rabbi Eliezer mounted the *bimah* and began to read from the Torah.

The Great Synagogue was filled with light. It seemed like the April morning sun had suddenly moved to illuminate the grand vaults of the holy prayer house.

"Do you like this?" Grandma Rokha asked, bending over and whispering into my ear.

"Yes, I do," I said truthfully.

"Will you tell that to your papa and mama?"

"Oh yes!"

Grandma listened to the Tilsit-born Rabbi Eliezer, who was wearing a white silk *talis* and a velvet yarmulke embroidered with gold thread, as if she knew ahead of time what he would say. She was bothered by the German accent that he had not succeeded in losing. But when he began to recite some of the blessings, the old woman paid complete attention. Her face began to shine and, as if hoping that the One Above would hear, she shouted loudly, "*Omein!*" the Ashkenazi Amen. Then she instructed me, her Hirshele, to repeat the word after her.

"*Omein! Omein!*" I repeated twice, imitating her, wishing to please her, with such a strange enthusiasm that our neighbours in the balcony turned toward us, frightened.

The reading of the Torah, it seemed to me, lasted far too long and, beginning to get bored, I began to fidget on the bench. I looked down on the men's section, paying no attention to what Rabbi Eliezer in his black yarmulke was explaining. The Rabbi, in his black trousers that could be glimpsed beneath his white *talis* and sharp pointed shoes, resembled a heron standing on one leg next to his nest. I expected him to pronounce once more the magic "*Omein*", spread his wings and fly up to heaven to join our *Gotenu*.

Below there was a noise as if someone had stirred up a beehive. After hearing the Rabbi say "*Omein,*" all the worshippers rose together, like soldiers, and recited a prayer. Candles were burning around the *bimah* and the smell of wax hung like an invisible haze over the densely packed prayer house. The service would soon be over, I thought, and the people would disperse and I would be able to go home, where Grandma's delicacies were awaiting me, but the Rabbi just continued to talk and talk.

"Don't fidget," Grandma said. "You're bothering the people who want to listen. The Rabbi is speaking about our troubles, about how no one in the world loves us and about how we Jews have to live in harmony with each other because we are still living in slavery to others."

Again, I understood very little of what she said but, for some reason, I piped, "But I love everyone: you, Grandma Sheyne, Papa, Mama. Everyone!" Then I quietened down. My attention was drawn to a butterfly that had somehow entered the synagogue and was circling around the top row, above the women who were yawning from lack of sleep. The creature was as bright as their holiday dresses and scarves.

I was totally captivated by its flight above the heads of the worshippers and the ark in which, my grandma explained to me, were kept the holy scrolls brought from Jerusalem itself. I followed the butterfly, not taking my eyes off it. The beautiful creature that had flown into the *Beit Knesset hagadol* rose sometimes toward the mighty vaults that smelled of holiness and then descended and landed on the rail of the *bimah*. I was fascinated by its light wings spotted with dark dots and, with great interest, observed its desperate flight, forgetting completely about the sermon of Rabbi Eliezer, about Passover and even about the fact that no one in the world loved us. I was overcome by the fear that some worshipper or other would swat the butterfly with their calloused palm. One blow and it would fall dead on the well-trodden rug that covered the floor.

"What are you staring at, Hirshele? Haven't you ever seen a butterfly before?"

"Yes, yes, I have."

"There's no reason to stare! Is that butterfly really so wonderful?" Grandmother chided. "We came here to pray, not to gaze at the ceiling. God forbid you should grow up to be a heretic like your Uncle Shmulik!"

However, I didn't listen to her or take my eyes off the butterfly.

"In our yard we have some like that and lots of other kinds. You'll have the chance to look at them later."

"But it's such a beauty!" I persisted.

"So what if it's beautiful?" Grandma Rokha remarked. "We're not in a field, or a garden, or a yard! Why are you filling your head with nonsense? A butterfly is a thing of a day, while our *Gotenu* is forever. Hirshele, think about Him."

I did not reply.

"Think, my dear, about us Jews who, as Rabbi Eliezer said, have been wandering in foreign lands as if we were still in the desert. And not just for forty years, but for thousands."

No matter how hard Grandma Rokha tried to get me to think about Him, no matter how she tried to explain about the Jews who wandered in a foreign land, all my thoughts were focused on the butterfly, which had disappeared somewhere. Since the doors and windows of the house where our *Gotenu* lived were firmly closed and the butterfly could not have flown out of the prayer house, I was certain that someone must have swatted her so that the worshippers' attention was not distracted. My sorrow was somewhat alleviated by the faint hope that the butterfly had perhaps hidden in some corner or other, or landed on the door of the ark, where the holy scrolls were kept. When the doors opened, she would burst out into the street and fly off to some field or land on a bush by the roadside.

After Rabbi Eliezer had once more blessed everyone and wished them a Happy Passover, the people slowly began to depart.

As soon as we left the Great Synagogue, I began to look around in search of my butterfly but, under the cloudless sky and above the fragrant chestnut trees there flew only the swift, free swallows, which turned the blue sky black with their wings. Avigdor Perelman was still standing in the front garden at the exit of the synagogue and, violating the sanctity of the festival, begging for donations from his fellow shtetl dwellers, who would be more generous leaving, he hoped, because of the parting words of Rabbi Elierzer.

"Have you forgotten that it is forbidden to either give or receive charity on the Shabbat and festivals?"

"I can accept it. I am an atheist, an apostate, and whoever is generous will give. The Lord will look the other way rather than blame those who give."

"You should come to us this evening," Rokha said. "You can try some honey liqueur. I remember when you were young, you were quite good-looking then, a real handsome fellow! You had dark curls to your shoulders, so long that you could braid them. You were an imp with light blue eyes. The girls used to melt at the sight of you. I too, it's no sin to admit it, had my eye on you."

"You, Rokha? On me?"

"On you. Who else do you think I mean?"

"You must be confusing me with somebody else. It wasn't me. I never had curls down to my shoulders and my eyes weren't blue. I was weak-sighted from birth," the pauper wheezed. "As for my best day, it's not in the past, but rather in the future." For a moment he stopped speaking, chewed his lip, and then added, "My best day will be when the grave-digger, Hatzkel Berman, covers my woes and my shame with his shovel."

"Come." Grandma Rokha repeated her invitation. "When Hennie had her misfortune, you came to us to share our grief. Now we would like to share our joy with you. Nobody should be alone, either in good fortune or in misfortune."

"Thank you for the invitation, Rokha, you are a marvellous woman, one who is often misunderstood. Excuse me for my directness, but sometimes you are a witch and sometimes an angel in a skirt," Avigdor said, shaking his head. "Still, I might come. At least to sit in a warm place and drink with you like a human being. And who is this here? Shleimke's son? Your first little grandchild?"

"Yes."

"He's a cute little fellow. What is your name, you little urchin?" he asked me.

Grandma Rokha answered for me. "Today was Hirshele's first time in the synagogue," she boasted before the atheist Perelman.

"Rokha, isn't it too early to drag him there?" Avigdor couldn't resist asking. "You might have waited a year or two before going to bow down before the One on High. Hirshele, if it's not a secret, what did you ask God for?"

I felt embarrassed.

"I didn't ask. Grandma always asks for me."

"That's what a grandma is for! After all, she and the Lord are old friends and everyone is always glad to do something for an old friend. But still, you must have some wish. Everyone wants something from the Lord. What would you like from Him?"

"I want . . . I want . . ." I babbled. "I want him to open the synagogue doors and let the butterfly go free!"

"Butterfly? What butterfly? Butterflies don't fly around in synagogues."

"They do!" I said.

"They fly, they don't fly! Hirshele, you are talking nonsense! Let's go home, we have already chattered too much," said

Grandma, taking me by the hand and pulling me after her. "Grandpa must be worried already. You, Avigdor, I am inviting once more to our *seder*."

On that *seder* night Perelman did not come, but my parents did. Uncle Shmulik, who was being kept under surveillance, also dropped in at Rybatskaya Street. For the sake of family accord and harmony he came every year on Passover to offer his greetings, which were sincere but as pale as faded daisies.

The house was sparkling clean. The previous day Grandma Rokha had put away all the work ordered by Grandpa's customers in the cupboard – the shoes, slippers and various kinds of boots. She also put away his work tools – his hammer, awl and cobbler's scissors. And she shoved his waxed thread and pins into a drawer of the bureau. She covered the shoe last with a white sheet that looked like a shroud. She aired out both of the rooms so they didn't smell of wax or leather. But before that, she put on the table the honey liqueur, the holiday matza and the other food.

Grandpa, whose hair had been cut for the holiday by the shtetl's wonder-working barber, Naum Kovalsky, looked much younger, resembling the bridegroom Dovid in the old photograph on the wall. Another thing that made him look younger was the almost unworn, double-breasted suit that had been tailored for him the year before from good-quality material by his son. Grandpa was so satisfied with his appearance that it seemed he had completely forgotton about his duties as leader of the Passover *seder*. Grandma was getting nervous and kept motioning for him to stop stroking his reddish beard and start the long-awaited Passover celebration without delay.

"Right away, right away," Grandpa repeated. Everyone sighed with relief when, tediously and haltingly, he began to recount what he remembered from his youth and repeated every year at the Passover table.

All those present repeated what he said in his weak, hoarse voice. Even Uncle Shmulik, that inflexible opponent of priests and rabbis who poisoned the people with religion, also muttered along out of politeness.

"Hirshele, repeat after Grandpa! *Ma nishtaana halaila hazeh mikol haleilois,*" Grandma ordered. Without any further prompting, mangling the words and having no idea what they meant, I raced along. "What a fine fellow you are! He grasps everything on the fly. Don't worry, when you grow up, you will understand what the night was Grandpa was talking about."

For me the Passover *seder* did not last long. Grandma Rokha cut me a big piece of gefilte fish and Grandpa poured some grape juice into a small cupro-nickel wine cup and everyone clinked cups with me. When I had polished off the food, everyone wished me a happy holiday and a good night.

"Let's go, I will put you to bed," Mama said, paving my way to bed with praise.

"It's not necessary, Hennie," Grandma stopped her. "He can take care of himself. There's no reason to spoil him. He will lie down and go to sleep by himself."

I didn't fall asleep right away. Before my eyes there flickered both the uniformed policeman and the pauper Avigdor in his cloth flat cap with its short, dirty visor that looked like a bird's broken wing. Before me slowly floated the image of the packed *Beit Knesset hagadol* and yarmulkes, prayer shawls, women's kerchiefs, melting candles, velvet pillows, prayer books, holy scrolls wrapped up like babies in nappies and a butterfly with dark spots on its wings.

Before I closed my eyes, the butterfly circled above my bed like an angel. Maybe it really had been an angel flying above the worshippers, waving at them with its speckled wings. Then off it flew to another shtetl, or returned to heaven, since no matter how hard you try, you cannot swat an angel or stop them with walls.

2

At that time I was going on seven and my family was giving serious consideration to which school I should attend.

As had been the custom among Jews throughout the ages, no agreement was reached. The family split into two uneven factions – the implacable Yiddishists and the ardent Hebraists.

From morning to night, passions flared on Rybatskaya and Kovno Street. From time to time fierce disputes broke out between the opposing sides, who could in no way agree on the main issue. Some insisted that I absolutely had to attend the Yiddish school, which was open to all. The others maintained that I should study at the elite Tarbut school. There instruction was in Hebrew and the students were mainly the children of those who in Jonava were considered by many to be the cream of society, although Uncle Shmulik referred to them as 'narrow-minded Zionists'.

My parents and their allies Grandpa Shimon and Grandma Sheyne, with the militant support of the revolutionary Shmulik, argued steadfastly that I should study in Yiddish. My other grandma, Rokha the Samurai, demanded that I be sent to the Tarbut school. Her cautious husband Dovid always avoided arguing with people who might become his customers, and in this instance had no good reason to cross swords with his wife, who would be the inevitable victor in such disputes, so he too voted for Hebrew, the prestigious language of our distant ancestors, which had never been very popular in the shtetls of Lithuania.

"Not Hebrew, that pitiful relic of the past!" Uncle Shmulik argued. "The boy should be sent to a people's Yiddish school! Only to a Yiddish one! After all, for his whole life he will have to converse not with the Lord God in the Great Synagogue, like our respected Rabbi Eliezer does, but with his fellows at work, with his beloved wife in a warm bed, or to quarrel with his shrew-like, peevish mother-in-law," continued my father's senior apprentice with his typical emotion. "Yiddish is the language of the proletariat, of the broad Jewish working masses. And this *mame-loshn* is the language of our own mother. Our Mo-ther!" emphasized Shmulik.

"And you, Rokha, why do you want the lad to study with obscurantists?" he asked.

"You are an obscurantist yourself, Shmulik!" Grandma argued. "You are just pretending you don't know why!"

"Do you really intend to make a rabbi out of him? A successor to that tongue-tied Tilsit 'German', Rabbi Eliezer?"

"And you want Hirshele to become a good-for-nothing like you?" Rokha shot back.

"Still, perhaps, you will be so good as to explain to me, obscurantist that I am, why you insist that your grandson go to that Zionist Tarbut school?"

"For his future!"

"For what future? Allow me, please, to ask," Shmulik said.

Rokha didn't reply, knowing that whatever she said to the loud mouth, he would still insist he was right.

Although Grandpa Dovid did not agree with the fervent seeker-of-truth Shmulik, he continued to maintain a rather shaky neutrality so as to avoid unnecessary disputes. All his life Dovid had kept to an unwritten rule not to become involved in a fight with anyone who was stronger than he was and, in the event that such a fight did begin, to step aside and wisely wait until someone came and parted the fighters. Having the reputation of a peace-maker, Grandpa Dovid always tried to convince disputants that no one, not even our infallible Lord God in heaven who judges the sins of those on earth, is always right in their decisions.

"Hirshele mastered Yiddish at home already, long ago; he jabbers away in it without making any mistakes. Let him study the language of the Bible, the guide book for every decent Jew," said Grandma Rokha the Samurai, continuing to press her argument.

She didn't want her beloved Hirshele to study in a common Yiddish school with the children of the poor of the shtetl, like the twins of the riff-raff water-carrier Gershon, the daughter of the night watchman Rachmiel and the two children of the widow seamstress Doba. Rokha hoped that her grandson's schoolmates would be the youngest son of the haberdasher Nisenboim, the shtetl Rothschild and a fervent Palestinophile, the nephew of the childless landlord, Ephraim Kapler, and the daughter of the owner of the furniture factory, Eliyahu Landsburg. Rich people have a refined sense of smell. They instinctively know who is who, just as they sense instinctively which school to send their offspring to.

Rokha caught her breath and then launched another attack against the enemy. "You know, Shmulik, what the far-sighted Nisenboim was thinking about when he sent his elder son Benchik to the Tarbut school, from which he himself graduated many years ago with a diploma of distinction? Do you think he was he thinking about Kaunas? Paris? America?"

"He was thinking about the Turks," Shmulik replied calmly, not at all deflected by the irony directed against him.

"Not the Turks, but our holy city of Jerusalem, the Promised Land, where you can't take a step if you don't know our ancient Hebrew language."

"Are you aware that Jews are being killed in the streets there?"

"That's nonsense! After all, miracles happen. At some point God will chase the Turks out of there, along with the Arabs, and gather us all into the Promised Land. All except you, of course. You, Shmulik, are not a Jew but a socialist!"

"Do you have any idea what you are saying? Not even two of our fellows can get along with each other and you're talking about thousands upon thousands? For Jews to live normally they must be mixed up with some other people – Lithuanians, or Poles, or Chinamen or Blacks. You say, 'God will gather us all together.' I can't imagine a bigger mess than that! And, in general, all your hopes about God and the rich man Nisenboim and your rosy, but impossible, ideas about Jerusalem have no relationship to the primary school where your grandson, my nephew, should study."

Rokha shifted tactics in despair. "Anyway, his parents will have to decide what school Hirshele goes to, not you and me. But they seem to be deaf and dumb. They listened to our argument but didn't put in a single word. It's clear that they must have reached a decision some time ago."

"Don't be angry at us," my mother said. "We've been racking our brains about this for quite some time."

"So what did that brain-racking lead to?" Grandma Rokha said testily, grasping from her daughter-in-law's tone what the answer was.

"Our Hirshke should go to the Yiddish school, where Balser is. He's a wonderful teacher and a real human being," Shleimke responded for his wife. "Who knows when our merciful God will finally gather us in the Holy Land? Meanwhile we are living in Lithuania, where we hardly need any other language except for Yiddish."

"Have it your way," Rokha sighed, making her disappointment clear. "I'm not concerned for myself. Dovid and I," she said, pointing her index finger toward her husband in a threatening way, "will soon be called by God to another place, you well know where, while you still have a long time to live. Does it really matter to each of you where Hirshke will go to school?"

"Don't take it so hard, Rokha," Shmulik immediately responded, attempting to calm Grandmother. "The main thing for a Jew is not studying a language, be it Yiddish, or Hebrew, or an African language, but accounting," he said, laughing.

I sat all this out, scarcely listening to the raging argument, as if the discussion was not about me but about some other boy. I looked at the ceiling and watched a huge spider slowly and uninterruptedly entangling its victim, a dead fly, with

thin threads. Although I was happy about my parents'
victory, pity for Grandma Rokha quietly welled up in my
heart.

There were still three weeks left before instruction began.
Nevertheless, Mama bought all the items I needed for school:
a primer with many pictures that inspired pupils to be excellent students, a useful, rather large school bag, pencils, a pen
and ink, notebooks with squares and with lines, a pencil
case, erasers and even a small blue tie to be worn on the
upcoming festive day.

On the eve of the first day of school, Mama ironed all my
little shirts and trousers and cut my hair. In the morning she
combed and parted my unruly hair and sprinkled it with my
father's eau de cologne. Then, at the long-awaited hour,
she took me to school with great fanfare, as if I were being
shown off to the whole shtetl.

The Yiddish elementary school was located not in the
centre of Jonava, but on its outskirts, in an unimpressive
one-storey building, whose dull windows faced an empty,
sandy lot. On one side there was a thick growth of thistles
through which field mice darted day and night. The miserly
autumnal sun barely peeked through the thick patches of
cloud and with its pale rays coloured gold the tin roof and
chipped brick walls.

Every Friday the soldiers of the local military garrison
passed by in line to bathe in the river, deafening the neighbourhood with the bold stomping of army boots or jaunty
folk songs about the sorrow of parting from a beloved girl.
Not far from the depressing and colourless school building
were some mysterious structures, which looked like orphans

huddled together; they were either temporary food store-houses or peasant huts. Behind them there extended a lawn that had been burned by the summer sun; for whole days in a row goats wandered back and forth across it. Sometimes they wandered around the school area and their pitiful bleating distracted the pupils.

Mama took me right up to the entrance of the school, kissed my cheeks, which smelled of eau de cologne, and, with a tender pat on my behind, pushed me toward the open entrance door.

"Good luck, Hirshele!"

A moment later I found myself among my noisy peers, whose clothes were not fancy, but apparently the best they had.

"Greetings, children!" A woman's loud voice rang out from the corridor. "You have had your chance to make some noise, now it's time to be serious. Please, without pushing enter the classroom. The fourth room on the left. Do you understand?"

"Yes!" said a redheaded boy, clearly used to giving orders. Giving his now quiet classmates an appropriate example of obedience, he was the first to enter the room.

The others followed him without rushing, like goslings after their mother.

"Quieten down, children. A school is not a market. If you shout you will be punished – you'll be taken out of the class-room and given a bad mark for behaviour," said our teacher-to-be. "You can make noise only after the bell that ends your day of studies and then, preferably, outdoors."

Our 'pack' quietened down.

As soon as we entered room number four the teacher delivered a short celebratory speech in honour of the start of the school year.

"Boys and girls, we, the teachers of the Yiddish school, are happy that you have chosen us. Thank you! Today for each of you, this is perhaps the most important day in your life. You are starting your long journey to knowledge, to understanding the world." The teacher paused, then continued. "Today there won't be any studying. We will spend most of the time getting to know each other. I will begin by introducing myself. My name is Esfir, Fira for short or Esther Bereznitskaya. You may simply call me Esther. I will not be insulted. I will teach you our native language, Yiddish, and also singing. Of course, you will love to sing."

"We already do," she was assured without hesitation by the redhead, even though not all of us loved singing.

I myself did not love singing. Nor did my father. "Unmarried women and synagogue cantors should sing," he used to say.

"The principal, Mr. Balser, will teach you arithmetic. Right now he is being treated at the Jewish Hospital in Kaunas. He will return when he is better. Do you understand?"

"We do," our self-appointed spokesman said, once again putting in his five *kopecks* worth.

Fira Bereznitskaya was a tall, shapely woman with hair cut short like a boy's. She wore small earrings shapped like apples of paradise. Her white satin blouse and dark blue skirt emphasized her thin figure. She spoke rapidly and abruptly and as if trying to get rid of the words stuck in her throat as quickly as possible, sometimes swallowing their endings.

Our classroom was small and rather dark, with a low, depressing ceiling, from which hung three electric lights covered with flies. The room had a total of ten shabby, old desks, five in each of the two rows. The first row was closer to the windows that faced the yard and had frames that were dark with age, while the second row faced the massive brick lopsided stove, which during the winter frosts and the fierce Lithuanian snow storms, was heated with a fire of dry birch logs that were stored piled up in a shed.

The teacher had us sit down behind the desks. The first desk was occupied by the redhead, who was distinguished from all the other new pupils by his size and strength. This desk was close to the blackboard, on which something was written that we were not yet able to read, probably, 'Best Wishes for the New School Year'.

Fira Bereznitskaya placed me in the middle of the first row, next to a quiet girl with huge, sad eyes and thin brown braids tied with bows. She was wearing a white pinafore and had a schoolbag that was stuffed full.

"Has everyone sat down?" Fira asked.

"Everyone," the redhead reported from the first desk.

"Good." Bereznitskaya smiled. "But it's disappointing that not all of us are here; for some reason two of our new pupils have not shown up. Perhaps they are sick. There's nothing to be done about that. Outside it's not summer with its heat, but winter with its cold."

At the back of the classroom on the long un-whitewashed wall there hung a large portrait of a man in an open jacket and pince-nez. This unfamiliar person looked at us slyly and ironically, as if hoping to find one of those who was for some reason, perhaps because of illness, missing the first day of classes.

"After we get acquainted," Fira turned to everyone, "I will briefly tell you about our school, which is probably older than your grandpas and grandmas. It was started in the last century, before Lithuania became independent, when it was part of Russia and everything depended on the Russian tsar."

After that Fira took from her desk a new class journal, opened it, put on her eyeglasses and, pronoucing the names clearly, began calling the roll.

"Abramson, Moshe!"

"That's me!" responded a chubby little fellow standing to attention with a frightened expression on a face lavishly endowed with golden freckles.

"Ainbinder, Chaim."

"That's right, I'm both – Ainbinder and Chaim," the neighbour of the stuck-up redhead asserted in a falsetto voice and with barely concealed joy, clearly proud of both his first and last names.

"Berger, Leah!" Fira Bereznitskaya continued taking the roll, bestowing a condescending smile on Chaim Ainbinder.

"That's me!" my neighbour twittered like a swallow, flashing her brown eyes bathed in sorrow. She straightened her white pinafore, stepped out from behind the desk and, to the amazement of all her fellow classmates, curtsied.

"Giberman, Mendel!"

"That's me!" shouted the redhead, jumping up from his place and, with pleasure, once again showing off to everyone his muscles and size, which were quite untypical for his age.

"Gindina, Mira!"

Another girl stood up and, without saying anything, bowed to the teacher.

"Dvorkin, Dov-Ber!"

"Dineman, Moshe!"

In response the covers of two old wooden desks slammed down loudly and twice there was heard another, "Me!"

But where was I? Had she forgetton me? I wondered, hurt deeply. I awaited my turn with anticipation, ready as soon as my name was called to jump up from my desk, like our redheaded leader, and loudly report, "Me!" But, as if on purpose, Fira Bereznitskaya did not call my name. Then, glancing around at the pupils, she counted us, apparently comparing the number of those in the classroom with the number indicated in the register.

"Why doesn't she call my name?" I asked myself. "Perhaps my name has not even been included in the list?"

How on the first day of school was I supposed to know the order of the letters in the Yiddish alphabet? Fira Bereznitskaya intended to teach us the alphabet in our upcoming lessons. But later, at home, my father explained to me that my name started with *kuf* and that was why my name was called only at the end of the list, not because of someone's ill will or negligence, but because there was no one in my class on that day whose last name began with the letters *reish*, *shin* or *tov*.

When I finally heard my name called out by the teacher, I sighed with relief, happy to feel myself an equal among equals.

As my Uncle Shmulik liked to say in similar cases, I 'had the honour' to complete the list of our class.

"I didn't forget anyone, did I?" asked Fira.

"No," the class responded in chorus.

"Are there any questions?"

Silence.

"Any at all?" she repeated.

Again there was silence.

"If you don't ask me any questions, you won't learn anything," she rebuked us. "If a person doesn't ask any questions, there is no reason for him or her to attend school!"

"There *is* one question," Mendel Giberman said, the first to express the desire to learn. "What is a tsar?"

"That is a Russian word that means ruler or owner," Fira explained. "But not a simple owner, not someone, for example, who owns a mill or a grocery store. The tsar owns the whole *tsarstvo*, the whole kingdom, the whole land from sea to sea. The tsar once owned our small Jonava too. Do you understand?"

"We understand," the redhead replied before anyone else could.

"Our school was founded with money given by generous Jews. One of them had a match factory in Kėdainiai, another traded in rawhide. At the beginning of the last century they bought this building. Then they brought from Kaunas two capable young teachers, may their memories be blessed, rented living quarters for them, gave them a good salary and said to them, 'Gentlemen, don't ever leave here, settle down in Jonava and teach the children to read.'"

"Did the teachers stay?" asked 'both Ainbinder and Chaim', beating Mendel this time.

"Yes, those benefactors said that if we Jews want to survive, then our children have to study better than anyone else in the world." Fira coughed and wiped her lips with her handkerchief. "Except for our heads, we really have no other weapon to defend ourselves from our enemies. For that reason we have to continue to sharpen and polish our minds. So, on this your first day of your school life, I ask you, will you sharpen and polish your minds, and by that I mean study better than anyone else, or not?"

"Yes! Yes!" there resounded from all sides. "We will, we will! Better than anyone else!" the class promised unanimously.

"Thank you. And who will tell me why we Jews have to study better than anyone else?"

"To defend ourselves against our enemies," was the first hypothesis, offered, of course, by Mendel Giberman, the most quick-witted of us.

"Maybe we shouldn't say so, but we Jews certainly have enough enemies and we can not defeat them with weapons like rifles and canons. Only with our minds, our knowledge, can we beat them. Do you understand?" the teacher asked.

"We understand, we do!" most of the children shouted.

This time Giberman did not express his agreement with Fira. The readhead had something better to do. Mendel was occupied by a matter that could not be delayed; he was devouring a sausage sandwich.

To tell the truth, none of us then understood what kind of defence or what kind of enemies Fira was talking about, but many of us decided it was better to agree with her completely in ignorance than to voice dissent. All of us were spared further duplicity by the one who, either jokingly or seriously, had presented himself as 'both Ainbinder and Chaim.'

"Tell us, please, that man in the pince-nez whose portrait is hanging on the back wall of our classroom, was he one of those teachers brought by the rich men from Kaunas?" he asked suddenly, pointing to the photograph beneath the glass, and then added, "He is dead already, isn't he?"

"Yes, Chaim, he is."

Fira Berznitskaya quickly and easily remembered everyone's name and made an effort to call the pupils by an endearing diminutive.

"My Grandfather Perets, my mother's father, is dead too and he's hanging behind glass on a wall as well," 'Ainbinder and Chaim' announced, to the amusement of us all.

Fira smiled gently.

"That, children, is Sholem Aleichem, a teacher of teachers," she said. "He is my favourite writer. When I read his books, I'm proud that I was born a Jew and that I speak the same language this great man spoke. Do you understand?"

"Yes, yes, yes!" was heard from all sides. Some of the words echoed like dried peas falling on the floor, while others ricocheted from the four corners of the classroom.

The bell finally liberated all of us from questions and answers. We ran outdoors, where there stood a tall maple tree that was a popular resting site for starlings and sparrows. With enthusiastic shouting the older pupils were soon chasing after a battered ball on the well-trodden empty yard. The gate served as their goal. Some friends of the players followed the match from a distance, while the goats, who weren't sporting types either, followed what was going on from the grassy area.

After the break Fira Bereznitskaya began asking each of us about our parents, whether they had been living in Jonava long and what their occupations were.

"My father is a hairdresser. His hairdressing salon is on Kovno Street. Fira, you can have your hair cut by him," Mendel Giberman volunteered first, just as one would have expected. "He will cut your hair in the latest style."

The other pupils were more modest. Of course, you couldn't invite your teacher to visit your father's work place if, for example, he was a man's tailor or a carpenter or a blacksmith.

"Leachka, why don't you say something?" Bereznitskaya said, approaching our shared desk.

"I don't have any parents. I live with Grandma Bluma," my neighbour, the girl with the sad brown eyes, replied, embarrassed.

It grew so quiet in the class that one could hear 'Ainbinder and Chaim' sniffing.

Fira couldn't find anything to say.

No one dared ask Leah anything else.

The mournful silence, the kind that you find only in a cemetery, lasted quite a long time. It wasn't interrupted by the teacher, or even by Mendel Giberman. It was as if a gust of unhappiness had blown into the room. We shivered involuntarily.

"Do you all have your primers?" Fira asked after a pause, trying to dissipate the bitter atmosphere of sorrow. "If you don't, please raise your hand."

Not a single hand was raised.

"Excellent. Tomorrow we shall begin, not with stories, but with our ancient alphabet. Do you understand?"

This time we really did understand her!

"Now, children, you are all free to go," Fira Berznitskaya announced, taking off her glasses and putting them into a leather case. She waved sympathetically to my desk partner Leah Berger, who left the room with her class notebook under her arm.

It's certainly no sin to say that the freedom at the end of that first school day was, for each of us, far more appealing than any of our teacher's stories or moral lessons. With a joyful hooting our class ran outside and immediately flew off in various directions like sparrows from a cat.

I adjusted my school bag on my shoulder and headed straight home, without noticing that Leah Berger, in her white pinafore, was walking behind me in the same direction, waving her bag full of who knows what.

"Where do you live?" I asked her.

"At the very end of Rybatskaya Street."

"Imagine that! I live there too, on Rybatskaya, but at the very beginning," I said joyfully. "At my Grandma's."

"Don't you have a father or mother either?" asked Leah, looking not at me but somewhere off in the distance, where one could see the fire tower and the local pump house.

"I do, but where are yours?"

"I don't know. Grandma doesn't say anything to me. I ask, but she says nothing and just gets angry at me and, especially, at my mother."

Leah stopped speaking. She didn't want to tell me anything more. Perhaps she herself did not know. That put an end to my curiosity, all the more so since at the next crossing I had to part with her and run toward my grandmother's house.

"Until tomorrow," I said.

"Until tomorrow," Leah replied sadly. "It's better at school than at home. If you don't mind, I'll wait for you tomorrow morning here, at this corner," she said, pointing toward a post with torn electric wires. "We can walk together. I will be happier that way."

"Agreed," I said and waved goodbye.

I also grew sad. I could in no way understand why it was better for Leah in school than at home. Home was the best place of all! It was always good for me there.

Grandma Rokha was busy in the kitchen, but when she heard my steps, she came out to greet me.

"*Nu?* Tell me, Hirshele, my golden one, what did they teach you at school?"

"Nothing yet."

"I just knew it! What can one learn in that school where your bright Uncle Shmulik simply wore out his pants?"

"Uncle Shmulik?" I said, my eyes opening wide at Grandma.

"When he was small, he went to that same school. But what was the good of it? The way he used to chase the wind is just the way he continues to this day. God willing, he won't end up in jail for the nonsense he spouts. All you hear from him is, 'Lenin-Stalin, Stalin-Lenin.' Soon he won't even remember the name of his own father. If his papa wakes him up at night, instead of Shimon, his father's name, he'll mutter 'Lenin'. Are you hungry? Do you want to eat?"

"Yes."

"How about potatoes in their skin with herring?"

I nodded.

"You're nodding again!" Grandma said angrily. "Don't you know that all nodders are deceivers?"

"With herring, that would be great," I exclaimed, as if I had not heard her last remark. When it came to food and presents I was not short of words.

Grandma Rokha put the potatoes in their skins in a bowl, cut up some herring and buttered a piece of bread for me.

"Eat, Hirshele! Eat it all! Otherwise, you'll be just skin and bones like your Grandpa Dovid." She said this heatedly, but then paused and asked, "At least tell me who you were seated next to, a beautiful little girl or a boy?"

"A girl. Her name is Leah Berger."

"That unfortunate orphan?"

"She said that she doesn't have any parents," I agreed. "How can it be that everyone else in our class has parents but she doesn't? Did her parents die?"

"You never know what life will deal a person," Grandma said, as if she hadn't heard my question. "Poor little Leah had bad luck. Her mother Rivka fell in love with a *goy*, married him and converted in a church."

"A *goy*?"

"I mean a non-Jew, a Catholic, a Lithuanian."

"So?"

"So Bluma, Leah's grandmother, cursed her daughter Rivka and drove her out of the house. She put up a gravestone in the cemetery for her living daughter and instead of giving up her little granddaughter to the *goyim*, kept her."

Then Grandma Rokha stopped.

"What happened next? After the church?"

"I'm not going to tell you any more. You'll sleep badly from such stories."

"Why?"

"Some day you'll know. Right now it's not a girl who is sitting with you on the same bench, but a big misfortune. Don't hurt her or insult her. Pay attention to what I am saying, even fortunate people shouldn't brag about their good fortune; no one can protect himself against trouble behind seven locks! Trouble can open any door without knocking and enter anyone's house, even ours. But, I see you've stopped eating."

"I'm eating, Grandma, I'm eating. But where did Leah's father go to?"

"Why are you pestering me? She doesn't have a papa or mama, that's all there is to it! They disappeared. Just eat! The potatoes are getting cold."

Grandma returned to the kitchen while I sat and idly stuck my fork into the now-cold potatoes. My thoughts revolved not around food, but around Leah. I wanted morning to come. I would meet her where we agreed, near the electric pole with its torn wires. We would set out for school together, me with my backpack and Leah with the briefcase that her grandmother had packed with who knows what.

"I won't ask her anything," I said to myself, "or try to comfort her with words, but for the whole way I'll look after her and think about 'the great misfortune' that sits at the desk next to me and touches me with its unseen tentacles. I will be silent because silence is better than words. When you are silent there is no need to lie or to demand that others tell you the truth that is painful for them."

Evidently, I was fated to become familiar with the alphabet of misfortune sooner than with the written alphabet that was illustrated with jolly pictures in the school primer.

After the departure of the Kremnitser family to France, Mama no longer had a job. She had no desire to hire herself out as a nanny again, taking care of a young heir of a local merchant or wealthy shopkeeper. Even if you looked with a lantern during the daytime you would be hard pressed to find such a warm, kind household as the Kremnitsers', or such a sweet, affectionate pupil as Raphael, Reb Yeshua Kremnitser's grandson. But nor was Mama attracted by the unenviable fate of a lifetime as a housewife.

"I will provide for you, Hennie," my father said to comfort her. "I have more than enough work, thank God. Don't trouble your head, take it easy and enjoy yourself. You and I won't have to go begging like Avigdor Perelman. I'm even thinking about getting some help, perhaps taking on another apprentice as an assistant, in addition to our revolutionary Shmulik."

"Why not take one? However, at my age I would be ashamed to be dependent and a freeloader. A person can choke on bread he doesn't earn," Mama said. "Don't try to convince me otherwise. You and my brother are both pretty handy and can cook, so you won't starve. But I still want to find some kind of work. If I don't, then I'll become a cook, put my apron on and cook and roast for you." She continued, "It's easy to say that I'll find some appropriate work, but if all I know how to do is look after children or prepare food, then God knows how long my search might last. It might lead nowhere at all."

Hennie was sorry that she hadn't listened to the advice of her benefactor Reb Yeshua long ago, before she got married, and had gone to Kaunas to learn to be a seamstress. If she had, she would have had no worries now, since seamstresses earned as much as men's tailors. But Hennie had been afraid of losing what was most precious to her, her Shleimke, even though she should have trusted that someone who truly loves another can wait years for the one he loves.

In the beginning her search was discouraging. Hennie had no idea where to turn, or to whom to offer her services. She suffered very much from her feeling of helplessness.

But, as often happens in life, success came by chance. One fine day, on Sadovaya Street near the Great Synagogue, Mama was suddenly stopped by her former employer, the owner of the roadside inn with the attractive name 'Drop in at Itsik's.'

"Well, who do I see here?" he said with exaggerated joy. "Is it you, Hennie?"

"So it seems. Up to now, no one has taken my place."

Meeting the tactless, uncouth Itsik Berdichevsky was unpleasant for her and she didn't attempt to conceal her hostility.

"Sweetie, I hardly recognized you!" continued the innkeeper. "You're even more beautiful, my dear, than you were before. You've filled out. In a word, you're like a ripe berry. Not a single peasant would pass by such a tasty treat!"

"Excuse me, Mr. Berdichevsky, I'm in a hurry. Someone is waiting for me in regard to an important matter. I can't be late."

"Where can you rush to in our God-forsaken shtetl? No matter where you hurry, you'll still end up in the same stagnant swamp. I envy those Kremnitsers! They said 'Adieu' to everyone and took off – and not just to anywhere, but to glittering Paris! How happy I would be if I had the opportunity to move there! But you can't get far with the amount of capital that I have. With such small change I couldn't even open a café in Paris."

"Don't make me cry!"

"There, every step you take there are luxurious establishments – restaurants, bars, and bistros. And what a fancy public! Not horse cabbies, not drunken peasants, but ballerinas, female singers, artists and actors. I saw that in a movie. It's not like it is at the inn of the insignificant Itsik Berdichevsky that attracts all kinds of trash! Stop twitching, I'll let you go wherever you want in a moment. Just tell me whether you're working somewhere or are you sitting at home taking care of your little hubby?"

"I'm not working."

"Well, would you like to come back to work for me? We've expanded, made improvements, got some new furniture, new tables and chairs and even put in a toilet."

"No."

"Why are you so negative, speaking as if I were your worst enemy? After all, I didn't criticize you for the way you worked and I didn't pay you with blows but with good money. I could up your wages if you returned to work for me. Who would turn down a good salary just become some drunken, loutish peasant tried to lay his dirty paws on you, or sized you up as a bedmate? You got angry for no good reason and left me in a huff! I didn't let anyone insult you in any way."

"Thank you," Mama said to Berdichevsky. "What can you do if a person's honour is dearer to him than money? God willing, I'll find another place."

Itsik Berdichevsky scratched the back of his head where his hair was thick as wild grass.

"Honour is a good thing," he said with considerable regret, "but in our time, to put it frankly, not a very profitable one. So, listen, I'm not the scum that some people think I am."

"I don't think you are."

"You can't eat a walnut whole. You need to crack it open to get to the essence. So what can you say about a person? His essence is not concealed under a shell but under his armour. Someone who is considered a hawk might, upon closer observation, turn out to be a dove. But let's talk instead about work. I know a good house where they need a housekeeper. Do you understand what I am talking about?"

"Yes, I do."

"Shall I give you the address?"

"Yes, please!"

"Kudirkos Street, number eight. That's the house of the Kogan couple. They're not poor, but they're all on their own. Last year their son Perets took off for the pampas of Argentina. If the Kogans ask who advised you to come to them, say Itsik Berdichevsky. I'm a distant relative of Reb Ruvim Kogan. Do you remember the address?"

"Kudirkos 8."

"That's right. Go see them straight away! They're good people. And good luck! But if it doesn't work out, don't cry, just drop in at 'Itsik's Place'. I'll always be willing to have you work for me and even ready to give your husband a guarantee."

Hennie didn't try to clarify what kind of guarantee the crafty Berdichevsky might give her husband. She thanked the innkeeper for his unexpected kindness, but headed home rather than to Kudirkos Street to discuss the matter with the lonely Kogans.

"What's going on, Hennie dear? You've begun to disappear mysteriously and you're spending much more time outside than at home," the inherently curious Shmulik asked his sister. "In my opinion, decent women don't exchange their home hearths for the gap-toothed cobblestone streets of their shtetl."

"Shmulik, did you only realize today that your sister is a dissolute girl of the streets?"

"Will you two ever stop teasing each other?" my usually calm father said, raising his voice. "My head is spinnng from your stupid skirmishes and, furthermore, the pedal of my sewing machine isn't working."

"What, can't we even joke around?" grumbled Shmulik.

"All right, all right, you know-it-all. Perhaps you could tell me whether you know the Kogans, whose only son left recently for Argentina."

"I know Perets, he's a sharp fellow. Don't put your finger in his mouth. But I never had any contact with his parents."

"Wait a minute! Is that the Ruvim Kogan who owned the Shell petrol station where you leave Jonava to head for Kaunas?" asked my father.

"Perhaps," said Mama, neither confirming nor rejecting her husband's suggestion.

"And why, my dear do you need a petrol station out of the blue?" asked Shmulik ironically.

"To tell you the truth, I don't need a petrol station, Shmulik," Mama smiled mischievously and added, "I have enough fuel to last me for the rest of my life."

"So what do you need from them?" her brother inquired.

"Nothing."

Mama didn't want to say anything prematurely. When the matter had been settled and she had agreed with the Kogans about the conditions of her employment, then she would explain everything. After all, it was shameful not to work, to spend whole days doing nothing.

But Shmulik would not have been Shmulik if he had not fought for a victory to the very end. "And what kind of work do you count on from those old Kogans? Will you dress them in the morning, wash them on Fridays, feed them and take them for a walk in the park every day?"

"Leave her alone," said Father, defending Mother. "While you're talking nonsense instead of sewing loops on the belt of someone's trousers you're sewing the fly shut."

Mama was in no hurry to reach a final decision. She vacillated, considering whether or not to go to the unfamiliar Kogans. After all, who would want to be the servant of two infirm old people, with their moaning and caprices, even if they were rich? Her uncertainty increased after she met the midwife Mina in at the market among the peasants with poultry in their carts.

"It's been quite a while since we've seen each other," the widow complained.

"Yes, it has."

"Your little fellow must be going to school already."

"He is. He's in the first grade."

"The children grow up like trees while we grow head down, like carrots."

"There's nothing you can do about that. You can't argue with time. You can't scare it off the way you would a horse."

"Whether you argue or not, all the same eventually you lose. I'm getting ready for my journey to my Gershon, may his memory be blessed."

"But you haven't finished welcoming the babies of Jonava into the world; just see how many pregnant women are waddling around town! Our husbands are putting the effort in, Mina."

"So what if they are trying their best? Their wives shouldn't count on me anymore. There was once a midwife named Mina, but she is not around any more. Her arms are not the same, nor her legs, nor her heart." Mina smiled, but her smile was a sad one. But then she perked up. "How good it is that I ran into you! I've been thinking and thinking about who could replace me when I am reunited with my Gershon. You, Hennie, you are the one!"

"Me?"

"You know what a price women pay giving birth. You yourself risked death twice. Every Jewish town, every shtetl, has to have not only its own rabbi, but also its own midwife.

Without us midwives the rabbi would have nothing to do. All the synagogues would be empty; there would be no one to pray there."

Although Mama was stupefied by such an unexpected idea, Mina continued. "You probably think I'm out of my mind, finding work for you! You won't get rich from what you earn helping women give birth; you won't be able to build a house with such earnings. You will be paid less with money than with gratitude but, on the other hand, you can't buy such gratitude with money. Basically, Hennie, that's the way it is. So Hennie, while I'm still alive, I will teach you."

"Mina, you have simply amazed me. I don't know what to say. I will have to consult with my husband," Mama muttered, perplexed.

"So consult, consult. I will wait. I'm not going to die while I'm waiting for an answer."

The meeting with Mina completely threw Mama. She couldn't get Gershon's widow's words out of her head about every shtetl needing both a rabbi and a Jewish midwife.

At home she didn't say anything about Mina's idea. She stayed silent, since she only needed to open her mouth for Shmulik to make fun of her and Shleimke would, she was sure, be angry.

No, definitely not. Hennie would not become a midwife. Even though seven years had passed, the memory of the suffering that had twice been her fate at the Jewish Hospital still tore at her soul. Jonava wouldn't be without a rabbi or a midwife; Mina would find another student among the Jewish women in the shtetl, while she, Hennie, would find an easier occupation.

"Get it into your head, it is not up to you to earn your keep!" her mother-in-law stressed when Hennie went to visit her. "During the day a woman should occupy herself with domestic matters like cooking, cleaning, ironing and washing and at night, excuse me for saying it, she shouldn't be idle in bed. What kind of husband is it who cannot provide for his wife? Thank God, your Shleimke has no reason to complain about a lack of clients. My Dovid was the same when he was young, he didn't straighten his back for days and nights. He would mend whatever came his way because he had ten mouths to feed. Listen to some good advice, sit quietly at home. You don't know what kind of people you might end up working for. We don't have any other Kremnitsers in town."

When discussing work conditions, everyone, relatives and non-relatives alike, insisted on that Hennie should be able to eat at her employers' house. The food would be enough even if she didn't receive any other benefit. However, Hennie had a secret dream, one she didn't want to share with anyone. Her dream had been born right after the departure of Isaac and her benefactors the Kremnitsers from Jonava. Hennie dreamed of scraping together a decent amount of money and then, one fine day, just saying to her husband, "Listen, Shleimke! You and I have lived our whole lives in just one place. Are we going to do so until we die? After all, life is hurtling past Jonava like an express train, signalling farewell with its whistle and leaving us only a memory of its faint smoke."

"Why in just one place? Next Saturday we can go visit Kaunas. We can visit my brother Motl and his Sarah and see our niece."

"Of course, we can visit Kaunas. But how about some place further?"

"What do you mean further? Let's visit Kaunas for a day or two and then return home, to Jonava."

"It's a simple matter to go to Kaunas and come home," Hennie replied. "But what, for example, would it be like to pack our bags and travel, not to your younger brother, but to your older one. To Isaac. Wouldn't you like that?"

"To Paris? To Isaac? But he hasn't had time to get settled there yet!" Shleimke's eyes widened, as if Hennie had put some drops in his eyes.

"Yes, to Paris," she said calmly. "What do you think we're living in this world for? Just to see the bend in the Vilija River and the Old Believers in Skaruliai? Or just to fill our bellies?"

"Apparently not even a policeman could stop you!" her husband would have grumbled, if he had responded aloud.

"Our bellies have got used to *tismes*, to gefilte fish and holiday pie with cinnamon, and that makes them happy," Hennie continued. "But you know very well where those culinary joys end up in the morning; in the latrine! But there are some joys that warm the heart for your whole life."

When Hennie, who still had no money, brought the conversation around to this topic, Shleimke listened and became more and more gloomy. His face suddenly appeared wrinkled like that of an old man, whether from dissatisfaction or from surprise.

"What are you frowning about? I don't intend to travel on the money that you have earned. Calm down! I won't spend a single one of your *litas*. I'm not a cripple; I'll earn the money for the trip myself somehow."

"Hennie, do you have any idea how much a return ticket to Paris costs?"

"When I learn the amount, then I will know. Every month I'll set aside ten *litas*," Mama said. "Within a year, I hope, I'll have the necessary amount. Imagine how Isaac and Sarah will be amazed when we appear together at their door, you in a felt hat and I in a new silk dress. I'll write to Ethel Kremnitser. I have her address. Perhaps she will meet us at the train station and we can stay with her and Mr. Aaron and see Raphael.

As often happened with my father, after he had vented his anger, he calmed down. His stern expression mellowed and his face became smooth and shone, like after shaving.

"And then where?" he asked with a barely perceptible smile.

"What do you mean?"

"Perhaps next year, after Paris, we'll have acquired a taste for travel and we'll cross the ocean to America? After all, we must taste the delights that Leah and Philip sell in their store!"

"Why not?" replied Mama smiling. "If you don't dream, why live at all?"

Father was silent, not having an answer to the question. Why live at all? He just shrugged his shoulders.

Mama didn't go to see the old Kogans right away. She thought things over, dealing with her doubts and pondering on the advantages. Finally she set off for Kudirkos Street.

It took Ruvim Kogan, the owner of the one-storey brick house, a long time to open the door because he had trouble inserting the key into the keyhole.

"Are you coming from the pharmacist Nota Levita?" he asked, when the felt-covered doors finally had mercy on the old man and opened wide.

"No," Mama replied.

"Forgive me, please. My old friend Nota promised to send the pills that Dr. Blumenfeld prescribed for Nekhama and me with his assistant Mirra. Alas, we can no longer walk such a distance. We have legs, but for some reason they refuse to move. 'Enough!' they say, 'we don't want to carry you any more, so don't beg us to.' And our eyes say the same thing. 'Enough, we don't want to serve you any more. Full stop!' Even our eyeglasses are on strike. 'For many years,' they say, 'you could see everything through us so you should just thank us for that.' So that's the way it is. Come in, please, don't hesitate! Except for Dr. Blumenfeld and that thief Hannah, whom we chased away in shame, no one has come to visit us recently. So we're glad even when the mice put in an appearence. I wait every evening until they come out of their holes and squeak. I greet them and thank them for being willing to spend some time with Nekhama and me. It's just a pity that we can't have coffee with them."

The tall, tanned Ruvim Kogan, who had a large head of white hair and wore creased trousers, a blue shirt and house slippers that flopped around like frogs, led mother into the living room and grandly gestured for her to sit down.

"Nekhama, we have a guest!" he shouted.

No one responded.

"Nekhama!" the old man called out once more. "A guest, I said."

Kogan's wife did not appear for a long time. Finally, the small, toy-like Nekhama appeared to float out from behind a screen. She extended her arms, excused herself for the delay, nodded and sat down opposite their guest.

"If I may ask, I'd like to know with whom I have the honour?" Kogan said.

"I'm Hennie Kanovich, the daughter of Shimon Dudak."

"Very pleased to meet you, Hennie Kanovich, the daughter of Shimon Dudak." Her host rummaged around in his dried up memory, as if in a purse where some old coins rattled around. "Dudak? Dudak? The cobbler from Kovno Street? Isn't he the one who mended my boots long ago?"

"Yes, the very one," Mama responded with satisfaction. "I'm his eldest daughter."

Mama was tempted to jog his shallow memory and add to it by telling him about her husband the tailor, or about her work for the Kremnitsers, but Kogan didn't give her the opportunity.

"Very pleased," he repeated and asked grandly. "How can I be of service to you, Mrs Kanovich?"

"I was informed that you are looking for a housekeeper."

"You were not deceived. We are looking. We have been looking for a long time. Nekhama and I cannot manage without help. We got rid of our previous housekeeper, Hannah, as I already informed you. Her hands weren't clean and she stole things from us."

"For several years I worked in the home of Reb Yeshua Kremnitser, serving as nanny to his grandson, Raphael, preparing food and sometimes even taking the place of Reb Yeshua in his hardware store when he was sick," Mama managed to put in.

"Oh, the Kremnitsers! Aaron always filled up his car at our petrol station. He was the first Jew in Jonava to have a Rolls-Royce! As for Reb Yeshua, he was really a righteous person. We are the same age; he was born in June and I in December, in 1859. We both appeared in the world, so to speak, before the new era. So that's the way it is! You have excellent recommendations."

Nekhama did not take part in the conversation, but dozed quietly in the soft plush armchair.

"You probably know that our son left for Argentina?" Mr. Kogan continued.

"Yes."

"He promised that as soon as he got set up there he would take us to join him, but, tell me, what would we do in Argentina? Nekhama, may God give her health, and I danced our last tango long ago." Ruvim Kogan sighed, then said unexpectedly, "I see that you have a kind face and good, honest eyes."

"Thank you," Mother said, embarrassed.

"I believe that we will get along. You'll be more like a daughter and not a servant."

"How can you say that?"

"We will not insult you. We'll give you a good salary. We aren't poor or misers. We don't intend to take anything with us into the next world, or to cover our graves with paper flowers made of banknotes of various denominations."

The sensible and talkative Ruvim Kogan gestured toward his dozing wife, who was curled up in her chair, and then again addressed their guest. "But since we are still alive, let's get down to business. We paid that thief Hannah twenty-five *litas* a month, but I'm prepared to offer you thirty-five. We will, of course, share our food with you. We will eat at the same table. It's a pity that you are much taller than Nekhama. In her wardrobe there is a whole store of all kinds of dresses, skirts and blouses, which she hasn't worn for quite some time. Her wardrobe is food for the hungry moths."

"What do you mean?" Mama blushed. "I don't need anything. I have clothes and shoes."

"Well, to be honest, giving you such things would hardly beggar us. However, there is one snag. If, God forbid, we become ill during the night, you will have to sleep, pardon me for saying so, not with your husband but with us. In a separate room of course. Think about it. Perhaps it doesn't suit you, in which case you'll have to seek work elsewhere."

"I have already decided. With your permission I will start work tomorrow."

"Wonderful! Nekhama, Nekhama!" Kogan woke his wife.

"What?" the old woman replied quietly. "Is there a fire somewhere? Did a child, God forbid, fall under the wheels of a carriage? I hear you, I hear you, Ruvim, I'm not completely deaf. I am a little deaf, it's true, but my dear, who said I was totally deaf?"

"Nekhama, please meet our new carer. Just imagine, she worked for Reb Yeshua Kremnitser!"

"My name is Hennie," Mother said.

"My Lord, how young she is! She probably doesn't even know how to cook yet," the mistress of the house remarked sceptically.

"I do know how. Not everything, of course. But what I don't know I will be happy to learn."

"I like your honesty. We expect you tomorrow. Here is the key," Kogan said, passing it to his new housekeeper like an engagement ring. "In the morning Nekhama will still be in bed, so you and I will begin by sitting down to coffee together."

Hennie went home quite satisfied.

"Well?" Shleimke said to his wife.

"Everything is fine."

"What kind of people are your new exploiters?" interrupted Shmulik.

"Wonderful people," Mama said.

"Oh, y-e-s," her brother replied. "With you, sister, it's hard to dream about a revolution."

As Mama had judged, Nekhama and Ruvim Kogan turned out to be wonderful, albeit very unfortunate. They needed a housekeeper less to cook them fancy dishes, or to scrupulously clean their luxurious home to the last speck of dust, , or even to take them for a walk, but rather to have someone to pour out their pained souls to and to save them from total isolation. What they really needed, as had been the case with Ethel Kremnitser, was sympathy. What they needed was an understanding and responsive companion who would lighten their sorrow until their son Perets got himself together enough to take them from Lithuania to distant Buenos Aires.

From her first days of work at the Kogans Mama discerned their sadness and great need. It turned out that, as in the home of Reb Yeshua and Ethel Kremnitser, she would be paid good money not for the pea soup and cinnamon pastry, for the *latkes* and potatoes with prunes that she prepared, but for her real, sincere sympathy that would, at least for a short time, alleviate their pain and brighten up their loneliness.

The Kogans were not fussy eaters. They ate little, mainly dairy dishes, occasionally lean meat, chicken and *latkes*. They paid no attention to how Hennie moved around with a broom or wet rag, preferring rather her healing conversations, which sometimes lasted until long after midnight.

"A good son should first of all bury his parents and only then leave for America or Argentina," said Ruvim Kogan. "How old is your little fellow?"

"Seven."

"May you and your husband enjoy him. You'll still have him with you for a long time. After all, he hasn't learned about Buenos Aires or New York yet, or about Rio de Janeiro." Ruvim took a sip of coffee from a porcelain cup and continued. "If I had the authority, I would first of all issue a decree that forbids an only son or daughter from leaving their parents' home before they die. That would be just. One can not remain only with the mice."

"Yes, that's right and just. But what there has never been and never will be in this world is justice."

"Justice is not available anywhere. And what does not exist, Ruvim, my dear, should not be sought," said Nekhama. "You can't chain people to you. You have to admit, we were unjust too. I think that only unjust people are happy because they don't think about others, only about themselves and their own welfare."

Mama couldn't believe her ears. Did the toy-like, old Nekhama, who spent whole days dozing, indifferent to everything, to Buenos Aires, to Jonava and even to her own house, really say that? Hennie hadn't heard such remarks even at the Kremnitsers or at home on Rybatskaya Street or from Ephraim Kapler, from whom she and Shleimke had long before rented living quarters.

The senile helplessness of the partially deaf Nekhama and the affected bravado of Ruvim, who dressed as smartly as a hussar and their bitter loneliness overshadowed Mama's dream of traveling to Paris. Who could she leave them with? If something happened to the old folks during her absence she would never forgive herself. At such an age the only one eager to offer help would come along with his scythe and then it would all be over and done with. It was clear she would have to forget about Paris, or at least delay the trip until the Kogans' son Perets showed up. But nothing was to be seen of him. Either his letters did not arrive or, for some reason, he didn't write.

The longer she worked for them, the closer Mama grew to her lonely employers and the Kogans responded to her in the same way.

"Without you, Hennie, we would have been quite lost. Definitely lost." Ruvim had very quickly begun to use the familiar '*ty*'. "Who still needs us old ruins except Dr. Blumenfeld and my old friend Nota Levita? You were sent to us by God Himself!" he said effusively.

Mama often returned home around midnight.

"*Nu?*" My father always greeted her in the same pithy Jewish manner.

"They held me back; they were unwilling to let me go. So I just sat there and sat there. I ended up sitting with them until the stars were all out. I feel so sorry for them," Mama said, justifying herself. "Kogan says that God Himself sent me to them."

"The God who sent you could have shortened your work day by a couple of hours," Father joked. "After all, we're still husband and wife as far as I'm aware, aren't we? I don't think we've divorced yet."

"And we will never divorce!" Mama replied.

Her brother also reproached her. "Hennie, you have no class consciousness. None! You are an incorrigible servant with petty-bourgeois pretentions."

However, Mama didn't care; she gave no thought to what kind of consciousness she might have. She did what her heart commanded her to do. She said to herself, "Can one possibly look on indifferently when on a nearby street someone is suffering and slowly fading away from unbearable solitude?"

"Are you starving here without me?" she asked Shleimke, hoping she wouldn't be interrogated any further.

"No. We're just bored. We miss you."

"So, be bored! What do I care? I'm going to bed."

Hennie undressed and lay down. Exhausted, she fell asleep as soon as her head touched the pillow. She dreamed of Paris, the light-filled city of her now abandoned dream, of the famous arch erected in honour of the Emperor Napoleon and the Eiffel Tower, both of which the newly minted Frenchman Isaac had described so enthusiastically.

From somewhere in the nocturnal haze there emerged in the dim light of the street lanterns the slim silhouette of Ethel Kremnitser in a mauve dress and a stylish hat. She was running toward Hennie, her high heels clattering on the pavement, while behind her trotted Raphael, older than she remembered, in a schoolboy's uniform and a stylish cap.

"'Ennie!" he shouted. He was the first to reach his former nanny and buried himself in her skirt, as he used to do as a child when he lived with his mother and grandfather in Jonava. "'Ennie!"

"Do you want to pee-pee?" she said with loving irony, recalling the words the child had used to ask to go to the bathroom.

"Pee-pee," laughed Raphael. "Pee-pee!"

Ethel Kremnitser squinted in the electric lights and dabbed at her tears with an embroidered handkerchief.

Meanwhile lights shone and were refracted. Cars honked and from somewhere came the sound of music, the beating of a drum and the melancholic roulades of a saxophone, while the flat Paris moon stretched over the city like a thin cake that had grown cold in the stove of the starry sky; a cake baked in the shtetl bakery of Chaim Gershon Fain.

4

Customers of various clans and tribes came to my father's workshop. His regular customers were mainly Jews with medium or even higher incomes. Due to the recommendation of Reb Yeshua Kremnitser, he had gained the business of clients who used to frequent other tailors. These included the pharmacist Nota Levita, Dr. Isaac Blumenfeld, Reb Ephraim Kapler, owner of the house where we rented a room, and the owner of the town bakery, Chaim Gershon Fain.

Christians also eagerly availed themselves of my father's services. He sewed an overcoat for the principal of the local *gymnasium,* who was a distant relative of President Smetona. He sewed a cassock for the young priest Bartkus, who was the successor of Vaitkus, the previous head superior of the Jonava Catholic church, whom the curia had sent to the religious academy in Rome. He didn't, however, decline orders from townspeople of little means either. For sewing or repairing he always took less money from them than from the rich. Father didn't pay much attention to compliments, which he considered exaggerated, and he rejected every tempting offer to relocate to Kaunas, the capital at that time.

On more than one occasion the owner of the well-known atelier on Svoboda Alley in Kaunas, Alex Ziskind, a frequent guest of Ephraim Kapler, buzzed in his ears about the excellent abilities of his tenant, attempting to lure Father there.

"Kaunas is the Paris of Lithuania!" exclaimed Ziskind. "My atelier sews clothes for diplomats, the ambassadors of England and America and for ministers in our own government. I guarantee that you will receive a fantastic salary. In a year or two you could buy a house of your own on Zelennaya Gora and live the good life."

It was clear, however, that Father didn't want to live the way the lords lived in Odessa. He was quite satisfied with his life in Jonava where his parents lived, where he knew every alley and every cow in the herd that the herdsman Eronimas drove out to pasture each morning to the simple tune of his reed pipe. Let his younger brother Motl live in Kaunas and sew overcoats for diplomats and jackets for their wives. In contrast to Shleimke, Motl had a particularly tactful and well-disposed manner with women.

Father looked for a second apprentice in order to be able to increase the number of customers he could serve and to lend greater solidarity to his flourishing business, as Shmulik referred to it. As strange as it may seem, he was suddenly aided in this search by Ephraim Kapler's janitor Antanas, who lived with his wife and son in the basement and continually bothered Shleimke with the same question.

"Saliamonas, do you really not smoke?"

"No, Antanas, I don't smoke."

"And don't drink?"

"No."

"But you must!" Antanas said in surprise. "What fine fellows the Jews are! They save money on everything. All of them are sober. Just take our house. It seems to be charmed. No one drinks and no one smokes. There is no one to drink with, no one to bum a cigarette from," he complained. "My own son Julius can't stand tobacco himself and refers to shag as a stinking poison."

"He's right."

"Julius is a good lad, but he's lazy. From morning to evening he wastes his time sitting by the river with a fishing line trying to catch bleaks and roaches."

"So maybe he'll become a fisherman."

"Since we're talking about it, it would be better for him to become a tailor. Saliamonas, perhaps you would consider taking the lad on for a trial period, at least to teach him to mend things. He's a quiet type, not a troublemaker. And he relates well to your brothers."

"To my brothers?"

"To Jews, I mean. People say that the Jews are the models for everyone; they don't wear out their trousers sitting in pubs, don't engage in fist-fighting, don't waste money on cigarettes and don't smack their women when they're drunk. They sit for days at a time, earning money. Try him! If it doesn't work, then send him packing, to put it mildly, and let him spend the rest of his life wth a fishing rod, providing fish soup for us and leftovers for the cat."

"How old is your son?"

"Seventeen."

"Well then, why not try and see what happens. If it doesn't work out, he can still run off to the river."

"Try him. Just try. I'll pray for you, Saliamonas, as God is my witness, I will. I will get down on my knees in church and for the first time pray for a Jew. I swear on my cross."

"Antanas, we should pray for everyone. The sun shines on everybody and the birds in the trees sing for everyone. Why shouldn't we take this as an example for us humans who want to do something good for our neighbour?"

"That's so, but we aren't birds, Saliamonas. And we hardly resemble the sun!"

"All right, so have your lad drop in and, meanwhile, pray for me in your church."

"Fine."

Julius turned out to be a capable fellow and mastered the basics of the tailor's trade much quicker than Shmulik had. Furthermore, without difficulty, indeed with enviable ease, he learned conversational Yiddish and became an irreplaceable translator for the flourishing business. Neither Shleimke nor Shmulik could boast of their linguistic prowess; both expressed themselves in Lithuanian with difficulty and with many grammatical mistakes and, after all, you can't speak with customers about style using just your fingers.

With the appearance of Julius the number of customers increased, as can be imagined, with the addition of local officials and well-off peasants who eagerly came from their farms to have Shleimke sew them new clothes for the major church holidays and the weddings of their offspring.

In contrast to Shmulik, young Julius was the silent type. He preferred answering questions to asking them. When Father was busy, Shmulik taught the lad, not only acquainting him with the secrets of cutting and sewing, but teaching him too, in a simple way, about the difficult fate of the workers of the world, who were forced to bend their backs for the benefit of their fat-cat persecutors.

"Why are you filling his head with all this nonsense? Persecutors-shmersecutors! You'd be better off talking about girls! After all, it's about time you started thinking about choosing a helpmeet, not the leader of the world proletariat!" my father remarked, trying to rein in his brother-in-law.

"But this green young fellow should know that not all bosses are such angels as you are, Shleimke."

"You'll end up badly, Shmulke, with your foolish chatter. You certainly will! I believe the *okhrana*, the tsar's secret police, have long had you under surveillance. In jail you'll be mending prisoners' uniforms, not sewing trousers."

Although Father was not a risk-taker by nature, he reacted to the authorities' attacks on the rebels with a deep-seated disgust, even though, in his view, the world should be improved not by rebellion, but by work. What advantage would there be if one lot of stupid and cruel rulers were replaced by others who were no different? A change in regime would not make a tailor a Rothschild or a Rothschild a tailor. The only ones to win would be those who thoughtlessly first shouted, 'Down with them!' and were the first to throw themselves into the embraces of any victor.

In the evenings Shmulik disappeared to the outskirts of Jonava where, it seemed, his secret meetings with his fellow-thinkers took place. In the morning he appeared at work angry and half-asleep, sometimes even falling asleep with a needle and thread in his hands. Father would call out to him, ironically citing the first words of the anthem of the Communist Internationale, "Arise, cursed of the earth!"

Being branded 'cursed of the earth', he would jump up from his chair, shake himself like a rain-soaked puppy and, in an effort to reduce the tension and minimize his guilt, apologetically, in a cracked baritone, sing the rest of the anthem in a loud and deliberately free manner. "The whole world of violence we shall destroy to its foundations and then . . ."

Shmulik stretched with enjoyment and yawned with pleasure.

"We shall destroy, destroy . . ." Father continued ironically. "You, hero of ours, keep a sharp lookout to see that they don't destroy you before you and your comrades suceed in destroying their foundations."

For a while Shmulik stopped giving sermons about the new, just world to Julius, who had no idea about politics, and devoted himself to work. But soon he would start up again on the same topic.

Finally Mother, who was busy taking care of the old Kogans, became concerned too.

"They might, God forbid, punish my brother. Geraitis has already warned him a number of times," Hennie said, as she made the bed. "It's not easy to find such a good fellow as that policeman."

"Shmulik just spits on all warnings. For him they are like water off a duck's back."

Shleimke undressed and lay down. Hennie quietly lay down next to him. The darkness was heavy with temptation, but they did not yield to it immediately.

"May God forgive me, but if fate has already decided that he be taken, let it be out somewhere on the street, just not in our house! The publicity would do us no good at all. The business of a tailor is to sew, not to wag his tongue. I've never heard of someone being thrown into prison for sewing. A tailor's jail is his work place. He is sentenced to that place for a life term."

"Perhaps our fears are groundless. We shouldn't panic."

"They're not groundless! How do you explain to that reckless brother of yours that Lithuania is not our land where we can do as we please?" Father said, coughing in his agitation. "How can one explain to him that if we are not asked, we shouldn't dig rows in someone else's garden or plant what the owner doesn't want planted?"

"Shmulik thinks differently."

"One shouldn't think differently, but correctly. The owner wants to plant onions and cabbages in his furrows, while Shmulik jumps in there with his own seeds and tries to plant something else!" continued Father.

"You can't change him. Whatever we say to Shmulik, no matter how we try to convince him, he still won't listen to us. Let's go to sleep instead."

"Yes, let's."

Then she cuddled up to him and felt their bodies merge into one as if they were fused together. They didn't separate until dawn.

Outside the autumn was dry, without the rain and fierce winds that would blow down from Finland in the far north. The trees stood in their silent dignity, clothed in green, while those trusting songbirds that had not sought winter refuge in foreign parts nested in them through the winter.

This was the second autumn of my studies at the Yiddish school. I was already a second-grader and lived not with Grandpa and with Grandma Rokha, but with my parents. I got up before sunrise and, afraid of missing my friend Leah Berger, ran to Rybatskaya Street to meet her near the electric pole with the torn wires to comfort her with my words and my silence.

Every morning I would bump into my now somewhat quieter Uncle Shmulik, who stopped me at the threshold, tenderly mussed my hair, pulled my ears and asked with a smile, "How are you, my little proletarian who is taking over the next watch?"

"Fine," I would answer.

Uncle Shmulik would reward me with two dull, painless taps on the forehead and, satisfied by my answer, which masked the fact that actually I had failed to understand his question, immediately disappeared behind our felt-covered door.

My father was amazed by the change that had taken place in his militant brother-in-law. "I don't recognize you, Shmulik. Almost an hour has gone by and you haven't uttered a single word about our parasitical persecutors," Father noted, almost with regret. "Has something happened with your parents?"

"No, I'm just in a lousy mood. Things are good for you, Shleimke. You're like a mole, you hardly ever come up out of your hole into the light of day, you don't listen to the radio and you don't read newspapers. You just ride along on your sewing machine and don't give a damn about anything else."

"What can I do? Evidently, that's what I was destined for, from birth, just to ride that thing."

"Lucky guy! If you just listened to the evening summary of events in Europe, to a broadcast about what is going on under your very nose, you would be terrified. Your face would be darker than the clouds."

"Has war broken out, then?"

"So far they've only declared war against us. Hitler threatens to destroy all of us like cockroaches in the nearest future and to free the world from 'the Jewish plutocrats.'"

"If my memory doesn't deceive me, he promised to destroy all of us a year and a half ago. You were the first to inform me about that promise which, it was claimed, reflected his love of humanity."

"I remember," nodded Shmulik.

"As it says in the Holy Writings, 'there is nothing new under the moon.' For thousands of years people have tried to destroy the Jews. Just tell me who didn't put their hand to the matter, starting way back in ancient times? There were the Romans and the Greeks. But despite all the killlings, we're still here! Maybe, God willing, we will also survive this monster Hitler and continue to exist."

"Maybe we will survive, if Stalin throws all the might of the invincible Red Army against him and halts the Nazis."

"What makes you think that Stalin will stop the Nazis because of the Jews? When someone murders us, the majority in the world usually rejoices and applauds."

"Stalin is for us, for the Jews."

"Shmulik, I couldn't vouch for the non-Jewish tailors, never mind for any foreign rulers. They won't risk having their heads cut off for the Jews. I believe that I know our fellow Jews rather well: when it comes to words we love our people ardently, but still business is dearer to us. But that's enough philosophy! Let's end things and conclude a peace treaty."

"Now that's an interesting proposal."

"For a year let's leave aside all chatter about politics!" Father stopped sewing and, focussing suddenly on some idea that had arisen from the depths, expressed it immediately. "This will be our pact by which, from today, we will send to all the devils both Stalin and Hitler and also our own President Smetona! You will agree to throw your dangerous radio out into the garbage and you and I will speak only about pleasant things, about those things we know and love best. I, Shmulik, for all the inconveniences I cause you, will raise your salary but, please, just leave aside your constant condemnation of the ills of capitalism since, in any case, you won't improve the world. As it was in the time of Adam and Eve, even so today; no one can stand alone. In short, shall the two of us make a peace treaty or not?"

"Yes! The conditions, of course, are servile ones, but what won't one do for a class-retarded relative?" Shmulik agreed and, as always, softened his words with a compensatory smile.

With this pact Father hoped to reign in his rash brother-in-law, whom he feared might suffer severely for his loose tongue, "Ending up in two shakes of a bull's tail behind bars, thus depriving the business of a diligent worker." Father, of course, doubted that Shmulik would be able to completely fulfill the conditions of the agreement. He would hardly throw his Philips radio onto the garbage heap; what was more likely was that he would conceal it from Sheyne and Shimon. And no matter how much he was forbidden to speak about politics, he wouldn't be able to restrain himself from bursting forth and criticising the exploiters.

However, Shmulik held out firmly. He ceased criticizing social problems and directing angry remarks against the parasitic persecutors. He suddenly began to focus all of his energy on education. In a light, mischievous tone that caught the imagination of the pious Julius, without any overt intention of undermining the religious beliefs of the Lithuanian lad, Shmulik undertook to acquaint him with the Jewish origin of his Christ.

Julius had no idea of this origin. Doubtfully, he focused his light blue eyes on the older apprentice and after each phrase, sighed deeply and murmured, "What are you saying? That can't be! In that case, what is your conclusion, that the Mother of our God, the Holy Virgin Mary, was Jewish? And that Christ was circumcised like you, *Ponas* Shmulik?" Julius crossed himself three times and then continued, "And that He had a father?"

"Yes, a father, as we all have, in order to continue the human race. And you continue to foolishly repeat, 'She gave birth without a husband . . .' Your virgin gave birth with a husband, a lawful husband. After all, even a hen doesn't produce an offspring without a rooster. Your god, the one depicted in all your churches, is a Jew! A real Jew, both on his mother's side and on his father's."

"What are you saying?" moaned Julius, pushing back his hair, which was the colour of dry straw, from his forehead. "That can't be! I couldn't say anything like that even to my own father, not to anyone! Not a single word!"

"Why?"

"Father would say I was drunk, or would simply pull out his belt to use on me. And for such blasphemy my friends would simply break my bones in some dark alley."

"When people beat you for the truth, you can stand it," said Shmulik, a smile once again shining on his sunken, unshaven cheeks.

My father chuckled.

"Julius, when you go to confession," Shmulik continued, "Quietly, so that the priest doesn't hear, first speak to Christ by addressing him, saying *'Sholem aleichem'* and then do the same with His mother. They understand Yiddish," Shmulik stated, then suddenly exclaimed in alarm. "But, my dear fellow, did you accidently overheat the iron? The room smells of burning!"

Sniffing the air, Julius rushed to the iron, lifted it up, spat on his fingers and touched the bottom of it. He sighed with relief. "It's all right. You can still iron with it." Then, forgetting about Christ and the Virgin Mary, Julius began to carefully iron the trousers of Dr. Blumenfeld who, for his seventieth birthday, had allowed himself the luxury of renewing his wardrobe by having a suit sewn for him from English cloth.

Although Shmulik had stopped fulminating against and criticizing the government, Father was still worried. He was certain that his brother-in-law was leading a double life. Mama was also uneasy.

Their intuition did not deceive them.

On the eve of Yom Kippur Vincas Gedraitis, who was known in the shtetl by the Yiddish expression, '*kimataytid*', almost a Jew, because of his positive attitude toward the Jews, stopped in at Father's workshop.

"Good day," he said, not addressing anyone by name.

"Good day," my father replied, already surmising that the day would not turn out to be a good one. "Sit down, *Ponas* Vincas."

"I'll sit down in the future," replied 'Almost a Jew'. "Soon I will be pensioned off and then I'll sit on a bench, gaze up at the sky and the clouds floating above Jonava and wait until the Policeman on High summons me."

"It's a shame my wife isn't home. She would have treated you to some delicacy," my worried father muttered, trying to delay the unpleasantness he was expecting.

"I've just dropped in for a minute," said 'Almost a Jew', putting his case on his knee and pulling out of it a document with the seal of the Lithuanian Republic on it. "Actually, I've not come to see you, *Ponas* Saliamonas," he said then, "but *Ponas* Dudak. Unfortunately, although people don't believe me, it is very unpleasant for me when I bring them bad news, for which the government pays me, not badly I must say." He paused, focused his gaze on Shmulik, handed him the document and said, "Please, sign your name where the mark is."

While Shmulik was slowly reading the bureaucratic document, 'Almost a Jew' explained the essence of the matter. "By order of the head of the Jonava police, Captain Ignas Rozgi, *Ponas* Shmulikis Dadakas is required to report to the police station on the third of each month. I'm very sorry. Out of friendship, I warned him several times not to wag his tongue or upset the authorities. I did warn him, didn't I?"

"Yes, you did," Shmulik confirmed.

"This measure, of course, is better than being arrested. But, I always ask myself, why do you Jews not keep your dissatisfaction hidden behind your back like a stone? Why do you have to shout it out on every street corner so that the whole world can hear you? We Lithuanians, to speak in confidence, are also not satisfied with the way things are here. Maybe we sometimes even curse the authorities no less than you do. But quietly! No matter how much you criticize someone who is lame, you won't cure him by cursing him in the town square. You too should learn to keep your mouths shut! Silence always pays off in life and is much more useful than crying, 'Down with the government!' I have to go now," 'Almost a Jew' said, getting up and saluting. He straightened his uniform and left.

"Shmulik, so far you've got off with just a small fright," sighed Mama. "It will be good for you to walk to the policestation once a month from the house you're renting from Ephraim Kapler. You'll breathe the fresh air and clear out your head."

I was sitting in the corner doing my homework to the accompaniment of the rattling sewing machine. When the Singer fell silent, I listened to the conversation between Uncle Shmulik and Gedraitis, whom I had previously seen in Grandma Rokha's house. At the Passover table he would munch greedily on the white pieces of matza, while the crumbs would fall on his grey worn uniform with its shiny copper buttons. But no matter how hard I tried to grasp how Uncle Shmulik had disappointed 'Almost a Jew', I could in no way imagine the answer since, after all, he had not robbed, killed or even crippled anybody.

I liked Shmulik far more than any of my other family members. Direct, responsive and jolly, he would joke with me or reproach me, caress me or slap me on the behind. The main thing is that he would always defend me from the criticism of my parents.

"Why don't you just let him be? You just give him instructions all the time. Let him figure things out for himself! He has a head on his shoulders, not a jug of sour milk!"

And in the process of speaking up for me he would refer to me portentously as 'the hope of the Jewish proletariat'.

Father would bcome angry at Shmulik and demand that he stop uttering such dubious compliments.

Shmulik tried not to break his agreement with his brother-in-law, but before two months had passed the necessity of reporting every third day at the police station was no longer relevant.

After Yom Kippur, Mama and Shmulik decided to take me with them on a visit to their parents, Grandpa Shimon and Grandma Sheyne, and my three unmarried aunts, Feiga, Hasya and Pesya, whom, I must confess, I rarely visited.

"Oh my beautiful! Oh you precious one!" Grandma Sheyne sang out as soon as she saw me. "What a handsome fellow you have become, may the evil eye not cause you any harm. My little sunshine, let me give you a kiss."

I offered each of my cheeks in turn and Grandma Sheyne brushed me with her dry rough lips.

Grandpa Shimon waited for a long time until she had finished kissing me and, as he was waiting, with fingers that had often been pricked by his awl, jauntily twisted the overhanging ends of his luxurious peasant moustache. Then he extended his hands, strong as a blacksmith's forge and pulled me to him, pressing me hard against the brass buckle of his belt.

"Little fellow, you have really grown," he exclaimed, rejoicing like a child. "Soon your ear will reach Grandpa's shirt and you will be able to hear how the peas are gurgling in my stomach and, then, you will grow even taller than I am."

My aunts approached ceremoniously as in olden times, strewing many compliments on the way. They then began to knead and pummel me like the dough of a holiday pastry.

At the same time, from a distance, Grandma continued to proclaim joyfully, "Oh you! Oh you!" as her happiness extended into the room like a quiet wave on a lake.

Grandma Sheyne set the table, putting out treats – apple pastry, ginger powdered 'lady fingers' and a small bowl of raisins – then she prepared the tea and poured it into porcelain cups with silver handles and, finally, sat down with Grandpa Shimon, who was silent, but radiant like a polished samovar.

"Enjoy!" she invited the company proudly, taking the first swallow herself. "The tea is homemade, from raspberries. I gathered the berries and dried them myself."

"Hirshele, you can learn to be brave from Gandma Sheyne. When she has no pains she goes out into the forest for raspberries. She has no fear of wolves," said Shmulik lightly.

"The wolves are afraid of me," said Grandma. "As soon as they see such an old monster, they immediately run away in all directions."

"Don't say such bad things about yourself," Hennie said, disapprovingly.

We stayed until late in the evening, when Grandpa Shimon suggested that Mama and I spent the night at their home on Kovno Street rather than going home.

"We'll put Hirshele on the sofa and you, Hennie, for old time's sake, on the floor."

Mama absolutely refused. "Hirshele has school in the morning and, as for old times, my heart still pains me from then."

It was not hard to understand Mama. When she was young there were not enough beds for the children and someone had to sleep on the floor. Hennie, the oldest and the nanny for her younger siblings, would lie down there with the youngest girl, the eight-year-old Hava. Once there was a disaster. One night Hennie accidently put her arm over her sister and suffocated the little one in her sleep.

"No, no! Father, it's time for us to leave," Mama objected again.

She got up from the table and told me to get ready. At that point somebody knocked on the door loudly and insistently. We all looked at each other in fright. Alarmed and fighting his premonition, Uncle Shmulik slowly headed toward the door.

"Who has the Devil brought tonight?" Uncle Shimon inquired of the darkness that had enveloped the room.

The darkness responded only with even more insistent knocking.

Shmulik opened the door. The first person he saw on the threshold was 'Almost a Jew', Vincas Gedraitis.

"*Gut ovt.*" Good evening, he said in Yiddish to the whole family, letting in ahead of him his superior, a round-faced clean shaven man in a coat and cap.

"Are you Shmulik Dudak?" he asked, addressing the person who had opened to door.

"Yes."

"I'm Ksaveras Grigaliunas, representative of the district department of state security. I ask the whole family to forgive me for such a late visit, but our work continues around the clock. I am obliged to serve *Ponas* Shmulik Dudak with an order for his arrest and to undertake a search of your home."

"*Vey tsu mir, vey tsu mir*!" moaned Grandma. Woe is me!

She could not grasp what her son might be guilty of, who had he killed or maimed? Who had he robbed? If she could have, she would have gone to prison instead of Shmulik.

The search did not last long. Neither the petrified sisters, nor their parents, had any idea what the conscientious and harmless Gedraitis was looking for in a room where everything was in full sight. 'Almost a Jew' rummaged in the cupboard and under the bed. For appearances sake he checked the pillows, looked into the old chest of drawers with the iron tools and then reported to his superior, "Nothing suspicious has been found, Mr. Grigaliunas."

For the county representative of state security apparent poverty was hardly sufficiently suspicious or serious evidence. The witnesses, neighbours who were called in to observe the search, shuffled from one leg to the other and looked on with unconcealed curiosity. It was clear they were viewing the inside of a Jewish home for the first time in their lives.

"Will you allow me a question?" asked Shmulik.

"Go right ahead," replied Grigaliunas coldly and super-ciliously, but politely.

"Is it permitted to take warm clothing for the winter?" the prisoner inquired. "A fleece jacket and a shirt, a woollen scarf, a cap with ear flaps, and, excuse me for the expression, underpants?"

"Yes, it is," Ksaveras Grigaliunas replied with aristocratic haughtiness. "Although, in general you'll hardly freeze. For your information our prisons and prison colonies are heated well all winter. After all, we are part of Europe."

"I'm glad to hear that," Shmulik snorted. "But, to tell the truth, I'm cold-blooded, like a finch."

It took Shmulik a long time to collect and carefully pack a big sack with all his *bebekhes* – his stuff. By his expression one could see that Gedraitis was trying to hurry him, but Shmulik was in no rush, as if testing the patience of the unwelcome guests.

"Shmulik," Grandma Sheyne said, alarmed, "Why are you taking so long? These people are waiting! Perhaps the sooner they take you away, the sooner, God willing, you will be released and return home to us."

Taken aback, Ksaveras Grigaliunas, the witnesses and 'Almost a Jew' Gedraitis stared at the woman of the house. In all of their service in the police they had never seen anything like it – a mother hurrying her son out of her house to go with the police! Oh those crazy Jews, those unpredictable madmen; you couldn't tell whether there was more desperation or hope in their eyes.

In the doorway Gedraitis turned and said quietly in Yiddish, so that his superior wouldn't understand, "Don't lose hope! Maybe he'll be released. After all he's not a murderer, just a fool who got mixed up in all kinds of nonsense."

When the strangers left, Feiga was the first to burst out sobbing. After her the other sisters joined her lament.

Grandma sat immobile, staring at the bureau and the eight-branched candlestick on it, as if she was trying to light the candles that were not there while her eyes were filled with grief. Grandpa sniffed with his big nose.

I was the only one who neither cried nor sniffed. I held Mama's hand, in no way able to comprehend why strangers were putting such a good person into jail, a joker and prankster like Uncle Shmulik.

"I will never put anyone in jail! I don't like it when grown-ups cry and sniffle. I don't like it at all!" I exclaimed.

Mama said goodnight to her parents and sisters. Depressed, we went out into the night and headed home.

Above us the stars were shining brightly and in the sky the moon shone like a piece of white peasant cheese.

"It's good that at least it is not possible to put behind bars the light that shines for us all," Mama said. When we approached our house, she said, "Tomorrow you will probably oversleep and miss school."

"I won't oversleep," I answered.

However, the next morning, during a lesson when we were busy with multiplication and were struggling to figure out what nine times nine was, I was thinking not about numbers, but about Uncle Shmulik, wondering when he would return and give me two taps on the forehead.

5

Shmulik's arrest stirred up the whole shtetl. Most alarmed of all were the law-abiding Jews who, for the sake of their own security, never lost an opportunity to try and dig out the truth. For what sins had their fellow Jews, the simple baker or mediocre tailor, been suddenly thrown into prison? If one Jew was put behind bars then it was possible, they logically concluded, that, God forbid, soon the rest would follow.

His fellow shtetl-dwellers tormented my innocent father with questions.

"So, what kind of thing did your apprentice do? Why was he carried off and taken to a place where a respectable Jew doesn't belong, where he could die of shame?" asked Ephraim Kapler, the owner of the house we rented, who was always sensitive to bad news. "Apparently he didn't kill anyone, or rob a shop, or blow up a bank safe?"

"God forbid! My brother-in-law never harmed a fly in his whole life. However, sometimes he talks too much and says what he shouldn't have," Father replied evasively.

"I tell you, Reb Shleime, all too often Jews have begun to say things that shouldn't be said, and to their own detriment, and especially to talk where they shouldn't. But are they really going to put every one of us in prison for wagging our tongues?"

"Not all of us, so far, thank God. Everything depends on who and what Jews talk about," Father said sadly. "It's one thing when a Jew curses the janitor who is drunk and does a lousy job of sweeping the street, or the bath attendant, Reb Shaya, who didn't give someone hot steam or was slow to give him a bucket before the Sabbath Queen arrived. It's quite another thing when somebody curses President Smetona for no good reason and, even worse, when some hotheads go so far as to call for his head."

"And please explain to me, old stump that I am, why do we need the head of President Smetona? He's not ordering anyone to bayonet the pillows in our homes. What is he doing? Is he stopping us from living a quiet and tolerable life?" asked Kapler. "However, I'm beginning to guess where the dog is buried here: apparently your brother-in-law was infected by that contagious Franco-Russian disease."

"Excuse me, Reb Ephraim, what disease do you mean?" Father inquired.

"The most shameful of all those that exist in the world, from my point of view. In French it is pronounced, *liberté, egalité et fraternité* and it mostly affects the Jews."

"I never heard of such a disease."

"In our language the disease is translated as, 'liberty, equality, and fraternity.' Your brother-in-law decided to save the world from the rich by making everyone poor. It seems he got too carried away and forgot that the rooster doesn't frighten off the hawk with his loud cock-a-doodle-doo, but only invites the predator to his prey. And we, what do we do?

Instead of keeping our tongue behind our teeth, we continue to cock-a-doodle-doo in someone else's poultry yard."

Shmulik's crowing led to him becoming the first political prisoner in Jonava and, indeed, the whole area. His arrest slowed down the work in the tailor's workshop, but it did not harm Father's reputation; there was no less business than before.

Father was unhappy about the loss of a good worker and awaited with concern news of when the court would pronounce sentence on Shmulik.

Shmulik was tried in the Lithuanian capital, Kaunas. The court session was a closed one. For illegal activity and agitation in favour of a foreign state he was sentenced to three years incarceration with the first two years to be spent in a strict regime prison colony somewhere in Žemaitija beyond Raseiniai. The last year would be spent in prison in Kaunas.

Neither Mother nor Father understood what kind of illegal activity Shmulik might have been involved in or what state he might have acted in favour of, but they were at least happy that in three years, in early 1940, the loose-tongued prisoner would be released.

Father did not seek a replacement for him. After the arrest of his brother-in-law he pinned all his hopes on Julius, who impressed him with his diligence and industriousness. The young Lithuanian not only quickly grasped almost all the fine points of the trade, but also amazed the Jews, who looked at the blond lad with an appreciation mixed with suspicion, because although he appeared to be a real *goy*, he spoke such excellent Yiddish that it was a pleasure to listen to it.

Mama also liked him. She treated Julius with considera-tion and warmth, almost as if he were a member of the family. He repaid her in kind, sharing with her his joys and sorrows.

"I was born underground like a mole," Julius admitted to her, as if he were at confession, "and I grew up in a damp basement. I thought I would die there. I had a single dream – no matter what it took – to get out of there, but I had no idea how to do so. I'm thankful to *Ponas* Saliamonas and *Ponas* Shmuelis! They are helping my dream come true. When I earn enough money, I will rent a room across the river, hopefully on the second floor. Every day I'll open the windows wide so that the sun can shine in and at night the light of the moon and stars can enter. What can I see from my tiny basement window? Only legs, legs, and more legs. I'll stand at the open window, look at the sky and quietly thank the Lord God, *Ponas* Saliamonas and *Ponas* Shmuelis for releasing me from those depths."

Sometimes pencil-written letters arrived from the colony in Raseiniai addressed to Hennie. Her brother did not write about the difficulties of prison life. To the satisfaction of both his family and the censor he described the beauties of nature, waxed enthusiastic about the eternal pines, the air that smelled of pine needles and the local wonder the Dubysa River, to the banks of which the prisoners were taken under guard to build a road. Shmulik also described the birds that landed in the yard to pick up crumbs of bread that had been dropped there. He stressed that he always asked them, in the event that they flew as far as Jonava, to tip their wings in greeting to his parents, his sisters and, of course, to his far-sighted brother-in-law Shleimke and the amiable Julius. He also wrote that he could not provide any help to his family from the prison colony, unfortunately, since prisoners do not receive a salary, may both his parents and sisters forgive him for forcing them to suffer deprivation.

"Did he really expect that they would pay him good money for being behind bars?" Father protested. "As if he were concerned for the situation of his parents and sisters! Where was Shmulik before? The only people he was concerned about were not his sick old folks, or Feiga, or Hasya, or Pesya, but with that other troika, the threesome of Lenin, Stalin, and Hitler. It wasn't us he was listening to in the evening on his lousy Philips radio."

"Maybe jail will teach him something useful," Mama said, trying to calm her worked-up husband.

"You can't teach a person who is too busy all the time teaching others," Shleimke said, cutting her off.

"So, in your opinion, he should perish there, in the prison colony, among the criminals?"

"Don't worry! Shmulik will be all right. Your brother is a survivor. He will manage."

"Perhaps he will manage, but it will be difficult for my parents and sisters. After all, Shmulik brought money into the house, not buttons and scraps of material."

"What is true is true. It wasn't buttons but Lithuanian *litas.*"

"Don't laugh, but after he was taken away I said goodbye to my dream of Paris forever."

"To Paris?" Father had forgotton about the dream she had long ago. Dreams, he believed, were only one of life's spices and in his youth life tasted so good in Jonava that there was no need for any spices. Oh, how good it was!

"Every month, as you know, I put aside part of my salary for the trip. A little bit, but still some money. Now I've decided to hand it all over to my poor parents, right down the last *litas*. It is hard for them to get by. You won't object, I hope? After all, quite recently, who was it that promised, in front of witnesses, to support me? It was you, Shleimke! Don't deny it," Mama said, trying to make light of her decision.

"I did promise and, as God is my witness, I will keep that promise. Do you doubt that?"

"No."

Mama threw herself on Father's neck and began to kiss him shamelessly, right in front of me and Julius.

"What are you doing?" Father muttered, fending off her kisses; he was not used to expressing tenderness in public. "If business is good, perhaps we really will travel to Paris sometime to visit Isaac and Sarah. If you only knew to what distant countries and magnificent cites my sewing machine takes me in the blink of an eye, almost every day! I've already travelled around half the world, but I didn't stop anywhere, except for Jonava."

Mama laughed and, encouraged, shared with him what she had kept from everyone. "Before we talk about travelling to Isaac and Sarah, I'd like to visit my brother in the penal colony in Raseiniai; I hope I can get permission to see him when I get there. Feiga will stand in for me at the Kogans' for the day; I've already agreed it with them."

"Go. Just so long as they let you back out of prison."

"If they don't, I'll escape."

"So tell me, who do you take after in your eloquence? Shimon, your father, scarcely says a word and your mother Sheyne has basically spent her whole life expressing herself with those half-moans, half-exclamations, like, "*Oy vey! Oy vey!*" so, who is it then that you take after?"

"Evidently, my irrepressible brother. However, unlike him, I was definitely not born for handcuffs."

The young apprentice Julius listened to their conversation in silence. He stared at Hennie with his incredible blue eyes, in which shone sparks of awed admiration. Being shy and modest, Julius didn't ask either her or *Ponas* Saliamonas how *Ponas* Shmuelis had brought the wrath of the authorities down on himself. Perhaps, he thought, it wasn't just to him that Shmulik had blurted out something about Christ, the Virgin Mary and the twelve apostles being Jews and they had gone and denounced him? Was it really possible that the icons looking down at Catholics from the altar in all their churches were Jews? It couldn't possibly be!

And since Julius didn't ask anything, Father wasn't going to initiate him into the details of Shmulik's illegal activity. Instead, he asked Julius to sew pockets onto the new jacket of the lame painter Eyne, who was going to marry off his old-maid daughter during Chanukah. Father asked Mother not to criticize her brother and she replied that his needle would be waiting for him.

It didn't take her long to prepare for her trip. Mama packed some leftover delicacies into her bag and wrapped an unopened bottle of wine in rags so that it would not break. Along with these she packed a deck of greasy cards, since

Shmulik was devoted to playing cards. Then she left the house and walked up towards the road, along which the shuttle buses travelled via Raseiniai all the way to the Palanga resort on the Baltic Sea.

Sitting at a window on the bus and looking out at the tiny houses lashed by the autumn rain, Mother recalled the trip she had taken with Rokha to Alytus to see her beloved cavalryman Shleimke. She was overwhelmed by that same feeling of pity toward those who worked from morning until night in those wet, swampy fields, without sparing themselves and huddled under those poor straw roofs. She tried to understand how it was possible, or indeed whether it was possible, to eliminate the long-standing enmity of the hut dwellers, which burst out now and again into outright hatred towards the Jewish tribe that had long ago descended upon their heads; that mysterious tribe which neither reaped nor sowed and was not soaked by the rain or frozen by the frost but lived in warmth and wealth.

Leaning against the dirt-spattered window, Mama wondered why it was that her relatively well-off brother Shmulik fulminated against those he called exploiters, while the farmers that worked the land were silent. Their silence was forced upon them; they had no time to rebel either during time for ploughing or for sowing, or during harvest.

In Raseiniai the rain stopped, the skies cleared and the sun revealed its rinsed face. However, it was quite a distance to the penal colony – ten whole *versts* along the water-soaked roads.

Hennie had not expected that she would have to plod along the winding road for so long. She walked slowly, guessing the way, her feet sinking into the mud. Fortunately, she suddenly heard the squeaking of wheels and soon a cart, travelling along the shoulder of the road, caught up with her.

"Where are you heading, young lady?" asked a voice hoarse from smoking.

The driver allowed his small light chestnut horse to rest. Then, not waiting for an answer from the young lady, he disappeared into a thick juniper bush and urinated. Sitting back down on his cart, he took out some shag from his tobacco pouch and rolled himself a cigarette.

"Visitors come to this blueberry patch either for berries or to visit the penal colony," he boomed, striking a match.

"I didn't come for the blueberries or any other berries," Mama replied.

"You wouldn't find any to pick now anyway. In August you can find berries by the thousands. So, if you haven't come for berries, that means you want to visit the prison colony. Why else?"

"Yes."

"Get in. I'll take you there."

While Mama was getting into the cart, the peasant gave her the once over and asked, "Are you going to visit your husband?"

"My brother," said Mama, having no desire to engage in a long conversation with the driver.

"Giddy up!" he shouted, urging on his overworked horse with the cracking of his whip. "I didn't think your people sat in jail."

Mama didn't say anything, allowing him the opportunity to sound off. "Just try explaining to him," she thought, "that jail is like the grave; it treats everyone equally, giving a discount neither to our people nor to his. There is complete equality there, the kind that Shmulik had espoused."

"You're Jewish."

"Yes."

"As I was saying, I thought that Jews sat in shops and stores, not in jails. They don't pull knives on each other over a bit of land, they don't steal their neighbours' horses and they don't beat their wives with a belt. They don't have any land, they don't own any horses and yet they live lives of ease. What a fortunate people they are! The jails aren't built for them!" Finishing his cigarette, he spat onto the road with relish. Before dropping Mama off, he said, "Do you see the two rows of barbed wire over there? Behind them is where your brother is languishing."

The peasant stopped the chestnut horse, jumped down onto the country road and helped Mama from the cart.

There was not a single person visible anywhere. Peeling brick barracks stretched out one after another. Standing among them was a gloomy two-storey administrative building. Mama walked along the barbed wire fence, but didn't encounter a single sentry.

Suddenly a young, unarmed man in rubber boots and a canvas jacket with a hood pulled over his head appeared in front of her. For some reason Mama took him for a forest ranger. He appeared not from behind the barbed wire fence but from a storm-tossed pine forest, which hid not only the strict regime prison colony from the world, but the whole horizon too, so that the place seemed to be lost in the wilderness.

Bowing his head under the broad hood, the man greeted the strange woman and, either bewildered or temporarily sympathetic asked, "Did you come to see someone?"

Mother nodded affirmatively.

"Who?"

"My brother."

"I'm very sorry, *Ponia*, but you confused the days. You can't possibly see him today."

"What do you mean I confused the days?" Mama exclaimed in a worried tone.

"You think I don't know when visits are permitted and when they are not? I've been working here for seven years now as a cook," said the unarmed man. "There's no visiting on Tuesdays and Fridays. A penal colony isn't a park you can wander into whenever you please to meet whoever you feel like without any permission."

"It didn't enter my head to ask and, anyway, who is there to ask in Jonava?" Mama mumbled. "What I am to do now, fool that I am? Do I really have to trudge back through the mud to Raseiniai?" She addressed the cook as if he were the Lord God himself.

"What should you do? Come on Monday or Wednesday," replied the cook, who was not God.

"It is not easy to travel from Jonava to here and back. I don't just travel around visiting penal colonies; I have to work. My employers won't let me go again."

"What can I say? It's certainly quite a distance to travel.

But it's the administration that sets the rules not me. It knows best. What's your brother's name?"

"Shmulik Dudak."

"Is he a criminal?"

"God forbid! He's a tailor."

"A tailor? We never had any tailors here. Who needs tailors in prison? We don't have any fashionable fellows here. Every one who eats prison food has one type of clothes here, the same striped uniform. That hasn't changed in the seven years I've been working here."

Mama didn't know what to say.

"I don't know how to help you," the prison cook said politely, as if to excuse himself.

"I would just like a short time. Ten minutes, not more. I'll just give him this bag and say goodbye right away."

"If you want, I can hand the bag over to your brother myself. I would need to check it. There isn't a bomb in it, is there?"

"No!"

"You should go back to to Jonava. The next time you come, you can collect your bag. Don't worry, you'll get everything back whole and undamaged. Perhaps you'll be back soon for the bag and your brother!"

"Not so soon. He still has two more years to spend alone here like a cuckoo and then another year to sit in jail in Kaunas."

"The politicals don't stay with us long. It's the violent ones and the thieves who serve their full sentences. Well, what have you decided?"

"All right. Since there's no other solution, at least my brother can enjoy some tasty treats. Tell him they're from his

sister Hennie. And also tell him that everyone is waiting for
him at home. Even his needle and thread miss him. Don't
forget!"

"I won't."

Mama arrived back in Raseiniai, under a fine, mischievous
light rain around four in the afternoon. She was upset at her
failure and blamed herself for starting out on such a long
trip in such a bungling and unthinking way, not bothering
to find out what she needed to know, since she naively
thought that jails would be open to the innocent.

The only thing that alleviated her sorrow was her meeting
with the peasant driver and the cook. She was sorry she
hadn't asked their names. After all, there should be a name
for both good and evil people; anonymous good is not
remembered, while time and time again anonymous evil
remains unpunished.

Mama decided not to inform anyone about her mistake;
not Shleimke,

nor her parents and not her sisters. Rather than hurting
them, it would be better to give them some pleasure by
making something up, even if it was based on falsehoods.
She certainly had the ability to fabricate something believa-
ble if she needed to, to substitute desire for reality. In addition to her fiery temperament, Mama had an innate artistic
gift; she knew how to artistically embellish everyday
situations.

Bouncing about in the bus on the way home, she imagined all the possible answers to the most difficult questions
her family would ask. By the time she arrived, she was

delighted to find that almost all the questions she was deluged with corresponded to those answers that she had already prepared.

Shleimke asked what Shmulik did all day long, how he looked and whether he was still as talkative as before. Without faltering, Mama calmly and thoroughly satisfied his curiosity. "Let me start with the main thing, he has no one to talk to there. You can't discuss justice with the wardens. Nor can you discuss equality with the violent criminals and thieves."

"How does he look?" Shleimke continued.

"He's thinner," Hennie said, "and he's grown a goatee and a thin moustache, which crawls under his nose like a worm and his hair is cut short. Once a month the colony is visited by a barber, a Jew named Sachs. Of course, he's not such a master as our own shtetl barber Naum Kovasky. I'm sure Sachs doesn't cut and shave as well as Reb Naum, but that's hardly surprising since every movement of his razor and scissors is carefully watched by the warder. I don't know how you would sew, Shleimke, if you were constantly being watched by someone wearing a pistol. I expect your hands would be trembling."

Father and Julius listened to her attentively.

"But do they at least work there?" her father inquired. "Or do they just twiddle their thumbs and read books?"

"They work and how! They lay roads and cut down trees. They hardly have time to read there."

"Instead of cutting down pine trees, Shmulik could be sitting with us now, singing his favourite song about the white baby goat that stands guard next to every Jewish cradle. Or he could be cracking the joke about how a husband returned home unexpectedly and found his wife's lover dead in the closet, after the poor fellow died of fright."

"He could," agreed Mama, tired of her fabrications. "Shmulik sent everyone his regards and asked you all not to forget him."

Mama didn't bother with the fantasies she had concocted for her parents and sisters. "He's alive and well. He doesn't complain about anything except being bored. They are surrounded by a forest and a swamp," she told them.

"Does he have to wear hand-cuffs?" asked Shimon.

"What hand-cuffs? He's still waving his arms around as he always did. He just speaks less and he's got a different audience to the one he used to have!"

"How's the food?"

"Obviously, he doesn't see any *teiglekh* or pastries from one end of the year to the other, but there's plenty of bread and pea soup."

"Oh, Lord, give me strength," old Sheyne prayed. "I doubt I'll still be alive when he returns."

"Of course you will!" Mama retorted. "We'll all wait out the time. Time flies. You'll hardly notice how quickly two years will fly by."

"When they transfer Shmulik from the penal colony to Kaunas, I'll travel to visit him," Shimon announced. "I have the right to lay my hammer and awl aside for a day, don't I, and leave my work for another kind of prison?"

"Yes, you do," his family chorused.

"After all, in all my life, I've only crossed from one bank of the Vilija River to the other twice; once to go to the Old

Believer, Afinogen, to buy some honey. I've never got any farther from my shoe-block than Giranai. Who wouldn't be bored just plugging away all the time on the same bank of the river?"

"You will go, you certainly will. I believe you have a distant relative there, a barber?" Hennie said to her father, encouragingly.

"Yes, Menachem Sesitsky." Shimon lowered his voice and added in an alarmed tone, "If only Mama's health holds. We need to get Dr. Blumenfeld to examine her."

"Don't waste money on me," Sheyne said. "A person isn't a shoe. With a shoe you can take your hammer, thread and tacks and replace the old sole. That's how it is. But you won't fix me; I am totally worn out."

The quiet, bent Sheyne interrupted Hennie's stories of her brother's resilience. She realised that her efforts to find work and Shmulik's arrest had distanced her from the person most dear to her, her selfless mother, who had never gone anywhere, even in town, except the road from their home to the synagogue.

It was right there, in her own home, that Sheyne had given birth to all her children, on the squeaky, termite-eaten bed.

"I'll speak to the doctor today," Hennie said.

"Have him come and examine her," her sisters agreed. "Let him prescribe some kind of medicine. She has sharp pains."

"Yes, let him come," said Shimon. "But do you know what she said to me last week?"

Everyone was silent as Sheyne made a gesture to her husband with her hand.

"Your mother said that she doesn't want to live any more, that she has lived long enough. She said that she thanks God for allowing her to live this long on His earth and that a person shouldn't ask from Him more suffering. That's what your mother said!"

"Nonsense!" shouted Hennie, unable to contain herself. "Mama, heaven is quite capable of deciding who should suffer and for how long without your participation! God has His own calendar. It hangs on a cloud not the wall and is invisible to the human eye and the angels guard it day and night. On God's calendar it notes what will happen to everybody and when."

6

Until the spring of 1939 Death, perhaps by the mercy of God Himself, spared the residents of Jonava, bypassing it and collecting its tribute in other, more distant places.

God-fearing Jonava, the locals joked ironically, was like an island of immortals. No one could remember when it had been so long since someone had been buried in the Jewish cemetery.

Providentially, though with difficulty, Grandma Sheyne lived with her ailments, even though her health continued to be a cause of serious concern for her family.

Due to the lack of work, the shtetl's burial society was forced to occupy itself with other matters than its usual task: its members cleaned up the cemetery, taking in barrows the fallen leaves and rubbish that had mounted up in the wet autumn to the abandoned sand quarry, lifting and repainting the sunken gates and diligently re-engraving the faded inscriptions on the moss-covered gravestones.

"I have a keen presentiment that the Messiah himself will come some day soon," Hatzkel Berman, the head of the gravediggers, joked gloomily, entertaining the others with his ideas. "What reason do people have to die if He's going to come and raise them back up? He'll resurrect them and proclaim joyfully, 'Jews! Quickly shake off the clay of the grave and go home – to sew, to shave, to build stoves, to sole shoes, to fall in love, to be jealous, to envy, and to betray each other . . .'"

However, *Mashiakh*, the Messiah, was in no hurry to visit Jonava; the happy time of the mass 'immortality' of its residents ended long before the arrival of the redeemer.

The first to force the burial society to take up its shovels was the pauper Avigdor Perelman. There were many in Jonava who believed that Avigdor had died much earlier. In his patched and repatched cloak he rarely left the blackened ruin of his hut near the Yiddish elementary school I attended to engage in his unprofitable business. For days at a time the infirm Avigdor didn't rise from his squeaky iron cot. Lying on the high goose-feather pillow in its long-unironed chintzy pillowcase that someone had given him, he stared aimlessly at the thickly cobwebbed ceiling. Perhaps, for this reason his end was not such a sad surprise to his fellow townspeople. All the more so since he hadn't been known for being particularly healthy; Avigdor had a variety of ailments, though they were known only to himself since he kept them concealed from everyone. The frail Perelman never complained. He rarely went to Dr. Blumenfeld, as he would strengthen his spirit and flesh by resorting to a glass of vodka elixir, as he used to say. When he did occasionally turn to Blumenfeld it was not for pills or tinctures, but for alms.

Not long before Perelman's exit from life, Grandma Rokha met him at his favourite Sabbath position, the synagogue courtyard. Before entering the stuffy prayer house, for politeness' sake Grandma asked him how he was.

The sharp-tongued Avigdor smiled guiltily and replied, "To you, my dear Rokha, as the gypsy women say, I will reveal a secret. I won't keep anything from you. The thing is I haven't collected the amount needed to pay that bull of a man, Hatzkel Berman, and his fellows. As soon as I do, I will immediately arrange a first-class funeral for myself. But without an orchestra. I would like to have the honour of inviting you and Dovid. If you have the time, please come. That will make me happy."

"Thank you for the invitation, but listen to me, if you don't stop spouting this kind of foolishness on every corner, then I swear that from today on you will not receive a single coin from me," Grandma threatened. "And, furthermore, I will trumpet it around the whole town so that others do not open their purse for such a fool as you too."

"I hear you, Rokha, but I wonder whether you're really so keen on living yourself? You passionately try to convince me that it's better in this world than in the other one, the one under the pine trees on the hillock, but even if you were to kill me, I wouldn't understand why you found this world so charming. You don't have a palace, or capital in the bank, or even a pitiful sawmill."

"I don't have a palace but I do have some capital," Grandma Rokha shot back. "After all, aren't children one's capital?"

"Yes, they are, but in my opinion they're not very dependable. Don't parents turn out to be totally bankrupt later? They do! Moreover, everyone, Rokhele, knows that I divorced my wife long ago. We've gone our separate ways. What could I have done if she became sick and tired of me? She simply became nauseated with me!"

"You're talking nonsense and you like it."

"Then, wise woman that you are, tell me who in the world needs me? A dog guards someone's home, a cat catches mice, during a heatwave a tree provides the passers-by with cool shade. But what use am I? I just spoil the air. I just groan and fart, fart and groan."

"Tell me, Avigdor, when you were born were you asked whether you wanted to live or not? You were not! You were given life as a gift. You didn't pay a *grosh*, a cent for it. So be grateful, live as long as you can and stop speaking foolishness. For this gift you don't have to thank our Creator. That's your affair. But just don't blaspheme the One Above with your stupid words!"

"Rokha, the Creator gave this gift totally in vain. In vain! For what, tell me, did He need us? After all, in addition to us, the Lord granted life to thousands and thousands of other unfortunates. He could have done well enough without us! Adam and Eve should have been quite enough for Him to amuse Himself with and get rid of His heavenly boredom, or to put someone on the right path."

The body of the no-longer-breathing Avigdor Perelman was found by his neighbour and old friend, the lame widower Eyne, who used to visit him not just to bring some food, but also to down a glass or two of vodka and listen to his host's account of the hard times he had endured.

The door to Avigdor's hut was always unlocked. Since he never closed it there was no need to ring the bell or to knock. Just push and it would open.

"What could anyone steal from me?" he used to say. "Nothing. The fleas and bedbugs all have something of their own, but I have absolutely nothing! My friend, Eyne, I'm not afraid of thieves or vagrants, or even of him who is represented by a skull. I'm not afraid of anybody! Locks and bars were invented by the rich or by cowards. Since I never had anything, I've never been afraid either in regard to my worthless life or to my worthless property," Perelman asserted with pride.

Eyne discovered his body in the morning. Avigdor lay on his cot, with his arms extended wide. A fly wandered around on his face, moving from his eyes to his child-like half-open mouth, undisturbed and self-importantly as if he were quite at home spreading his glass-like wings. At first the painter thought Avigdor hadn't recovered from a drinking bout. Eyne approached and bent over to see if his friend was alive. Suddenly, springing back from the bed, he cried out in grief. After standing for a while, petrified, he took his sorrow and despair out on the fly, slamming it with his hand. Eyne closed the squeaky door behind him and rushed immediately to the Great Synagogue with the bad news, to the synagogue's *gabbai*, Osher Kobrin.

"Reb Osher!" he cried when he found him. "You won't believe it, you won't believe it!" Eyne was unable to say anything coherent, either because he was out of breath from running or because he was upset. The words seem to be caught in his throat. "Avigdor Perelman is . . . dead," the painter finally managed to say. "Can you believe it?"

"Why shouldn't I believe it, Eyne? Everyone, without exception, believes in death. Much more than in the Lord

God," the corpulent Kobrin said calmly. Then he added, "The matter is clear – he lived and he died. Now, in regard to the ceremony of his burial . . ." He paused, leaving a meaningful silence, then continued. "We have to think seriously here, to ask the advice of Rabbi Eliezer and of Hatzkel Berman about how to send Avigdor on his last journey."

"He doesn't need any special honours. Just to have a grave dug, to have the *kaddish* recited, and to be wept over," Eyne said.

"That's the way it will be. May God not punish me for unnecessary words, but the burial society doesn't bury dead people for free. Whatever you might say, their work is heavy and sad and for work one should be paid. As far as I know, Perelman didn't have any relatives, no wife, or children? And not a penny to his name?"

"That's true, Reb Osher, it's true. No one and nothing," Eyne said, hanging his head.

It did not take much time for Rabbi Eliezer to convince Hatzkel Berman, the head of the gravediggers, to waive payment for the burial. The gravedigger was even hurt. "Rabbi, how can there be any question of money here?"

It turned out that in his youth, a long time before, Hatzkel Berrman had befriended Avigdor. They had even studied together under the reknowned *melamed* Reb Nison Grinblat from Salant.

"Everything will be done as it should be. I won't conceal the fact that it was painful to see Avigdor when he was alive. Who could have imagined that he would one day be extending his hand, begging for charity?" said Berman. "He never asked me, clearly he was ashamed. Don't criticize me, Rabbi, for my sacrilegious words, but not everything – in fact far from everything – is in the hands of our omnipotent God. Even He can not do everything. Once Avigdor was a model student and knew all the Psalms of David by heart. Our *melamed* Nison Grinblat referred to Perelman as a real *ilui*, a genius, and predicted a radiant future for him – as the rabbi of a fine Jewish city like Smorgon or even of Vitebsk. But things turned out differently. It's sad that a person who was supposed to be a luminary in the skies of Israel spent his life as a vagrant and a beggar."

Perelman's funeral was a modest one.

While the gravediggers were preparing the last terrestrial refuge for Avigdor, Hatzkel Berman counted with an eagle's eye the number of people who had come to say farewell to Perelman. Ten men are required to fulfill the Jewish burial ritual, but there was one lacking. Both my grandfathers, Shimon and Dovid, had turned up for the funeral with their wives. Even my sick Grandma Sheyne had gone. My father and mother went, along with the lame painter Eyne and the large wagon-driver Pinkhas Shvartsman. To make up the necessary quorum they included me, a nine-year-old lad, who was at the cemetery for only the second time in his life.

The first time I had been there had been in the autumn of the previous year, with Leah Berger, my desk-partner, my 'bride', as the joker Mendel Giberman referred to her in front of my classmates. When we were second-graders and could read our last names without difficulty, she and I agreed to run off after our last class in order to seek, among the graves at the Jewish cemetery, the moss-covered gravestone of her mother, who had died young and whose grave Leah's grandmother had never visited.

"If we don't succeed in finding her the first day," I said to my classmate, "next week you and I will run off again after our last class and then we will be sure to find her. After all, our grandmas Rokha and Bluma said that your mother Rivka died and all the dead Jews of Jonava are buried in this cemetery unless, of course, they are *goyim* and not real Jews."

I really wanted to help Leah and to impress her with my determination and devotion.

However, neither on that day nor later did our search lead to anything. Who didn't we find? There was Dvoire Birman and Zipora Bernshtein and Hanna Bronevitskay and Taibe Binshtok, but the first and last name of Rivka Berger was not on any of the gravestones.

I remembered that autumn; our fruitless search, our confused wanderings around the cramped cemetery. I remembered how we had sounded out the names carved into gravestones, both the new and old, and the childish or, perhaps, rather mature question that I addressed to my mother after our unsuccessful search, "Tell me Mama, is love really a disease? Do people really die of it?"

"Yes, they do," Mama replied.

While I was recalling that previous sunny autumn, unusually warm for Lithuania, the worried Hatzkel Berman was looking with concern towards the cemetery gate. Suddenly he sighed with relief and triumph, seeing the figures of Dr. Blumenfeld and the *gabbai* Osher Kobrin. Together with the two regular gravediggers and me, a mere boy, the number of males came to eleven, saving the burial society from committing a sin.

When the eternal abode had been prepared for the deceased, the gravediggers carefully removed the light body of Perelman from the cart to which a gentle horse had been harnessed, which made its way to the cemetery without either being whipped or prodded. Then they lowered the deceased into his grave.

Fighting against his shortness of breath, Reb Osher Kobrin slowly recited the memorial prayer, hoarsely and emotionally ending with the word "*Omein!*"

"*Omein,*" repeated those following the prayer and then they placed on the hillock pebbles the size of the small out-of-circulation coins of the kind that people used to give to beggars.

"In the presence of the grave worm all are equal, both kings and paupers and we will all end up there," the heavy-set Kobrin said. "No one can avoid that one way journey from under the roof of the sky to a roof of earth."

The crows cawed, the horse neighed and the pines, those eternal witnesses to grief, murmured assent. Then the gravediggers threw their shovels into the cart and all the others headed toward the graves of their family members.

As was his custom, Dr. Blumenfeld went to visit his father. He went to every funeral so that, when everyone had left the cemetery, he could go over to the grave of his father and speak with him heart-to-heart. In the more than forty years that they had been parted, it seemed that they had not said all that they had wanted to say and still had something important to share. Reb Osher Kobrin hobbled over to his wife, Elisheva, who had died on the eve of Rosh Hashana from a haemorrhage in the brain. The wagon-driver Pinkhas Shvartsman walked over to his sister, who had perished in the flower of her youth after eating poisonous mushrooms.

Our family headed all together for the hillock where the grave of my brother Borukh stood, whose peace was guarded devotedly by two stately thuja or aborvitae trees that had been planted there soon after his burial by my distraught mother, almost out of her mind with grief.

Many tears were shed on the hillock. Loudest of all cried my pale, wizened Grandma Sheyne, who could hardly stand on her feet. Mama and Grandpa Shimon sobbed, while the stern Rokha the Samurai, my father, and the gloomy, taciturn Dovid looked at the unmarked grave of my elder brother, Borukh, and bit their lips.

I looked at them and my eyes flowed with involuntary tears that I didn't wipe away with the sleeve of my new calico shirt. A shadow seemed to cover the whole world. I experienced a feeling of helplessness that made it hard for me to breathe. I was confused because I didn't know for whom I was grieving. I had never seen my brother, nor had anyone told me what he had looked like. Neither a sigh nor a cry remained of him. I was filled with pity for all my family, especially for my deeply suffering mother, who stood like a statue before the unmarked grave of her first-born.

Grandpa Dovid, bent over and shivering, as if from the cold, indistinctly mouthed the mourner's prayer. This quietly muttered grieving seemed to satisfy him more than an obvious act of turning to God on high.

The burial society's cart creaked past the hillock, drowning out the barely audible words of prayer. On the cart, in addition to the driver, there sat the hefty Pinkhas Shvartsman, the lame Eyne and Osher Kobrin.

Berman waved goodbye, raising the arm that had just engaged in hard work to those who remained at the cemetery. My father responded for us all by raising his hand to the gravedigger. There had long been a custom in our shtetl that, when parting from the head of the burial society, his fellow townspeople superstitiously avoided saying, "Until we meet again." And, when parting with these mortals, Hatzkel himself also tried to avoid using that simple phrase which, when he said it, resounded unintentionally with an ominous double meaning.

"Our Borukh would have been ten this year," Mama sighed, when the squeaking of the cart wheels had grown silent in the distance and the quarrelsome crows had quietened in the pine trees, as if on command.

"Time flies quickly," whispered Grandma Rokha, pulling tight the knot of her black scarf. "When my time comes, I would like to lie next to Berele here and have the stonemason, Yona, engrave on my gravestone his name together with mine, 'Here are buried Rokha Kanovich and her grandson Borukh Kanovich.'"

"I feel that my turn will come sooner," said Grandma Sheyne in a barely audible tone. Rokha didn't argue, since Sheyne was far better endowed than she was when it came to all kinds of illnesses. "When my turn comes, and it isn't as far off as the mountains, I also want to be buried next to him here and for the stonecutter, Yona, to engrave his name on my gravestone like this, 'Here are buried Sheyne Dudak and her grandson Borukh Kanovich.'"

"They're cawing like the crows!" Grandpa Shimon burst out. "With such words you only summon up trouble. Where was it ever seen that Jews wrote such things on gravestones! Just stand at the grave and that is enough. Now it's time to get back to work, me to my hammer, and you to your pots and pans to make a pea soup or a casserole."

"Best of all would be *kreplekh*!" my father said, in support of his father-in-law, a great lover of meat dumplings.

"Everyone should go home!" interjected Mama. "I'll stay here a bit longer."

"Why?" Grandpa Dovid asked her. "We have already buried Avigdor and remembered Borukh."

"I want to wait for Dr. Blumenfeld. I need to speak to him about something."

Before leaving the deserted cemetery, our whole family, according to ancient custom, went to a tin basin attached by large rusty nails to a ring sunk into the earth so that people could line up to wash their hands under a lazy cold stream of water. Grandma Rokha explained to me that everyone who visited the cemetery should do just so in order to ensure that they did not carry home some unseen fatal dust that scattered death among the living.

After washing this fatal dust from our hands, we slowly trudged toward the cemetery gate. For some reason, at the cemetery gate, I suddenly turned and saw how the tall, thin Dr. Blumenfeld took off his velvet yarmulke, put it in the pocket of his jacket and approached Mama.

"After a funeral you shouldn't look back into the cemetery," Grandma muttered, noticing me turning. "It's a bad sign, Hirshele my dear. If you look around you unwittingly summon the one who has no skin on his skull, may he not come our way!"

"I was looking back at Mama," I mumbled, attempting to justify myself, but Grandma Rokha viewed any attempt to justify yourself as nothing but deception.

"And why do you need to look back at your mother? Has it been so long since you last saw her? I've always been able to see my mother, both when she was living and when she was dead, without having to look backward. She will always be before my eyes, until they're closed for the final time. Do you understand what I am saying?"

"Yes, I understand," I lied. "Whether I understand something or not, at school they always ask if I do."

"So what? If they ask, it's because they want the best for you. I've lived almost all my life and still understand little, while right away you kick up and say, 'I understand, I do,' even though your eyes look blank."

"Word of honour, I understood!" I cried, trying to defend myself.

Grandma Rokha stopped, caught her breath. "Hirshele, would you happen to know why your Mama needed to speak to the Doctor so urgently?" she asked suddenly, as if by the way. "Especially in such an inappropriate place?"

Grandma Rokha had to know everything about everything and everyone in town – about matchmaking and divorces, about births and deaths, about departures of fellow townspeople for places abroad and arrivals of guests from

America, about the prices at the market for lime and buck-wheat honey, for rye flour and eggs and for veal in the butcher's shops. But most of all she was interested in other peoples' ailments, which in her mind she compared with her own and which she imagined herself suffering from. Obtaining various bits of information was her insatiable passion. Grandma could have been an excellent police investigator. One had to answer all her questions precisely and correctly, without any evasion or silences. Anyone who didn't answer Grandma Rokha was put down on her list of inveterate deceivers or thieves.

"Mama doesn't need him, but Grandma Sheyne does. Do you know what she said?"

"What?'

"Grandma Sheyne said that she doesn't want to live any longer. 'Everything hurts, here and there,' she said." I began to poke at my stomach.

"That's hardly surprising. Find me a Jew who doesn't have a pain somewhere. Search all over the world, you won't find a single healthy one. With one it's the stomach, with another, like me, it's the kidneys and the spleen and with yet another everything hurts almost from the time he or she was born."

"But with me, for example, nothing hurts," I said.

"Hirshele, you're young yet. You still have everything ahead of you. God grant that nothing will hurt you," muttered Grandma Rokha, as she closed the door of her house on Rybatskaya Street.

On the day after the burial of Avigdor Perelman, at Mama's request, Isaac Blumenfeld, who was considered not only a wonderful physician, but also quite a unique character, showed up on Kovno Street to see Grandma Sheyne. Despite his age – the doctor was older than Grandma Sheyne by five years – he looked young. With a large nose and quick eyes, his broad-brimmed beret cocked jauntily over his right eye and in a long cloak resembling that of a priest, Blumenfeld gave the impression of being a foreigner who had somehow dropped into town. The people of Jonava marvelled at his goodness – in the town the doctor treated all the large families as well as the disabled for free. The townspeople were struck by his idiosyncrasies; every morning, in all kinds of weather, he jogged in the nearby woods in short linen pants that reached to his knees. All year round the doctor bathed in the Vilija River, slipping into the water in the winter through a hole in the ice, as the local Old Believers did during the Christmas holiday. He also avoided eating meat, nourishing himself only with fish, milk products, vegetables and fruit. He attended synagogue rarely; only on Rosh Hashana and Yom Kippur, and never prayed, but sat somewhere to the side and silently counted his patients who, together with God, he tried to care for and protect from troubles and misfortune. The doctor did so with the medicines he prescribed.

Mama's sisters – Feiga, Hasya and Pesya – viewed the doctor with obvious, almost shameless, adoration. They simply had to. "He was such an outstanding man. What a waste that he's a confirmed batchelor!"

"Well, so now, let's see, let's see," he repeated in a singsong voice, "and then, we will be able to say what the matter is with you, respected Sheyne. What complaints do you have? What bothers you?"

"And what do all Jews complain about? About life," Grandma Sheyne replied in a sincere, if somewhat petulant and melancholy manner.

"Mrs Dudak, I cannot cure life," the doctor said regretfully.

He removed his beret and cloak, hung them on a nail and followed the patient into the room. Dr. Blumenfeld opened his little bag and took out his stethoscope. As during his previous visits, he placed it on Grandma's flat chest and pronounced the familiar words, "Breath deeper, exhale. Lie on your right side, now on your left and now on your stomach." The doctor probed her with his experienced fingers, asked about her appetite and whether she suffered from heartburn, or had difficulty exercising, 'excuse the expression', her natural functions. Grandma Sheyne, like a soldier, executed all his orders and answered all his questions. Then she asked, "Doctor, tell me honestly, what do you hope to find and hear in this empty vessel that has been cracked for a long time already?"

Blumenfeld was taken aback. He stared at her and then asked, "What prevents you from living peacefully?"

"Doctor, in general I haven't lived a single day in peace. My children, just imagine – I gave birth to ten of them! Every day I cooked for them, fed them and ironed for them and hardly slept. Despite all this care I buried four of them. It was probably easier for Samson the town blacksmith to work at his forge every day than for me. That's why it is not worth looking for something in this old worn-out vessel now. You'll find only cracks and mold on its walls. You won't find anything else."

"What I'll find I'll find. Be patient," said the doctor. For a long time he palpitated her stomach and sides with his slender fingers. "Mrs Dudak, I don't think it would do you any harm to be examined in the hospital in Kaunas at least once in your life," he said. "Unfortunately, you can't hear everything with my stethoscope, all the more so since, it's no sin to admit it, my hearing, like the rest of me, isn't what it used to be and I can't perform an X-ray with my eyes illuminating everything inside a person."

"That's true, it's true," said Grandma Sheyne. "Even with young eyes you can't see everything inside a person. God has closed our bodies with seven locks and, in my opinion, He did the right thing."

"Yes, indeed, He closed us with seven locks," agreed the doctor. "Meanwhile, my dear, I will prescribe some pain-reducing medicine for you. But still, don't delay too long in going to the hospital. Let them examine you there. Your daughter will take you there and bring you home."

"Of course I will!" my mother said, sadly. She had stood at the head of the bed during the whole examination.

"And the quicker the better!" added Blumenfeld, putting his stethoscope back into his bag and closing it.

"Thank you, Doctor, thank you for your kindness and attention, but they'll hardly help me in Kaunas," said Grandma Sheyne, leaning back on the pillow.

"Where did you get the idea that they won't help? The doctors who work there are very experienced!"

Grandma Sheyne thought a bit, ran her hand through her grey hair and said softly, "I was born in a rural area. I grew up, one could say, in the country and from childhood I understood that you can't pick a faded wild flower from its place and send it somewhere to be healed. And that an old bird has no reason to abandon its branch and fly off to be examined in a hospital. When the time comes the flower will no longer exist and the bird will fold its wings and fall to the ground. Won't the same thing happen with us decrepit old folks?"

"You're right, of course. Basically, there's not a big difference. But, in contrast to a wild flower, a human being is a rational, thinking creature. If he cannot help himself, others need to help," said Dr. Blumenfeld, discouraged by Grandma's words.

"A thinking being, perhaps, but I haven't yet met a single living Jew who had his health the least bit improved due to thinking."

"Unfortunately, that is true."

In a hurry the doctor wished the patient well and, turning to Mama, said, "Please, be so kind as to see me out."

Accompanied by the vigorous sound of the hammer of Grandpa Shimon, Isaac Blumenfeld took his time putting on his outer garment, at first having trouble getting his long arms into the sleeves of his cloak and returning his elegant black beret to its place over his right ear.

When they were out on the street, Dr. Blumenfeld sighed deeply. "I suspect the worst. She has to be taken to the hospital immediately."

"Is it a tumour?"

"I can't exclude the possibility. What is worrisome is her significant loss of weight, her unexplained temperature and her lack of appetite. I'll be happy if my suspicions are proved wrong. Come to me in the evening. I will prescribe some pills. Goodbye."

In the evening Mama took the prescriptions to the pharmacy and got the medicine from Nota Levita, but Grandma Sheyne flatly refused to take it.

"You're wasting money on me," she insisted and, to avoid her family bothering her with questions about how she was feeling, she tried to sneak out of the house and hide in the copse of lime trees close by.

When I left school, I would sometimes, at Mama's request, head not for home or for Rybatskaya Street with Leah Berger, but to Kovno Street, to Grandma Sheyne's and Grandpa Shimon's house.

"You shouldn't forget her," Mama reproached me. "You have two grandmothers."

Mama would look at me sadly, apparently expecting me to admit my guilt. But I was wrong in assuming that the situation would carry on as it always had.

"I'm afraid, Hirshke, that you will soon be left with only Grandma Rokha." Mama sighed sorrowfully and then added quietly, "Grandma Sheyne loves you very much and you hardly ever visit her, hardly ever spend time with her. Son, hurry to her and tell her how much you love her. You can't put off expressing your love for someone who is old and unwell; you might be too late."

Grandma Sheyne really loved me. As soon as she caught sight of me, she would immediately cry out, "Oh, my golden one, my handsome one! Oh you!" But I was bored when I was with her; it was much less interesting than it was to be with the hot-tempered, unpredictable and imperious Grandma Rokha, who would give me a smack with Grandpa's belt or a slap on the back of the head and then, suddenly, shower me with kisses. Rokha the Samurai was loud and critical, while Grandma Sheyne was easy-going. She was as quiet as a bird that had fallen out of its nest and broken its wing, making pitiful sounds and trying to fly, but not being able to.

Grandma Sheyne loved to sit for long stretches on an enormous blackened stump amidst a copse of lime trees and quietly talk to herself. Often, from a distance, I would notice how, although not addressing anyone, she would whisper something. When I would approach, Grandmother would no longer rise to greet me. She did not, as she used to, shower me with ecstatic exclamations that were as sweet as caramels, like, "Oh you, wonderful you!" Instead she would look me over from head to foot and praise me without restraint in order to conceal her pain and embarrassment. "My golden one, how tall you have become! You are already a man! Just without a moustache yet!"

"I will grow even taller, Grandma, I will. And I will have a moustache too. But why are you sitting here alone whispering to the lime trees? Are you tired? Do you need to rest?"

"I am resting. Feiga is cooking supper, Hasya is ironing the laundry and Pesya is washing the floor. I'm doing nothing."

"But who were you just talking to?"

"With the one who always listens attentively to everyone and never interrupts anyone."

"The lime tree?"

"No, of course not. You won't ever guess, Hirshele. When you grow old, you'll want to talk alone with Him too, and ask Him about everything. But don't count on getting any answers. The one I talk to never gives answers."

Grandma Sheyne spoke in riddles. Her conversation, which I could not understand, soon bored me. Not wanting to hurt her, I would take off my knapsack and, looking at the grass around the tree stump, ask how she felt and whether Uncle Shmulik had written to her from prison.

"Yes, he writes," Grandma Sheyne nodded affirmatively.

"What does he write?"

"What can he write from prison? He writes, 'Wait for me. I will return home soon.'" Then she would grow silent and listen to the spring wind playing with the leaves on the lime tree. Then quietly, so that only the wind and I could hear, she said, "Maybe Shmulik will return sooner than he thinks."

"That would be great."

"Of course it would be. It couldn't be better. People say that prisoners are allowed several days leave for the funeral of their father or mother. Maybe, they will do that for him. At least he would be able to recite the *kaddish* at my grave."

"What are you saying, Grandma?" I exclaimed. "I don't want him to recite the *kaddish* at your grave! I don't want that!"

"Oh, my treasure, my clever one," Grandma exclaimed. "What can you do, since everyone has to leave for the other world at the appointed time? God makes no exception for anyone. A human being is born to die."

"But I don't agree with Him," I burst out, as if I were speaking about my know-it-all classmate, Mendel Giberman. "I do not agree!"

"With who?"

"With your God. You are good. Mama and my aunts will ask Him and He will have to make an exception for you. You'll see, He will."

Grandma burst suddenly into tears. The tears trickled down her face like rain down a window on an autumn day. She covered her wrinkled cheeks with her hands. Then, surprising me, she rose from her rotten stump throne, approached me and began to caress my long, black, curly hair.

"When you are very very old, you will understand that everyone, whether he wants it or not, will have to do this work."

"What work?"

"Dying," Grandma said calmly. "It's hard work, but no one has yet been able to avoid it."

"When I go to the synagogue with Grandma Rokha, I will certainly ask God to help you. I will, I promise!"

"Oh you angel, you want to intercede for me!"

No matter how hard Grandpa Shimon tried to convince Grandma Sheyne, no matter how the rest of her family insisted that she had to travel to the hospital in Kaunas without delay, she would not agree. She insisted that if the time had come for her to bid farewell to her dear ones, she wanted to leave them intact, without cuts or scars on her body.

Grandma Sheyne held on steadfastly, without complaining, not discussing her ailments with anyone. She busied herself in the kitchen for half the day and fed Shimon. Then after lunch, without being noticed, she went out to the lime trees, sat on the stump and, closing her eyes, listened to the amiable chirping of the birds in the trees and the gentle rustling of the leaves. Sometimes her daughters would run out of the house, ostensibly to ask her something about the housework, but mainly to be sure their mother was still alive.

Out of pity I began to visit her more often and to boast to her about my successes in school, reporting that I could now read with ease and write my own name and more, I could add and multiply.

"Good boy! But still, did you drop in to see me on your own initiative?" She smiled weakly. "Did your mother insist on it, or do you feel sorry for your old grandma?"

"No, no!" I shouted, but then immediately corrected myself. "I do feel sorry for you. I feel sorry for everyone."

"Oh you fibber, you little fox! You don't have to feel sorry for me, Hirshele. I sit here and think that I could have been born a lime tree. They live a long time. If I were a lime tree, I would rustle my leaves in the autumn and wear a warm coat of snow in the winter. I wouldn't fear any illness. But, on the other hand, I wouldn't have you all. I wouldn't have you, or your good mother, or your aunts, or your Grandpa Shimon with his awl, hammer and the tacks in his mouth. Do you understand what I am saying?"

"I understand," I said, since there was nothing else I could say.

"If you don't understand me now, there's no harm; you will some day," she said. "Only fools don't have the time to understand things in life." Grandma Sheyne consoled me. She didn't look ill to me then, only tired and thoughtful. "Stay with me a bit," she said. "Then, before I bore you completely, go do your lessons and I will sit here a while longer."

In parting I gave her a peck on her flabby cheek. She continued to sit on her stump and gaze at the lime tree where, amidst the thick green leaves, a little bird was rejoicing in song. Chirp, chirp, chirp. The copse resounded to its song.

In the evening Aunt Feiga found Grandpa Sheyne dead in the lime copse, seranaded, perhaps, by the chirping of the same little bird.

Grandma was buried, as she had requested, on the hillock next to my brother Borukh. Rabbi Eliezer reminded everyone that it was a sin to add the name of anyone else to the gravestone apart from the name of the deceased; neither in the Torah nor in any other of our holy books was it written that it was allowed and since not a word was said to that effect, it was prohibited.

All was done in complete accord with the Torah – the reciting of the *kaddish*, the tears and the words of consolation. All that was missing was Shmulik, who could not get even one day's leave from the prison colony authorities.

The whole time Mama held Grandpa Shimon under the arm. Grandpa was in no hurry to leave; it was as if his feet had grown into the ground. With eyes blinded with grief he looked at the fresh clay mound and repeated in a hoarse voice, "You should die together with the person you have spent your life with." He inhaled, exhaled and, sniffing in a manner that indicated he was holding back tears, continued to wail. "When you're old you should die at the same time.

Why does God separate couples who have lived together for so many years in peace and harmony? Why does He take us away separately?"

Not one of Grandpa Shimon's family members was able to reply, nor did Rabbi Eliezer open his mouth. Everyone remained dejectedly silent.

"Perhaps He parts us and takes us away separately because He himself is a bachelor," Grandpa Shimon persisted, "an eternal bachelor."

This sacrilegious remark hung in the air like a dark cloud for a long time, refusing to dissipate among the gravestones. One of the mourners laughed quietly, but quickly covered his mouth with his sleeve, while someone else gestured disparagingly at the blasphemer Shimon. Mama poked him in the side and, unhappy and ashamed, he slowly made his way from the grave to the cemetery gate.

The spring sun shone full strength on the cemetery. It seemed as if the heavens were trying, with their brilliance, to do what they could to dissolve the heavy darkness of despair that had overcome the soul of the bereaved Grandpa Shimon.

The year 1938, which had begun with two deaths, slipped into oblivion without any further shocks or noteworthy events. Life in Jonava flowed along in its old, accustomed current and, like the Vilija River, as Grandma Rokha used to put it, continued to provide us with water and food. No one murdered anyone, or attacked anyone, or robbed a shop-keeper. More Jews, thank God, were born into the world than died and the Jews, may the evil eye stay far away, did not just equal the number of the members of the other faiths, but even exceeded them. Not for nothing did the homeowner Reb Ephraim Kapler, who valued quiet, uninterrupted sleep more than anything else in life, refer to our comfortable shtetl by the German word *Yidishstadt* or Jewish-town.

My father insisted on trying to convince everyone that Jonava was indeed the best example of how the members of various groups should and could get along. He claimed that the world would be saved not by coups, bloody revolutions or wars, but by honest daily work. He believed that when a person worked, it never entered his head to overthrow the king or ruler, which would always result in the victors hand-ing over the reins to another tyrant, who would have no qualms in shedding the blood of innocents.

Thank God, Father and Julius had plenty of work in that blessed *Yidishstadt*. Neither were interested in any matters that were not directly connected with sewing, so they pushed themselves hard, working diligently from morning to evening. Perhaps for that reason, even they, who paid no attention to the news, were alarmed by the words of the baker, Chaim Gershon Fain.

"Fellows, I fear that a great war will soon break out in Europe! Is it possible that we in Lithuania will not feel its effects?" said Chaim Gershon, who, on the advice of Reb Yeshua Kremnitser, had his clothes tailored not by Gedalya Bankvecher, but by the former cavalryman Shleimke Kanovich.

Chaim Gershon Fain was a notable personality and, by local standards, well informed about what was happening beyond the bounds of the sleeply shtetl. The resourceful Reb Chaim Gershon offered not only *challa*s for the Sabbath, sweet rolls covered with cinnamon and stuffed with imported raisins and Chanukah *latkes*, but also world news 'fresh from the oven.' Every customer received the latter free in addition to the amazingly tasty items made from flour. Fain drew his hot news not from his capacious red-hot stove, but from the three-lamp radio set bought in Kaunas, made by the very same company as the one that had been used by the now jailed Shmulik Dudak.

"At the beginning of last year Germany gobbled up the innocent, defenceless Austria, like a delicious roll. The Austrians, who have never been distinguished by courage, surrendered without resistance to the mercies of their conqueror. What are we talking about? Resistance? It was capitulation to the accompaniment of waltzes and exultant shouts of 'Heil, Hitler!' I would say."

"Reb Fain, I beg of you, be quiet for a moment. Don't say anything more right now. I can't measure your sleeves while you're moving around and waving your hands."

"Reb Shleime, how can one stand in one place while such outrages are taking place in our own time in the very heart of Europe? Germany is acting impudently before our very eyes. Last year, with the complete passivity of other countries, the Germans forced Austria to its knees and, in the not too distant future, our native Lithuania will also fall at their feet, even if it is armed to the teeth."

Although Father was less concerned with Austria than with the length of the sleeves of the new coat for the baker, his customer was eager to share the news that Lithuanian radio presented dispassionately on its morning and evening broadcasts.

"First of all, as one would expect, after capturing beautiful Vienna the Germans have occupied themselves with us Jews there. People say that in the public squares of Vienna you can see the bodies of the wounded and the murdered. Soldiers have been looting the shops of wealthy Jews along the main streets."

"So they looted . . . Anyway, Julius, the sleeves need to be shortened a bit, by one or two centimetres, not more," Father said to his apprentice and, then, without entering into a long argument, tried to calm the excited Chaim Gershon. "It may be that the Germans won't reach us here in Lithuania. Austria is one thing, with its beauty and its wealth, but our poor defenceless homeland is something else entirely, even if the national anthem proclaims that Lithuania is a country of heroes."

"Shleimke, you underestimate the danger. After all, the Germans are already very close, just across the Neman. They can reach us easily within an hour and a half in their tanks over the bridge at Pagegiai."

Even though Chaim Gershon's arguments were irrefutable, Father did not give in. "But do the Germans need Lithuania?" he asked. "Anybody listening to you would think that the only thing of value here are the Jews. However, you can count the wealthy ones among us on your fingers. There really is no one here to rob. Perhaps everything will work out for the best and the Germans will stay on their side of the Neman and not move their tanks over to our side."

"God willing!" the owner of the bakery boomed. "Let's hope so. What remains for us to do?"

"You're right, Reb Chaim Gershon, hope has been our main protection against all evil over the years," Father agreed, adding, "Until now we haven't had any other type of weapon. But as far as your coat is concerned I believe I'll soon be able to congratulate you on having a new one."

He was sorry about Austria, with which he had no personal ties, but a far greater shock for Father than its occupation by the Germans was the news that his able assistant Julius, son of the drunkard caretaker Antanas, was about to be called up by the Lithuanian military command to the army.

"What kind of 'attack' is this? One of my apprentices sits in jail, the other is being taken into the army and there's a mountain of work to be done," he complained to me, even though I was just a lad. "Hirshke, how will I cope with this mountain? I can't imagine who will help me deal with it. Perhaps you can become my assistant," he joked. "Then the two of us will be able to do such a good job that everyone will envy us."

I didn't say anything, because I had no idea what I wanted to be when I was older. Grandma Rokha dreamed that after I completed Yiddish school I would study to become a rabbi in the famous Telshe Yeshiva. As she said, "A rabbi would be an ornament to our family; so far we've only had tailors and shoemakers multiplying like mice."

However, I didn't want to be either a tailor or a rabbi; I dreamed of becoming a devoted dove-flyer, like our neighbour the furrier Tsemakh Libkind. His Caesars, Tumblers and Ring-necked doves had circled over my head from my very first days on earth. I very much wanted to have the same kind of splendid flock that he had and a dovecote in my attic.

Grandma Rokha made fun of this dream.

"A dovecote isn't a trade, it's entertainment, Hirshele," she informed me. "In any case, you're not our ancestor Noah, who became famous due to the good news he received from the dove. There's not going to be another universal flood. Even if it overflowed its banks, our little Vilija wouldn't drown the world and you won't need to tell the Lord God that we here have been saved by a miracle."

I really did sympathize with my father; it was difficult for him to get by without an apprentice, but I still couldn't help him.

But Mama answered the call. She suggested that she could do the kind of work that didn't require any special mastery;

she could iron trousers, sew buttons on and attach pockets to jackets. She could even, if necessary, sew in a satin lining. But Father resolutely refused her help.

"You have enough work with the old Kogans! Hennie, a man can be an unsurpassed women's tailor, but where in the wide world have you ever seen a woman being a men's tailor?"

Father was bent over by himself in his workroom for days and nights for a year and a half. But, as Grandma Rokha used to say, a person can sometimes be lucky in his misfortune. Fortunately, the rattling of his Singer did not disturb the precious sleep of Reb Ephraism Kapler. He no long threatened to immediately throw us out onto the street because of the noise. He wasn't even in Jonava; Kapler had left for the Czech resort of Carlsbad, where every day he drank the healthy spring water in an attempt to get rid of a stomach ailment he had long suffered from, along with the unbearable heartburn he was plagued with. In his absence, my father was able to ride his Singer day and night.

A week remained until Kapler's return when Chaim Gershon Fain showed up in the workshop to be measured again. Without a word of greeting, he exclaimed from the doorway, "So what did I say to you, Reb Shleimke? What have I been telling you? Only a little time has passed and things have already started!"

"What do you mean? Excuse me, Reb Fain, we've spoken about so many things. I can't remember them all. My head is busy with other things," my father said, cooling Fain's enthusiasm.

"My most gloomy predictions have come true; everything is starting to get serious! We won't be able to stop it. I saw it as clear as water! If England and France don't get involved, if they don't bridle Germany, I wouldn't vouch for our security. Everything has been turned upside-down!"

"What is starting? What has been turned upside-down?" asked Father, concerned.

"Everything in Europe is going haywire. Get it into your head, a major war has begun. The Germans aren't satisfied with their one tasty roll, Austria, now their troops have invaded Poland. Polish Jews are fleeing from there in droves; families with young children and old folks are seeking refuge wherever they can. Perhaps they will soon flee to us, to our quiet Lithuania. They're only a stone's throw away. In good weather you can get here in a couple of days, even on foot."

The news that Germany had attacked Poland immediately made its way through the shtetl. Some people wondered what would happen if the refugees did flow into Lithuania, even in small numbers. Where could they be housed? What work would these unfortunates engage in? Others wondered how they would pay for their lodgings and food, since they wouldn't have a single *litas* to their names.

"So, Shleimke, what do you have to say about this whole terrible nightmare?"

In such cases Father preferred a long, thoughtful silence to a wise answer.

"What, Reb Chaim Gershon, can one say about such nightmares? A nightmare is a nightmare. You can't add anything to it or subtract anything from it," he uttered, after a short pause.

"The problem is that autumn is on its way," the owner of the bakery continued. "The interminable rains are coming, then they're always followed by winter's cold and storms. And what kind of luggage do the refugees have? Only a little sail-cloth suitcase, if that. Many of them, most likely, fled in what they were wearing. I've already managed to speak with Rabbi Eliezer about it. 'Jews,' he said, 'should not stand aside when others are in trouble. We are obliged to help our suffering fellow Jews.' We've to set up a committee of wealthy members of the community to aid the Jewish refugees."

"There is no doubt that we have to help those who have fallen into trouble," Father agreed. "But isn't it often the case that our help is limited to sympathetic exclamations and sermons? We moan and sigh, drop a brotherly tear of pity, and that's the end of it."

"I don't know," Fain replied, "but I've already made a decision of my own. When the refugees appear, until they get settled and find some work, my bakery will undertake for this initial period to bake free tasty black bread for them daily."

"That's great!"

"We shall try to bake enough for everyone. Rabbi Eliezer told me to reach an agreement with all the heads of the small synagogues and they promised to provide shelter for the homeless, to provide temporary housing for them. Each of us should do something," said the owner of the bakery with some self-satisfaction, looking at his taciturn, gloomy interlocutor.

"Free bread and a temporary roof over peoples' heads are wonderful possibilities," Father agreed.

"My head is brimming with ideas, thank God," bragged Chaim Gershon, whose character included the contradictory qualities of true piety and self-satisfied braggadocio, of generosity and stinginess.

Always elegantly dressed, clean shaven and smelling of eau-de-cologne, for days at a time he went nowhere near the heat of his bakery. All the work was done by hired employees – a two-metre tall Lithuanian from Zagare and a local, broad-chested Jew with prominent cheek bones named Yehezkiel. They were the ones that dragged bags of flour, kneaded the dough in tubs and baked the bread and pastries for every taste – for rich shop owners and poor peasants, for rabbis and for priests; for everyone who paid, that is.

"Reb Chaim Gershon, you know well that one doesn't bake bread with a needle and as for a roof, to this very day not only do I not have any extra room, but I don't even have enough for myself," Father said. "But what I can happily do for my fellow Jews is to employ two refugee tailors and provide them with a decent salary."

"What a fine idea! Let's try to find them together. I'm sure that some tailor like that will turn up and make his way to my bakery. Bread, let me tell you Shleime, is a great magnet, it attracts everyone!" the self-satisfied Fain responded to Father's proposal.

The young apprentice Julius, who had until recently been totally occupied with preparations for his military service, learned about the war that was raging in Europe later than everybody else. He first heard about it from my father on the day he came to say goodbye.

"I don't think that we Lithuanians will be fighting against anyone. We don't have tanks or planes, or cannon, or any extra people. Someone who is weak shouldn't interfere in the affairs of those who are strong. He shouldn't wave his arms around, but wait to see how the scrap will end," said Julius, trying to console both himself and his mentor.

"May your words reach God's ear," Father said. "Sometimes it happens that thunder roars close to your house, but the storm passes you by."

"I will pray that it does!" exclaimed Julius and then suddenly he asked directly, "Tell me, *Ponas* Saliamonas, when I finish my national service and return to Jonava, will you take me back?"

"Yes, I will. Of course I will. You're a capable and diligent student. You can be expected to make something of yourself."

"Thank you. That will make it easier for me to carry out my service. May I ask you one more question?"

"Yes."

"I heard that if a soldier serves very well, he might be sent home for a short leave. If they really let me go for a couple of days, may I come up to you right away out of my cellar?"

"Of course, you aren't a stranger, you're one of my own. Just come right up and I will be glad."

"But what I mean is, not simply to come up to chat with you about one thing or another."

"So then what do you mean?"

"I would like to spend my leave, so to speak, usefully, you know," Julius said, with some peasant shrewdness. "To sit, *Ponas* Saliamonas, together with you, in my usual place, over there, on my stool and exercise my fingers for a day or two. And also, to tell the truth, to earn a bit. Dad continues his drinking and Mother can't deal with him or even stand him. I would like to leave her something so that she can put some bread on the table. I'm ready to do anything. I hope you will agree."

"I've never had anything against a person who wants to work and earn some money."

"To tell you the truth, army life doesn't suit me. My friend Petras Kliausas from Skaruliai used to say that you can go off your rocker from army drills. Every day its: 'Attention!', 'At ease!', 'Lie down!', 'Get up!', 'Present arms!', 'Rifles ready!' It's better to be a tailor than a soldier. It's probably not going to be too easy for you now either."

"Julius, no work in the world is easy if you work conscientiously. A master is a master because every day he needs to make it clear that he works better than anyone else."

"What do you hear about *Ponas* Shmulik?"

"He's still in prison."

"For how much longer?"

"If he grows a little smarter and doesn't cause trouble again, maybe he will be released before the end of his term."

"*Ponas* Shmulik is smart."

"Smart people, Julius, don't sit in jail eating their bread under the watchful eyes of a guard, but under the protection and care of God."

After crossing himself, the recruit said goodbye. In the doorway Julius encountered Grandma Rokha, who as her son was now quite alone had brought his lunch. It consisted of soup with dumplings and braised veal with potatoes.

"Sit down and eat it while I'm here!" she ordered. "Have you put anything at all in your mouth today?"

Father smiled guiltily. "No, of course not. I die of hunger at work."

Grandma Rokha made my father sit down at the table. She sat opposite him and, perhaps ironically, said as one would to a small child, "Eat, Shleimele, eat! If you eat you'll grow up to be big and strong. No one will dare lay a finger on you. But if you're naughty and don't listen to me, I'll give you to the gypsies and they'll carry you off to their camp."

"Mama, I don't want to be given to the gypsies! I'll be good!" Father imitated her ironic manner, but was really touched by her care. He gobbled down the soup and meat, licking his lips with pleasure.

"Obviously it's hard for you to manage by yourself. It would be a good idea to find some assistant," said his mother.

"I'm looking. I'm looking. There's not one candidate in our whole shtetl, but perhaps someone will show up soon. You must have heard about how the Germans have invaded Poland; Jews are fleeing to wherever they can. You'll see, some of them will end up in Jonava. It's not for nothing that it's called Jewish Town. They'll have a place of refuge here. I expect there will be some tailors among the refugees."

"I heard about the war and that the Germans were putting matches to rabbis' beards. What won't you hear at the market! More than from Shmulik's radio!" Rokha said, looking at the empty plate and smiling. "Good boy! You polished it all off!"

"It was very tasty! Thank you."

"Now then," Grandma continued, "I also heard about these refugees and about that damned Hitler. When I was young, before there was a bridge over the Vilija, everybody had to cross the river on a ferry. The ferryman was a cross-eyed beanstalk of a fellow with long arms that were like oars. His name was Khitler, Meishke Khitler and he came from Kedainai. So what is the name of that cut-throat from Germany?"

"He's Hitler, not Khitler, and he's certainly no Jew! His first name is Adolf."

"What can you say? During rotten times even people's names sound like those of dogs!" But then Grandma Rokha grew serious. "I just hope we won't have to run from here. People are fleeing from Poland to Lithuania, but where shall we run if they invade us? To Russia? They won't let us in. They will trap us all like rabbits at the border. Into Latvia? They have plenty of Jews of their own and don't know where to put them."

"If you try to figure out where you might go, you simply won't be allowed in. As long as we live, we won't be able to escape from this lousy place. There is no refuge. Tell me instead how Father is."

"He continues to make holes with his awl and bang with his hammer."

"Is he still coughing?"

"And how! And spitting up blood."

"Blood?"

"Sometimes."

"He should go to Kaunas. He could stay with Motl and Sarah on Zelenaya Gora and see his granddaughter Nekhama and be examined by doctors there. I can go with him. As our Old Believers say, work is not a wolf, it won't run off into the forest."

"You can't even mention Kaunas to him. You know what he would say, 'Why drag myself such a distance just so they will feel me over like a horse. Kaunas isn't next door; at home bed is just one step away and in two steps you are in the courtyard, at the outhouse.'

"I reply, 'Dovid, it's also not far from the house to the cemetery!' Speak with him, Shleimke," Grandma Rokha pleaded. "Maybe he will listen to you and let himself be examined by doctors."

"Speaking to him is like speaking to a wall. Father listens only to his customers."

Rokha washed the dishes and was just about to leave when suddenly she grasped her head. "My memory is going fast, I forgot the main thing. Yesterday Kazimiras brought a letter. It took two months to reach us."

"A letter? From where? Who sent it?"

"From Paris. From your brother Isaac. Read it to me and then I will retell it to Father, so he can pull his behind away from his shoemaker's last for a while. What a stubborn fellow he is. He seems intent on presenting himself before the One on High just as he always is, with a hammer and an awl in his hands!"

My father took the letter and concentrated on reading it.

"There are only two pages, but you're studying it like the Torah. What does Isaac write already?" grumbled Grandma.

"What does he write?" repeated Father, rushing through the text, speeding up. "He sends greetings to everyone

– from him, from Sarah and your grandsons Berele and Yosele. Thank God, in regard to housing and work everything is not bad. Monsieur Kushner has once again raised Isaac's salary. Only Sarah is worried."

"Worried?"

"They are afraid that war will break out. The French have taken the side of the Poles and the Germans are furious at them for it. Isaac fears that they might move their army toward Paris and that the Jews there will be in big trouble."

"May their seed be cursed!" swore pious Grandma Rokha.

"Isaac isn't afraid for himself, but he is for his boys. Very afraid. The next time, he writes, if everything quiets down, he will send photographs of Yosele and Berele in wooden frames."

"He could have sent them earlier," Rokha said, pursing her lips. "Then I would have had three grandsons right at my side – one real one and two in frames. I would have liked to look at them before I went to sleep. But now, I will just have to wait."

"He writes that the situation in the world is such that they won't come to visit Lithuania this year, unless the danger passes, which he and Sarah very much doubt."

"And that's all?"

"Well, he sends kisses and hugs, as one does in letters from far away."

Rokha left, carrying the empty dishes, promising her son that the next day he should expect no less tasty dishes: bean soup, chicken breast and a compote made from dried fruit.

There were still no refugees in Jonava. Father had to make do without assistants and, to his loss, turn down new orders in order to be able to complete the old ones in time. Father considered it below his dignity to lure apprentices away from other masters.

"Hirshke, if you would only hurry up and finish school," he would joke with me, "you could work with me and we would order a sign that said, 'Shleime Kanovich and Son'." He laughed. "It wouldn't take me long to teach you my trade. I suspect, however, that you don't care that when I was still a youngster, at the height of World War One, I went to learn from our old fellow townsman Shaya Rabiner. I wasn't much older then than you are now. I was going on thirteen. Rabiner was my very first teacher; he not only sewed remarkably well, but he also played the fiddle."

"I would like to help you, Papa, but . . ." I hesitated. Father wasn't happy at my lack of interest, but if I lied, even though he wouldn't take off his belt to use on me, he wouldn't spare hurtful words.

"Wouldn't you like to be a tailor, son?" he continued.

"But a tailor has to sit the whole time in just one place. I like to run, to climb and clamber around."

"I used to run and climb trees when I was your age, but then life forced me to apply a certain part of my body to a chair," said Father, slapping himself on that very place. Since then I don't run but sit, but by sitting I earn bread for all of us."

My father was a fanatic. My mother claimed that he loved work more than her, and, as God was her witness, for many years he had been betraying her, not with another woman, but with his sewing machine. As my mother put it, "The machine never grumbles or complains to him, it never curses or fights with him about petty matters and it always yields to him."

I was too young to understand Mother's complaints, but as I grew older I was convinced of the justice of her words. It was perhaps due to Father's diligence, his painstaking labour both on holidays and on weekdays, that he lived longer than any of his relatives, dying at a very advanced age. It seemed that even in his sleep, until his final hour, Father cut cloth and pressed down the pedal of his sewing machine. In the morning he would laugh and ask Mama, "Did you hear how I was still stitching away on my Singer while I was in bed?"

Although it was late at night when Mama returned from the Kogans, she was always eager to help him. However, with good-natured pride Father turned down her offer of help.

"Go to sleep!" he said. "I'll manage without you."

"Your mother Rokha knows how to attach soles and glue on heels," she replied. "No one taught her the cobbler's trade; she taught herself. I want to teach myself, like she did, but to be a tailor. I don't want to spend my whole life serving people. I made a mistake when I rejected the offer Reb Yeshua Kremnitser made long ago to pay for me to go to Kaunas to take a course and learn how to be a seamstress. I was afraid of losing you!"

"You made a mistake in refusing. You were afraid for no reason," he replied in a softer tone. "I wouldn't have disappeared anywhere. I would have come to find you myself."

"Oh, we know how you search and what you find," Mama shot back.

"There's no reason for us to fight. All right, so you know the peasants better than I do," Father conceded. "Just rest a

bit, then we can begin your lessons. First you will measure
me."

"Measure you?"

"Why are you surprised? That's how a real tailor starts.
Measuring correctly, my teacher Shaya Rabiner used to say,
helps make the reputation of a tailor. If you take an accurate
measurement, you can make a garment for any man, for a
giant or for a dwarf. If you make a mistake of two or three
centimetres, you can be sure that it will be ruined; you'll just
have to sit down and do everything all over again. A good
customer will leave you if his order has to be redone. You
won't get him back even if you try pulling him back with a
rope!"

"Really? So that's the way it is?"

Recalling Shaya Rabiner, Father suddenly relaxed, sinking
into fond memories of his own apprenticeship. He remembered how his master, although he always approved of his
efforts in every way, took the measurements himself for a
long time, not trusting his well-thumbed measure to a
youngster. "To learn to sew," Rabiner would say, "doesn't
require merely a year or two, but one's whole life, because
every client is an original model that requires an individual
approach."

Mama listened and looked at Father with genuine sympathy, thinking, "What can you expect from him? He's just
trying to distract me."

"Please understand, Hennie," he said, "being a good wife
and a mother is also a profession. Perhaps the most difficult
and important one in the world. To outfit a person is one
thing; to give birth to a person and feed him is something

else entirely. Would it be worth it for you to change such a profession?" Father asked. He paused a while, then added, "I don't believe it would."

"I don't intend to become a tailor and I don't have any objections to you always taking the measurements, but until you find an assistant I can still learn something and try to be of some use."

"Thank you, but you already tire yourself so much at the Kogans that by the evening you can hardly stand. Isn't that enough for you?"

"Don't worry about me! And don't try to win me over with your outrageous compliments! You would be better off just agreeing!" Mother insisted, smiling.

Father knew her nature well. By constantly undermining his apparently solid position she would get her own way. She was thinking that if her faithful partner didn't yield and continued to reject her request, she would, one day, God forbid, resort to extreme measures; she would just sit down and ride away on his sewing machine.

"Let it be your way. I give up," Father said, succumbing.

That's the way it was with us. No one except Mama could win such rapid and easy victories over Father. A white flag always fluttered over our house right until the day of her premature death.

"If only 'Lenin-Stalin' would come home from Raseniai soon," the quick-witted Mama repeated, as she usually did to distract Father. "Maybe they will let Shmulik out from the prison colony before the end of his term. Dr. Blumenfeld was at the Kogans to examine Nekhama, who had the beginning of an acute attack of asthma. And do you know what he said? At first I didn't believe him, but a doctor can't lie!"

"Everyone can make things up. So what unbelievable thing did our dear Dr. Blumenfeld say?"

"He said that, in accordance with an agreement with our President Smetona, the Red Army entered Lithuania without any resistance. More than twenty thousand men. At night tanks with red stars on them passed by our Jonava and took up position five kilometres from here at a field at Gudžioniai."

"Did we sleepy-heads really doze through such a major historical event?"

"Yes, we did."

"And you're thinking that the Russian tanks will boldly advance against the penal colony of the old regime in Žemaitija in order to free our 'Lenin-Stalin'?"

"I don't think so," replied Mama. "Dr. Blumenfeld said that the Russians came to Lithuania in order to protect us from the Germans." She concluded, however, more somberly, "If the Russians come, then it's for a long time. Maybe forever."

8

Soviet officers, or Red commanders as they were called at that time, appeared on the streets of Jonava much earlier than the Jewish refugees from devastated Poland. At first they tried not to stand out; they kept to themselves, wandering aimlessly in small groups around the town. On rare occasions the Russians looked in at some factory or haberdashery store or had themselves photographed against the background of the old brick Roman Catholic Church, the sharp steeple of which pierced the sky. The soldiers photographed the peaceful Vilija River, which poured its waters conscientiously into the Baltic Sea, through farms with shingled or straw-thatched roofs, past lone pines, flowing placidly by idyllic scenes of cows grazing on the river bank.

Except for the Old Believers, who brought their goods to the market, no one in the shtetl could communicate with the uninvited guests without a translator. The Jews did not know Russian, except for several 'ancients' who had served in the tsar's army or who, during World War One, had been deported as German spies from the border area and sent deep into the Russian and Belorussian hinterland by an edict of Tsar Nikolas I.

At first the tank crews who strolled around town seemed to the old-time residents to be deaf and dumb. They communicated with the local population mainly with their hands, gestures, gentle smiles, or looks that indicated they were asking for something. But relations were soon established. Gradually, along with the tank brigade, Gargždai began to fill up with other vehicles and with new recruits, rank and file Red Army soldiers and their commanders. Among the new recruits, either by chance or for the purpose of communicating with the local population, Senior Lieutenant Valeri Fishman, a Jew from Gomel, appeared. He became the guide and translator for his fellow Red Army soldiers. But since he had rarely had recourse to his native Yiddish in his Soviet environment, his *mama-loshn* was quite impoverished.

At the beginning of their stay in the *terra incognita* of Jonava, the Red commanders displayed only a pale and disinterested curiosity in regard to the items on sale. They were ordinary onlookers whose glances were caught by the wares on display that were of foreign, rather than local, manufacture. However, before a couple of months had passed, the new arrivals became accustomed to the new situation and on Sundays, in the company of Senior Lieutenant Fishman, began to enter shops more often, especially the haberdasheries and the ones selling manufactured goods to inquire about prices in a tentative manner.

Among other places, they wandered into the store of Reb Ephraim Kapler. The store owner, who had returned rejuvenated from his cure at Carlsbad, was a merchant by birth. Reb Ephraim divided humanity up not into races and nationalities, but into buyers and non-buyers. He dealt with the military and police officers with special respect and politeness. His philosophy was 'A smile works better than a frown with those in power'. He didn't think it a sin to behave politely to the Soviet officers who had alighted on the town like snow on the roof. In his long-distant youth, Kapler had served in the tsar's army, in Ryabinsk. Since then, by some miracle, he had retained in his memory a modest number of Russian phrases, mainly curses, that he had brought back home with him to Lithuania after the Bolshevik Revolution. "*Zdravii zhelai!*" Wishin' you health! He would greet his Russian customers. "I now not much good Russian speak."

"*Ir kent reydn yidish, ikh vel oystaytshn ayere verter.*" You can speak Yiddish; I will translate your words," one Russian officer replied.

"Oy!" cried Reb Ephraim. It wasn't clear, however whether the cry was more due to feigned joy or to well-concealed perplexity.

The Red commanders took a long time to look over the goods on the shelves in their bright, multicoloured packaging. With Lithuanian money, small change, they bought toothpaste, shaving cream, or perfumed soap. As a sign of respect Kapler gave Valeri Fishman and each of his companions a lovely comb made of bone. As they took their leave from the courteous owner, he tried to say something "*po-russki*".

On Saturday, as usual, Grandma Rokha took me with her to the Great Synagogue. I had to part with her, however, at the entrance; she went up to the women's balcony and, as she always did, sat down in the first row so she could see the whole hall and hear those who were down below. I, a lad of ten, rightfully took a place in the men's section and settled on a bench close to the *bimah* where Ephraim Kapler and the bakery owner Chaim Gershon Fain presided. Grandma impressed upon me the importance of people seeing that not all the males in our family were out and out atheists. Before Rabbi Eliezer had time to begin chanting the weekly Torah portion *Toldot*, 'The Generations,' Genesis XXV to XXVIII, about our patriarch Isaac, our matriarch Rebecca and their twins Jacob and Esau who had fought with each other for their birthright, news about the Soviet Jewish tank-crew member who was serving in Gudžioniai quickly made the rounds of the entire house of God, almost overshadowing the Sabbath sermon. The news of 'the Jewish officer' distracted the worshippers from the story of how, when Rebecca was giving birth, one of the twins beat the other out into the world, grabbing his brother by the heel in order to gain the birthright of the firstborn. The men began to quietly debate the mission or secret assignment that had led to this commander's sudden appearance in Jonava. After all, until that time the only Jewish officer to have served in the Lithuanian army was its chief rabbi with the icy family name of Sneg – snow.

"Even if you deal me a death blow I still won't be able to understand how a normal Jew can become a member of a tank crew," Chaim Gershon said in his bass- voice, bending toward his neighbour Ephraim Kapler, who was immersed in his prayer book.

"You're asking me? I've always preferred Jews who stand on their feet and without military rank," Reb Ephraim replied. "Let's talk about this in detail when the service is finished; it's not right to gossip in the house of God. I'm sure that a Jewish tank crew member is of very little interest to Him."

"What is true is true," Fain sighed. He was an avid observer and interpreter of important world events.

Finally, as the service ended and the worshippers began to disperse, Grandmother came downstairs and sought me out in the crowd in order to take me home.

"I will hand you right into the hands of your parents and then I can sleep peacefully tonight," she said and then trailed off after Kapler and Fain in order to, in her expression, "catch with the corner of her ear" what was being discussed, not by simple cobblers but by solid, knowledgeable people.

"Do you really believe that the Russians have come to defend us from the Germans?" the worried Chaim Gershon asked, not letting Kapler catch his breath.

"No, I don't. It's enough that we're tolerated in some countries, Reb Chaim Gershon. I'm not so concerned about whether they will defend us or not, but by something else entirely; I'm concerned that these guests of ours might suddenly become our masters."

"God forbid!"

"The Russians broke off diplomatic relations with God during the revolution in 1917. If they become masters here, then goodbye to your wonderful bakery and your fancy house above the Vilija and to my three-storey house and haberdashery shop and all our savings in the bank. The Bolsheviks will take away everything. As I'm sure you know, there is no private property in Russia."

"I know, I know," echoed Chaim Gershon. "The only person who owns anything there is that Georgian son-of-a-cobbler with his moustache and pock-marked face."

"The common man is master among them only in songs," said Reb Kepler. "As long as the Germans and Russians don't bother each other and peacefully divide the booty, we don't have to worry, but who can be sure that in the near future those wolves will not be at each others' throats?"

Kapler extended his hand in farewell to Fain and disappeared into the entrance of his house.

Reb Ephraim's gloomy predictions of the Russians becoming masters were not realized. The tank crew members behaved in a friendly manner, quite unlike masters. On their days off, to the unalloyed delight of the public, they held concerts in the market square. On an improvised wooden stage soloists and a choir of Red Army soldiers sang about a border above which "dark clouds pass," and about Katyusha, who went out "to a steep bank", while they danced the lively *hopak* and the *lezginka*. For two weeks running, the Helios movie house of Evsei Klavin showed a film about the Soviet military hero Chapayev. The audience shivered when the brave Red commander charged the White Guard troops; it seemed like he was raising his dagger not at the fierce enemy on the screen, but at the viewers themselves.

Applauding every number performed, some of the crowd made their hands red with clapping. As they exited Klavin's packed movie house, many viewers wiped tears from their faces, mourning the bold Chapayev who had drowned in the Ural River. Still others, songs ringing in their ears as they made their way home, crooned lines about Katyusha who, on the mysterious river bank, swore to stay true to her love for her soldier who was guarding their beloved Soviet homeland.

As a rule, there were more Jews at these performances than Lithuanians. The latter tended to avoid the Russian singers and dancers in their forage-caps with their five-pointed stars. It was clear that few of them considered the Soviet leader to be "their own beloved Stalin" or the "mighty and unconquered" representatives of Moscow, their own dependable defender.

"Why don't you just stay home?" 'Almost a Jew' Vincas Gedraitis asked Grandma Rokha when he met her near Chaim Gershon Fain's bakery. "Why do you Jews crowd in to the square to be offered God knows what kind of entertainment? You are doing it as if your joy over some 'Katyusha' or other won't have some kind of consequence. Rokha, you have known me for a long time, I wish you no evil. As much as I have been able to, I've always tried to protect you from all kinds of unnecessary, unpleasant things."

"Yes, *Ponas* Vincas, I know you have. May God grant you health for your good heart and your good relations with us!"

"That's why I don't want to ever have to conceal anything from you. But what I'm going to say must remain just between us."

"You can be sure it will!"

Gedraitis, the 'Almost a Jew', paused, took a deep breath and then said, "Our top authority is very unhappy with you; that is, with your people. Think about those you are becoming so friendly with so soon! How have those Russians so enchanted you? But, for God's sake, don't mention my name! I didn't say anything, because if my superiors find out that I have blabbed what I shouldn't have, they'll throw me out of my job before I reach pension age."

"I don't go to the concerts myself," Rokha said. "Nor do those close to me or the members of my family. Ephraim Kapler doesn't go, the owner of the bakery, Chaim Gershon Fain, doesn't rush off to the square and Dr. Blumenfeld doesn't show his nose there," Rokha continued. "Half the shtetl stays home. Clever people, *Ponas* Vincas, don't stand around listening to songs, but earn money."

"Not at all, not at all," replied 'Almost a Jew'. "In any case, let your fellow Jews know that they had better not be too friendly with the outsiders. They would be better off singing their own songs. You never know what might happen in this world."

Grandma Rokha was telling the truth. Neither Ephraim Kapler, nor Chaim Gershon Fain, nor Dr. Isaac Blumenfeld, nor the barber Naum Kovalsky, nor my father had any interest either in the love-struck Katyusha, or the 'turbulent, mighty, invincible' country of the Soviets, or in its leader, 'the people's own beloved Stalin'. Or, in fact, in the tank-crew member Fishman. This, despite the fact that, according to Grandma Rokha, the latter's job was a profitable profession for normal Jews, including me.

Father stitched away on his sewing machine as he always had, awaiting not the Messiah, but the first refugee tailor from Poland. I imagined how his face would shine when Chaim Gershon Fain appeared on the threshold of his workshop with the good tidings. Any day now the owner of the bakery would enter and, smiling broadly, announce, "Shleime, I've found an assistant for you!"

When Fein did next appear, the bakery owner said, "Let us rejoice: four families from Białystok have been saved from death and have arrived safely in Jonava!"

"Reb Chaim Gershon, have you perhaps managed to find a tailor for me among them?" Father asked.

"Unfortunately not, but I'm sure we will succeed in this matter. I have a good nose for success. You just have to have some patience, which is something we Jews just don't have. We always say, 'I want it right away, just give it to me.' Don't be despondent. In a little while some tailor will show up. The flood from Poland is just beginning."

"So then, I will just have to wait."

"Shleime, I hope you won't have to wait long. Meanwhile, we have to take care of those who have managed to escape from the German hell."

The flood of refugees did gain force, but grew only to a small stream; fifteen people arrived in Jonava. Throughout the ages Jewish exiles and refugees have turned first for warmth and protection to the house of God. Rabbi Eliezer prepared for their arrival. The synagogue committee that he formed decided unanimously to provide financial help from the mutual aid fund to every refugee. Furthermore, the community assumed the responsibility for providing housing and work, to arrange schooling for the children and to send the ill to be examined by Dr. Isaac Blumenfeld. They would also make a list of all the newcomers to present to the local police so that each refugee would receive permission to reside in the Lithuanian Republic.

Finally my father's hope was realized. At long last there turned up among the refugees a taciturn man who had worked as a cutter in one of the sewing workshops in a suburb of Warsaw and had fled from the Germans to Lithuania with his Polish fiancée.

"Shleime, you owe me a commission! Here is your assistant! A tailor from Warsaw!" said Chaim Gershon Fain, pointing to an embarrassed refugee. "Introduce yourselves!"

"Melekh Tsukerman," said the newcomer, rooted to the spot.

"The sugar king," my father said, smiling, translating the Yiddish name into its non-Jewish equivalent.

"A naked king," replied the bearer of the royal name.

"For how many years have you been sewing?"

"Fifteen," said Melekh concisely. "I began at the age of fifteen," he added.

"I started at thirteen, right after my *bar mitzvah*," Father boasted. "When can you start at the sewing machine?"

"Tomorrow."

"Then tomorrow it is."

"Well, I won't bother you further," said Chaim Gershon. "My mission as intermediary is finished. Good luck!"

When the satisfied owner of the bakery who, following the departure of Yeshua Kremnitser for Paris, had inherited the flattering title of major local patron and benefactor, had left the workshop, Melekh turned to my father.

"It might seem somewhat immodest to say so, but when I fled from Warsaw, I managed to take along with me a rich basis for my future life; I took my scissors, my needle, my thimble and my young fiancée."

Both of them laughed and this laughter drew them together.

His new assistant greatly pleased Father. Tall, sturdy, with a mop of wheat-coloured hair and long muscular arms, the refugee looked more like a Polish carpenter than a Jewish tailor.

In contrast to Julius, the new assistant was not merely sparing with words – it appeared to be painful for him to even open his mouth. He spoke briefly and unwillingly about himself and about what was happening in Poland. Melekh was totally involved in his work. Rarely distracted by extraneous matters, he tried not to ask about anything. He replied briefly to questions and avoided speaking about Warsaw, as if he had never lived there and never fled from there.

"Work is like a bunker; you descend into it and forget everything else in the world. You slam shut an iron door, sew away and are in bliss," he said, making it clear that he would appreciate it if no one pestered him with any inquiries, but simply allowed him to be.

"Did any of your family remain there?" my curious mother asked Melekh, even though Father had warned her that the new arrival did not like to talk about his recent past.

"No one. My father and mother died before all this terror started. You could say that they were lucky, may God not punish me for such words. If they had been alive, it would have been hard for them to leave."

Father soon came to appreciate Melekh's ability and easily came to terms with him about his salary. Father offered him more than he paid Julius and then began to rack his brains about where to set the young couple up so that they could spend their nights in a decent way.

But it was Mama who got the fine idea of persuading the elderly Antanina, who had many years before been the housekeeper for Abram Kisin, to rent the long-empty room in her house to them. It would have the benefit both of being more cheerful for her with them living there, and they would no longer feel so destitute.

When she learned that Melekh's young fiancée, Małgozata, was Catholic, Antanina agreed with alacrity, since she was almost blind and would have someone to take her to church.

Melakh came to work with his fiancée. With Mother's permission, Małgozata took care of the kitchen duties in her absence, preparing food, cleaning up, ironing and hanging up the laundry in the yard. Sometimes, in a wave of half-forgotten emotions, when he had drunk too much, the janitor Antanas would take off his cap before the attractive Polish woman and even blow her kisses.

"*Ale smacna, cholera jasna!*" Damn it, what a tasty bit she is! He would exclaim in Polish, smacking his lips. Wanting to encourage Melekh and to show his approval of his choice, Father missed no opportunity to praise Małgozata and even borrowed from his new apprentice one of his favourite Polish words, "*kochana*", my beloved. As soon as he learned what it meant, Father would use it to Mother. When she was delayed for a long time by the old Kogan couple, Father would always use the term, "Kochana, why are you returning home so late? Maybe you're just pretending to be at the Kogans, but are really fooling around with someone else on the side?"

Mama didn't bother replying to such jokes. She wasn't angry. How could she be angry when she correctly translated the Polish word into Yiddish as *meyne teure*?

Father was more satisfied with the refugee than he had been with any of his previous assistants. "Melekh has golden hands," he assured everyone. "He won't remain an apprentice for long."

Melekh also pleased Mama and Grandma Rokha. They both, however, expressed their unhappiness, sometimes openly and sometimes indirectly, that of the thousands of possible brides in Warsaw he had chosen a Pole not a Jewish woman. Not only had he chosen her, but he had run away with her to another country.

"It's hard to be a non-Jew and a good person, but just wait and see – Małgozata will become a Jew. What won't a person do out of love? One person will be baptized while someone else will replace his cross with a yarmulke," Father said, in defence of the Polish refugee.

When I heard these conversations I thought of the orphan, Leah Berger, and how her strict Grandmother Bluma had cursed her own daughter, Rivka, and driven her out of the house. She drove her out because she had fallen in love with a Lithuanian. I agreed with every one of my Father's words, but I couldn't in any way understand how one could curse and drive somebody out of the house because they loved someone. If Bluma had not driven Rivka away, there would have been one less orphan in the world. Let Mendel Giberman tease me as much as he wanted and call Leah and me bride and groom, it didn't stop me from leaving with her after our lessons or waiting for her each morning at the pole with the torn wires, until the day I finished school. And when nobody could see or hear me, I would secretly call her *'kochana'* – just as Melekh referred to his Małgozata.

The year was drawing to a close. The constant hum of saws from the sawmill heralded a new day in the age-long history of Jonava.

As always, the warden of law and order, 'Almost a Jew', conducted his morning tour of the town. And in the Market Square, on their days off, the tank men continued to sing and dance, the only difference being that their lively Georgian *leginka* had been replaced by the spirited Russian *Yablochko*, the Ukrainian *hopak* by the Lithuanian *klumpakois* and their Russian dance by the proud Polish *krakowiak*. The Red Army men had even learned to sing a choral version of a Jewish wedding song that the appreciative audience welcomed with shouts of "Bravo!" and "Encore!" Simultaneously, at Yevsei Klavin's overflowing movie house the heroic film 'Chapayev' was replaced by the popular 'Circus', in which the star of the Yiddish stage, Solomon Mikhoels, sang a touching Yiddish lullaby to a small black child.

The only person to voice his opposition to these concerts was Rabbi Eliezer since, instead of spending the end of the Sabbath meditating on God's commandments and preserving its holiness, some of those who attended his synagogue rushed to Market Square and sang quietly along with the men of the Red Army. The performances also upset Reb Ephraim Kapler, who couldn't bear the noise.

"My head is bursting from that tararam on the square," he complained to my father, when he came to collect the monthly rent for the apartment. "These songs and dances will end badly for us."

"Why do you say that, Reb Ephraim?" Father said, challenging his landlord's dire prophecy. "As long as soldiers sing, they don't shoot. Meanwhile we're under no threat. The Germans have stopped in Poland."

"Oh, there you go with our Jewish 'meanwhile'. 'Meanwhile' our bellies are full, 'meanwhile' they haven't released a pack of dogs on us, or smacked our faces, 'meanwhile' they haven't brazenly taken our property away from us. All is fine, everything is wonderful and we are satisfied. That's the way we live 'in the meanwhile.' But you should know, Reb Shleime, that it's not in the German nature to stop halfway to their goal."

No matter how Reb Ephraim tried to instill a fear of the Germans in him, Father was more disturbed by his fear for Grandpa Dovid. His family urged him to travel to the hospital in Kaunas, but it was to no avail; the old man would not hear of it. "At home," he said, "your own walls heal you."

Grandpa generally listened to Rokha without contradicting her, but even her threats didn't convince him.

"There are shoes that one can fix, but there are also ones that, no matter how you try, cannot be mended. They have to be thrown out onto the rubbish heap," Grandpa Dovid said, with a smile, faced with the onslaught of his family. "As long as I hold my hammer in my hand and hammer away, I'm healthy."

Grandma Rokha stopped talking to him. She said that if she were younger, she would turn to the rabbinical court for a divorce and marry someone who didn't hammer away every single day; she would marry someone who had a head on his shoulders rather than a cabbage.

Father wrote a detailed letter to his brother Isaac in Paris about their father's illness and sent him the prescriptions written out by Dr. Blumenfeld. Father asked that the medicines should be sent as soon as possible as their father's lungs would not stop bleeding.

Grandpa Dovid had no idea about the correspondence with Isaac. To escape his illness he worked, banging away with his hammer. Indeed, he coughed less and, surprisingly, spat up blood less frequently.

"Perhaps work is the best medicine," his family said, trying to encourage each other.

Nothing presaged the sad outcome.

Grandpa Dovid began to work less. He hammered away less briskly than before. Sensing the onset of an attack, he went outdoors where there was a shady maple tree, leaned against its rough trunk and tried not to attract his wife's attention. For a long time he watched the clouds flying by, which reminded him of his life. They soon disappeared beyond the horizon. "That is how," he thought, "my life will disappear when my turn comes."

However, Grandpa Dovid's unexpected and to her mind unwarranted excursion outside didn't escape the watchful eye of Grandma Rokha. "Thank God, at least you didn't take your hammer and awl out with you," she remarked positively.

"It's time, Rokha," he said, "to breathe some fresh air, not leather, or wax, or glue and not, if you'll excuse the expression, what people's lower parts smell of. I've smelled enough bad smells for a lifetime."

"What are my ears hearing?" Rokha said. "It's a real shame you didn't say that long ago and take your wife by the arm and promenade with her along the main street so that everyone could see that some time ago you married a woman, not a slipper with holes in it. But, instead, for so many years – so many that you could go out of your mind – you didn't get up from your stool."

"I was a fool," Dovid agreed. "A complete fool!" He pointed at his head to emphasize his words. Then he exclaimed, "What a pleasure, the light wind refreshes the soul, the birds pledge their love to each other and the clouds swim by like white geese! You see these wonders and you really don't want to . . ." Grandpa Dovid suddenly hesitated, trying to find the right words, "and you don't want to spoil this beauty with your coughing and spitting."

Then he was silent.

The wonder-working medicines sent by his son Isaac in France took more than a month to arrive in Jonava. The eternal labourer Dovid Kanovich couldn't wait.

On that clear, sunny day, celebrated by the birds, intoxicated with their freedom and the warmth, Grandma Rokha set out, as usual, with a lunch she had prepared, not just for her son but also for the refugee couple. For some reason, she insisted on referring to the fiancée as "that Polish woman" rather than by her name.

Since Grandpa Dovid's youngest daughter, Hava, had not long before moved to Kaunas to train to be a manicurist, Grandpa was at home quite alone with his hammer, his awl and his last.

There was no one in the room but the cat and the tin cuckoo in the clock, which marked the time. Grandpa Dovid sat on his throne, a three-legged stool, carefully covered with felt, humming his favourite song, '*Yidl mit zayn fidl, Shmerl mit zayn bas*', 'Yidl with his fiddle and Shmerl with his bass', tapping with his hammer in time to the jolly tune. At first, the sound was loud, but gradually it became rarer and quieter, until it stopped completely.

Only the cat, who always cuddled up to her master, noticed how, with his hammer still in his hand, he silently slipped from the stool onto the floor, surrounded by unmended shoes scattered like little mice from their holes. The cat focused its shining green eyes on Dovid, then purred affectionately and hurried to him. The old man did not respond to its caress, but he did not push it away. The cat inserted its face into Dovid's unmoving hand and then caressed with her paw the sparse hair that surrounded his bald spot. The hair seemed to be alive as it moved in a mysterious manner.

The master of the hammer and awl lay on the floor until evening, among the boots, the shoes and the slippers.

Above him, on the wall, there sounded every half hour the voice of the cuckoo, but Dovid no longer heard it. The devoted cat rubbed her warm side against the shirt of her master. For the first time, however, he didn't pick her up and put her on his bony knees as he used to do during his occasional moments of rest, to share wordlessly the secrets he had concealed from his wife and children for his entire life.

In the evening Grandma Rokha arrived back at Rybatskaya Street with my father. He had decided to accompany his mother home to try once more, before it was too late, to convince his father to stop being stubborn and travel to Kaunas to the doctors there.

Before they had time to enter the room, Rokha's frantic scream so startled the cat, who was guarding her master, that she ran away at full speed.

"*Vey tsu mir*!" Woe is me! Grandma uttered. "Who did you leave me for?" Tears flowed down her dark dress. "Who needs me now? Only you needed me, Dovid! Everyone else deserted me. Everyone. But now you have left me too. God, in what way was he guilty before You? He had only one sin, he prayed more often to his hammer and awl than to You!"

Father held her shoulders and drew her to him, trying to calm her a little, to save her from a state close to madness. But Grandma tore herself from his embrace and fell to the floor next to her dead husband.

"Get up, Dovidl" she urged the deceased, swallowing her tears and, as she had in her distant youth, long before their marriage, calling him by the affectionate, diminutive form of his name. "Dovid, please get up! I beg you."

"Mama! Take pity on yourself! You can't help him any more and you're just hurting yourself," her son urged, choking as he heard her pleading and hating himself for his pitiless moralizing. "That's the way it is in the world; some sooner, some later. You're not a child. You know well that a wife and husband do not leave the world together. Shrouds are not sewn for two, nor is a bed of earth prepared for a couple at the same time."

Overcome with grief, Rokha did not hear her son's words. Feverishly she caressed her husband's head, repeating through her tears, "What a curly head of hair you had, Dovid! What curls you had! I would never have married someone who was bald! Never!"

Overwhelmed by the calamity, the helpless son did not know how to help his mother. No words of consolation held any meaning; they were worthless and only made her angry.

At that point, worried by Shleime's long delay in returning home, Hennie rushed over to Rybatskaya Street. Seeing her mother-in-law prostrate on the floor, she rushed to Rokha and joined her sobbing.

"How will I live without him?" Rokha wailed, though it wasn't clear who she was asking. "How?"

What could her son and daughter-in-law reply?

"We will live together," Mama said, drying her tears, not realizing it was that very simple answer that her mother-in-law wanted to hear. "We will not abandon you in your distress," she added.

"Hennie, you are good but still very young," whispered her mother-in-law, overcoming her sobbing. "When you get older, you may understand how terrible it is to wake up in your house with no one to greet but the cat and no one to chide, 'The sun is not yet up but you, old fool that you are, are already hammering away like a woodpecker.'"

They didn't light the kerosene lamp; thick darkness hid their tormented faces like a curtain and muffled the inarticulate wailing and moaning of the suffering Rokha. The cuckoo on the wall insisted on marking the time, even though it seemed that time had stopped long before and turned to darkness. It felt like there would never be another dawn.

Nevertheless dawn did come and Mother returned home so that I wouldn't wake up frightened and alone in an empty room.

"You're not going to school today," she said. "A great misfortune has happened to us. The funeral will be after lunch."

"Funeral?" I muttered, stunned.

"Grandpa has died."

"Grandpa Dovid?"

"While you were sleeping, his heart suddenly stopped beating. Papa is with Grandma now. He won't move a step from her."

I had turned ten the year before and I had thought that death had nothing to do with me or those close to me. I had thought that only other people, like the beggar Avigdor Perelman and the apostate Rivka Berger, Leah's mother, died. But suddenly it was the turn of Grandma Sheyne and Grandpa Dovid. Who would be next? Some day would someone say about me, "Did you hear? Hirshke died, his heart stopped beating?"

"Mama," I asked, "tell me honestly, will I die too?"

"It's not something you need to think about. Just do what you need to. Study well. A person who knows a lot is rarely sick and lives longer than others."

* * *

As is the Jewish custom, Grandpa Dovid's funeral was the day after he died. He was buried on the family hillock, next to my brother Borukh and Grandma Sheyne. Motl and his wife and his sister Hava, the manicurist-to-be, came from Kaunas, but Isaac and Leah, who had left Jonava seeking happiness in other countries, were absent. For them, in France and America, Grandpa Dovid would still be living for a long time, hammering away as he used to do; after all, letters take months to reach such destinations.

The shade of the two tall arborvitae trees fell over the hole dug by the gravediggers.

Although Grandma Rokha stood by the grave, she was not able to respond to the words of condolence and gestures of sympathy.

It was rare to have so many people at a funeral in Jonava. It seemed that everyone for whom Grandpa Dovid had skilfully mended shoes throughout his long working life, at a reasonable price, was present.

My atheist father haltingly recited the *kaddish*, which he had learned the night before the funeral. As Grandma Rokha listened to the distorted recitation she threw threatening, critical glances at her favourite child, as if to say, "You might be an atheist, but you could at least have remembered it right!"

Rabbi Eliezer always excelled at funerals, expressing eloquently, in superlative terms, appreciation for the labour of all those who had died. He recalled Grandpa Dovid with kind words, calling him a Jew who was worthy of imitation.

"He was an industrious and wonderful person. I recall how once Reb Dovid came up to me and said, 'Rabbi, allow me to make a remark. You would be better off standing on the *bimah* before God and His faithful children barefoot than in such awful shoes as those antediluvian clod-hoppers of yours. Please, come to me on Rybatskaya Street and I will make for you new shoes from the best leather.' And he kept his word. He made a wonderful pair for me and I wear them to this day," Rabbi Eliezer concluded, looking down at his feet.

Among the people in the cemetery, but far from the grave, the policeman 'Almost a Jew', Vincas Gedraitis, who on a number of occasions had happily eaten matza at the Passover table with Grandpa Dovid, shifted from one foot to the other.

When the crowd began to disperse, Gedraitis approached Grandma, bowed his head and said quietly, "Be strong, Rokha. You lost a husband but the rest of us also lost the best Jew in Jonava. May he enjoy eternal peace!"

His fingers moved to make the sign of the cross, but then he caught himself, realizing that it was inappropriate to cross oneself in a Jewish cemetery. He quickly put his hand into his pocket.

The seven days of mourning passed. My mother temporarily moved into Rokha's house to keep watch over her. Every evening, after work at the Kogans, she rushed over to Rybatskaya Street to spend the night with her mother-in-law and then, in the morning, ran off to work again.

During the day Grandma remained by herself. But she was not called Rokha the Samurai for nothing. Idleness was both alien and distasteful to her nature, which required constant activity. Gradually Grandma began to recover from the grief that had overwhelmed her. First of all she forbade her daughter-in-law to come to her, sending her back to her husband, while she herself sat at the last on the stool that her husband had left behind.

"There's no reason to bother about me!" she announced. "Go back to your faithful spouse; don't try his patience. Men don't need just work and food! As you know, they have other important needs. You're not a young girl; you know what I'm talking about. I don't need care. If you're still alive you need to work, not cry. There's never been a demand for tears; no one in the world ever gave a bent penny for them."

Soon the sound of a hammer was heard in the house again. Grandma Rokha decided to repair some of the footwear that remained after Dovid's death herself, while some she sent over to her in-law, Dovid's competitor, Shimon Dudak, who had gone downhill since the death of his Sheyne.

Rokha wasn't interested in new customers. With God's help she could manage the orders that had already been placed. Perhaps it was for that reason that she was startled by an insistent knocking on the door.

"Who's there?" she asked.

"It's me, Kazimiras the postman. I have a package for you."

Grandma opened the door.

"A package? From where?"

"From France. For Dovid Kanovich from Isaac Kanovich."

"Kazimiras, it's too late. Unfortunately, our Dovid is no longer with us. He's at another address where neither packages nor letters can ever reach."

"I know. It's a pity, a great pity. For some reason good people do not live long." Kazimiras handed the widow the receipt and asked her to sign it. Grandma made some squiggles on the paper with the stub of a pencil.

"Thank you. I wish you health," Kazimiras said, bowing low.

Grandma Rokha opened the package and saw packets of medicine and a letter. She looked at them for a long time, then broke down, sobbing.

9

Every day the presence of the Red Army units had an increasing impact on daily life in Lithuania. Out of the way Jonava was no exception. The residents increasingly felt that the foreigners were settling in, not to defend them from attack by the Germans, but for some unexpressed purpose of their own.

Wives began to arrive from various corners of Russia to join their officer husbands. They settled with their spouses, not on the military base in Gargždai, but in rented apartments in the very centre of town. The unmarried lieutenants, who did not wish to appear to be celibate like monks, began to court local girls and, in this delicate matter, achieved some undeniable success.

My youngest aunt, Pesya, was not one of those who resisted the temptation. She fell in love with a Russian officer, Vasili Kamenever, a native of the Urals with two stripes on his collar. Of course, by doing so Pesya shocked her whole family.

Although my aunt didn't know any Russian, by the summer of 1940 she had managed, albeit with innumerable serious mistakes, to learn words and phrases such as "*tovarishch*" – comrade, or "You are a very good *chelovek* – person", required to flirt or develop a relationship. Pesya's Russian was also catastrophic in regard to the letter 'ch', which she had trouble pronouncing, just as she did in her native Yiddish.

Grandpa Shimon took a different attitude towards her infatuation to that taken by Leah Berger's grandmother, the stern Bluma, over the love of her only daughter Rivka. He didn't curse Pesya or drive her out of the house. Nor did he consider her to be dead to him while she was still alive. Grandpa only warned Pesya and her sisters Hasya and Feiga that an officer of the Red Army was, one might say, not the best gift from a Jewish daughter to her old parents. Pesya's choice only pleased one member of the family, her brother Shmulik, who had always proclaimed that the members of the various peoples and religions were equal in battle, in work and in bed. Shmulik, however, was still serving his jail term, though no longer in the backwoods of Žemaitija, but in Kaunas.

Grandpa Shimon had travelled there to visit him but, just as was the case with Hennie, had not succeeded in seeing Shmulik. For an infraction of prison discipline and for constant talking back to the warden, Shmulik was not only deprived of the right to see his father, but was also at that time in solitary confinement. It was strictly forbidden for any relative to meet him.

An old friend of Shimon, the barber Sesitsky, collector of all kinds of rumours and gossip, with whom Shimon was staying, tried to console Grandpa, saying, "Don't be upset, Reb Shimon. The times are changing and not to the benefit of the jailors. It just may happen that they themselves will soon be sent to sleep on the wooden prison plank-beds while your fiery Shmulik will be released. Our helpless president, Smetona, is like a fish bone in the throat of Stalin. I'm willing to bet that the Russians will get rid of him and put their own man in his place."

Sesnitsky had no idea how soon his prophecy would be realized. Who could have believed that in less than a month, at the height of summer, Lithuania would wake up and fail to recognize itself? It no longer had a president, who had fled abroad, or an army, which hadn't fired a single shot at their supposed friends and defenders, who turned out to be their occupiers.

The changes that took place awoke even Jonava, which had long been accustomed to an unchanging way of life. And how! The mayor fled, the soldiers of the local garrison left their barracks without permission and headed to their native villages. Of the local authorities in our town there remained only the postmaster and that long-time guardian of law and order, Vincas Geidraitis, who immediately exchanged his old uniform for civilian clothing. He still walked around Jonava with his old forage cap with its badge and in uniform trousers inserted into calfskin boots that were polished to a shine.

The Jewish upper class was disturbed by the recent developments and didn't know which way to turn. "No matter how bad President Smetona was," they whispered covertly, "the Bolsheviks will be a hundred times worse!"

"We would be better off getting out of here," the furniture factory owner Ephraim Kapler remarked to Eliyahu Landburg, unafraid to utter this in the presence of witnesses in the synagogue. Not long before Lithuania was incorporated into the Soviet Union, Eliyahu Landburg became the first person in Jonava to request a visa from the American consulate, which had not yet been closed down.

Father, however, had no intention of getting out of anywhere. As always, he continued to insert his needle into some cloth, stitch away on his Singer and, during his brief moments of rest, to ask Melekh whether he thought what was going on was good for the Jews or not.

"In my opinion, it's more good than bad," the refugee replied. "The Russians are not the Germans. They're not killing Jews yet."

"Are they killing others?"

"As for how the Russians are treating others, I don't know. The others are probably others because those in power can't tolerate them and so oppress them."

"Whatever happens in the world, Melekh, one has to sew," Father said. "No power in the world can abolish the needle and thread."

Father usually reduced all the complexities of life to matters relating to his own profession. He was most concerned not by what was happening in the world, but by what was going on under the roof of his own home. It was as if he and the world existed separately from each other. Father liked to say that he wasn't responsible for what God sewed, only for what he sewed himself. And no matter how the rebel Shmulik tried to convince his brother-in-law that a person was responsible for everything in the world, Father just shook his head and muttered through his teeth, "Whoever is responsible for everything, is responsible for nothing."

This time, my father, who was indifferent to politics, worried about how everyone, as if by common agreement, had grown agitated and couldn't stop conjecturing. Conspiratorial whispers covered the town like snowflakes.

Reb Ephraim Kapler, who generally avoided talking to his tenants and customers on topics unrelated to questions of renting, buying and selling, suddenly began speaking to my father in an alarmed manner about the change of rule in Kaunas. "You, of course, had no premonition that our guests would start by singing and dancing in the square to lull our worthless government to sleep and then take matters into their own hands."

"What do you mean, Reb Ephraim?"

"About this habit of theirs of starting out as a guest and then taking over as masters. You tailors and cobblers have nothing to lose; what can they take away from you? A needle or an iron, a hammer or an awl? Don't be angry at what I'm saying, but they won't even cast a glance in your direction. But from us they will take away everything, our houses and our shops, as they did after the revolution in Russia, leaving us to wander the world naked. Can you remember when I was incredibly angry at you once and even wanted to throw you out of my house because the terrible chattering of your sewing machine prevented me from sleeping? Do you remember?"

"Yes, I remember. How could I forget such a thing?"

"But now I can't fall asleep until the morning. Of course, you wouldn't dare ask why, but I'll tell you anyway. Uninvited, terrible, really terrible thoughts crawl into my head! So, Reb Shleime, I'm prepared to give you written permission to sew away, to your heart's content. Sew as much as you like! It's easier to while away the night listening to your machine's chatter, not doing anything stupid and waiting for the dawn."

"Perhaps the new rulers won't dare put their hands on property that doesn't belong to them?"

"Don't make me laugh, Reb Shleime. God's commandments were not written for locusts."

Father was sympathetic about the nocturnal worries of Ephraim Kapler, but didn't take them to heart; after all, neither his needle nor his Singer would be taken away from him. He was more worried by something else – whether or not they would soon release Shmulik from prison and whether he would soon return to the workshop. Perhaps they would appoint him to some high position or other, seeing as he had been a fighter against the *ancien régime*? They might, for example, appoint him head of the prison where he had sat out his three-year term and where the victors would now lock up their sworn enemies and opponents. Father also tried to guess what they would do with Julius; whether they would shift him from the disbanded Lithuanian army to the Red Army, even though he didn't know a single word of Russian. Or maybe he would decide to desert? In which case he might make his way to Jonava, knock on the door, as he had promised his mentor he would before going off to become a soldier, and once again begin to sew for him?

However, neither Shmulik nor Julius showed any signs of appearing and it wasn't either of them who knocked at the door. The drumming of fingers on the door was Chaim

Gershon Fain who, following a decision of the synagogue board, was now dealing with the needs of all the newly arrived Polish refugees. Fain asked Melekh whether he had any complaints, whether he was having any difficulties or lacked anything? He also asked whether he was satisfied with his work. Melekh answered the questions briefly, shaking his head, while his fiancée, who was busying about in the kitchen, left the pots of jam on the stove for a moment, poked her head out of the kitchen and mirrored precisely, like an official seal, the words of her beloved.

"*Tutai u vas v Janove zycie piekna!*" – Life is wonderful here in Jonava!

Satisfied with their answers, Chaim Gershon turned to my father.

"Who would have thought that our lives would take such a sudden turn? Apparently God himself has allowed these developments to take place. Just see how our Lithuanian leaders, who couldn't stand the Jews, have run off to Germany – his excellency, President Smetona, the generals, our top-ranking police officers and the heads of government departments, while the lowly bureaucrats and bosses have gone into hiding. Here, in our town, the only one who has stayed is 'Almost a Jew' Gedraitis, who looks like a plucked chicken now when he goes around without a uniform."

"And you, Reb Chaim Gershon, are you sure that those who have come to replace them will like us any more than the previous lot did?"

"Since I haven't lived in Russia, I can't swear that such will be the case. But I did hear that in the Soviet Far East, in Birobidzhan, they've established a Jewish republic in accordance with an edict of Stalin. The carpenter Aron Katz, a friend of your apprentice Shmulik, secretly crossed the border and, while Smetona was still in power, moved there to build a new life."

"Reb Chaim Gershon, I've heard that there are as many Jews in that Jewish republic as there are Tatars in Jonava. One or two and you're finished counting. We have such republics here in Lithuania headed by a rabbi – in fact we have one in every shtetl!"

"Perhaps things aren't sweet there. We'll live and learn," Fain remarked more moderately. "One thing is clear," he continued, "you'll have more customers and I will have more buyers. Everyone needs bread, the Reds, the Whites and even the Greens."

"You can't argue with that," Father replied.

The bakery owner followed up on this thought. "But tailors sew for everyone, even the hunchbacks and the maimed. Moshe Leibson, our magician in tailoring women's clothes, boasted that two Russian women officers have already come to him with pieces of material and I have no doubt their husbands will be coming to you soon. You won't chase them away, will you?"

"No," Father replied. "I won't chase them away. Although, to tell you the truth, sometimes I would like to show some customers the door."

"Whatever happens, the Germans won't dare cross swords with the Soviet Union," Chaim Gershon Fain proclaimed, repeating his old refrain. "In town people are talking only about the new rulers. The Jews of Jonava, like Jews throughout the world, have always hoped for mercy from new rulers.

However, rulers change but hostility towards the Children of Israel remains and gets worse."

As should be clear, if Father was waiting for anyone it was Shmulik, not a new president of Lithuania. A rumour to the effect that all political prisoners had been released from prison had reached our town. Father assumed that Shmulik would be returning at any moment, but his wife's brother didn't appear in his native Jonava. Father was disturbed, trying to guess the reason. It shouldn't have taken so long for him to get home from Kaunas!

"Hennie, do you know anything about Shmulik?" Father asked. "Where can he be?"

"No, I don't," Mama replied, "but I think that if he appears, he won't come to us first."

"I know. As a loving son, he'll first visit his mother at the cemetery."

"But Shmulik doesn't know that she has died."

"Do you think that he wasn't told?"

"If his jailers had told him, they would have let him go, at least for a day, to say farewell to her."

Mama was silent and then, wanting to put an end to her husband's interrogation, remarked suddenly, "I don't think that he is going to go back to being your apprentice. It's highly likely that my militant brother will be appointed to some committee or assigned to some post. So, my dear, don't count on your brother-in-law returning to work for you."

"God help him! He didn't have the time to become a real master. He wasn't bad at making trousers, but that's all."

"But maybe the new rulers don't need tailors; perhaps they need masters of a different kind. No special skill is required to shout, or to issue orders, or to cart people off to jail. You just need to shout, order and drag people by the hair," Mama said with bitter irony.

The idea had not even entered Father's head. But then he started thinking, what if she was absolutely right? Shmulik had spent three years in jail, not for stealing and not for brawling. In winter he froze in isolation, in summer he was drenched in sweat, dragging lengths of pine trees that prisoners had cut down to a sawmill. He had suffered because he had fought for justice the way he understood it. He wanted to ensure that the proletariat would not be controlled by their greedy, thick-headed persecutors and that the selfless, downtrodden workers should rule themselves. For the sake of his brothers in the working class he had, for almost three years, borne deprivation and eaten prison fare. Now, as a victor and in the name of justice, he deserved some sort of reward for his services.

"You have the quiet, industrious Melekh working for you. The hardworking Julius will come home," Mother said, to console Father. "Don't break your head over this! Who knows what Shmulik will end up doing, but those two will never sit in jail. They'll be with you for a long time."

"You smart little wife of mine!" Father said.

"Smart-shmart . . ." she said. "You could at least ask once in a while how things are with me, and how, after the death of your father, your mother is holding up. But you just think about yourself."

"So? Since you mention it, you might as well tell me!"

"Mama, thank God, is holding out. She sits in her dead husband's work apron and spends the whole day hammering away. When I come in, Rokha always shows me her purse and counts out how much she's earned in the past month. According to her, it's no less than her Dovid earned!"

"It was only by a mistake of fate that Mama was born a woman," her son said.

"And what kind of man are you?" Hennie burst out and then bit her tongue. "Please don't get angry! You are a man, a real man! Only, for God's sake, have patience and hear me out. I want to share some news with you that isn't very pleasant for me; Perets, the wandering son of the Kogans, has reappeared."

"He's come back from Argentina?"

"He hasn't arrived yet. He sent a letter a month ago. He wants to take Nekhama and Ruvim to live with him. His conscience seems to have finally woken up. According to him there's nothing for them here in gloomy Lithuania, where they're more likely to die from loneliness than from illness. As far as death is concerned – God forbid that it should relate to them – there's a Jewish cemetery in Buenos Aires like in all big cities.

"Is that what he wrote?"

"Well, not exactly, but that was about it."

"What do Nekhama and Ruvim say about it?"

"Ruvim says that they won't go anywhere, that their travelling days are over. 'What do we need Buenos Aires for?' he asks. 'The people are foreign and so is the language. It would amount to house arrest for the rest of our lives.' Or, as Nekhama puts it, 'We would be like two canaries in a cage, who had lost our voices'."

"They're certainly not stupid."

"They're not stupid, but that flighty son of theirs might still manage to convince them to move and then I would lose my job."

"I'll take you on. I'll pay you the same amount that you get from your Kogans," Father said, trying to raise Mother's mood with words and a smile.

"You're just joking; I'm being serious. Meanwhile, it's too soon to get upset. The old Kogans don't want to move. According to Ruvim, they'll die much sooner in Argentina than in Jonava. When you hear what the old fellow says, your heart weeps. 'Here, Hennie,' Ruvim says, 'I just have to stick my grey head out of the window and right away I see our youth; I see a shapely, dark-haired Nekhama in a polka dot dress and wearing high heels. I hear her tapping across the cobblestone street toward me, a restless stallion. In our own country everything smells of life, while in a foreign place – it smells of death. There, even your love for your children and relatives from whom you have been parted evokes a requiem.'"

"No one will allow Perets into Lithuania at the moment," Father remarked, hearing what Mother had said. "Nor will Isaac and his Sarah be able to keep their word, as much as they want to visit us from Paris. All the country's borders have already been tightly sealed."

"Why?"

"That you will have to ask someone else. When your brother arrives, he might be able to explain in detail and with his normal passion why a crane or a rabbit can freely cross the border, but you and I cannot. Or perhaps we can, but only in our dreams."

Mama was embarrassed to admit that in her dreams she had already been to Paris, the city of light.

Just as she was preparing to leave for work, round-faced Aunt Pesya, looking more Russian than Jewish, to whom the good-natured oaf Vasili Kamenev, Red Army commander with two stripes on his sleeve, had offered his hand and his heart, rushed up to us. She dashed in, out of breath, and shouted, "Shmulik is back!"

"At last!" Father rejoiced.

"Imagine how thin he is and his hair is so short you'd think he's bald! And he looks as stern as a policeman!" the overjoyed Pesya added.

"So what is he doing?" the older sister asked the younger. "Why hasn't he come to see any of us yet?"

"He's catching up on his sleep. He just sleeps and sleeps, like a groundhog. He says, 'For three years I've slept on planks not a normal bed, laying my head on a paltry pillow in a torn pillow case and covering myself with a threadbare cover'," Pesya recounted, cackling away like a birch log in a fire.

"Has Shmulik been to the cemetery to visit his mother?" my mother asked.

"He says he will, just as soon as he catches up on his sleep. Mother won't be angry at him. People say that the dead are more patient than the living," said Aunt Pesya, somewhat guiltily straightening her colourful short dress and glancing worriedly at the unhappy Shleimke. "I also told him about the death of Reb Dovid," she continued.

"You did the right thing. And how are your affairs?" Father asked. "When will you be inviting us to your wedding?"

"I don't know yet. I can't go to the rabbi and although people say he's a good person, the priest Vaitkus won't give us his blessing either. He would send us to a Russian Orthodox priest, but there aren't any in Jonava. Furthermore, none of those options is possible for Vasili."

"That's not a good situation," said Father, sympathetically.

"Shmulik says that the rabbis and priests are no longer in charge. He says we're the bosses now. He says, 'We'll register you as a married couple in two shakes of a lamb's tail and issue you a marriage certificate with an official seal!' He's joking, of course."

"Maybe he's not," said Mama. "You can continue talking, but it's time for me to go to the Kogans. I really don't know whether it will make them happy or upset when I tell them that the borders of Lithuania are closed and that Perets won't be able to come for them."

"I'm coming with you," Aunt Pesya said, joining her sister.

Father remained alone, but he was in no hurry to start working. He stared at his sewing machine, which had a cover thrown over it, like a horse blanket. He opened the window wide and for a long time watched how, indifferent to all the changes in the world except those related to the price of alcohol, the sluggish janitor Antanas perfunctorily swept the street with his huge broom.

The arrival of his sister-in-law had only aggravated Father's bad mood. He didn't have any idea what was upsetting him so much. Father no longer had any doubt that Shmulik had bidden farewell to his needle, but something else disturbed and agitated him. Even though he never touched alcohol, in some ways Shmulik resembled the janitor

Antanas. Perhaps the similarity between them, Father caught himself thinking, was the fact that each of them always insisted passionately that he was always right. Antanas had the same reverence for the old regime in Lithuania as he did for his beloved vodka; he just wanted it to continue being there. The janitor didn't want anything in life to change. Rather than being the new broom that would sweep clean, he was an old broom that would not stir anything up. Whatever was new seemed to him unpredictable and hostile.

As for Shmulik, he was intoxicated not by strong drink, but by novelty itself, by change, especially by the downfall of the old.

Sunk in his reflections, Father didn't immediately hear someone knocking insistently at the door.

When he opened it he saw before him, to his great surprise, the usually stern and taciturn owner of his house, Reb Ephraim Kapler, smiling affably.

"Good day," Reb Ephraim said to his tenant, his broad smile not faltering. "There's no reason now, I believe, to lock your door. Locks and latches won't protect you from the plague. If those . . . comrades . . . want, they can open any door without bothering to pick the locks and take whatever property they want."

"Excuse me, Reb Ephraim, but what are you talking about? About whom are you speaking so heatedly?" Father said, playing the simpleton.

"About whom is everyone speaking now? About these new masters of our life. By the way, how is your brother-in-law? Has he returned?"

"Yes, he has."

"My, how three years have flown by!"

"When you're free, time flies quickly, but jail seems to clip time's wings, I think. Anyone who has been thrown into prison knows that time moves at the pace of a tortoise," Father replied.

"I'm sure the Russians will recompense your brother-in-law for all his deprivations. He will hardly return to being a tailor now. They'll fix him up somewhere. They'll find a warm spot for one who has suffered."

"He's a shrewd fox!" The thought popped into Father's head. "Reb Ephraim Kapler is trying to pave a level and safe way for the immediate future for himself, via Shmulik." However, Father gave no indication that he had surmised the intention of his landlord and listened respectfully, not interrupting his visitor.

"For you, Shleime, it makes no difference what the regime in charge is," Kapler said frankly, twisting his lopsided moustache. Then he added meaningfully, "But for us it's a noose around our necks. One movement and they will strangle us. I'm telling you, all hope rests on the fact that sometimes we Jews have been able to buy ourselves off. Perhaps, God willing, we shall do so this time too. No rulers are indifferent to gold. When your brother-in-law shows up, let me know. I want to discuss something with him. I will be very grateful to you."

"If he shows up."

"He will. He has nowhere else to go. We'll soon hear from him, have faith in my intuition."

Three days later, on Saturday, when even my father, who didn't believe in God, maintained the tradition of his ancestors and didn't touch his needle or saddle his faithful Singer, Shmulik finally turned up at the workshop.

Saying nothing, he rushed to my father and hugged him in his muscular arms, almost crushing him in his embrace.

"We've won! I told you we would win and you didn't believe me!" Shmulik exclaimed triumphantly. "Is it possible that you're not happy? Your face looks like sour milk."

"I am happy that you are free, even though you are hardly recognizable. If I saw you on the street, I would simply pass you by," Father said, avoiding a straight answer. "You look younger and thinner."

"After being in the fresh air in a pine forest for that amount of time, watched over by a reinforced unit of guards, anyone would look younger. But how are you? How is my dear sister? Where is our wonderful workhorse Julius? Are you working by yourself? There are so many questions after three years! It's terrible! There's not enough time in one life to ask and get proper answers to all of them."

"How are we? We are living," Father replied. "And working. Hennie, as you know, works for the old Kogan couple, the ones who used to own the petrol station. She won't be home until the evening."

"So she likes the bourgeoisie!"

Father gave the impression that he had not heard his brother-in-law's aspersion. "I have a new apprentice," he continued, "a refugee from Poland, Melekh Tsukerman. Julius was called up into the army."

"Which one?"

"The Lithuanian one."

"There is no such army any more! You can forget about it! Its commander-in-chief ran off, the soldiers deserted and went home. But you're so involved in your sewing that you don't even know about the important events taking place right under your nose."

"Some things I know, some I don't," Father replied, not insulted. "To tell you the truth, I've never been particularly interested in commanders and presidents; they're not my customers, Shmulik. But let's not talk about me; I am the way I am and I'm not likely to change. Better that you should talk about what you will be doing now."

My father might as well not have asked. From Shmulik's bravura tone and his good mood from the first moment he had appeared, Father realized he would not be returning to work with him; he would apprentice himself to the new regime and 'sew' according to its instructions. With chagrin, Father suddenly recalled how, when his wife had travelled to see her brother in the strict regime prison colony, she had embroidered a fairytale out of thin air when she returned home. She said that Shmulik had asked some migratory birds to carry his greetings to everyone from behind the bars and that he was sorely missing his needle, thread and thimble. Fool that he was, Father had believed her.

"I'm awaiting an assignment," Shmulik said proudly, "to wherever the Party sends me."

"So," Father uttered in a drawn out way, having no idea what parties were or what they did.

"They have already made several offers," his brother-in-law added casually. "But I will probably stay here, in Jonava, with you and Hennie, my sisters and my father and my mother, may her memory be blessed. Believe me, Shleimke, you won't think me a liar if I tell you that the last time I cried was when I was a child. But when I stood at her grave and asked her forgiveness for being such a lousy son, for not even accompanying her on her final journey because I was stretched out on a plank bed in prison, tears fell from my eyes and I couldn't stop them."

"Angels don't live under every roof," Father said. "Sheyne was an angel who settled under the roof of your house."

"Yes, definitely. Everything on earth can be replaced – a regime, a religion, a country, a husband, a wife – but a mother cannot be replaced," Shmulik said with emotion.

"If I had my way, I wouldn't change anything. Let things remain as they are. As one of my customers used to say, 'it will be better but it will never be good.'"

Father was silent for a while, then, feeling that the impatient Shmulik was in a hurry, said, "As soon as you get your assignment, let us know right away. After all, we are family."

10

It was clear to everyone that there was a new regime when the authorities ordered all house owners, even those who lived in modest little houses, like Grandma Rokha, to fly the new red flag, with its image of the hammer and sickle, rather than the old state flag of Lithuania, on all holidays.

The demand for red material was so great that there wasn't enough for everyone and the residents of Jonava had to travel to nearby towns to buy some.

Our whole town first turned red in November 1940, when the defeated Lithuania first celebrated the anniversary of the October Revolution. Red flags fluttered over all the homes and buildings, except for the Great Synagogue and the Catholic church.

Setting out for school early on the overcast day before the holiday, I saw Julius's father, the janitor Antanas, raise a red flag up the bare flagpole over Ephraim Kapler's haberdashery store and then spit energetically on the frozen pavement.

After greeting Antanas, I intended to pass by, but having not yet sobered up from the previous evening, he stopped me suddenly with a tirade.

"Our three-coloured flag, damn it, was prettier than this red rag. So, am I telling the truth or not?"

Enveloping me in his alcoholic fumes, he awaited my reply. Since I didn't speak Lithuanian very well, Father had once advised me to reply only with gestures or to simply agree when our janitor posed a question when he hadn't recovered from a serious round of drinking.

In keeping with my father's advice, I nodded affirmatively.

"That flag is the colour of blood!" Antanas continued. "The prophetess Mikalda has prophesied that it will flow in rivers. *Du farshteist? Blut, blut!*" he added in his modest Yiddish. "Do you understand? Blood, blood!" He made a slashing gesture with his hand, as if it were a knife at his neck.

"All the best," I said politely in parting and, as if trying to signify something important, straightened my school bag, which had slipped from my shoulder, and rushed on.

When I approached school, I was not surprised to see the same red flag waving in the freezing wind above the entrance. In the school corridor there was an exhibition timed to coincide with the great October Revolution; the walls were adorned with the famous image of Lenin standing on the front of the armoured train and of Stalin with his cohorts at the mausoleum of Lenin, and a photograph of athletes marching in identical white trousers and shirts.

Preparing for the anniversary of the Revolution, Fira Bereznitskaya studied with us a short poem by a local poet, taken from the Yiddish press and dedicated to the 'wise and beloved' Joseph Vissarionivich. Stalin. Our teacher announced a contest for the best recitation of the poem.

The winner turned out to be my classmate who had, on our first day, introduced himself at roll call to the general amusement of the pupils and the smile of the teacher, saying, "It's me – both Ainbinder and Chaim."

More than seventy years have passed since then, but his cheerful voice and the striking rhythm of that poem still echo in my ears. My memory still recalls the first stanza, which I cite here in a rough free translation:

"Everywhere they hurt the Jews

To whom the whole world was unkind,

But then there appeared Comrade Stalin

And protected all of them."

Unfortunately, Comrade Stalin did not protect the winner of the competition devoted to the 'wise and beloved one' himself. Less than a year later, "Me – Ainbinder and Chaim" along with many others, was shot by Lithuanian nationalists in the Green Grove near Jonava for the imagined sins of the Jews. And, perhaps, for some of their real ones.

Earlier, the simple melodies of Lithuanian folk songs had resounded in the Green Grove. There, with his homemade flute, the shepherd Jeronimas had enthusiastically entertained his ill-disciplined herd of cows with his playing. Before that fateful midday in June, in our classroom, as in all others, a thrice-enlarged photograph of the Leader and Teacher of all people was exhibited on the whitewashed wall, glued to a broad piece of card. In the photograph Stalin was wearing a white tunic, filling his famous pipe with a jaunty gesture. Opposite 'Our Protector', behind the last row of desks and almost level with the ceiling, there hung a sad image of Fira Bereznitskaya's favourite, the thoughtful Sholom Aleichem in a massive wooden frame, in a photograph taken shortly before the writer died, by an American photographer. Sholem Aleichem's eyes were lit up with a farewell smile, while the great Stalin looked as if he were wondering how he had found himself in the same building and, even more surprisingly, as a neighbour of that four-eyed Jew.

Before the beginning of the lesson our self-proclaimed leader, Mendel Giberman, tried to ask Fira Bereznitskaya a question.

"Why did the portrait of President Smetona hang only in the teachers' room, while that of Stalin . . ."

But the teacher didn't allow him to complete his sentence.

"First of all, Giberman," she said, "learn how to speak correctly. We don't say Stalin, but Comrade Stalin. Do you understand?"

"Not really," replied the insistent Mendel. "Why does Comrade Stalin hang everywhere?"

"Because he is the friend of all the people of the world, including our Jewish people, while Smetona was never our friend. Now do you understand?"

"Yeah," muttered Giberman, "but I still don't understand."

Much that was not understood took place in Jonava and all of it met a lively response from the pupils of our school. We were no longer the same thoughtless children who had first crossed its threshold. That was the case even though my patient father had often repeated to me that whatever happened in the world, one should always remember that there were never as many answers as there were puzzling questions, and that it was better to avoid unnecessary unpleasantness by not asking them.

The portraits of Stalin did not apparently concern our teacher Fira Bereznitskaya very much. "Who cares if they have been put up? Perhaps sometime soon they will be taken down and replaced." She was more concerned and worried by the news that the new authorities apparently intended to close the Tarbut Hebrew school, where Grandma Rokha had wanted, with such militant determination, to send me.

"They will start with the Hebrew school and end with the Yiddish one, and then we can go hang ourselves," Fira muttered despondently.

When she informed our whole class of the closing of the Tarbut school, I abruptly forgot my father's advice and followed the example of my worst enemy Mendel Giberman, posing a question to her that less expressed my own view than that of my grandmother, who had dreamed of my studying in the Tarbut school and nowhere else.

"But why did they close that school?" I asked.

"I don't know. You had better ask your uncle. I heard that he will soon be a big shot in Jonava." In order to end the discussion about the closings and bans, Fira added, "Children, let's talk about something happier. In honour of the twenty-third anniversary of the October Revolution, about which I will tell you later during our lessons, you are going to have a three-day holiday."

"Hurrah!" our class shouted in unison, like soldiers. Even the girls shouted and clapped their hands.

After school, near the building, Mendel Giberman grabbed me by the sleeve and with impertinent irony asked, "So where is your Leahchka? Where, bridegroom of hers, are you hiding her from us?"

"She's sick. She probably caught a cold. It's freezing outside," I replied, not suspecting any ill will on his part.

"A cold . . . freezing," Giberman teased me. "You're lying, aren't you? Maybe she waited and waited for you on Rybatskaya Street near the pole with broken wires and then stopped waiting and went off, like her mother, with some *goy*?" He grinned, satisfied with his buffoonery.

"Mendel, you are a fool!" I replied.

"You are a fool yourself! You don't know anything about that 'beauty' of yours. Everyone knows but you. Because of you, you blockhead, Leah won't hang herself and you won't throw yourself under a train from grief!"

"What nonsense are you spouting, Mendel? Why are you talking such nonsense?"

Taken aback by his nastiness, I found it hard to restrain my anger and my desire to punch him, but I didn't want to be the first to start a fight in school.

"Why am I telling you this? So that you know what kind of nest your little bird comes from!"

I don't know what came over me at that moment, but I turned suddenly and slapped my insulter across his ugly face. Giberman didn't let that pass and launched his fists into action. Suddenly I felt blood streaming out of my nose and tried to lick it from my lips, but no matter how much I tried the taste of blood remained.

Two of my classmates, the tall "Me – Ainbinder and Chaim" and the freckled, plump Dov-Ber Dvorkin, came running into the yard. They separated us while Fira Bereznitskaya stopped my bleeding nostrils with some cotton from the school infirmary.

In that state, with blood-stained cotton wool sticking out of my nostrils, I appeared before my family.

"What happened?" Father asked.

"Holiday," I muttered.

My father and Grandma Rokha, who happened to be at our house, along with the apprentice Melekh and his Małgozata, all burst into laughter.

"Did you get into a fight?" Grandma asked.

"No," I responded, trying to brush the incident off.

"Your friends evidently don't know yet that it's better not to tangle with you. You have the kind of protector now who will take care of you immediately in all your scrapes in town."

The only protector I could think of was the one hailed in the verses that Chaim Ainbender had recited more expressively than any one else in class.

"You mean Stalin?" I burst out.

At this, the laughter became uproarious, rising like a wave, pounding through the wall of the house to disturb the sleep of Reb Ephraim Kapler.

"Oh, Hirsh, how you've made us laugh," Father said several times, unable to stop laughing. "Grandma wasn't referring to Stalin, but to your Uncle Shmulik. Hirshke, he's not a tailor anymore; he works in quite a different profession."

"What does he do now?"

"You would never guess. He does what people used to call police work. No, that's not it, he works at something higher, he's not simply a policeman. He's not like 'Almost a Jew' Gedraitis. He's almost like a police chief. In the new order here he's assistant head of the Jonava department of the

NKVD. He's a big shot now! Shmulik used to spend all his days and nights with us, but now he hardly even drops in on his own father, Shimon. He lives by himself in the three-room apartment of the former head of the tsarist police, Ksaveras Grigaliunas, the one who arrested him some time ago in you and your mother's presence at Grandma Sheyne's."

"Will Shmulik visit us?"

"Maybe he will and maybe he won't. He has a lot of work to do. Some things in Jonava have to be opened right away and some things have to be closed down immediately."

"Our teacher says that the authorities have closed down the Tarbut school, where Grandma wanted me to study, for some reason," I said, recalling what I had just heard.

"That can't be!" Rokha said, upset. "Who was that school harming? Who?"

"Calm down, Mama. Anything can happen in life, even what shouldn't happen."

"Those are holy words," said Melekh, supporting his boss. "Who could imagine that we would ever end up as homeless refugees in Lithuania?"

"A new broom sweeps clean. The main thing is that it doesn't sweep us away too," Father said. "Meanwhile, let's just sit and sew. It's a sin to complain about your fate."

Fortunately the new regime did not touch the tailor's workshop. In fact, it was overwhelmed with orders. As Father put it, "the Russian season" commenced. It seemed that all the commanders of the Red Army who were quartered in Jonava decided to celebrate their service in Lithuania by putting together a collection of civilian clothing sewn by local tailors.

The first to come to Father were Senior Lieutenant Vasili Kamenev and his future wife, Aunt Pesya.

"Vasili would like you to sew him a double-breasted jacket and trousers from English material," Pesya explained in Yiddish. "Here's a bolt of the material."

Her hero from the Urals didn't understand Yiddish, so he restricted himself to a few signs of agreement. His conversational Yiddish consisted of three or four easily acquired expressions like, "*Ye, ye, ye,*" "*A gutn tog aich,*" and "*Zait mir gezung*". Yes, yes, yes, Good day, and, Good health to you.

"Does he at least know how much I will charge?" my father asked his sister-in-law. Just as he was in regard to all of his customers, Father was scrupulous in making business matters clear to his relatives.

"Yes, he does."

"And does he know that I give discounts only to family members? Since you're not yet husband and wife, I won't make an exception in his case. When you're married, that will be another matter."

The whole time Vasili Kamenev shifted his gaze from the master tailor to my embarrassed aunt and back, scattering his, "*Ye, ye, ye,*" around the room like peas. After they had agreed when the suit would be ready, the good-hearted Vasili demonstrated, to the pleasure of Father and Melekh, his knowledge of their language. "*Zait gezunt, a gutn tog eikh!*"

Kamenev's fellow officers' pilgrimages to the tailors of Jonava continued. A week later, following the future brother-in-law, there appeared at Father's workshop a captain and a major, together with their translator Valeri Fishman. Each of them brought with him a measure of English material that had been purchased at the haberdashery shop of Reb Ephraim Kapler.

While Father was measuring the Red commanders, Senior Lieutenant Fishman remained silent, but before leaving the workshop he couldn't contain himself any longer and turned to Father.

"You can't find such wonderful material by day or by night in Gomel or in Bobruisk. Not even in Minsk could you find such material! What wonderful English cloth, such a fine quality!"

In order to cope with the orders Father and Melekh had to work until late at night, trying as hard as they could, as Shleimke joked to Hennie and Małgozata, to reclothe the whole Red Army quartered in Jonava in civilian dress.

Father continued to wait for reinforcements in the form of his apprentice Julius. He asked Antanas whether he knew anything about his son.

"My son has disappeared," replied the janitor and with a drunken smile added, "Maybe he made off to Germany with his Excellency the President and all his ministers and generals."

"*Nu*, don't be so upset," Father said, trying to calm Antanas. "He's probably fooling around with a girl somewhere. He'll have a good time and then return home."

"God willing, *Ponas* Saliamonas! The prophetess Mikalda predicted that the world will fall apart this summer. Since you Jews don't believe that, you'll suffer more than anyone else."

Superstitious Antanas always had an aura of destruction and hopelessness about him, compelling Father to think about what had already happened. After all, the old world had already collapsed in both Poland and in France. Banners with the swastika had already been raised over Warsaw and German soldiers were marching in triumph along the Champs-Élysée. Father wondered whether Isaac and Sarah and their boys Berele and Yosele were still alive in Paris.

As twilight fell, Antanas would have continued to talk for quite some time about the wise prophecies of Mikalda if Shmulik's familiar figure had not appeared in the distance. There were no family embraces and kisses. Only my mother wept.

Father introduced his brother-in-law to Melekh and Małgozata, the refugees from Poland.

"Very pleased to meet you," Shmulik said. "I hope you will never have to flee anywhere again. We're not helpless like Poland and we're not the former toy state of Lithuania. We're the mighty Soviet Union, whose army is the most powerful in Europe and will not allow you to be harmed."

"As we used to say in Warsaw, let's hope so," said Melekh with a grudging smile.

"Understood," Shmulke replied coldly, having evidently expected the refugees to show more gratitude to the Soviet Union and its glorious Red Army.

Mama set the table and everyone drank tea from the decorated cups and devoured her special pastries with black raisins.

"Eat, Shmulik," Mama urged her brother. "You certainly didn't get pastries like these in jail; try to make up for those lost three years! If you come to us more often, you'll be able to make up for them."

Shmulik frowned, looked at my father, then turned to Małgozata. "Those were good times, when you could just sit and thread a needle and sew away. But they're gone now! Now you have to sew a different kind of life. And it's not always enough to arm yourself with a needle; sometimes you need a gun."

Everyone drank their tea quietly, not responding to Shmulik. Who, they wondered, would Shmulik try to 'sew' in a new way? Perhaps the factory owner, Eliahu Landburg, who was still in Jonava because he hadn't succeeded in getting a visa to America, because the new authorities had ordered the US consul to leave Lithuania within forty-eight hours. Or perhaps Reb Ephraim Kapler, who had unfortunately inherited from his father Rakhmiel the three-storey brick house and two shops, the haberdashery and the one selling manufactured goods.

Although the silence didn't last long, it was strained. Shmulik did not conceal his irritation. "The Lord Himself was willing to get his hands dirty to create the world, so why look down on us? The world won't be rebuilt by those who keep their hands clean. Sometimes you just have to get your hands dirty."

"With blood?" Mama said, looking at her brother with alarm, and then, wanting to calm the situation, she added immediately, "Perhaps, after you remake this rotten world, you will sit down on a stool once more, stretch out your long legs, put someone's unfinished trousers on your knees and complete them?"

"When it comes to people, Hennie, anything is possible. Maybe I will return to sewing. If so, I hope your husband won't turn me away," Shmulik said, smiling. "But then, he might. During my three years in jail my fingers lost their agility. I can no longer thread the needle on my first try, or sew or cut the way I could. After all, in the penal colony my hands were occupied with the rough work of cutting down timber."

He relaxed then and began to quiz Melekh about how he and Małgozata had made their way to Lithuania. "How many days did it take? How did you end up in Jonava and at the workshop of Shleime at that?" Mama didn't take her eyes off her brother. The whole time she seemed silently to be repeating, "Ask, my dear, ask away!"

After listening to Melekh, Shmulik turned to his taciturn brother-in-law.

"Shleime, you have nothing to be afraid of. No one will lay a finger on you. You are prepared to sew for any government. No rulers should go around with bare arses; they like to look attractive so they always turn to a good tailor, not a lousy one. You really are a skilled tailor, the kind one has to search high and low for! Believe me!" Shmulik raised his index finger. "You could sew for the highest authorities. If I were asked, I would recommend you without hestition even to Comrade Stalin in the Kremlin."

"That's the way to talk! I can recognize my brother now! You are a fine fellow! A very fine fellow, even when you utter nonsense!" exclaimed Mother.

I listened to Shmulik, who not so very long before had given me, whenever he left, two affectionate slaps on the forehead. I really wanted to ask him why the Tarbut school had been closed down. Who was it disturbing? But I decided it was better not to interrupt the adults' discussion. I recalled the fierce argument Shmulik had had with Grandma Rokha, who had not even wanted to hear about any Yiddish school, just the Tarbut, only the Tarbut, since that was where the children of the town's elite studied. Had it really been closed down to take revenge on the rich, on the orders of my good Uncle Shmulik?

Though they drank their tea in peace and polished off Mama's tasty pie, I had lost my appetite for asking questions. No matter how many questions you asked my uncle, who had apparently reached great heights, the Tarbut school would still not be open.

Shmulik was preparing to leave when Grandma Rokha entered the room, which served both as a workshop and living room, with full pots.

"Who do I see here?" she asked in surprise. "I thought that you had already found quarters with your fellow police-men and forgotten us."

Shmulik embraced her with a sad tenderness and, bowing his head, expressed his sorrow for Grandma's loss. "I was at the cemetery. My mother and your Dovid are lying next to each other on the hillock. You shouldn't forget your parents, either when they're alive or when they're dead. But the reason we see each other so rarely is my own damned business."

"They say that you are something like our former police chief Rozgi now except that, forgive an old woman for mentioning it, you're circumcised."

"What's true is true. I am circumcised but I'm not a police chief," Shmulik said.

"So then, what are you?"

"How can I explain it to you, Rokha? My boss is Aleksei Ivanovich Vorobev from Mordovia. He's only been in Jonava for three weeks. I have to help him get a sense of what is to be done here, who should be supported, who repressed and who we should keep a good eye on so that they won't cause any harm to the new authorities."

"And why did you repress the Tarbut school? You repressed it. Now there is a barn lock on its doors, Shmulik. You were always against us, always. I remember how you cursed me four years ago for wanting to send our Hirshke there because no one speaks Hebrew in Lithuania. And in what language will everyone speak now? Russian?"

"In Lithuanian, in Yiddish and in Russian. But I still don't take back my words. No regime in the world will pay out of its own pockets to encourage the studies of its sworn enemies."

Suddenly the fire, whose last coals were glowing, flamed up with redoubled strength.

"What enemies are you talking about? The schoolchildren?" Rokha exclaimed, unable to control herself.

Noisily, almost triumphantly, I banged my spoon against my empty cup, proud, even exalted, at Grandma's boldness.

"Schoolchildren? They are not schoolchildren, but the Zionists of tomorrow. Let them go to Palestine and study as much as they like in the dead language of King Solomon. Such schools are not needed in the Soviet state. Who in Jonava will its graduates speak to, except for Rabbi Eliezer? In what university will they be able enroll with that language? Why should they bury their heads in the ancient past? They would be better off directing their thoughts to the future," said the newly appointed boss, employing the rhetoric of the Soviets.

"You say, 'Let them go to Palestine', but who will let them go there?" Father burst out. "The owner of the furniture factory wanted to leave for America, but its embassy was gone with the wind; Reb Eliahu Landburg was turned away from the gate."

Exhausted by the attacks of his family members, Shmulik deflected the conversation. "What can be done if none of you have any class consciousness? I dropped in only for a minute and have already spent a whole hour with you at the expense of my work. I have a last question, has Julius turned up?"

"No," Father replied.

"The fierce Lithuanian military, with its two tanks borrowed from the Latvians and its single artillery piece that's fit only for shooting fireworks, has fallen apart. And Julius is basically illiterate; he doesn't know a single word of Russian. He's hardly fit for the Red Army. He's got nowhere to hide; he'll be found, it's not like looking for a needle in a haystack."

"Listen, Shmulik! Perhaps on Sundays you can help Shleimke with his sewing?" Grandma Rokha suggested ironically. "He'll pay you well."

"I would help him with great pleasure." Shmulik laughed. "But we work on Sundays too. Rokha, we basically work the whole week long."

"But don't you at least sleep at night?" Grandma responded.

"When our service requires it, we are awake at night as well," Shmulik replied without malice, as he got up to leave.

Father recalled Ephraim Kapler's request to facilitate a meeting with the assistant head of the town's NKVD, but he decided not to mention it. Let Reb Ephraim make contact with Shmulik himself. His brother-in-law would hardly bite at Ephraim's golden bait.

"I'll come visit you and have tea and pastries," said Shmulik, their family member who was now a boss, and then departed.

"My dear brother will go far," said Mama. "If he doesn't stumble."

"His work is dirty!" Father exclaimed suddenly, annoyed by Shmulik's supercilious words, "Don't worry, they won't touch you." He had no idea why they could possibly want to touch him; from the age of thirteen, he had bent his back working from morning to night without oppressing or humiliating anyone.

"Why is it dirty?" Mama asked, trying to defend her brother.

"He believes that it's pure and noble. He thinks that it's possible to serve a good cause and, at the same time, without any twinge of conscience, to engage in evil and indulge in hatred," Father explained. "I don't know about you, but I wouldn't be able to fall asleep in a three-room apartment that had been taken from someone else. But Shmulik doesn't give a fig about that. Well, anyway, that's enough about him!"

"I'm worried about Isaac," Rokha said, when passions had calmed down. "Yesterday I went to Fain's bakery to buy *challah* for Shabbat and Fain said to me, 'What's the news about your older son?'"

"'What's the news?' I said. 'There's no news. Not a rumour, not a sound.' Then he frightened me, saying, 'The Germans are in Paris and people say that they're marching down its main street.'"

"The Champs-Élysées," put in Melekh.

"Really?" asked Father in surprise.

"Yes. It's just as I thought. Oh why did Isaac have to stay in France? At first he was planning to go to America. It's one thing to flee from the Germans from Warsaw," Grandma Rokha said, looking askance at Melekh and Małgozata, "but it's quite another thing from Paris! You'd be done for before you could get from there to us in this out of the way corner. If Isaac hadn't got so carried away, he could have stayed here in Jonava, curing animal skins and making fur hats from them. There's always a big demand for them, and for fur collars. And now how many officers' wives there are who have come here for the winter!"

"Perhaps they managed to escape to some other place, one that isn't so dangerous," Mother said, trying to comfort her mother-in-law.

"What times these are!" Grandma began to wail. "There's no place to flee from trouble. You run away from one only to have another catch up with you and grab you by the collar."

Outside dusk had descended on Jonava. A solitary star shone between the clouds. Stars too, it seemed, could be alone.

Mama put on her warm, quilted overcoat to accompany Grandma Rokha home; her eyesight was poor even in daylight. Nor did the polite Melekh and Małgozata stay long either. Their landlady Antanina didn't like the night-owls arriving home late.

I remained alone with Father.

"What about our school? Will they close it?" I asked.

"God only knows what the new authorities are planning," he replied.

I wasn't about to ask God. If you ask Him something, you shouldn't hold your breath for an answer.

"Go to sleep, Hirshele. I want to sew a bit longer."

In bed, I heard the voice of the janitor Antanas.

"Excuse me, *Ponas* Saliamonas, for coming so late, but, damn it, my Julias has finally come back! He plans on coming to see you tomorrow."

"Thank you."

"Do you, maybe, have a bit of wine around?"

"Sorry! We have wine only on Passover."

"It's a long time until Passover!" said the janitor and, disappointed, bade Father goodnight, throwing in one of his few Yiddish expressions. "*Zayt gezunt!*"

11

As Antanas had promised, the following morning, before Melekh had arrived for work with Małgozata, there was a knock at our door. It was the young apprentice Julius, who had disappeared without a trace.

"Here I am," he said simply.

"Welcome, brave warrior!" Father greeted him. "Somehow you seem to have completed your army service quite quickly."

At first Julius hesitated. He wiped the perspiration from his brow, blinked, his eyes still clouded with traces of sleep, and then grudgingly confessed, "Well you see, *Ponas* Saliamonas, in fact I didn't serve for a single day."

"How did that happen, you were drafted into the army? You found a clever way to get out of it?"

"I didn't serve a single day or carry a rifle. I wasn't a soldier in the Lithuanian army, or in the new Red Army either," he replied, embarrassed.

If Father had met his assistant on the street, he would scarcely have recognized him. To disguise himself, the lad had grown a short reddish beard, a thin Spanish moustache that curled like a snake as if slithering under his large meaty nose with its wide, sensitive nostrils. Julius was dressed scruffily in a worn flannel shirt, broad patched trousers and a shabby old belt and greasy cap.

"So where have you been holed up then?"

"When this whole mess began, when they were searching for the Red Army soldiers who had been kidnapped in broad daylight and with the letters-shmetters on both sides, going from one country to another and threatening ultimatums from Moscow and Kaunas rejecting them, I said to myself, 'Scram, Julius, before it's too late! Disappear! Things aren't going to end well.' So I ran away from the recruitment point, made it to Prenai and then to the resort of Birštonas, where I found a job as an odd-job man in the Tulip Sanatorium. What didn't I do in that period of time? I worked as a loader and a cleaner, I even cleaned floors, but I ate for free and lived rent-free in a deserted bathhouse on the bank of the Neman. Nobody was looking for me, nobody asked anything. Nobody wanted to know who I was, or where I had come from. They only wanted one thing from me – work! And I worked."

Father didn't doubt the truth of his story, but he couldn't imagine how the mild-mannered Julius was capable of such a decisive act as desertion. The clever lad had taken advantage of the chaos all around and taken a risk. The new authorities had declared the previous government and its army illigitimate, while maintaining its own rule by intimidating the majority of the citizens, through the use of bayonets.

"So, dare-devil, have you returned for long? Or will you take off again back to your resort in the bathhouse on the Neman?"

"I've returned for good. What will be, will be. I felt sorry for my mother. When I'm not here Pop skins her alive. When he gets drunk, he immediately starts to beat her and shout, 'You slut, you!' *Ponas* Saliamonas, I can begin work today. My hands may have become a little rough and unused to handling needles but, please believe me, I won't let you down. I have a special feeling for the tailor's craft."

"So tell me, I'd like to know, what feeling is that?"

"A positive one. To sew, *Ponas* Saliamonas, is quite different from working as an unskilled labourer. You can't imagine the jobs I had! I washed the floors in the sanatorium buildings, swept the rubbish-strewn areas, unloaded heavy packages of washed bed linen from trucks for those staying at the resort and dragged them up to the third floor on my back." When Father didn't say anything, Julius caught his breath and continued. "Maybe I could start by working for free? After a trial period, you can decide whether to take me back or not."

"Why for free? Julius, you know that the only place people go for free is the outhouse."

"Well, *Ponas* Saliamonas, as you say!"

"We'll do without the trial period. Have you had breakfast?"

"Yes."

"Then sit down and get to work. My future relative, Senior Lieutenant Vasili Kamenev, ordered a suit with a double-breasted jacket. Sew the sleeves onto the jacket. He's coming to try it on this Sunday."

"May God grant you good health! I'm constantly trying to reeducate my father. As soon as he has drunk too much, he begins to talk rubbish, saying, 'Son, watch out for those non-Christians, they're all repulsive liars.' But I reply, 'That's ridiculous, you just don't know them. You can learn a great deal from them. They should be an example for us. It's just your envy that makes you curse them mercilessly. Envy and jealousy never made anyone happier or richer.'"

Having got himself worked up, Julius was going to say something more, but at that moment Melekh arrived.

"We'll all work together and try to help each other," Father proposed, introducing them. "Julius, you speak Yiddish fairly well, *Ponas* Melekh will teach you some more and you can both teach Małgozata, who only knows one Yiddish expression, '*Vos hert zikh idn?*' What do you hear, Jews? By the way, where is your *kochana*, Melekh?"

"She stayed home with our landlady. Antanina is sick again," Melekh replied. "The old woman is really in bad shape. It's hard for her to get out of bed and she doesn't go to church with Małgozata any more. She whispers her prayers every day and asks that the priest comes to see her. She's afraid she won't live to receive the last unction."

"I am sorry to hear that. I've known Antanina since I was young, from the time when, after the death of my first teacher Shaya Rabiner, I became apprenticed to Abram Kisin," said Father. "Except for us, she didn't have anyone else in the world – no husband, no children. Harvesters found her wrapped in a nappy in a pile of hay, and took her to a Catholic orphanage. It's terrible to say it, but there will be no one to bury her."

"Several times Małgozata and I intended to turn to you for help to get a doctor to see Antanina, but she refused. She says, 'God is my doctor. My whole life He has come to me without being called, healed all of my sicknesses and strengthened my spirit. He will come and take me, His true servant, to Him.'"

"You can't change her," Father said. "She's an old woman who has always been alone. More than once she's told me, 'Only solitary people cause no harm and do not fear death.'"

"If she dies, how will we pay for the apartment?" asked Melekh. "Or will we be put out onto the street?"

"Abram Kisin left the house to his nephew in Riga. He came to his uncle's funeral and then went back to Latvia, where there's no trace of him now. You'll pay the new owners, Melekh, the new government; it's taken over almost everything and is happy to get money wherever it can. You won't be left without a roof over your heads."

Julius took no part in the conversation, but settled down to attaching the sleeves to the double-breasted jacket for Vasili Kamenev. Leaving off his bad-mouthing of the government, Father took up a pair of scissors and began to cut a length of material for another customer, while Melekh, who was a little more relaxed, sat at the sewing machine. The rest of the day the quiet was interrupted only by the cheerful humming of the machine.

Close to evening, a rare guest dropped in unexpectedly – Mother's widowed father, the cobbler Shimon, who was well known in the shtetl for being an incurable stay-at-home. Only on the major holidays did he dress up in his best clothes and set out for the synagogue with Sheyne; the rest of the time he sat at home tapping away with his hammer.

"The Almighty in heaven will hear you hammering away without a pause like a woodpecker and punish you and all of us for having allowed your unheard of rudeness," Grandma Sheyne used to say.

Father had no idea what had brought his father-in-law to visit him so unexpectedly. Nor did Mama. Since the matter seemed to be serious, she immediately went into action, taking an embroidered tablecloth from the cupboard and putting some treats on the table, but Grandpa Shimon didn't touch the pastries, the plum jam, the Lithuanian cheese or the chamomile tea from the porcelain teapot.

"I am only staying a short time," he said.

No one doubted that; Old Dudak never stayed long at anyone's house. He always justified himself, citing a reason that was indeed worthy, "It's a sin to steal time from others, just as you shouldn't waste your own time. No one has ever opened a store where you can buy hours and minutes wholesale or retail."

"I've come because of Pesya and her young man," Grandpa Shimon stated briefly and frowned, raising thick eyebrows that resembled hornets. "I came to pour out my heart."

"What's wrong with Pesya?" Mother asked in alarm.

"Nothing, but do you know that she intends to marry a *goy*?" Grandpa asked.

"But, Reb Shimon, a *goy* is a human being, not an animal," my father replied.

"No, he's not an animal, but he's not one of us either. What's a wedding without a *chuppah* and without a rabbi, just Red Army soldiers in blouses and caps askew at the wedding table, dancing the *kazachok*?"

"Still, according to the Torah the grandchildren will be ours – Jews," his son-in-law consoled Grandpa Shimon.

"We Dudaks have never had any Russians, much less Russian officers, in our family. I don't know whether you approve of Pesya's choice, but she'd better not count on receiving my blessing. And it seems to me that my late Sheyne is crying in her grave, 'Shimon, talk to the foolish girl, talk to her!' Only Shmulik keeps repeating like a parrot, 'there's no such thing as Russian love, or Turkish love, or Jewish love. Real love has no . . .' Something. Damn it, I can't remember the word, even in Yiddish, it just falls out of my stupid head . . ."

"Has no nationality," my father prompted him.

"That's the word. That's what Shmulik said," Grandpa said. "And now Pesya's sisters Feiga and Hasya say that if this Russian lieutenant really loves her, then you can make a Jew of him."

"It's better to be happy with some Russian named Ivan or Vasili than unhappy with some pure-born Isaac or Chaim," Hennie said, daring to stand up for her younger sister.

"The devil brought these Russians to Jonava! Why, I ask you, didn't they just stay home?" asked Grandpa Shimon, sighing deeply. "Just where is the good Lord God, the arranger and matchmaker of all weddings, now?"

"Don't despair, Papa. Perhaps Vasili and Pesya will go their separate ways," Mama said, trying to lighten her father's dark mood. "As for God, it's imposible to know how He manages things. Is it even possible for Him to keep an eye on everyone?"

Her efforts to comfort him not only didn't cheer Grandpa Shimon up, they upset him even further. He hadn't expected Hennie and Shleime either to criticize Pesya or totally support him, but he had hoped they would promise to help change her mind. Instead, both of them had launched into tiresome observations about the vagaries of life. He wondered what they would have said if Pesya had been their own daughter. No doubt they would have had something different to say. Their hearts were not tormented by a parent's pain.

Grandpa Shimon thanked them for the lavish spread, of which he had not partaken, arose and headed for the door.

"I'll go with you," Hennie said, putting her coat on and going to the door.

"You don't need to," he said. He put on his cap and, taking a deep breath, said without any reproach, "I'll find the way by myself. Nothing will happen to me. After the death of your mother I stopped being afraid. As for that sister of yours who has fallen for the Russian officer, Hennie, I have to say, it's clearly the way of the world now for young people to sow foolishness and helpless old age to reap the woes."

Grandpa disappeared into the night.

When she returned home, Mama repeated her father's words to her husband.

"You can't help but sympathize with him a little," replied Shleimke. "Bluma Berger cursed her daughter and chased her out of the house. We all know full well how that ended. But now there are much worse troubles than an unsuccessful marriage and these troubles affect just about everyone, regardless of age. People are suffering from wars, pogroms and are being driven from their homes."

"Thank God that for us things are still quiet for now," Mother said.

"Quiet for now?" Father said. "With the Kogans it's like you're behind a brick wall; bad news doesn't reach you. Here, in my workshop, all kinds of ugly rumours stream in, making you want to plug your ears up."

"Why haven't you ever told me about them?" Mother rebuked Father.

"I didn't want to upset you. What if all the rumours were a lot of hot air?"

"Which rumours?"

"All kinds. People say that the new government intends to close down all the artisanal synagogues – the butchers', the cobblers' and the others. They say one is enough for everyone."

Mother listened without interrupting.

"And they also say that some kind of secret lists are being compiled."

"Lists?"

"Yes, lists," said Father, no longer hiding his anger. "Lists of those Shmulik always used to call the bourgeoisie."

"What do they intend to do with them?"

"I've no idea. I do know that when that know-it-all Chaim Gershon Fain came to pick up his new item of clothing, he said he would probably close down his bakery and move to join his cousin in Gargždai. He didn't hide the fact that he would willingly sell it at a loss, but where could you find a buyer now?"

Mother's eyes widened in amazement.

"Chaim Gershon said that in the Soviet Union all bakeries are owned by the state, not by individuals."

"But if he leaves, there won't be any more rolls and *challot* like his. There won't be anyone to buy them from," Mother said.

"He said that the time has come when it's better not to try to cling on to your property, better to forget about it as if it never existed. Head for some hole in some out of the way place rather than to trying to protect your property. 'The Russians,' Fain reckons, 'favour the poor more than the rich.'"

Less than a month had passed when the rumour about the closing of the small prayer houses in Jonava was confirmed.

In the spring of 1941, my uncle Shmulik, officially Shmuel Dudak, asistant of the head of the local NKVD division for operational affairs, brought Father a new customer, his direct superior, Major Vorobev.

"Alexei Ivanovich," he said, introducing his boss.

"Shleime," my father said.

Following this introduction, Uncle Shmulik conducted the rest of the conversation in Yiddish.

"Samuil Semenovich recommended you to me as a first-class tailor," the major said. Vorobyov looked around the room with the eye of an experienced investigator. "My old overcoat is worn out. I decided to have a new one sewn before I'm transferred to another location."

From a large package wrapped in paper the major took a swatch of grey cloth, a lining and the other items needed and put everything on the table.

Father looked in perplexity from the tall Vorobyev to Shmulik, who appeared frozen in the pose of an obsequious matchmaker, then at the cloth and the other items.

"I have never sewn an overcoat before," the first-class tailor admitted frankly to his brother-in-law.

"Don't even think about turning down this order," Shmulik said in a hushed voice. "You'll do it. I'll come in the evenings to help you, like I used to do. And not just with idle chatter or advice, but to work. I didn't forget everything in prison. I can compete with Julius and that sympathetic refugee with the sweet name."

"But does your boss know what I will be charging?" Father said to Shmulik, posing his usual question. "After all, we're dealing with an overcoat, not something simple like a suit."

"He knows. He knows. Stop trying to act as if this was some kind of bazaar and get on with measuring him," said the sly Samuil Semenovich, forcing a smile. Then, in Father's name, he invented a compliment for Alexei Ivanovich. "My brother-in-law says that the material you brought is excellent. It will be a pleasure to use it."

While my dumbfounded Father was doing the measuring, Mama called her brother aside and asked in a whisper, "Shmulik, people in the shtetl are saying that the authorities are closing down all the synagogues. Is it true? Tell me the truth!"

"What do you care if the authorities close them down or not? You don't attend any of them. Nor does Shleimke, nor do your three sisters. One hearth of obscurantism, the Great Synagogue, is enough for the old people."

The closing of the small synagogues began a series of events in Jonava that shook all its residents, regardless of whether they were religious or not.

Trucks with armed soldiers began to roar around the shtetl at high speed, not sparing the cobblestoned streets. They stopped at the homes of former government officials, leading members of Smetona's party and of groups that had fought for the freedom and independence of Lithuania. At the houses of overt or covert Zionists and owners of the large stores, of tracts of land and of factories. The soldiers forced people from their houses, along with their families, pushed them with their hand luggage and meagre food supplies into covered trucks and took them to the railway station, where empty freight cars were awaiting them.

The prudent Chaim Gershon Fain had not waited for something bad to happen; he had dismissed his workers, shut the door of his profitable bakery and got out of Jonava to a place where, he hoped, he and his wife Perle and their twins would not be found. When he got to Gargždai, he didn't prance around in his new coat or the suit tailored for him by the skilful Shleime Kanovich. The dandy Chaim Gershon donned an old coat, grew a beard and forgot about listening to the daytime and evening news on his Dutch radio. "Damn the news, anyway!" he said. He made every effort not to stand out, or to let anyone suspect that with the profits of all the *challot* and rolls he had sold over the years, he had bought ten *dunams* of land in Palestine.

It seemed to Fain that by avoiding being deported to the Arctic Circle he had outwitted fate. The owner of the bakery had no idea that instead he had doomed himself to certain death. A half year later, he and his whole family would perish, not as members of the bourgeoisie, but as Jews. If they had been exiled to the Arctic Circle or to Siberia, they would have had a chance to survive.

The naive Reb Kapler, who didn't believe he was guilty of anything, didn't follow the example of his old friend. Unlike Chaim Gershon, he didn't abandon his property – his three-storey house and the haberdashery and manufactured goods shop – to seek refuge in some hideaway. He stayed in Jonava with his wife, the full-bodied Fruma and their Doberman Pinscher, Jackie, and with his stomach pains, heartburn and insomnia.

One morning a truck stopped beneath our windows, its brakes screeching, polluting the air with its exhaust fumes. Behind the wheel was a driver in a green shirt, who was either a Kalmyk or a Buriat and next to him a young officer with a red, girlish face. Father said, either to himself or to Melekh,

"That's it!"

Father stood at the open window and watched as the jaunty young soldiers jumped out of the truck and headed for the shop, going not for Danish toothpaste, or shaving cream from Latvia, or eau–de-cologne from Switzerland, but for the owner.

"I pity Reb Ephraim and Fruma," Father murmured. "Woe to the country where the poor are exalted while the rich are persecuted like criminals," he added.

I went up to the window, snuggled against Father's warm side and looked at the military truck and its driver with his high cheekbones who, lifting the hood, began fiddling in a calm manner with the engine.

For some reason, like Father, I was sorry for Ephraim Kapler. Perhaps because sometimes, when complaining about the pains in his legs, he would hand me the leash of Jackie, his beloved Pinscher, and allow me, under his supervision, to walk her near the house. I couldn't understand how the pious Reb Ephraim, who sold dry goods, had earned the ire of the Russian soldiers. It was evident that something bad was happening if Father was stood looking out of the window for so long, forgetting completely about his sewing machine. I was tempted to ask what had happened, but he turned to me angrily.

"Go read your book, on the double! You need to develop your mind! There's no reason to waste time looking out the window!"

Melekh and Julius continued to work on Major Vorobyev's overcoat, while Father decided to go out into the street to, by either word or gesture, bid farewell to Reb Ephraim and to ask his forgiveness for having disturbed his sleep so often with the annoying, monotonous hum of his Singer sewing machine.

Father wanted to tell Kapler not to lose hope. To tell him that, God willing, he would return to Jonava. The soldiers barred his way with their rifles, not allowing him to approach the bent Reb Ephraim and the distraught and frozen Fruma. Nor did the Red Army soldiers permit the childless old couple to take their beloved dog with them in the truck. The Pinscher, with his leash around his neck, ran around the truck and barked angrily, as if to say, "Let my master go! Why are you taking him from me?"

"*Mir veln oif euch wartn! Zait gezunt!*" Father shouted in Yiddish so that the Red Army soldiers would not understand. We will wait for you! Keep healthy!

The Kaplers, prisoners with bundles in their hands, did not turn to look either at the home they were leaving, that had been locked by other people, nor at the shop that had been sealed shut. Nor did they pay any attention to the cry of their brave tenant. Reb Ephraim simply raised aloft his wrinkled hand, which he formed into a fist – as if to not only bid farewell to his home and apartment, but also to remind the Lord God that a glaring injustice was being committed right before Him. The Almighty was angry, but remained silent in the face of the actions of the soldiers, while the red-faced lieutenant who was in charge of the operation to take the Kaplers turned out to be more powerful than the Ruler of the World, shouting loudly,

"Stop that immediately!"

Father was forced to be quiet. But the official's order had no effect on the Pinscher. Dragging his leash behind him, the dog barked furiously at the mightiest army in the world, who did not know what to do with him. They tried chasing him away with their rifle butts and attempted to intimidate him with foul curses, but Jackie lurched toward his master and howled pitifully.

"Get it out of here!" screamed the lieutenant, losing his temper, though he was generally more tolerant of animals than of people. "Otherwise my boys will take care of him."

Father bent down, picked up the leash and led the Pinscher back into his workroom. Having stopped sewing, Melekh and Julius tried to caress the orphaned dog, but he was afraid of their affection and tried to hide in the corner of the strange house. Trembling, the dog began to whine quietly. It was just at this point that Major Vorobyev turned up for a fitting accompanied by Shmulik, his assistant for operational matters.

While Father was marking out with chalk the flaws and the parts that still had to be completed, the former trouser-specialist Shmulik whirled like a spinning-top around his smartly dressed superior, examining the unfinished overcoat, which still had white threads sticking out of it, exclaiming, "Brilliant! They've worked magnificently in such a short time! What fine fellows they are!"

After a pause Shmulik added, with a sly chuckle, subsuming the Catholic Julius into the Jewish workers in order to appear more convincing, "Comrade Major, you will have an excellent gift for the First of May from the Jewish working class."

Vorobyev smiled broadly and laughed with pleasure.

"Thank you, thank you!" Alexei Ivanovich said after the measuring had been finished, and he shook the hands of the Jewish working class. Saluting, he turned to his assistant and said, "Samuil Semenovich, undoubtedly you would like to spend some more time with your relatives. I will send a car for you at six."

Did you hear that? They would send a car for him! How could he possibly not stay? So Shmulik stayed, even though he had no interest in being lectured, or in being interrogated by his brother-in-law, who was not impressed by his former apprentice's new job or by what armed foreigners were doing with impunity in someone else's country. Shleime had never shared the views of his brother-in-law. In contrast to Shmulik, who had only completed *heder*, the traditional Jewish elementary school, Father had his own firm convictions. These were expressed in maxims like, do your own work and don't interfere with the work of others. Don't urge on someone else's horse with your own whip. Don't make your master's bed according to your style and certainly don't try to lie down in it!

Despite the fact that the people he had worked with often made fun of Shmulik and sometimes criticized him for his categorical and militant ideas, he had felt more protected in the tailor's workshop than anywhere else. Sometimes he even caught himself thinking that he couldn't explain why he felt so lonely in his new job, despite the fact that he was constantly receiving visitors and, it seemed to him, was working not for the bad but for the good.

Trying to avoid an argument and not thinking there was anything negative or problematic in his question, Shmulik asked my father who owned the lovely four-footed creature with the leash around its neck that was quietly whining in the corner.

"Don't play the fool and pretend you don't know whose it is."

"I swear to you I don't!"

"It belongs to Reb Ephraim."

"Ahh!"

"They didn't allow him to take the Pinscher with him into exile. They showed mercy on the dog, they let him stay home. But, Shmulik, why did they take Reb Ephraim? What did he ever do?"

"Shleime, that's not connected with my department. I deal with other quite different matters."

"The man simply inherited his father's house. He rebuilt it and opened some stores. Every year he contributed to the poor house and prayed fervently to God. For what good reason did they carry him and Fruma away in a truck like they were taking them to their grave?"

"Why are you asking me about this?"

"You deal with other matters but, looked at soberly, you are associated with these soldiers. Reb Ephraim wanted to speak to you; obviously he foresaw trouble. It's a good thing that he didn't. In any case, you wouldn't have defended him."

"Do you want me to go?" his brother-in-law threatened.

"No, no I don't, but, Shmulik, you can't escape being yourself. Perhaps the time will come when somebody should stand up for you, but he won't. In the future that truck that ferries people to the grave might get much bigger, and perhaps it won't be driven by your fellow thinkers and fellow workers."

Melekh and Julius pretended that they weren't listening to the conversation. Perhaps they weren't. Perhaps they really were concentrating on sewing the Major's overcoat. Anyway, they were more concerned about their own fate than that of the landlord Ephraim Kapler.

Father fell silent. Perhaps he had gone too far in his heated dispute with Shmulik. Father respected his wife's brother for his integrity, for his self-sacrifice, selflessness and love of life. He was sorry that Shmulik had given up being a tailor and was getting involved with what a Jew shouldn't get involved with – establishing order in a country where he himself was an outsider.

"I know that you're a good person. You're not bad in any way, but you're mistaken if you think that you can throw your lot in with violent and evil people and still reap the good. You'll almost be able to smell the good, but suddenly your nose will be assaulted by the smell of someone's blood."

The argument stopped when Mama returned from the Kogans'.

"Who do I see here? Shmulik, will you eat with us? I just bought some sausage, I'll fry some eggs and you'll be able to eat some food fit for human beings for once. I heard that all you do is gallop around the shtetl with the Russians fighting disorder rather than thinking about your health. Listen, just as He didn't create a human to exist forever, God didn't create a government to last forever, either. Today you're sitting on the back of your horse and tomorrow someone else is in the saddle. Take my advice, the hell with everything, sit down and eat."

"I'll eat, I'll eat," her brother gave in.

"But what is Reb Ephraim's dog doing in our house? He's made a puddle in the corner!" exclaimed Mama.

"They've taken away Fruma and Reb Ephraim," Shleime said without going into details.

"Where to?"

"As one of my customers put it, to join the polar bears. I took Jackie in. Our Hirshke will take him out for walks; the dog can run around in the fresh air and urinate outside to his heart's content."

It turned out that Shmulik didn't have time to eat. A jeep arrived for him at six exactly.

12

As the Passover of 1941 approached there was no sense of the normal excitement in the shtetl, of the mad, joyful rush that always preceded the bright spring festival of freedom. Everything seemed routine and dreary. Fear, dressed in a green shirt and military cap with a five-pointed star, strolled carefree along the lanes and streets of Jonava. The tightly locked synagogues of the artisans were intimidating to both the religious and non-relgious Jews alike, as were the army trucks that functioned as jails on wheels and the boarded-up windows of the shops, on whose doors were purple, wound-like seals stamped with a hammer and sickle.

Jonava suddenly appeared shrivelled up and abandoned.

The pre-Passover market, which had always dazzled the eyes with its wealth of goods, was bare.

Grandma Rokha, who had invited all our family for Passover, complained non-stop. For one thing, this year at the shtetl market there were far fewer carp, smelling of life and underwater mysteries; the fishmongers brought far fewer fish fresh from the nearby ponds and lakes than they had in previous years. That was scarcely surprising, however; the new regime had deprived them of many of their regular customers for God knows for what sins, sending them off to freezing barracks which never smelled of gefilte fish and horseradish.

Even though it was only days before the Russians joined the conflict that would later be known as World War Two, neither the Jonava residents, busy with their daily cares and their preparations for the holiday, nor the young Russian officers who wandered around the town without a care, looking regretfully at the boarded-up store windows, sensed its fatal approach.

Despite the closure of the 'superfluous' synagogues and the purge of the shtetl's wealthy, unreliable bourgeoisie like Ephraim Kapler, the Jews of Jonava were still able to get their matza in time and make the special preparations for the first two nights of Passover.

The fact that the world had not yet collapsed and that the practices commanded by the Torah were still observed was confirmed when 'Almost a Jew' Vincas Gedraitis, old friend of the cobbler Dovid, having been fired without receiving the pension he had counted on from the previous regime, appeared, as was his custom, at Rybatskaya Street to sample this year's matza.

Vincas stood at the door for a long time, his rumpled cap stuffed under his arm, wiping the soles of his boots on the doormat. "But perhaps you weren't expecting me?" he said, as if to excuse himself. "After all, I've nothing to do now. I'm unemployed and just wander around town. I was passing by and thought to myself, maybe I'll drop in for a minute, they won't kick me out. We'll say some good words about poor Dovid."

"Come in, Vincas! What is Passover without you?" said Grandma Rokha, smiling. "You used to come to our in-law Shimon, didn't you?"

"And now it's your turn. Let's remember Dovid. After all this is the first Passover without him," said the former guardian of law and order, sighing sympathetically.

Vincas Gedraitis was no longer the self-confident, well-groomed young man who had grown up among Jews, dealing with them without prejudice, with curiosity and sympathy, characteristics his fellow policemen didn't often show. The man standing before Rokha the Samurai was elderly, with a flabby, wrinkled face and eyes like burning embers that appeared to be constantly seeking something. The civilian clothes didn't suit Vincas at all; they hung on him like sacks. The only thing that recalled his former state were his boots, made by either Shimon or Dovid, although they lacked their former polish.

"Dovid always treated you to matza and enjoyed discussing life with you."

"Yes, he did. He always did," Gedraitis agreed. "We often spoke together about the temptations of life. Who could have imagined that everything would be turned on its head?"

"Yes," Grandma agreed, surmising what he was alluding to.

"Life, Rokha, if you'll excuse the comparison, is like a dissolute woman; at first she falls madly in love with a man and then, suddenly, the very next day, she betrays him."

Grandma Rokha wasn't prepared for the turn in conversation. Though she felt sorry for Gedraitis who, following the change of government, was totally bankrupt, she had no idea how to express her pity. Grandpa, however, resorted imediately to the most common means of consolation.

"How about a nice glass of mead Vincas? It'll go well with the matza. Let's drink a toast to the memory of Dovid and in the hope that things will improve for you."

"Sinner that I am, I've never refused a drink, although I've always drunk in moderation. I hate extremes. I wasn't a big shot in the police force, just a messenger delivering summons. I never arrested anyone or sentenced anyone to a jail term. I tried to be decent and I hope I was. Many of my fellow policemen were deported, but for some reason, I was spared. It might be that your wife's brother spoke up for me, that he put in a good word for me to the Russians."

"Shmulik?"

"Yes, Shmulik. More than once I gave him a friendly warning about not shooting his mouth off. It's no good shouting, 'Down with them!' on every street corner and risking being sent to prison," Gedraitis said, singing his own praises in a mixture of Yiddish and Lithuanian. "Now look how high he has flown! Perhaps he whispered in someone's ear, 'That harmless old man can be left alone, no need to deport him!'"

"He's basically a good fellow," Rokha said, "just a fool sometimes. He gave up a good profession and for what, I ask you? But why aren't you drinking? You're just holding your glass in your hand."

"To you, Rokha!" toasted 'Almost a Jew' and downed his glass and followed it with some matza.

Rokha thought that having drunk a toast 'Almost a Jew' would thank her for her hospitality and say goodbye. Instead

Gedraitis lingered, shifting from one foot to the other, glancing at the last where Dovid used to sit. Aimlessly, he turned the now empty glass around in his hand.

"Well, I'll be going now, Rokha." It was obvious Vincas wanted to add something to his toast, but hesitated.

"No one is chasing you away," Grandma said.

"Thank you for the matza, Rokha, and for the drink. May God grant that we all live until next Passover!" Gedraitis thanked his hostess.

"We will unless we die first. That's what Dovid, may his memory be blessed, used to say."

Gedraitis didn't respond immediately. He straightened the worn jacket that hung on him like a sack, raised his nose like a hunting dog that had smelled some prey and then said, "Who knows how everything will turn out? Yesterday, after morning prayers, Burbulis, who is substituting for our priest Vaitkus, who is sick, remarked that rumours are circulating about the Germans being on the move and, what's more, coming in the direction of our border! If they cross it, you realise that someone will suffer."

"Someone?" Grandma's eyebrows rose like swallows fleeing a crane. "By someone you mean us Jews, of course?"

"The priest said nothing about the Jews. He said that when the Germans occupy Lithuania, it will be the way it used to be here, an independent state without foreigners or traitors."

"The way it used to be? I don't think so! The Germans will rid Jonava of us Jews. And I've no doubt some of your fellow countrymen will lend them a hand."

"I won't act against my conscience. You can always find people who want revenge for the life they feel they were robbed of. That is why I am telling you what the priest said."

"Not everyone is like you, Vincas. You wouldn't harm a fly. So come on, did your mother perhaps commit a sin with a Jew when she was young?"

"Rokha, why are you insulting my mother?"

"Don't get upset. It was just a joke." Grandma suddenly frowned. "You can't bargain with fate like you are at the market," she said seriously. "Maybe the Germans will cross the Lithuanian border, maybe not. What will be, will be. Such is our cursed fate – to flee from wherever we were settled to somewhere else from where there's no where else to run."

Gedraitis didn't drop in by chance, Rokha realised. He hadn't come for the matza or a glass of mead. Having listened to the vicar, he had decided to warn the whole family about the danger that threatened them. He was implying that they should be prepared for being attacked from two sides, from the Germans and from the Lithuanians.

Just as Vincas Gedraitis was about to take his leave, the whole company arrived all together, her son and his wife, Melekh and Małgozata, and Shmulik too, accompanied by a guest – Senior Lieutenant Valeri Fishman. And along with them all there was I, who that very evening was supposed to ask the eternal question of the Passover *seder*, about the Exodus of the enslaved Jews from Egyptian bondage.

"So then, I'm off," Gedraitis said. "I've stayed quite long enough as it is."

"Where are you rushing off to?" Rokha said, trying to hold him back.

"My wife is expecting me at home, she's probably wondering where I have got to," Gedraitis muttered in dismay, glancing sideways at Shmulik and the Russian lieutenant who had shown up to celebrate Passover.

"*Ponas* Vincas, why not drink a glass with us as a sign of our reconciliation?" Shmulik proposed, detaining him with a laugh. "Personally I don't have anything against you. You weren't the one who issued the order for my arrest, nor were you the one who handcuffed me. When I was in the prison colony, I often remembered how you had warned me to stop shouting, 'Down with the Government!' at full volume on every street corner. 'Sew trousers and robes,' you advised, 'and the long coats all you Jews wear. There is no greater justice than work.'"

"True, true. May God protect you all!" said 'Almost a Jew' Gedraitis, clinking glasses with Shmulik. He left then, satisfied.

After a struggle, Grandma got everyone to sit down at the holiday table, which was covered with an ironed white tablecloth and laden with the food that had been prepared.

After the death of Grandpa Dovid, my father was in charge of the Passover *seder*, though he barely knew the order and details. He began the ceremony not at the beginning, but with the phrase he had learned by heart in *heder* and, for some reason, remembered best of all. Wanting to get on with the feast, which everyone had been looking forward to, Father hurried to ask me the main question of the festive evening – "Why is this night different from all other nights?" Because on this night God had saved us from Egyptian slavery, I responded without difficulty. My answer didn't elicit the usual unanimous joy and admiration that it had when I had answered in the same way before I was in first grade.

Grandma Rokha gazed at me with eyes full of pride. Melekh and his not yet bride Małgozata whispered something to each other, probably about the Warsaw suburb they had been forced to flee. Shmulik and the lieutenant discussed the international situation, talking about some Molotov and Ribbentrop rather than our ancestors Joseph and Moses who had taken us Jews out of Egypt.

Before the meal began, as it began to grow dark outside, I got the chance to sing, in my boyish soprano, the Hebrew Passover song, '*Bekhol dor vo dor*' which Grandma had taught me.

"In every generation
There arise those who want to destroy us,
But the Holy One, blessed be He,
Saves us from their hands."

Father, with Melekh's help, translated it from Hebrew into Yiddish for Fishman, who stood out at the Passover table with his military bearing and uniform.

"What a fine lad!" the senior lieutenant exclaimed, taken with the song. "You won't hear anything like that in a single home in my native Gomel. The synagogue is a flour warehouse now with a red flag on the roof and you can't buy any matza anywhere in the city. Some black-hatted emissaries came from Vilno and opened a bakery on the outskirts of town to prepare matza without getting permission from the authorities; they paid for it with their freedom though. We don't even have a rabbi. There was a self-proclaimed one once; he was really a former manager or a salesman from the city of Gorky, but he died of a heart attack.

"It seems like God Almighty has been banned in your country," Melekh commented.

"In the Soviet Union the Jews are protected by the Red Army and Stalin, not God," Shmulik corrected the Polish refugee.

Shmulik's militant spirit was not as fiery as usual that evening. The released prisoner didn't mock and undermine the tales of the wonder-working effects of the Almighty on the fate of the Jews. His thoughtfulness and calm manner evoked vague suspicions among those seated at the holiday table. He seemed to know something that he wasn't keen to share with his family.

"So you think the Red Army will save us from the Germans if they try to invade Lithuania?" Grandma Rokha asked her daughter-in-law's brother, recalling what 'Almost a Jew' had said – that people were saying that the Germans were already moving their troops up to the border.

"It's nonsense! It's just gossip! The enemy is trying to sow panic among our population," Shmulik responded testily. "Moscow and Berlin have concluded an agreement saying that neither of their countries will attack the other."

"Agreement, shagreement . . . Two wolves agreed to divide up a poor lamb and, for the moment, they don't tear each other apart," Rokha the Samurai said sharply.

"Shmulik, this is just rumour you say. However, who could have imagined that the Germans would take Paris? It's been almost a year now, since we got any letters from Isaac and his family. We don't know whether they're still alive,"

Father broke in. "No one can be sure of anything now. A peace agreement is only a piece of paper. And when you need to, you know what you can do with a piece of paper."

The Passover *seder* seemed suddenly to be descending into a fight, but peace-loving Mama saved the day. "Please, my dear ones, the gefilte fish is waiting and you can smell the horseradish. And don't let the wine turn to vinegar. As long as we're alive, let's eat and rejoice!"

Mother's invitation was accepted by all; the guests devoured the delicacies Grandma had prepared. Fishman was particularly enthusiastic, stuffing himself with the treats he had never seen in Gomel, carp stuffed with horseradish, chicken liver paste and crunchy matza.

"Delicious!" he kept repeating in praise of the treats. "Wonderful! I'll remember this Passover evening as long as I live."

It may be that Valeri Fishman did indeed remember it as long as he lived; unfortunately, he didn't live very long. Only a month and a half later his tank brigade stationed in Gargždai near Jonava was bombed by German Junkers and the senior lieutenant from Gomel was killed. Not only did he not receive any military honours, he was not even buried properly.

When it was dark, Grandma Rokha lit the large kerosene lamp. Everything quivered in its wavering light, appearing unreal, as if they were ghosts not living people gathered around the table. The silence added to everyone's sense of alarm.

"I'll be able to give you all a lift," Shmulik said. "A military vehicle will be coming for me soon. But before we part, I'd like to make a short announcement."

Everyone was taken aback. The silent room shone yellow in the light of the kerosene lamp. "I want to say farewell," Shmulik said, frightening us. "In a week or two I'll be leaving for a long time. I'm being sent to Moscow on an officer training course. We shall not be seeing each other for quite some time."

"To Moscow? For a course?" my father said, concerned. "What will you be doing there?"

"Studying."

"At your age?" Grandma Rokha said, bitingly.

"Study, like death, never comes too late. I'll be there for three years. Lithuania needs new, young personnel. I'll come home to visit during holidays, of course, so you won't be getting rid of me so easily."

They were shocked; Shmulik Dudak, who it seemed only a few days before had specialized in sewing trousers and then been a prisoner, was today the assistant head of the local NKVD and would soon be an officer. Wouldn't an officer's overcoat look like a tuxedo on a scarecrow on him?

"Well, is everyone ready?" Shmulik asked.

"Yes," they said.

"Hirshke will stay with me tonight," Grandma said. "And as for the rest of you, go with God!"

"By the way, in regard to God," said Shmulik, with a smile, "before I leave for Moscow I will still have time to do one more thing – in a single person I'll combine an Eastern Orthodox priest, a Catholic priest and a rabbi and bless the marriage of my sister, Polina Dudak and Vasili Kamenev and, then slightly later, that of Melekh Tsukerman and his beautiful Małgozata Brezinska. All the documents have already been drawn up. You can congratulate them on their upcoming marriages and wish them long and happy lives."

"*Mazel tov!*" exclaimed Mama. "As soon as the weather gets warmer we can hold a joint wedding outdoors!"

"*Mazel tov!*" everyone repeated and then began to take their leave.

I remained alone with Grandma. The kerosene slowly burned down in the lamp. In the dark room the shadow of the cobbler's last and, on it, a boot with high sides, stood like a monument to Grandpa. Since I didn't feel like sleeping, I helped clear the empty plates from the holiday table. Deep in thought, for quite some time Grandma didn't say anything.

"Hirshele," she said suddenly, with barely restrained anger, "Can you tell me why Jews need officers?"

I didn't know how to respond.

"Tell me, who are we planning on fighting? The Turks? What on earth does a Jew need to go on an officers' course for? Baron Rothschild didn't get rich through military operations and he didn't wear any officer's bars. And the only weapon Rabbi Elijah the Gaon of Vilna used was the law of Moses, the Five Books."

"Yes, you're right," I said, even though I didn't know anything about either the Gaon of Vilna or Baron Rothschild.

"You just completed fourth grade. What do you plan to do now? You don't want to study the Torah at the Telshe Yeshiva and you don't want to be a tailor like your father. What do you want to be?"

I shrugged my shoulders.

"Maybe you'll grow up to be a Soviet officer like your Uncle Shmulik?"

"No."

"That lifts a burden from my heart. A Jew shouldn't be giving orders in someone else's country – except to his wife and children," Grandma said, as she washed the dishes.

"Listen, my golden one," she mused aloud, pouring water into a bucket. "Maybe you would like to become a barber? I could speak to Naum Kovalsky, a relative of ours. As you know, our Motl is married to his Sarah. The only thing a person has that always grows is his hair. Hair, Hirshele, is definitely a treasure." Grandma spoke more to herself than to me, forgetting the burdens of slavery in Egypt and why this night differed from all other nights.

"Shall I speak with the 'matchmaker' Naum?"

"I'll talk to my parents about whether I should go after it or not."

"After what?"

"The treasure."

"If you're going to joke around like that, you'll stay as poor as Avigdor Perelman, who died recently."

After finishing the dishes, but not having to come to any agreement about my career, we lay down to sleep. In bed, with no one quizzing me about what I would be in the future, I fell into a deep sleep undisturbed by dreams.

Grandma woke me early in the morning and we set out for the Great Synagogue. People were packed like herrings, so that it seemed not one more worshipper could be squeezed in. The usual crowd was swelled by the worshippers from all the small houses of prayer that the authorities had closed down.

Everyone wanted to hear what Rabbi Eliezer would say. After all, he came from 'the other side.' He was considered a German since he came from Tilsit.

"Thousands of years ago we were freed from slavery," the Rabbi began solemnly. "Let us pray that the Lord God will not allow anyone else to enslave us once more, which might prove even more terrible than the slavery of Egypt."

Suddenly, the lame painter Eyne jumped up from his bench in the third row, interrupting the lofty sermon. In a voice hoarse from many years of drinking, he shouted out, loud enough that the entire synagogue could hear, "Rabbi! Is it true that your countrymen are going to attack Lithuania and slaughter the Jews?"

A din filled the house of worship. The clamour of condemnations was mixed with shouts of approval.

"Quiet!" Rabbi Eliezer commanded. "A Jew who has no questions isn't a Jew. Somebody just asked whether the Germans are going to attack and slaughter us. They shouldn't be silenced; they deserve an answer." The Rabbi breathed with difficulty. Abandoning the sermon he had prepared for Passover, he said, "That, if you want to know, is not simply the truth, but one thousand times the case! Who in the course of the centuries has not attacked us and attempted to destroy our people? There were the Greeks and the Romans, the Turks and the Arabs and the Russian Cossacks. What prevents the Germans from attacking us? They could certainly attack and slaughter us. It's quite probable. Like in Poland, like in France."

The worshippers could not believe their ears. The mild Rabbi Eliezer, father of six children, had suddenly been transformed into a fearless warrior. He knew from his own experience what the Germans were capable of. At first a foreigner, then a Lithuanian subject and now a citizen of the USSR, Rabbi Eliezer had been in Germany several times. In Hamburg he had seen with his own eyes the *Kristallnacht* pogrom.

"So, Rabbi, what are we to do?" A voice rang out. "We won't frighten them away with our prayers!"

"Unfortunately, I have no other weapon," the Rabbi said. "And even if I did, I would not use it. It is forbidden to kill one of God's human creatures. There is no sin as serious as murder. Whoever kills an innocent person loses his humanity and adds to the number of wild beasts. Pray, and may God send all of us peace and quiet." After ending his remarks with those inspiring words, he stepped down from the *bimah*, clasping the Torah scroll to his chest like a shield.

For a long time the agitated worshippers did not depart. Once outside, they continued to discuss the Rabbi's words.

Grandma Rokha, who loved listening to what intelligent folk had to say, greeted Dr. Blumenfeld and, as if she was a patient inquiring about her health, asked, "Doctor, what do you say about the Germans? Are they our deadly enemies?"

"What can I say?" Isaac Blumenfeld said, not knowing how to reply. "They're neighbours from whom we haven't got much hope, unfortunately, of protecting ourselves or from whom we can escape, no matter how much we might want to, by resettling in Africa or the North Pole. They dream of only one thing – how to round up the Jews and resettle them in the cemetery."

The Jews of Jonava were alarmed to learn that the NKVD had summoned Rabbi Eliezer after his Passover remarks. The authorities might not only decide to shut the Rabbi's mouth, they thought, they might also decide to close the Great Synagogue.

Rabbi Eliezer was interrogated by Major Vorobyev and his assistant for operational matters Samuil Semenovich Dudak – Shmulik!

"We have learned from reliable sources, my respected teacher," the Major began, "that in your sermons you're inciting your worshippers against our friend the German state. We would be very grateful if, in future, you were more cautious in the way you express yourself and limit yourself to matters related to your religious creed."

Slowly, with some omissions, Shmulik translated while Major Vorobyev appeared to listen attentively, giving the impression of a benevolent and well-educated person.

"My religion, Sir, obliges me not to lie, either to myself or to my worshippers. I will always say what I believe to be true and will not say what someone orders me to say if it is opposed to my conscience or my own will. I will answer to God for all that I say. And to Him alone. If I did not, my service, which is dedicated to Him, would be meaningless."

"That's fine," agreed Vorobyev. "But don't forget that in addition to God there are also other judges in the world – and sometimes they are more severe. It was a pleasure to make your acquaintance. You may go now."

No matter how the authorities attempted to calm the fears of the town's residents, the feeling grew that there was a catastrophe imminent – a clash between the Russians and the 'friendly' Germans. This was caused not only by the interrogation of Rabbi Eliezer, but also because suddenly the wives and children of the Russian officers began to leave Jonava in droves, returning to their own country. Major Vorobyev sent his wife and son back to Mordovia.

On more than one occasion, Father asked his new relative, Vasili Kamenev and the as-yet-unmarried Senior Lieutenant Fishman to explain this change. He wondered whether it might be related to the threat of the Germans invading Lithuanian territory. As if they had agreed their story ahead of time, both replied evasively. The problem was, they suggested, that Lithuania lacked Russian-language schools and that the living quarters were being constructed at a snail's pace.

Moreover, they agreed, "It's better to be at home than to be a guest somewhere else."

A clear indication that war was looming was received unexpectedly by Julius at the end of April. He brought a piece of paper to the workshop, which had been pinned to the front door of Ephraim Kapler's house; it had been discovered by Julius' father, the janitor Antanas, that morning as he was cleaning the street.

"I'm no great reader," Julius confessed, "but what I think is written here terrifies me. It speaks about you Jews."

He handed the piece of paper to his master.

Holding it in his hand, Father looked at the typed text and then returned it to Julius. "You studied in a Lithuanian school. Read it again and tell us briefly what it says about the Jews. Unfortunately, I can't read Lithuanian, since I never studied the language. I can speak it in a muddling way but I never really made friends with its letters."

Julius put the paper on the table and began by translating the title into Yiddish. It was headed, "Lithuanian Activist Front."

"A reliable organization!" Father said ironically.

"A Proclamation," Julius continued.

From the apprentice's clumsy translation, Father and Melekh understood that a fierce revenge awaited the Jews for their many years of sins. The decree of the Great Prince Vytautas granting Jews the right to settle in Lithuania and to engage in trade and crafts would soon be repealed. Within a very short time, every Jew would have to leave Lithuanian territory. If any of them was considered guilty of a crime against the now independent Lithuania, or any of them attempted to hide, to seek refuge or hide from justice, then it was the duty of all honest Lithuanians to personally detain them. Under certain circumstances, they would immediately carry out a severe and just punishment.

"Is that the whole thing?" asked Father.

"Yes, all of it," said Julius, breathing easier. "I don't know who wrote this or stuck it up, but, believe me, I've got nothing to do with it and completely disagree with it. In my opinion, I believe that the Jews have always been good neighbours to us here in Jonava. Always."

"Rip that inflammatory scribbling into shreds and toss it into the slop bucket!" Father said scornfully. "Isn't it too early for the German flunkeys to begin settling accounts with us and holding victory celebrations?"

"Still, maybe we shouldn't throw it away; we should show it to one of the authorities?" Melekh said in his bass voice. "It was a bad time for *Ponas* Samuil to leave for Moscow."

"Well, I don't know whether it was a bad time for him to go or not. How, in your opinion, could *Ponas* Samuil, as you call him, have helped if he had stayed in Jonava? Would he have comforted us, reminding us yet another time of the might of the Red Army?" Father asked. He continued, "For more than 500 years men of our tribe have repaired shoe soles and sewed clothing in this land and then, suddenly, we're ordered to get out with our wives and children, we're forbidden to seek shelter here, and forced to abandon our homes and the graves of our ancestors."

"For the moment it's just threats," Melekh said, trying to reassure himself.

"This isn't just empty threats. I have no doubt that the Germans have approved it and even given their blessing to carry it out."

13

On June 22nd the pre-dawn quiet, smelling of lilac blossom and of the fresh milk that had been delivered in buckets the previous day by saucy peasant milkmaids, was shattered by the falling of bombs.

Mama was the first to be awakened by deafening thunder. She threw the window wide open and gazed up at the brightening sky that was filled with fearful flashes of distant fire. Listening to the roar of the incomprehensible, uninterrupted thunder, Mama suddenly made out an approaching squadron of airplanes marked with swastikas. They flew over the mushroom-rich woods, beyond which a Red Army unit was positioned in Gargždai. From there one after another, almost without pause, wave after wave of planes rained powerful explosives down onto the still sleepy town.

Frightened, Mama tried to wake Father. He muttered something in his sleep, turned on his side and pulled the covers over himself, burying his head in the pillow. Mama stubbornly beat him with her fists.

"Get up, Shleimke! Get up!" she screamed.

"What happened?" he asked sleepily, looking reproachfully at his wife.

"It's war!"

"What war? What have you been dreaming about?"

Just then, as if in response to his question, a thunderous sound shook the windows and lightning-like flashes illuminated the skies. It was as if an insane tailor had mounted a cloud and was stitching away on his sewing machine without stopping to catch his breath.

"That, Hennie, really is a nightmare! Everyone was waiting for the Germans and Russians to start bashing each other's heads in. Listen to that thunder; that's what they're doing now!"

"The Lithuanians have been waiting for this; unlike us Jews, they were always more afraid of the Russians than the Germans," Mama commented. It's not myself I'm afraid for, but our Hirshke. He's so young; may he live long!"

"He'll live," Father said. "Just make sure that he doesn't leave the house. And don't stick your own nose out either, or anything else for that matter, without good reason. Any wrong step now might be the last you make."

"Of course I'll watch out for him," Mother said, "but what shall I do about the helpless old Kogans? They'll die if I don't look after them. They can hardly move as it is. I even have to take Ruvim by the arm to help him to the bathroom. They need help getting undressed and getting into bed. Their hands tremble so much they can barely raise a spoon to their mouths."

"I really feel sorry for them," Father sympathized, "but what can you do? Right now, as merciless as it sounds, everyone has to think about themselves and their own old folks, not about the unfortunate Kogans. I don't think my mother will leave Jonava. No matter what happens, there's no way that she, Rokha the Samurai, will abandon her Dovid. As she says, she's 'betrothed to him both in life and death.'"

While with lowered voices they discussed what to do first, whether they should pack some suitcases straight away or wait a bit longer and see whose force would prevail, the bombing of the army unit in Gargždai didn't cease for a minute. Rather, it became stronger and more ferocious and the residents of the town had no idea how to escape from the terror.

"Poor Valeri Fishman!" said Mama, thinking suddenly of the senior lieutenant from Gomel. He may have been killed."

"Poor all of us. If the Red Army doesn't stop the Germans, we'll have to get out of here. There is no alternative. We'll just have to get out!" Father said.

"But where to?"

"To where there are no Germans."

"Perhaps they still won't reach us. Shmulik said more than once that the Red Army is the mightiest army in the world; it can beat back any enemy, no one can overcome it."

"Your brother said quite a few things! Quite a specialist he is in military matters! He couldn't tell an infantryman from a pilot!" Father shot back.

Father and Mother had not noticed that dawn had broken.

The streets of Jonava, which were always filled in the morning with people, were empty. Heavy locks hung on the doors of the shops. Not a single worshipper could be seen rushing to the morning service at the church or the synagogue. Only stray dogs chased stray cats who were trying to hide in the gateways.

From time to time army vehicles roared through the deserted streets of the town carrying wounded tank crew members from Gargždai to the district military hospital in Kaunas.

"I have the horrible impression that our life is about to change," Father said glumly. "Evidently a tailor, if he wants to stay alive, might have to say goodbye to his profession temporarily, or possibly forever."

For a while my parents were silent, trying to conceal their feeling of hopelessness and despair. They took turns going over to the window, but what they saw did not change – a void threatening God knows what unpredictable dangers.

Only at midday did some of the Lithuanian shops open. In the anarchy and chaos, fearing violence and pogroms, the Jewish shop owners stayed at home, dug in, as if in the trenches. Their fears were not baseless. Here and there, groups of young men with white armbands began to appear on the streets, taking the place of the guardians of law and order from the institution in which Shmulik Dudak worked. While the German units were still engaged in combat far from Jonava, the young men hid their intentions; they left people alone, contenting themselves with examining each passerby carefully, judging by physical appearances whether they were of the tribe of Jews, from whom they felt obliged in their patriotic zeal to free their long-suffering Lithuania as soon as possible.

A red flag still waved over the two-storey brick building of the town's executive committee and, occasionally, a truck with Russian soldiers drove down the cobblestone main street, heading in an unknown direction.

Julius and Melekh were tired and depressed. Nor could Father concentrate after the pre-dawn bombardment. Work did not go well. Was it possible to calmly thread a needle and sew when bombs were raining down nearby and fires were burning and people were dying?

"As if there weren't enough woes, another has been added," Melekh said, excusing himself for having arrived a little late. "The war has ended already for *Ponia* Antanina. She passed away quietly in the night to the accompaniment of the bombing."

"She was a real saint! She never hurt anyone in her whole life. When will her funeral be?" Father asked.

"Małgozata ran to the church early this morning to make the arrangements with the priest, who speaks good Polish," said Melekh. "Antanina lived such a long life that there is no one, it's hard to believe, to bury or mourn her."

"Loneliness is a grave that is dug with one's own hands. If the situation doesn't get worse, perhaps we can drop by the cemetery for five or ten minutes to see Antanina off on her last journey, but I can't promise it," Father said. "The Russians are fleeing and the Germans are hot on their tail. They will take Jonava either today or tomorrow. I have no idea what to do about the orders of my customers. I have so many it would take me a month or two to complete them; I don't want to leave other people's property to the whims of fate, or to be carried off by looters. Maybe it would be better to return all the items to their owners and to just worry about myself?"

"Here's Małgozata!" shouted Melekh, catching sight of his *kochana* in the doorway.

"*Pani* Antanina's funeral will be on Tuesday," she announced as she stepped into the room. "That's what Father

Vaitkus decided. The Church will take care of all the details and expenses."

"Well, I don't think we will still be in Jonava on Tuesday. Hennie is giving me no peace; she insists that we get some things together, pack some food for the way and get out of here. Otherwise, she says she'll just take Hirshke and leave while I stay here with my sewing machine."

"Women have a keener sense of danger than men," said Melekh, taking Hennie's side.

"You can't argue with the truth. The Red Army turned out to be stronger on paper than on the battlefield. The Germans are moving toward Kaunas and they're meeting hardly any resistance. You know from your own experience what will happen when they enter Jonava." Father licked his dry lips and turned to Julius. "As for you, my friend, you have nothing to worry about. After all, if I can put it this way, you were only a temporary Jew, not a permanent one, and the victors won't harm somebody who has been baptized like you, while permanent and irreversible Jews, like Melekh and I, have to think very hard about when and where we can go so we don't fall into the clutches of the Germans or their volunteers. You understand?"

"Yes," Julius said. "But what do you want me to do, just sit and watch you get ready to leave?"

"While we stay here making a plan, you and Hennie go and give back to our customers the things we haven't managed to sew yet. Apologize to them and advise our Catholic customers to go to Pranas Gaidis, who is a master tailor. He's not expensive and, you could say, he's got Jewish hands. You just have to look at his work and a smile comes to your face. I'll return the material to the other customers and say farewell at the same time."

While Mama and the disheartened Julius set out to return the materials, Father and Melekh sat down at the table and began to plan where they might go, deciding which way offered the best hope for people fleeing.

Melekh decided, after a short time, to head to Lida via Vilnius, where Małgozata's cousin, a nurse called Teresa, lived, while Father decided not to argue with Mother; he resolved that we should head without delay for Latvia, to the rail junction of Dvinsk and from there into the depths of Russia, perhaps even to Siberia, since the Germans clearly would not reach frozen Siberia.

Meanwhile a fierce, bloody battle was taking place at the approach to our town.

There was no more time to think. The residents of Jonava, some on foot, some in carts, set out on their long journey, which promised nothing good.

The wagon-driver, Peisakh Shvartsman, and his twin brother Pinkhas, also a driver, were in great demand. Places in their carts had to be paid for with silver or gold, not with rubles, which had replaced the Lithuanian *litas* but were useless now.

Father discussed the price with the gloomy, solitary, large-headed and solidly built twin, Pinkhas, who had been a friend of Grandpa Dovid, to whom he always brought his oversized boots to be repaired. Among the other drivers he stood out for his piety and his strength, which was like that of the Biblical Samson. He always wore an embroidered yarmulke under his rumpled cap and, sometimes seriously, sometimes jokingly, tried to convince his customers, whatever their ethnic identity, that horses didn't just chew oats and decorate the town's streets with their droppings, but also believed in God, their Creator.

"How many of you are there?" Pinkhas asked my father, scratching his broad, hairy chest.

"Three."

"Three others have already reserved places with me – the cobbler Velvl Selkiner, his wife and son. They already have some experience as refugees; they've come from Białystok," Pinkhas said. "My bay horse can't pull more than seven passengers with their baggage."

"Tell me, Reb Pinkhas, what kind of baggage can a tailor have? A needle, a thimble, a couple of spools of thread and some material to tailor a suit, in the event that in some quiet place a customer happens to turn up," Father said. "In any case, he can't take a sewing machine with him."

"There's a lot one can't take" Pinkhas growled. "Of course, it would be better to save people from those monsters rather than cold metal objects. I would take your Singer, but my old cart isn't a two-room apartment."

"I'm not greedy. What I can't take in the cart, I'll take in my heart. There's room there for a sky full of stars, for the fields and the swift flowing Vilija. May God grant that we arrive safe and sound," Father said.

"Shleime, the road is not a Jewish bank, it doesn't give guarantees. I've been traveling through Lithuania for forty years, day after day except for the Sabbath and I won't hide the fact that I've had various kinds of scrapes."

"Of course! Draymen are people who have seen many things."

"Whether we have or not, our passengers don't pay us to run them into trouble, but to get them to their destination in one piece," Pinkhas said. "That's why I always collect my payment at the end of our trip not the beginning. God willing, you can pay when we get to Latvia."

"Whatever you prefer."

"Early in the morning, tomorrow, I'll drive my cart up to Reb Ephraim Kapler's house. On the way I'll pick up that Polish refugee with his family. We'll say our prayers and then 'Giddy up, old girl' and, if she doesn't let us down, with God's blessing, we'll find somewhere Jewish blood isn't about to be shed!"

Father didn't close his eyes the whole night.

He sat until morning at his Singer, which had been presented to him at his wedding by Reb Yeshua Kremnitser, just pressing the pedal without sewing. He pressed the pedal and whispered quietly.

When I awoke, I saw his back bent over the machine. I could not then understand what he could be whispering so passionately to his sewing machine in the darkness. Now, however, after so many years have passed, I think he was whispering with such tenderness and fierce passion what anybody whispers when they're forced to part from the woman they love dearly.

Then it was dawn.

The day of our departure had arrived. It was June 23rd, 1941.

Mama and Papa packed some belongings, two pieces of English woollen material and some food and we set off for Rybatskaya Street to say farewell to Grandma Rokha.

No matter how Father begged her and assured her that she would have a place in Pinkhas's cart, Grandma refused. "Who would waste a bullet on an old woman like me? Will the Germans kill everybody? It's a sin to abandon the dead. Yesterday I went to the synagogue to pray that disaster would pass us by. I prayed and I asked Rabbi Eliezer what he intended to do, since he has six children and Haman the executioner is at the door. The Rabbi was silent for a long time. He swayed like an ash tree in the wind and then finally he answered that as long as a single Jew remained in Jonava, whether he was an atheist or a believer, dead or alive, he would remain with them. So, in the same way I'll stay with my Dovid. And I don't want to be a burden to you."

Father couldn't change her mind.

Julius saw us off.

"You'll come back. I will pray to Jesus Christ that he brings you back. One morning I'll awake and I'll hear a sound like that of the twittering of birds breaking the silence and I'll say, it's a miracle! Thank God! *Ponas* Saliamonas has returned and saddled his machine and is up and running!"

"More than once miracles have saved us Jews from disaster," Father said. "But now it seems that God has turned away from us because of our sins. Thank you, Julius, for trying to give us hope. If you stay in Jonava, don't give up the needle for a rifle; carry on sewing. May you enjoy good health! Don't abandon Jackie. Feed her and take her out for walks. But remember, she doesn't understand Lithuanian and with the Germans around it could be dangerous speaking Yiddish, even with a pedigree dog."

"I'll think up something."

"Who could imagine that the day would come when we would envy an abandoned dog? The Pinscher will be allowed to breathe the same air as the rest of the citizens are and it won't even be forbidden from barking at the Germans on the street."

Then, to the surprise of them all, Julius began to cry.

"Good luck," Father said. "As I said, don't betray your needle. It will bring you success."

They embraced.

We climbed onto Pinkhas' cart just as dawn bathed us in its rays, like a naked peasant girl jumping from a bridge into the soft embrace of the waters of the Vilija. Father and the twice-exiled Velvl Selkiner settled in the front, Mendel, the six-year old son of the cobbler and I in the middle, while the cobbler's wife, Esther, with her family's trunks and my mother were in the back. Nobody spoke. It seemed that words were no longer any use; they had been replaced by silence.

Behind the cart there dangled an empty bucket. Its rattling filled our hearts with a vague sense of alarm.

Pinkhas and his obedient horse were calm. The driver smoked one hand-rolled cigarette after another and watched silently as the circles of acrid smoke polluted the clean blue sky and vanished in the warm summer air.

Soviet tanks occasionally rolled past the cart with a grinding noise. Combat shattered Red Army men in unbuttoned shirts and heavy canvas boots also passed by. The soldiers eyed the cart jealously.

"What will happen to us?" Selkiner wailed. "There's no time to stop and warm your feet up and earn a crust of bread before, yet again, you hear the words, 'Get out of here while you're still in one piece!' What I want to know is, why do people treat us as though we're guilty of something? Is it because my mother, Esther-Rokhl, was a Jew, not a Lithuanian or a Tatar?"

"Who are you asking?" Pinkhas asked, sucking on another hand-rolled cigarette. "Me or my horse?"

"What do you mean, who are you asking?" Velvl the cobber reproached the driver. "Were you born yesterday?"

"For one thing, if you are asking in regard to God, then this is what I think, my friend. Like all of those in power, He loves being praised and acknowledged for His might, rather than being cursed or pestered with endless requests. It's enough to drive you mad with so many people asking for so many things. Secondly, if you had been born a Lithuanian or a Tatar, you would never have been forced to flee from your home in Białystok."

Making our way through the crowds, allowing the Red Army soldiers with full packs and their weapons on their shoulders to proceed ahead of us, along with the Jews fleeing on foot with their pitiful hand baggage, the seven of us moved slowly towards the town of Zarasai. Pinkhas promised that we would rest that night at an out of the way farmstead, so that he and his passengers and his bay horse could rest. We would bargain with the owner, Pinkhas's old friend Vladas Doveika, to give us a bit of food without having to pay too much and a place to sleep for the night in one of his sheds and then be off in the morning.

At the entrance to a farm a military patrol with two burly Red Army soldiers, rifles at the ready, stopped our cart.

"Who are they?" one of them, apparently the senior in rank, asked our driver.

"Jews," Pinkhas replied, and added with irony, "We're retreating like your glorious Red Army."

The soldier was not amused by our driver's joke.

"For your information the Red Army is not retreating; it is temporarily relocating to positions that are easier to defend."

"Yes, we too are trying to occupy positions that are easier to defend. We're only fleeing from the Germans temporarily," the driver said, poking the terrified Selkiner with his stiff index finger. "This one is a cobbler from Poland who has already fled from the Germans before and this dark-haired one is a tailor. The others are their wives and children."

The senior Red Army soldier ordered us to get out of the cart and stand at the side of the road. When we were out, he used his bayonet to turn over the hay that covered the bottom of the cart.

"What are you looking for?" asked Pinkhas, surprised.

"None of your business! I don't have to explain myself to every passerby."

"Comrade, if you're looking for explosives, God is my witness, there aren't any in this cart," Pinkhas said. "Where did you ever see a Jew who carried non-edible things like bombs or explosives with him on a long trip?"

As it happened, the broad-cheeked Red Army soldier, a native probably of Buryatiya or Yakutia, had never seen a Jew before in his life. He looked us over suspiciously, turned over the straw again with his weapon and then said disdainfully to Pinkhas, "You can go, but you'll never make it to Russia with that worn-out nag and that cart."

"Russia?" Pinkhas replied. "What are you talking about?"

Our journey would have been over ludicrously quickly, well before we had even reached Zarasai, if it had not been for the resourcefulness and quick-wittedness of my practical mother. That same day, on the far side of sleepy Utena, at God knows what fork in the road, another miliary patrol appeared.

A soldier in a wide open overcoat presented himself. "Sergeant Ulyukaev," he said. "Where are you heading?"

"To Russia," Velvl said.

"It's a long way from here to Russia. Is the horse yours?"

"No," said the cobbler.

"Then whose?"

"The owner has just stepped into the woods. He's praying."

"Well, praying isn't pissing. It's allowed. According to an order from our commander, all horses and carts on the roads our troops are moving on are to be requisitioned for the use of the Red Army," Sergeant Ulyukaev told us. He made us all get out of the cart and then, as if he owned it, took the obedient bay horse by its bridle and led it after him.

At that point Pinkhas reappeared.

"This comrade wants to take your horse," Mama said in Yiddish, which the soldier did not understand. "Make him show you the order that he has the right to do so!"

"You need to show me the order," Pinkhas said, approaching the sergeant.

"You want to see the order? Perhaps you're going to tell me that I need to pay you for this old nag too?"

"Whether she's a nag or not, she's mine!" yelled the furious Pinkhas. With an iron grip, he grasped the soldier by the throat. There was no doubt that Pinkhas would have strangled Ulyukaev if the other soldiers hadn't separated them.

Fortunately, the soldiers didn't attack the cart driver. As we continued our journey, we praised Shvartsman for his fearlessness and willingness to sacrifice himself.

"Reb Pinkhas, he could have killed you," Velvl said, breathless from fear.

"But what could I do? She's been my bread and butter for my whole life; without her, without my old nag, I would have died long ago from grief. Simply died! Word of honour, I would have. What I've shared with her and how many miles I've travelled with her!"

As twilight began to fall the cart drove up to a farmstead surrounded by a grove of chestnut trees. Its owner, thick-set and with broad shoulders, was Vladas Doveika. In his youth Vladas had worked at the forge of a relative of Pinkhas. The cart driver became friends with him, often dropping in as a guest, returning to Jonava with gifts: honey and potatoes, a basket of blueberries or apples, fresh cream in a large clay jug and a bottle of moonshine that was as pure as tears.

"Drink a glass and it'll knock a year off your age," Doveika used to say as he clinked glasses with him.

Although Pinkhas did not become younger from drinking a glass or two, his friendship with Vladas was strengthened.

The table was set with country delicacies and a jug of kvas and a carafe of top quality homebrew. The farmer poured each of the men a glass of homebrew and the women and children some kvas and proposed a toast to our health.

"If all the Jews flee Lithuania, Pinkhas, what will happen to the Sunday markets in Utena, Ukmerge and Zarasai?" he asked the cart driver. "Who will buy what we grow in our fields and in our vegetable gardens, or the fish from our ponds? Half of all that food, maybe more, will have to be thrown out or used to feed the animals."

"And I suppose we Jews are to blame for that too?" Pinkhas said.

"Guilty." Doveika suddenly scowled. "What did you expect? You didn't expect to be killed? You should all have converted long ago. As converts you could have lived together with us and not had any trouble."

"*Ponas* Vladas, God didn't create Lithuanians and Germans and Jews. He created humans. Unfortunately, however, He didn't create somewhere where people could just live their lives without a label on their chests, where you wouldn't be murdered by your neighbour just because you wore a yarmulke on your head and prayed to God in a different language."

"What a fancy way you've got of expressing yourself," Doveika said, unaccustomed to sophisticated thinking. "Whatever you think about the way God has arranged the world, He isn't about to start redesigning it. So, anyway, we're better off having another drink; to your safe return from Russia. And to the old Jewish woman who would come up to my wagon at the Sunday market in Zarasai, squinting at my wares and ask me in our dialect, "Tell me, are your eggs kosher?"

Even though no one felt like laughing, the adults chuckled.

As the meal came to an end, Doveika's portly wife, who hadn't uttered a single word the whole evening except to say, "Eat!" began to clear the table. Afterwards she prepared a bed on a broad bench and from a row of sturdy country chairs. It was after midnight when the six-year old Mendel and the women were sent to sleep in the clean outhouse, while the men and I were put in the hay loft.

A deep, impenetrable silence fell upon the farm. The sky was lit by bright June stars while around the farm a line of ancient chestnut trees protected the pristine peace like knights of old. There were no Germans or Lithuanians or Jews, just human beings. Beneath the bright nocturnal firmament there was only the pungent, peaceful scent of cut hay and a vision of a world not desecrated either by ungodly hatred or bloodshed.

14

In the morning, before we started on our way, Pinkhas and Vladas Doveika looked carefully over the bay horse resting in the stable.

"It wouldn't harm you to re-shoe your mare," the farmer said after the examination. "It's a long journey and if one of its shoes flew off, that would be the end of the trip. You wouldn't make it to Dvinsk. It might take me a while to shoe her since I'm long out of practice, but I'll do it for free. I wouldn't know, in any case, what money to take these days – *rubles*, *litas*, *marks*? That's why I don't bother taking my goods to the market; I'm waiting to see how the fighting will turn out and whose portrait on the money will win out."

Doveika led the horse to the shed and we soon heard the blows of a hammer.

"That makes me feel a bit better now," the jack of all trades said when he had finished. "You'll make it to Dvinsk; you might even get as far as Moscow, like Napoleon."

"If we return, we will show you our gratitude, Vladas. Jews never forget the good done to them, maybe because we are met with hatred everywhere we go. That has been our fate – to become as familiar with evil as with our own name."

Vladas accompanied us to the main road. For some time he walked alongside the cart in silence and then he fell behind and waved his large hand. Pinkhas raised his worn cap in the air like a flag.

At the end of the second day of our retreat we saw the sparkling of a river. From a distance Pinkhas caught sight of a rope extended over the water and a small pine-board ferry-boat with a signal bell. The boat was protected by a small iron canopy resembling a boletus mushroom.

From the crumbling slope of the bank, a deserted forest path, covered with wind-fallen branches which protected it from rain, led to the ferry landing.

There was no ferryman in sight.

Our cart descended the slope.

"Hey, is anybody here?" our driver shouted.

The sound echoed in the silence. "Hey!"

Out of the bushes crawled a sleepy beanpole of a man with rumpled red hair.

"What are you hollering for?" he asked, yawning broadly.

"Are you the ferryman?" Pinkhas asked, while the peasant yawned.

"Yes, that's me," the man said.

"Will you take us over to the other bank?"

"I will if you pay," the ferryman said, thick with drowsiness. "Just hand over the gold."

"Where are we supposed to get that from?"

"Jews without gold are not Jews." The beanpole covered his mouth with his hand and, pulling up his trousers, headed back to the bushes.

"Wait!" shouted Velvl the cobbler, taking the ring off his finger.

"On one condition; you give me the ring before we go over!"

"Fine," agreed Velvl.

The cart rolled onto the ferry. The beanpole put the ring into the pocket of his creased trousers, pulled the signal bell and, with some creaking, the ferry moved off.

As the ferryman was navigating the rapids, a German fighter plane appeared overhead.

"It's heading straight for us," Father shouted, looking upwards.

Before he had time to look away, the air was filled with bullets.

The plane descended, then ascended.

It seemed as if the pilot was playing a diabolical game with us, aiming not at the people or the horse, but at the rope extended across the river, trying to break it, as if to take pleasure in how the ferry, caught by the current, would be carried away down river. Even as his bullets struck the wooden bottom and the sides of the ferry and the water around it, the German did not stop.

Huddling against the warm bodies of our parents, Mendel and I were afraid to move. Peasants, who were loading their fragrant, dry hay into carts on the other bank, threw down their pitchforks and stared helplessly at the cloudless sky that rained down death.

Finally the pilot succeeded; the loose ferry was carried swiftly by the current and crashed against the opposite bank. The barefoot ferryman lay unmoving in his rolled-up trousers beneath the now-silent bell. A thin stream of blood trickled down his unshaven chin. Pinkhas was squatting before his dead horse, caressing the hair of its mane, which fluttered like the broken strings of a musical instrument.

Recovering from their fright, the peasants ran down the slope to the water, crossing themselves at the sight of the dead man and, without uttering a single word, rushed off to the village. They returned some time later with shovels to bury Pinkhas's mare in the warm earth. They removed her collar and traces. They would have removed the bridle too, but Pinkhas had tossed it over his own neck before they returned.

"Perhaps we should take care of him first?" said my mother, pointing at the ferryman lying nearby while trying to avoid looking at his body.

"We'll bury Jonas; he won't be going anywhere," a frail peasant with a bandaged cheek muttered. "We'll bury him when the straw's gathered. It's easier to bury a horse than a man; you don't need to read a burial service for a horse or mourn it. You just take a shovel, dig a pit, cover it over and that's that."

With the bridle around his neck, Pinkhas stood at the edge of the large grave and began almost inaudibly, to the sound of falling clay, to recite the *kaddish*, the memorial prayer.

"What is he doing?" asked the pious Esther, wife of the cobbler Selkiner, appalled. "God doesn't allow us to recite *kaddish* for animals."

"Who said I'm reciting *kaddish* for a horse, Esther? Who said that? Aren't we all animals? Animals, animals . . .

Domestic, wild, all kinds?" Pinkhas exclaimed and then said nothing more.

Left without a horse and cart, we moved on to the road and plodded along behind the disorderly straggle of Red Army soldiers and refugees heading towards the closest Latvian railway station at Rezekne, or Rezhitsa as it used to be called in Russian. We were hoping to find a passing freight train to take us to Dvinsk, and from there, God willing, to Russia.

Exhausted, crushed by defeat, the soldiers looked at us with a mixture of condescension and pity. They had never seen such a flood of Jews. Sometimes, at short stops and halts, out of decency, one of the soldiers would strike up a conversation with the refugees who had attached themselves to the military column. While this did not provide the refugees with complete security, it still offered them some protection from the armed German collaborators that had begun appearing in areas abandoned by the Red Army. Even during daylight hours it was dangerous to try to reach Rezekne by the back-routes, since Jews were beginning to be murdered everywhere. Someone hiding in the bushes could easily pick them off with an automatic weapon or a rifle along the road.

The cart driver, Pinkhas Shvartsman, knew how to express himself in Lithuanian and Russian, albeit not as fluently as in his native Yiddish, since for many years he had driven people of various ethnic groups around the towns and villages of Lithuania. However, after the loss of his horse, which had provided his living, it was clear that he did not wish to engage in conversation or respond to questions.It was just at this point that, as if out of spite, he began to be interrogated by a talkative, simple soldier who looked like a schoolboy but carried a grenade launcher on his shoulder.

"Hey, where are you going?" the soldier asked. "You going to visit your auntie to eat pancakes?"

"We're not on a social visit. We're fleeing from the Germans, like you," Pinkhas said, not for the first time.

"For your information, Pops, we're not fleeing the Germans; we're carrying out a planned retreat, at the order of our high command, to lines that have already been prepared for defence and counter-attack. There will be reinforcements there – tanks, anti-aircraft guns, cannon. We're going to pay the Germans back and also go back to your Lithuania. We'll be back; we'll defeat the fascists! It was nice in Lithuania. It's clean there and the girls are pretty. Also the stores are full of goods, not like in Yelets."

"Then we'll be able to go back home to the graves of our dear ones," Pinkhas said, trying not to anger the soldier with his reticence and his gloomy look.

"Go back from where?"

"From Russia. Our ancestors were born in Lithuania. You can abandon everything in life except the graves of your dear ones. Whoever leaves them to the crows and field mice will never be forgiven."

"Do you have any idea how far it is from here to Mother Russia? You might, God willing, get as far as Rezekne. You don't have anything; you haven't got a horse or food for the road even for such a short trip. Your women folk and the kids won't hold out for a week. They'll die on the way from starvation."

"We had an intelligent, long-suffering horse and a cart too and provisions, but when we were trying to cross a river a German fighter pilot, damn him, destroyed it all."

"Son of a bitch!" swore the talkative Red Army man. "If those bastards don't bomb our field kitchen, I'll ask my buddy, the cook Pavlik Sizov, to give some hot cabbage soup to your kids. He won't refuse. The soup might be fatty, but when you eat it, it's like you're back home in Yelets and there's no war on. That's the town in Russia I come from."

"Cabbage soup is always good," agreed Pinkhas.

Father and Velvl the cobbler didn't say anything. What could they say, since they had never eaten cabbage soup in their lives?

"Well, I wasn't actually born in Yelets itself, but in the village of Osinovka on the banks of the Bystraya Sosna River. When this damned war ends and if I'm still alive and not a cripple, I'll go back home and you'll never guess what I will do first!"

"You'll celebrate with vodka!" Pinkhas laughed.

"Wrong! The first thing I'll do is to strip naked and jump into the river to cleanse myself from this hatred for the German scum that has eaten into my soul. Then I'll put on a white shirt, sit down at the table with my sisters Frosya and Klava and polish off a glass of Moscovskaya vodka along with a pickle."

He spoke without stopping. It was as if his words would distance him from imminent danger, or repress his growing fear for his life. The soldier's outpouring was like the incantation of a shaman that would ward off all woes and troubles.

"We've covered a lot of ground together, but we're still not acquainted. My name is Fedor. Fedor Proskurov. What are your names?"

"Pinkhas."

"Shleime."

"Velvl."

"What strange names you have," Fedor said. "Like some rare animals. I can hardly remember them. In school I studied with a Jew. His name was was almost like one of ours – Slavik Levinson. I used to copy his homework. He had quite a head! His mother would punish him if he got only a B in a subject."

The column advanced slowly. The refugees decided to stay with Fedor rather than continue on their own, fearing losing their last shred of defence in foreign territory. Pinkhas, who had never trusted anyone except his horse, was desperate now and counting on the goodness of the cook, Pavlik Sizov. He might not give anything to the adults, but the driver hoped he would at least give a bowl of fatty soldier's soup and a piece of bread to the kids – that was, to me and Mendel Selkiner.

By noon, when the June sun was scorching hot and there was no shade at all, Pinkhas saw in the distance a light chestnut horse harnessed to a two-wheeled cart unexpectedly emerging out of the summer haze. It was the long-awaited field kitchen. It pulled over to the side of the road and immediately, in single file, exhausted by the heat and their long journey, the soldiers formed a line behind it.

"Now march behind me to Pavlik," Fedor Proskurov, our compassionate guardian and grenade-thrower, commanded in a jovial manner. "Hurry up, comrade Jews, or the others will eat everything and lick out the bottom of the pot."

As soon as we approached the long line behind the cart carrying its big-bellied aluminum pots containing the much-desired soup, we heard a faint, alarming whining noise from above. It quickly grew louder and sounded closer. For a few moments longer the sky remained a freshly laundered, deep, blinding blue, unsullied by a single cloud. Then, suddenly, German planes broke through the pristine backdrop, flying towards the road along which the Red Army soldiers straggled, accompanied by the refugees from Jonava and all the other doomed Jewish shtetls.

"The sky! The sky!" a young officer, commander of the retreating unit, shouted at the top of his voice.

The column disintegrated. Soldiers rushed toward a thick hazelnut grove, hoping to hide in its thickets and wait out the bombardment.

Mama grabbed me by the hand and Father and I ran after her to the haystacks in the field and jumped into them head first, as if we were diving into a bunker.

The heavy set Pinkhas and the Selkiners raced after the soldiers to the hazelnut grove to shelter in the trees and the juniper bushes to which, just a few minutes before, the soldiers had been hurrying to relieve themselves, unbuckling their belts on the run.

It puzzles to me to this day how, in that fateful moment, my mother got the idea of seeking shelter in the sheaves of dry hay in the open field rather than the hazel grove. Her gamble that we would be more likely to survive in those vulnerable shelters turned out to have been the right one.

When the bombing stopped, shaking off our fear and dirt, we emerged from the haystack intact and unharmed. The Germans hadn't wasted their bombs killing beetles in the peasants' hay, which had not yet been collected in for threshing.

For a long time the explosions shook the hazel grove and the nearby ravines that were overgrown with high grass. The blue sky belonged to the Germans. Except for Mosin rifles and automatic weapons, the retreating infantrymen had nothing to return the fire of the Junkers and the Messerschmitts. And, no matter how good a shot they were, they would have only shot down some crows in the hazel grove, while subjecting themselves to enemy fire.

Having used up all their ammunition and satisfied with the results of their attack, the German aces turned their planes around and abandoned the sky above us.

The effect of the bombing was horrific. A third of the soldiers and the refugees did not return to the ruined road.

No one buried the dead. Their mutilated bodies, torn to pieces by German metal, remained lying in the hazel grove and in the sharp-smelling juniper copse. Crows, eternal witnesses of the departure of human life, circled above the scattered bodies cawing ominously, their loud cries sounding like a funeral lament.

Mama and Papa looked around hopefully, trying to catch sight of any familiar figures heading for the road, on which there was a large puddle of the soldiers' soup. However, they couldn't spot a single one of those they were so eager to see – neither the cart driver Pinkhas, nor the Selkiner family from Białystok, who had been trying to escape death a second time.

Like people leaving a cemetery, the surviving soldiers moved slowly and silently, not looking at each other, to rejoin the much-reduced column. The surviving refugees trudged after them. Why had God not saved Pinkhas and the Selkiners? And for what sins had He punished that naïve, simple Fedor Proskurov? Why did He not show mercy on him and allow him to return home to Osinovka? Fedor would have thrown off his overcoat and uniform, removed his worn canvas boots and plunged naked into the small river with the strange sounding name of Bystraya Sosna, the wwift pine tree, and, in honour of the victory, he would have downed a glass of fiery Moskovskaya vodka in the company of his sisters Klava and Frosya.

An officer was already getting ready to issue the command to line up the surviving soldiers when suddenly, out of the hazel grove, there emerged the cobbler Velvl and, after him, Esther and six-year old Mendel.

My father raised his arms and began to wave to them joyfully. Velvl, however, did not react. He limped slowly towards the road, over the prickly dry grass.

"My heart tells me something bad has happened," Mama sighed.

"Why do you say that?" Father said.

"There's a reason Velvl didn't respond to your greeting."

"Pinkhas?" asked Father, assuming the worst.

"It must be. Fortunately, all of the Selkiners seem to be alive."

When the Selkiners came closer with Mendel, Mama understood from Esther's tear-stained face that Pinkhas was dead.

"Here we are," said Velvl, but he didn't embrace us. "We were guests of the Grim Reaper; it was only by a miracle that we escaped his clutches. And without a scratch . . ."

"Let's be thankful that Death, thank God, let you go," said Father, breathing more easily. "But what about Pinkhas?"

Velvl was silent for a moment. "Unfortunately," he said, in a stifled voice, "Death didn't let him go. He got it into his head to run from one shelter to another, hoping to find a better place, and shrapnel from a bomb hit him in his head."

"If he hadn't, he would still be here with us," Esther said, shivering as if from the cold. "It's as it says in the Holy Scriptures, there's 'a time to sow and a time to reap, a time to live and a time to die.' Now the time has come to bury and to weep. It's shameful not to be able to bury the dead, but it's not possible with your bare hands. I covered Mendel's eyes so that the sight of Pinkhas's dead body, God forbid, wouldn't damage him permanently."

Esther choked on her words and once again broke down in tears.

"We wiped the blood from his face with leaves," said Velvl, rushing to his wife's aid. "We covered his body with dry branches and asked his forgiveness, then came back up to the road, to join you and our defenders. We were afraid we would be left behind . . ."

"May his memory be blessed," said Father.

"Pinkhas has joined his horse," Velvl Selkiner joked bitterly. "It's a great loss, but we have to carry on," he added, moving with us to join the column, which had finished lining up. "We'll await the coming of the great liberator, the messiah, who will resurrect all the dead – both cart drivers and their horses. All of them."

"But not the Germans!" exclaimed Esther, stroking her son's head.

Dusk had begun to fall when the column of Red Army soldiers entered Rezekne with the refugees. An eerie silence greeted them as they entered the city, as if there were no war going on. Rezekne was surrounded by large hills that resembled prehistoric mammoths; its houses seemed to be resting on their strong backs. From the hills there wafted a pleasant, refreshing coolness.

"Even though the Germans are coming, it doesn't seem like any one is fleeing," said Father. "Or perhaps there were no Jews living here."

"Well, no one is fleeing. They're sitting on their eggs, waiting to see what trouble might hatch. But we won't stay here," said Mama, who was not inclined to exaggerate.

Staying with the column of soldiers, we passed through Rezekne to the train station, where we decided to spend the night in the waiting room. The next day we would wait for a freight train to take us to Dvinsk, which was at a major railway junction.

Mendel and I were exhausted and fell asleep immediately on benches at the Rezekne station. Our parents dozed sitting up.

In the morning Father set out for town on a mission to obtain some food. He took along a length of woollen material in the event that he might be able arrange a trade. He did have some *rubles*, but back in Jonava merchants were not willing to accept them. It turned out that here too, far from the front lines, the shopkeeprs looked dubiously at the devalued currency and were unwilling to accept it, preferring silver or gold, which are good under any regime.

Father did not have either silver or gold, but he did succeed in exchanging the length of cloth for three loaves of fresh caraway bread and some pieces of liver sausage. The portions Father distributed for lunch were of different sizes; the children received a larger amount while the grown-ups got less, but no one complained. Everyone hoped the *rubles* would be accepted in Dvinsk and awaited the next freight train.

The trains, however, arrived only rarely.

The waiting room was like a jail without bars or wardens; not a single refugee had any idea how long a term they would have to serve there. Nevertheless, neither we nor the Selkiners despaired. We believed that we would be fortunate – that some engineer would take pity on us and allow us onto his train.

Not long before fate was indeed kind to us, a thin young man approached our benches. He was wearing a long black coat and a cap that covered his eyes. From his temples there hung curly whisps of coal black *peyos* and threads of *tsitses* emerged from under his outer shirt. The stranger was holding a prayer book with a leather binding.

"My name is Meir Zhabinsky," he said, caressing his *peyos*. "I studied at the Panevezh Yeshiva. Excuse me a thousand times but allow me, as one Jew to another, to ask one delicate question."

"Go ahead and ask. Everybody knows, Jews don't charge for questions," Velvl replied.

"Tell me, please, in Russia are there yeshivas, synagogues, and *hevra kadishas*, burial societies? May we not need the latter!"

Father shrugged.

"What?" said the cobbler Velvl, his voice laced with irony. "Are those things your main concerns now?"

"Perhaps they are the main things, perhaps not. Of course, it's not forbidden to pray alone. You can praise God everywhere. But it's better when there's a whole quorum joined in prayer in a house of God."

"We have no idea whether there are synagogues, yeshivas or burial societies there," Father said, shrugging again. "We've never been to Russia before this current nightmare."

"No one I ask knows the answer. What will I do in a place where there is nothing for me?"

"In order to pray, one first has to survive."

"Those are holy words!" exclaimed Meir.

Meir joined us, waiting for a train to take him to mysterious Russia where, perhaps, there was not a single synagogue or a single burial society, but, at least so far, Jews were not being arrested on the street or killed.

As evening drew close we succeeded in getting onto a freight train travelling to Dvinsk, in a car constructed to carry cows to slaughter.

The car had a pungent smell of manure and urine. For the whole trip we had to stand. No one was interested in sitting on the dirty floor. The stuffiness made us nauseous and our heads spun, but the doors were closed tight with iron bars and no one dared open them in order to get a breath of fresh summer air while the train was moving.

Our new travelling companion, Meir Zhabinsky, prayed quietly the whole time. The sound of his devout whispering made us sleepy, but there was no place to put down our heads.

Snuggled against Mama's warm side, I stood in the half-empty car; its tiny ventilation window didn't allow in any light. Listening to the prayerful muttering of the graduate of the Panevezh Yeshiva, I thought of Grandma Rokha. I remembered how she had made a place for me to sleep on the squeaking trestle-bed on Rybatskaya Street and, as if uttering a charm over me, whispered, "My golden one, may your guardian angel fly down to you while you are sleeping and give you his blessing." Grandma could hardly have imagined that in less than five years I would be dreaming not of heavenly angels, but of German bombers and of Latvian cows, who, like us, were unable to foresee their fate as they were being transported in these cattle cars.

Before we arrived in Dvinsk, Father suggested we fortify ourselves. The supper for six was a modest one – each of us got a piece of liver sausage and a chunk of fresh caraway bread. The Orthodox Jew, Zhabinsky, who had joined us on the trip, refused to eat our non-kosher food.

"I'm sorry, but I don't eat *treif.* Give my portion to your boys."

"If you follow the rules so strictly, you'll perish in Russia," said Velvl, rolling his eyes. "Tell me, my good fellow, what do you intend to eat there? Manna from heaven?"

"Whoever believes in God, will be nourished by Him."

It didn't take long to arrive at much-awaited Dvinsk. The freight train was shifted to a side track because the train station was full due to the cancellation of long runs. The ticket offices were not working. There were signs over their windows in Latvian and Russian, "Temporarily closed." The official on duty at the station only sent eastward specially designated trains – those with industrial equipment or high-ranking personnel.

There were crowds of refugees in the train station square. Some of them darted around the station building and along the tracks, trying to find some information, or to catch sight of at least one engineer through the window of his locomotive.

"It looks like we're stuck here," lamented Selkiner, who was easily depressed.

"God rescued us from Egypt, He will rescue us from Dvinsk," Meir Zhabinsky said, attempting to encourage his fellow travellers.

"When?" Velvl demanded.

"You can't rush in on our Heavenly Ruler and ask on what day and precisely at what hour Heaven will do this for you. You can only ask the One Above what you would like Him to do, with sincerity."

There's no doubt that Mendel and I, more than anyone else, wanted to get to Russia as soon as possible, where we could sleep in a proper bed with a pillow and a cover, not standing up in a smelly cattle car. Grandma Rokha always used to complain that God had never, in her whole life, fulfilled any of her wishes, even though she believed in Him more than Grandpa Dovid did. However, He did fulfill my wish. A rumour circulated among the refugees that on the third track a train was being prepared to leave with women and children and that some empty places could be seen through the lit-up windows of the compartments.

"All the passengers are VIPs," Mother said. "They have special tickets and they won't allow us on without special documents. Maybe we should wait?"

"For what? For death?" Father said. "Maybe they will let us on. After all, we're not thieves or looters."

Esther agreed with Father. "What do we have to lose? If they let us on, good! If not, we can either accept that or we can force our way on. For Mendel's sake I'm ready to do anything."

Esther determination surprised everyone.

The rumour about the empty seats on the train from Dvinsk to Velikie Luki and then to Yaroslavl spurred the refugees into action. They immediately rushed from the platform to the third track, but what they saw from a distance cooled their enthusiasm.

Armed guards stood along the whole length of the train. It was easy to guess that the reason for them was to safely evacuate the families of Party members and high-ranking officers to the Russian hinterland.

The soldiers guarded the approaches to the train, while women conductors with pocket flashlights scrupulously checked the tickets and the special passes which only the big shots and their children possessed.

Over all, there were no more than two hundred refugees attempting to flee the Germans. At first the guards viewed them with puzzled sympathy, but then, when some of the refugees began to approach the train, the guards grew alarmed.

"Comrades," the deep bass voice of a commander shouted. "I ask you to quickly move away from all the access tracks so as not to put your lives in danger or to interfere with the arriving trains!"

However, there were no trains arriving and the refugees were in no hurry to carry out the order.

"Citizens, I am asking you politely to disperse," the bass voice called out. "Please wait for your own train in the waiting room!"

It was easy for him to say, "Wait for your own train." We didn't have our own train, and perhaps never would.

Whether from the increasing, humiliating hopelessness, or from an audacity aroused by despair, instead of retreating, the first rows of refugees moved closer to the train.

"Perhaps it's not worth making them angry." Velvl hesitated. "If the train is guarded by soldiers it means they have the right to open fire on those who threaten law and order . . ."

"You should be ashamed!" Esther said, cutting him off. "We don't support the Germans, we support the Red Army; do you think they would dare use their weapons against us?"

"If we're doomed to die, what difference, tell me, does it make at whose hands it will be? Of Soviet or German atheists?" whispered Meir Zhabinsky and, as if he had discussed the matter with God, added, "God commanded human beings to fear disgrace, not death."

"People are cowards and most choose disgrace," Father commented. "But Meir has a point. What is there for us to fear? We're not escaped criminals and these guards are people, not animals."

"We'll find out soon enough," Mama quipped.

Caught up in an outburst that pushed aside all doubt and fears, the crowd of Jewish refugees approached the train. Demonstrating loyalty to his oath and devotion to military discipline, one of the guards shouted out.

"Stop or we will shoot!"

The soldier fired several shots over the heads of the desperate refugees.

"What scum!" someone shouted. "Shooting refugees!"

The shooting did not stop the crowd. Rather than turn back, they advanced on the train like kamikaze pilots, risking not only their own lives, but also those of their children.

The stunned guards seemed to conclude that if they opened fire on the refugees there would be a considerable amount of bloodshed and no guarantee that they would able to establish order. What's more, there might well be consequences, since it wasn't Germans they were shooting, but their own, albeit new, Soviet citizens.

Encouraged by the indecisiveness and confusion of the guards, the refugees broke through the cordon and began to storm the train. By the force of their momentum they pulled the helpless conductresses with them into the train cars and occupied the empty places in the compartments.

We too found seats, but none of us were ready to rejoice yet.

"What about the others?" we wondered. Hopefully, no one had been killed, crushed, or wounded.

"God willing, we won't be thrown out of here," sighed the sceptical Velvl, who was accustomed to the unexpected twists of fate.

"Rather than throwing us off, they might simply move another train onto the next track, put all the Party officials and commanders' wives on board and leave us here. It's possible, isn't it?" my cautious father said.

"Everything is in the hands of our merciful God. What happens does not depend on us," said Zhabinsky, who was praying in the corridor. I was shifting from one foot to the other next to him. The thought occured to me that if the Russian passengers and their children were indeed put onto another train and we were left here and the doors were closed, this car would become our prison and, maybe, even our grave. The German pilots would appear in the skies and in two minutes bomb us to pieces. However, I recalled the advice of Grandma Rokha. She used to say, "It's not right to share bad thoughts with others, since everyone has plenty of their own and it's a sin to add yours to them." So I kept mine to myself. Perhaps, for that reason they disturbed me even more.

What had happened to Grandma? Clearly God wasn't going to grant her last wish to lie in the cemetery next to Grandpa Dovid. She had probably already been killed. I trembled as my mind conjured up the most terrible pictures. Grandma Rokha lying in a pool of blood at the entrance to her home on Rybatskaya Street, a gunshot wound in her head, while people passed by as if she were a cat that had been run over. Why had Mother and Father not mentioned her once during all the time of our forced wandering? Had they forgotten her? It couldn't be! To calm myself, I thought, "It's just that they are not speaking about her aloud, but blaming themselves silently and suffering because they didn't manage to convince her, or simply force her to go with us."

We waited for a very long time for the train to start moving, thanks perhaps to Meir Zhabinsky, who prayed non-stop and must have been able to push even God into action. After all, wasn't it by His will that, having heard the whistles of many other trains, the engineer finally pressed down the lever and our train jolted forward and we departed from Latvia?

Late on that deep June night, exhausted but full of hope, we crossed the border into Russia.

In the morning, Mama recounted how that during the night all the refugees, except the children who had slept like logs on the rough benches, had put their heads out of the train windows and gazed at the starry Russian sky. Shamelessly they wiped the tears of joy from their eyes.

Only Meir Zhabinsky rocked from side to side, holding his prayer book. "Is there really not a single yeshiva in Russia?" he asked again.

For four difficult years Mother and I lived in an alien country (Father was drafted and sent to Balakhna for training). First, we lived deep in the countryside near Yaroslavl, where there were only six-month-old infants, the elderly and women, along with the men who had not been drafted into the army because of some handicap. Then we moved to a Kazakh village at the foot of the Tian Shan mountains. And, after that, we moved to the Urals, to the coal-mining settlement of Emanzhelinskie Kopi.

We returned to Lithuania in 1945. One year later, finishing the General Cerniachovski Gymnasium, I went to Jonava on my own. My father and his younger brother Motl had already visited.

I wandered for a long time around my native shtetl, which felt like a cemetery. From the house on Rybatskaya Street to the house on Kovno Street; from tree to tree, from the store that used to belong to Ephraim Kapler to the stable where the cart driver Shvartsman used to keep his horse; from the primary school where I had studied to the Great Synagogue. Other than a stray dog that attached himself to me, I had no one with whom to share the sadness that welled up in me. Not a trace remained of my dear Jonava, which had once been such a populous Jewish island.

When I got back to the station and heard the announcement that the Riga to Vilnius train would be four hours late, I decided to walk over to Rybatskaya Street, to the house of Grandma Rokha, who it seemed had just the day before accompanied me to the Yiddish school that she had little affection for. Perhaps I would see someone in the window? Maybe someone would come out onto the porch? However, the windows were covered by curtains and the porch was empty.

Strangers rushed by me on the street. I gazed at their faces, hoping to recognize one of the old residents, but I didn't recognize anyone. To tell you the truth, I already regretted that I had not stayed at the largely deserted provincial train station with my copy of the stories of Maupassant that I had not read. But suddenly, inevitably, a familiar face appeared at the corner of Rybatskaya and Kovno streets, near the pole with the torn electric wires that I remembered so well; the place where I used to meet my classmate Leah Berger. At first I thought I was mistaken.

"Oy!" I exclaimed, surprised when I looked carefully. And, in an unseemly loud voice, I shouted so the whole street could hear, "Julius!"

The man turned and ran toward me. "Oh Lord! Who do I see?" he exclaimed. "It's Hirshke! Shleime Kanovich's son, the son of my old master!"

Julius embraced me with his calloused 'worker's hands', as Uncle Shmulik loved to say, and pressed me to his chest as if I were a baby.

"How glad, how happy I am! Imagine meeting you! Are you here for long?"

"I have a train in four hours."

"I won't let you go. I have a house of my own with three rooms and my own Singer sewing machine. Do you know what I am in Jonava now? You'll never guess."

"What?"

"I am the top tailor here, you could say, like *Ponas* Shleime Kanovich used to be. Come and have supper with us. My wife Danute will make some tea. We'll have a drink and eat some peasant cheese and cranberry jam. You can sleep over at our house and leave in the morning."

"Thanks, but I can't. I don't want to worry my mother."

"We can go to the post office and call Vilnius so that *Ponia* Hennie won't worry. She will just be happy that we have met."

"Another time. Is that all right?"

"Of course. Without you Jews our Jonava isn't the same, of course," Julius said. "Almost all of your tribe stayed here in Zelenaya Roshcha, the Green Grove, and in the surrounding ravines and sand quarries. They were shot to death there. No one was spared."

"What about you? Did you just stand by and do nothing?" I said bitterly.

"If anyone had tried to save them, he would be lying with them now. I had to move from Jonava to Kupiškis. Those fellows with the white armbands said that I was a

Jew-lover, so they could easily have done away with me too."

Our conversation wasn't pleasant for Julius and he hurried to change the subject. "How is *Ponas* Shleime? How is *Ponia* Hennie?" the former apprentice asked.

"They're well, thank God!"

"My father got himself involved with those with dirty consciences. He was arrested right after the war for collaborating with you-know-who and exiled to Siberia. He doesn't sweep Kapler's courtyard now; he sweats away cutting down trees and the sweat dilutes any wine he might have got hold of. My mother died of cancer in '42."

After a while, I said goodbye.

"Where are you rushing off to, Hirshke?" said Julius. "We still have a lot of time to spare. Let's go down together to the Vilija River. I haven't been there for five years."

"The Vilija?" I said.

"Yes. The river's shallow now, but you can still swim there. Opposite the weeping willows there are some dangerous whirlpools. Let's go together. We'll dive into the water and have a race!"

"All right, let's go," I said. I had so many memories connected with Julius.

Father's faith in him hadn't been misplaced. Unlike his father, he hadn't participated in the pogroms against the Jews in the town, nor did he join the murderers. He sat at home and sewed diligently away on his Singer.

We descended the slope to the river of my childhood. Before returning to Vilnius, I had decided to pay my respects to it and stand in silence on its familiar bank. As we approached the very edge of the water, I suddenly felt that my grandma Rokha the Samurai had descended with us.

Some of my readers might find it strange, but even today as I approach the God-set limit beyond which there is only the silence of the next world, in my imagination I sometimes descend with Grandma that steep slope, overgrown with prickly thistles, to the Vilija, the river of my childhood that flows irresistibly into eternity.

In satin underpants that reach my knees, I stand before the overbearing, implacable Rokha, who has a large cane made of ash grasped in her wrinkled hand with their swollen veins. Her dark eyes, keen as a hawks, do not leave me for a moment. She was mercilessly at the ready to strike my bare back with the sharp point of the cane if I dared enter water higher than the level of my underpants, or, to her horror, begin doggy-paddling away from her, my stern and gentle angel, towards the far bank.

"Don't you dare swim! Do you hear me? Are your ears plugged up? Let the others swim!" Grandma Rokha screamed in anger, as she traversed, with the aid of her cane, the sand on our bank of the river. "Get out of the water this instant!"

"Grandma," I would beg my strict guardian, "I want to learn how to swim and go at least once over to the other bank of the Vilija, like Mendel Giberman did."

"What do you want to see on the other side?"

"Please, Grandma, I really want to . . ."

"To see what?" Grandma interrupted me. "Believe me, Hirshele, there's nothing different on the other side. Not a single thing! The same Jews as us live on the other side. Is it worth jumping into the water and risking your life just to see the very same thing?"

As always, Grandma Rokha was right. The same Jews lived on both sides of the Vilija. Both here and there the whole galaxy of the shtetl, with its inimitable inhabitants, revolved around the pale Lithuanian sun; skilled stove makers and tinsmiths, teachers of religion and atheists, rich men who were poor compared to the famous Baron Rothschild, amateur philosophers who predicted the end of the world and melancholic madmen. In the fateful year of 1941 that galaxy exploded under the impact of hatred and violence and its fragments scattered across the world. And, no matter how hard you try, no matter what effort you might make, you could never collect the pieces and fit them back together as a whole.

On a starry night, if you go out of your house you can hear familiar voices in the tranquil silence. It is the dead talking with each other in the sky and whispering to us: Grandma Rokha the Samurai with Grandpa Dovid, the landlord Ephraim Kapler with the baker Chaim Gershon Fain, Dr. Isaac Blumenfeld with Rabbi Eliezer, the gravedigger Hatzkel Berman with the cart-driver Pinkhas Shvartsman. There are hundreds, even thousands of them. One shtetl, one Jewish town that was wiped from the face of the earth, converses with another.

Since the Riga-Vilnius train had not yet arrived, I decided to while away the time in the stuffy waiting room alone. I sat on a rough bench and my thoughts revolved around that extinct Jewish galaxy. How many times I tried to quell my sadness. I hoped to convince myself that if we did not wall up our souls, overcome, as they were, with misfortune, and continued to talk to those we had not been able to mourn or accompany on their last journey, we could prolong their lives through memory. After all, memory is the shared roof under which all of us settle – the living and the dead, the righteous and the sinners, the murderers and the victims. No matter how much you want to, you will never evict anyone from your memory.

My sad musings were interrupted by the whistle of a train. Soon I would be bidding a last goodbye to Jonava, where, in the expression of my wise Grandma Rokha, it was fine to be born a Jew and not bad to die a Jew in one's old age.

"Fine to be born a Jew!" I repeated Grandma's words as I stepped onto the train. However, you can not bring back what has gone. In Jonava, as in the other shtetls of Lithuania, there was no longer anyone to give birth to Jews, or anyone to bury them in its broken cemeteries.

It was bitter to realize the truth that from now on it was the fate of that dead tribe to be born and live only in true and painful words and impartial memory, in which it was impossible to drown out the echoes of love and gratitude toward our forebears. Whoever allows the dead to fall into oblivion will himself be justly consigned to oblivion by future generations.

The train approached Vilnius, the city where my fellow Jews and I had taken refuge after the war and where we searched in vain to find traces of that long, rich Jewish presence, which had, with good reason, earned the city the lofty title of the Jerusalem of Lithuania.

September 2011-June 2012

Visit us at

www.noirpress.co.uk

Follow us

@PressNoir